About the author

Jean Robinson was a textile technologist with the Wood Industries Research Association in Leeds when she and her new husband, together with her brother, made the life-changing decision to take on, unseen, *The George* in Upper Wharfedale.

With no experience in either the licensing trade or in farming the 22 acres of moorland that came with the near derelict pub, Jean became the driving force behind the successful business, the basis for *George and Me*.

After nine years the Inn was sold from under them, and Jean returned to her original work, rising to become Technical Director of an international company. Now with her family and a menagerie of ex-racehorses, dogs and cats, she enjoys 'retirement' in a village in East Yorkshire.

GEORGE AND ME

DEDICATION

For my brother, David.

Jean Robinson

GEORGE AND ME

AUSTIN & MACAULEY

A CIP catalogue record for this title is available from the British Library.

ISBN 978 1 84963 043 6

www.austinmacauley.com

First Published (2011)
Austin & Macauley Publishers Ltd.
25 Canada Square
Canary Wharf
London
E14 5LB

Printed & Bound in Great Britain

ACKNOWLEDGEMENTS

With thanks for their patience and support to Shirley, Jean, Sue, Robin, Richard, and especially Linda Acaster for her expert tuition.

CHAPTER 1

The garden path was greasy after the brief downpour. Sylvia Bainbridge trod deliberately to miss the broken flag with its protruding edges. It had caught her out a few times, but not today. She reached the Iron Gate, flaked with rust accumulated over the years, and lifted the lop-sided latch. The metal complained as the bottom bar dragged an arc on the stone path. Pushing the gate to its limit she half turned to look back at the dilapidated Victorian semi. Perhaps once it had been quite a grand abode, but now it was a money-spinner for some property shark, coining in three substantial rents every week. She and John had rented the ground floor flat since their wedding a few months earlier. In spite of a couple of rude awakenings, they'd had fun and she'd been able to fulfil her childhood dream with the purchase of a whippet pup, Cassie. She bent down to stroke the silky head snuggling close to her knee.

'It's alright Cass. You're not going to be left behind. You're going to think you're in Heaven. You'll be with me all day, never to be fastened in alone again.' She'd felt terrible having to leave the pup when she set off for work every morning, even though she dashed home at lunchtime to walk her in the park. Cassie had frequently shown her disgust by causing havoc in some form or another, usually refusing to be caught when time ran short for Sylvia's return to work. The pup would run Hell-for-leather round and round the football pitch, reminiscent of a Whirling Dervish, seemingly with one intent, to keep her owner captive. And eventually late, Sylvia would return to her desk hot, sticky and rather flustered.

'Are you going to stand there all day? Your brother's here with the removal van.'

John looked impatient, but Sylvia ignored the call. Her eyes filled as she whispered a quiet goodbye to the place that had briefly been their first home, then dutifully she followed his gaze.

The green removal van was trundling down the tree-lined road. It didn't appear particularly steady as it hit the frequent pot-holes. Robert hung out of the window waving eagerly, his fair hair bouncing with every bump. She was relieved to see him. He gave her a feeling of stability, oddly absent since her marriage. Thank God he's coming with us. Guiltily she cast a quick glance at John. He too, appeared to be pleased to see Robert.

'Hey Sis. My stuff's hardly taken up any room at the front of the van, *and* I've got my motorised bike in, *and* there's still masses of space left for your load of baggage.'

The bike was a joke between the two of them. Sylvia always insisted it was an old man's means of transport.

He jumped out of the cab, laughing, but Sylvia noticed he briefly covered his left eye with a protective hand as the door swung towards him. She hugged her younger brother, happy she had managed to persuade him to thrown in his lot with her and John. He needed a worthwhile distraction, and they certainly needed his help on this, their first business venture.

'These two fellows aren't exactly bright sparks. You'd better make sure they know what's what before they start loading your furniture.'

The men under scrutiny, glared. Sylvia smiled sweetly.

'Thanks, boys, for leaving us plenty of room in the van. I'll show you what's to go. The delicate things are packed in tea chests, so you've no worries there. It shouldn't take long to load up.'

Her tone took them off guard and the pair had no choice but to immediately bend their backs and get into action. Robert joined in to help, while John looked on, puffing his pipe. The sweet smell of his favourite tobacco, hung round him like a sensual woman. Sylvia knew he wouldn't help and even if she chivvied him on, he'd soon find an escape route. She'd had to seriously fall out with him before he'd condescend to help decorate the flat, so there was no hope now.

14

'Sylvia, we'd better get going. It's a long drive and the vicar has arranged for us to take over at midday.'

Robert, catching the words, piped up. 'You two get off. I'll make sure everything's properly packed and I'll leave the key as arranged at the flat upstairs.'

'Just the job. Come on wife, get in the car.' He playfully slapped her bottom.

The black Ford Popular, sprang into life. Sylvia grabbed Cassie and waved to her brother.

'We'll see you later. Make sure those two fellows behave, and don't get lost.'

Eager to be off, John, put the car into gear and gradually let it creep forward, increasing the speed as they turned the corner out of sight. They were on their way!

The suburbs of Leeds were soon left behind. As they passed the fancy houses in Bramhope, Sylvia nostalgically wondered when she would see the place again. They'd often walked from there through to Arthington, where they'd swim in a pool formed by a bend in the river. Nervously, her thoughts strayed to what they were about to take on. It was a bit overwhelming.

'John, we are doing the right thing, aren't we?'

'For Heaven's sake, you're not having second thoughts now. You do pick your moments. We've left. There's no going back.'

'No, no, but I'm just a bit apprehensive, that's all.'

She felt hurt, some encouragement would have been nice. The Church-owned George Inn, high up in Wharfedale, was soon to be theirs and she would have the full responsibility of building up the catering and residential side. Her training on that score was nonexistent. Her background was technical; analysis of cloth manufacturing faults hardly constituted useful experience, and, to make matters worse, they were short of cash. They'd had to scrape the barrel bottoms to raise the ingoing valuation and a month's rent in advance. John never seemed to worry about anything, so he couldn't possibly understand her periodic bouts of coli-wobbles.

She took a peep at this handsome husband of hers, twelve years her senior, confident and charming, though she'd soon realised hard graft and reliability weren't in his vocabulary.

Perhaps this was why he hadn't been opposed to her brother joining them, solid, reliable Robert. Was she being unkind? John couldn't help the way he was made and she loved him to distraction. She glanced out of the window to rid herself of such thoughts and was surprised to see they had already reached Ilkley. And it had started to rain.

It seemed only yesterday that her best friend, Anna, had had her eighteenth party at the Troutbeck Hotel, up there, on the edge of the moor. What a night it had been: the food, the music, the dresses, she would never have known such delights if she hadn't met Anna at college. A mill owner's daughter, used to the best of everything, they had become firm friends, in spite of very different backgrounds. Sylvia had been welcomed into the family and had enjoyed many a wonderful weekend with them in their beautiful home, so different from her parents' little house in Pontefract.

It was on one of these visits she had first set eyes on John. She and Anna had decided they would support a couple of college friends who had been chosen to play for the Ilkley rugby team. The game, that afternoon, was at home. The opposition was a team from Horsforth, the village where Sylvia stayed with her aunt during term time. The two of them knew nothing about the game, but had giggled and drooled over the hunky warriors, especially one from the visiting side.

At half-time, this muddy God smiled at Sylvia.

'Don't I know you? I'm sure I've seen you before.'

Her legs went to jelly and weakly she acknowledged the possibility.

'I stay in Horsforth during the week. Perhaps you've seen me there.'

'I'll look out for you.' With that, he was gone, but not from Sylvia's innermost thoughts. Well, that was then, and now, she was married to the man and everything was about to change again. They were off to the top of Wharfedale, wild and glorious. It was going to be oh so different.

She had been to the George Inn at Hubberholme once during a visit to John's farmer friend, Gerald, who lived about half a mile from the Inn. They'd walked to the tiny hamlet that Sunday morning. It was hot and sunny, harebells bobbed at the base of the stone walls edging the road, the river tumbled happily alongside, gurgling as it broke into glistening, miniature fountains where lurking rocks surfaced. The Inn, low and white, nestled at the foot of the steep fell on one side of an old pack-horse bridge. On the other bank the church sat squat and square, its battered studded door flanked by two yews. What a view! She knew it was one she would never forget. She remembered feeling quite jealous of those who lived amongst such beauty. The Inn was open. Apparently, it was a requirement of the church that refreshment should be available to the congregation after the morning service. In the past, church-goers would have walked many a mile for their prayers and would have needed sustenance before the return journey. She and John hadn't gone inside, instead they'd had their coffee sitting on the garden wall absorbing the sunshine and the surroundings.

'You're quiet.'

His words made her jump.

'I was remembering that morning we had coffee at the George. I still can't believe we're going to live there. Do you think it'll take long to get the business on its feet?'

'Stop worrying. We've everything going for us. The business is at rock-bottom, so it can only go up. The rent's low, that's why we've the odd duty to carry out for the church, like ringing the bell for morning service. Look well if I end up hanging from the bell rope at the top of the tower.' He laughed and gave her leg a squeeze. 'Everything will turn out right. You're a super cook, you'll be fine. You watch, in no time at all Joe Public will be beating a path to the George.'

She laughed, pleased he had faith in her ability, even though she had never cooked for more than family and friends.

Sylvia watched the countryside change as they drove up out of Addingham, past the reservoir, where coots and the odd duck bobbed on the scuttling waves. The grass became ragged and untamed, and bedraggled sheep took shelter under the grey stone walls. Not the best of days, she thought, as rain intermittently blasted the windscreen. She shivered pulling her collar up round her ears and drew the sleepy Cassie close as though to protect her from the blast. Late February didn't appear to be a good time to up-sticks and move to a remote part of the dales. Even the bustling market town of Skipton had taken on a certain starkness in the unannounced downpour, as folk disappeared into the welcoming shops for cover.

The scenery became more rugged. Higgledy piggledy stone walls, like crazy jigsaws, protected small meadows. It didn't seem long before they reached the huge lump of rock with the unbelievable overhang, Kilnsey Crag. She had seen it a couple of times before and the sheer might of nature's hand thrilled her. It seemed close enough to the road to be able to reach it with the throw of a stone. She had tried on a college expedition, but without success, though some fit-looking lads had jubilantly managed the feat.

'For Heaven's sake stop fidgeting will you.'

'I'm just looking at the Crag, it's awesome.' Her voice came in gasps as she twisted over the back of the seat to get a last glimpse of the view.

John laughed at her. 'Sit down for Heaven's sake. The road's a bit twisty just here, you'll be sick.'

Flushing, she sat upright and straightened her skirt.

'Why Sylv, you've gone pink. It suits you, you should do it more often. Just look, you're steaming up the windows.' He grinned and briefly touched her hand.

'We're just coming into Kettlewell. When we came before we dropped down from Hawes, so this is new for you. They get plenty of visitors here in the summer and quite a few in winter. There's even a Youth Hostel.'

She noted the attractive Racehorses Hotel sitting beside the river. Now that was some spot... perhaps one day? The road from then on ran more or less straight and level, past a little school, on through a very pretty village, then Buckden came into view. As they entered the village, a large house surrounded by trees caught her eye.

'That's the Methodist holiday place. They get lots of visitors. They often walk to the George for coffee on Sunday mornings.'

'Has the house always been a holiday home?'

18

'No. Years ago it was owned by some man who bought the upper part of the dale and made the place a private estate. If you look across the way, you'll see rhododendrons planted. He had it laid out like parkland. There were deer roaming, but it's all gone now, only the rhododendrons are left.'

'I bet it looks lovely when they're in flower.'

Silently she absorbed the view. The village seemed to nestle in a bubble of safety. A tiny village green bravely sported a signpost pointing Heavenward to a place called Cray. There were quite a few little cottages, a rather nice looking pub and thank goodness, a shop-cum post office. That would come in handy, only a mile or so from Hubberholme. She felt a lot better knowing there was a nearby source for essentials.

'Does the shop sell bits of everything John?'

'Everything from bundles of firewood to butter and bacon.'

'Good, we won't starve then?'

Her husband laughed out loud.

'Anybody would think we were going to the North Pole.'

She didn't answer, instead watched the road they had turned onto at the low side of the green. It was narrow and the stone walls on either side gave the feeling it was hardly wide enough to let the car pass through. She could see the river in places where the eerie light gave silvered flashes as it kissed the edge of the low-lying meadows.

Gerald's home appeared on the left. It was plain and gaunt, a good distance back from the road. A short way past, on the opposite side, was the vicarage. It was completely different, a pretty, low building, with a quite impressive drive and a well kept front garden.

'We're here.'

Sylvia caught her breath. Even in the drizzle the place looked a picture. This was to be their home.

'Oh John, aren't we lucky.' Her fingers gently curled round her husband's wrist.

He swung the car onto the pub car park, turned off the engine and gave her a hug, big enough to make her squeak. She eagerly looked about her.

A row of stone out-buildings faced them, they seemed to grow out of the fell rising steeply behind them. The tallest looked like a coach-house with its arched double doors, half opened, displaying a couple of barrels, a pile of beer crates and, what appeared to be years of discarded rubbish. It had an air of neglect, yet nothing could detract from the absolute beauty of the setting. John had told her that artists often painted the view, and she could see why.

'Reverend Fullerton's waiting at the door. The rain's nearly stopped. Come on.'

The vicar stepped out onto the drive to greet them. Small and stocky, his pale face accentuated by a dusty cassock, he had an anxious air about him.

'Hello John, are you going to introduce me to your lady wife?'

To Sylvia's consternation, John put his arm round her waist, moving her towards the vicar.

'Reverend Fullerton, meet Sylvia, my wonderful wife.'

'How do you do Sylvia, I may call you Sylvia? I feel as though I know you already. I must tell you, I've had a glowing account about you from your college tutor. He happens to be a dear friend of mine. Now isn't that a coincidence?'

Sylvia blinked. 'You mean… Mr Oversby?'

The news surprised her. She'd been frightened to death of the man. Strict and fearsome, he'd reminded her of an undertaker. Not a sound was ever heard in his lectures, everyone behaved. She never imagined he could be complimentary about her.

Smiling politely, she looked directly into the searching blue eyes, strangely enlarged through the lens of the spectacles askew on his switchback nose. She took her husband's hand.

'I hope I live up to Mr Oversby's opinion.'

She realised his recommendation must have had some influence in them getting the tenancy. She didn't know whether to feel pleased or worried. Glancing at her husband, she searched for some sign that he was happy with it all, but he didn't look her way. In reality it was a bit late to do much about it anyway, their fate was sealed. The realisation of how remote the place seemed, now clothed in winter's trappings, and the enormity of what they had taken on, suddenly hit home. The amenities of city life were a million miles away, it was as though they had stepped into the late 1800s and left 1957 behind. A black hole in her stomach yawned, a chasm that would not ease. She'd always enjoyed a challenge and yearned to live in the country, but this was a test like no other. John was strangely quiet. Perhaps he had changed his mind when faced with the cold light of day.

The three of them had lapsed into one of those uncomfortable silences that Sylvia always felt obliged to break. This time it was the vicar who took a deep breath.

'Come through to the dining room, John. You've been here often enough, you know the Inn well. Are you ready to sign the tenancy agreement?'

As he spoke, he forcibly ushered John inside. Sylvia was unceremoniously dismissed.

'Perhaps you would like to wait in the bar, Sylvia, until we've finished with the formalities. John has to sign the tenancy agreement, witnessed by my two Church Wardens, they're waiting in the dining room. We won't be long.'

She felt as if she'd been slapped, and then, as she stood on the threshold in the dying drizzle, she grew resentful. It would be her who would shoulder most of the load, her who would be cleaning and cooking and doing the running about after visitors. It was all so unfair, but what had she expected? The female of the species seemed to be considered as second class. She'd seen it happen so often, if a woman became pregnant there was no job to return to. It was one of the reasons she'd welcomed the tenancy of the George. No one could sack her from her own work, even if they would not allow her to be in on the signing of the agreement.

Growling under her breath, she walked back to the car.

'Blow it, I'll stay here, they can damn well come and fetch me.'

She pulled at the door handle with unnecessary vigour and clambered over the front seat into the back to join Cassie, clutching the dainty creature close to her. 'Oh Cass. You're shivering.'

Sylvia opened her coat and drew Cass inside. All warmth in the car had long gone. She snuggled low in the seat and thought about her parents. Her father had been opposed to her marriage to John, but had finally relented after some heavy persuasion from her mother, who, like her, had succumbed to John's charm.

'You'll do what you want in the long run, but don't come crying to me when it all goes wrong,' was his final comment.

Deep down in her heart, she knew this dashing, carefree, love of her life, would not be a rock, she would have to find the strength to hold them together and prove her father wrong. This chance of their own business was really a godsend. She'd miss her job and friends, but if a baby came their way they would be lost anyway, and she would be totally dependant on John. And that would never do. Perhaps up here he'd buckle down to the work and not get bored so easily. Everyone liked him and that should make him a good landlord. She wiped the window with the back of her hand to clear the damp away, it gave her a camera shot of the hills beyond. There and then, she knew she had made the right decision. Now she felt positive and welcomed the task waiting to be taken on.

The door of the Inn opened and she was called to join the party. Cassie was asleep, lost in a doggie Heaven chasing imaginary rabbits. Carefully she extracted herself from a wet nose and a collection of elegant legs, then hesitantly made her way down the drive. At one time it must have been the road, for it looped round the front of the Inn, leaving the main road at one end, then connected again on the car park. Cyril, Gerald's father was standing in the doorway waiting to greet her. He was one of the churchwardens and had been instrumental in them getting the tenancy. He held out his hand in welcome and stood aside to let her through into the kitchen.

A gaunt man, his lank hair topped a bone structure reminiscent of an Apache Indian in a John Wayne film. He was shy and seemed ill at ease in his blue suit. Nervously he tugged at the bottom buttons of his waistcoat to make the fronts lie smooth and un-furrowed. Intermittently he ran a finger round the inside of his collar as though wanting to be out of the constraints of serge and into his 'muck'. Politely, he introduced her to the other churchwarden, Anthony Holdsworth, another farmer. He towered above her, the tallest man she had ever seen, who stooped to compensate for his height under the low ceiling. A scarecrow of a man, Sylvia half expected straw to creep out of his collarless shirt. His huge hands hung from hairy forearms, not hidden by the sleeves of his brown suit. He proffered his hand in greeting. Her own was not small, but it completely disappeared in his giant, calloused grasp.

'Pleased t'meet thi' lass. Tha's teken a lot on wi' this spot. I wish thi' well.'

The greeting rankled, she already had a good idea of the mountain to be climbed and didn't feel like being reminded. The vicar quietly took her elbow.

'You'll be alright, don't worry. They're a queer lot, these 'up-dalers', but they'll do anything for anybody. Hearts of gold, though they'll never call you one of them, you've to be born here for that privilege.'

Then with an encouraging squeeze of her arm, he turned to John.

'By the way, don't forget you have to ring the church bell for morning service on Sunday and you my dear,' he said kindly to Sylvia, 'make sure the church is nice and clean, I know you will.'

Clean? The word caught halfway across her lips. She knew there were some duties tied in with the agreement, but this was more than bell-ringing and lighting the boiler in winter. How long would cleaning the church take? She daren't look at the Reverend for fear of showing her horror, but glared at John, who ducked his head to avoid any confrontation.

'I'll leave you to explore the bedrooms on your own, and John, you know downstairs well enough. Come outside and see the land tied in with the tenancy. It is expected you will keep it in good heart and follow correct farming practises.'

Sylvia seethed. She wasn't to be given the courtesy of a tour of the domain that would be hers, the kitchen, just so long as she was informed of her 'cleaning' duties.

Reluctantly, she followed the men outside into the damp air. The ground was soaked, a good excuse for the brief outline given by the hasty cleric. She guessed the man must be hungry for his lunch. He pointed out a croft above the garden, an 18 acre mountainous pasture and a pretty 4 acre meadow leading down to the river on the other side of the road.

This amount of land seemed incomprehensible. She felt suddenly excited at the prospect of it being theirs, but overawed by the vastness of the undertaking. She tried to ask what the previous tenants did with the land, but was rushed into rapid farewells.

The vicar and his wardens took their leave, and Sylvia wondered if they felt the need to escape before any awkward questions arose. Watching the holy trio toddle down the drive, she quelled the desire to stick out her tongue. Instead, standing tall, she marched to the front door. A tiny flagged square formed the entrance, just big enough to turn around in. Immediately facing was a narrow, closed-in staircase leading up to a black hole. A nicotine stained, part-glazed door led to the public bar, and an open door on the right revealed the kitchen. Beyond was the dining room. Sylvia stepped into her new domain.

It was really more than a kitchen, for it stretched the full width of the building. It was bare, devoid of any furnishings and languished in an air of mustiness. The outer walls, built to withstand a siege, cradled small windows. One, housing a seat within the stonework, overlooked the garden and the fell rising behind. Its mirror image had no such luxury. Instead a faded stone sink with a lonely brass tap sat in isolated splendour. There was no room to move, but a view to inspire any artist. The window framed the swirling, peaty-brown waters of the Wharfe and the bridge leading to the ancient church, a view to die for. This end of the room seemed to be designated the working area. A well used Aga sheltered in an alcove, alongside a battered wood-burning stove. A narrow gap between the Aga and the wall was rather more than off-putting. A catacomb of dust webs, so impregnated with dirt that they sagged under the weight, formed a delightful backcloth for, who knew what? She recoiled with apprehension at the thought of cleaning out the den of any livestock that might have residence there. The lamps were calor gas fed and the heating, such that it was, fuelled by coke as was the cooker. Then it dawned upon her – *Oh no*! – There was no electricity. No fridge, no electric iron, no washing machine. How in God's name could anyone be expected to cater and take in guests under these conditions? Hiding her plummeting spirits, she warily turned to John.

'Is...is electricity likely to reach us soon?'

He swallowed. 'It could be a few years yet love. Buckden has it, but the cost would be prohibitive any higher up, as homesteads are too far apart.'

Her heart sank. There seemed to be a blow at every turn. Without a word she left the kitchen and climbed the stairs to see what was awaiting there. On her left was one very large bedroom, the window, deep in the wall, housed a seat where she sat for a couple of minutes looking out onto the garden. The only piece of furniture left by the previous tenants was installed in the alcove formed over the staircase. It was a big, dark wardrobe with a narrow mirror in the single door. A great drawer filled its base. Sylvia viewed it with some apprehension. It was forbidding, but she wasn't sure why. Perhaps it was the colour. Perhaps it was the overpowering size. She moved to open its door, but changed her mind and left the room in some haste. A long passage faced her. There were two rooms to the right and one at the end. They were pleasant and, happily all could take a double bed or two singles. An apology for a bathroom was the only room on the left. She had to smile. A Victorian bath hooked under a small window overlooking the river filled one wall. Tucked next to it was a washbasin, not of generous proportions, and an airing cupboard. There was just enough space to stand a towel-rail. The loo was separate next door. At least she'd be able to have a bath and watch the river flow past on its way to civilisation.

Satisfied she could make the bedrooms look pretty at minimal cost heartened her. The floorboards were in good nick and would look well stained and polished with bright rugs. Feeling better she returned to the bar.

The fireplace wasn't exactly welcoming. The grate was too small, more in keeping with a tiny living room. At one side, two wall mounted cases of fish caught her eye, despite their thick coating of dust. A wet finger rubbed on the glass revealed glittering scales of pink and red through to delicate blue and silver. Rainbow trout, and well named, Sylvia had a feeling they were a bit special. They'd make a good talking point, a feature to show off when made more obvious.

There had been very little 'stock at valuation'. The cases of trout, five round topped-tables with curved cast-iron legs, Windsor chairs painted indiscriminate colours, an 1890s American coffee grinder and the wardrobe. The place had potential, but Sylvia wondered how their meagre amount of available cash would stretch to do all that was necessary.

Rather than face John again she decided to leave the dining room till later, instead she stepped outside. The rain had stopped, finally, truly, and the cool, damp air caressed her cheeks and soothed her. Calmer now, she walked up the rough drive back to the car to collect Cassie who was gazing expectantly through the window. Seeing her mistress, she placed her front paws on the sill and pressed her nose against the glass.

'I'm here, Cassie. Come along, we'll go exploring.'

Her pet gleefully bounded out as Sylvia opened the car door and immediately began sniffing the exciting smells of the new surroundings.

The garden, retained by a dry stone wall, was about five feet higher than the drive. A narrow passage, between the garden and the dairy, which was beautifully shelved out in stone, led to a flight of steps. She eagerly climbed the green-slimed staircase where tiny ferns struggled to climb out of every available crack, then up onto a muddy path sunk in the turf. On her left was the garden, on the right a tiny building, half hidden by a shaggy growth of dead nettles. Curiosity led the way through a rough jungle to discover it was a derelict dry-closet. Mother Nature, in her wisdom, had grown a variety of pale, tangled stems that reached for the light out of the hole in the wooden loo seat. *Oh my God*, her hand shot to her mouth as though to stifle the gasp of horror. She recognised the design from the one at a holiday cottage her mother rented for childhood holidays in Wales. She smiled as she remembered their howls of laughter at each visit to the scrubbed, wooden plank. Ruefully rubbing her legs, snagged

26

by the undergrowth, she looked beyond the garden to a small croft, walled off from the steep eighteen acre pasture. In one corner was a corrugated steel shed next to a gate that led into the pasture, climbing to meet the grey sky where dark clouds scudded across the horizon. The vastness of 'their' land seemed to stretch forever before her.

Somewhat subdued she turned onto the garden, where the stream tumbling down from the hills beckoned her. There, wedged between two rocks, was a piece of wooden guttering, one end submerged in the water that cascaded down its length into a two-foot square, brick, catchment-tank. She stared at it for several moments before the truth dawned. This was the water supply to the pub! As she viewed the contraption she became aware of someone watching her. Lifting her head, she saw a pair of amber eyes in a black and grey face framed by dangerous-looking horns. Startled, she realised the sheep was standing in the stream on higher ground. The animal, with total disregard didn't flinch. Instead, it had the audacity to lower its back-end and piddle in the bubbling waters.

'Oh my giddy aunt, shoo!'

Sylvia tried to climb towards it, wheeling her arms in an attempt to drive it off, but it stood its ground and glared at her. She halted. Only then did it amble off up the fell to join its fellow polluters of their water supply. She realised this wasn't a one off incident and at best they'd all probably get the trots. She wondered how long it would take to become immune, though, happily they were all hardy souls, but what about the guests?

'Anybody home? Sylvia, Syl.'

Hurriedly she made her way down to the car park, surprised that she had missed Robert's arrival. Her brother was standing on the drive, his youthful face looking anxious.

'Robert.' She waved furiously. 'Did you have a decent ride up? What do you think of the place then?'

He spotted Sylvia as she galloped down the garden steps to meet him, and his worried expression lifted.

'I thought we'd never get here, it's taken forever and the road lower down seems about to flood. Lord knows how we'll make a living in winter up here. It looks as though a fortune needs spending on the place to make it decent. I've had a quick nosey whilst waiting for you. Have you seen this?'

He took her arm and led her to a small building sandwiched in the middle of the row of out-houses. He kicked the door. The top hinge complained and, in slow motion, parted company with the rotting jamb.

'Crikey Robert, you've broken it. What will we do?... What's inside?'

Shifting the door, they peered into the blackness. There were stained, stone slabs on three walls closeting the most unbelievable stench.

'Hell's bells. It's the gents.'

After everything else Sylvia couldn't keep from giggling. 'Well at least there's the tap and the stone trough at the door. Perhaps the idea is to grab a ladle of water on the way in, then swill down when the job's done.' This set her off into fits of hysterics.

'Be serious sis. I can't see people coming up all this way in winter. It's not exactly the Ritz. And the place...' he gestured to the gents behind them '...well, it's filthy, Sylv. There's no other word for it.'

'Look on the bright side, Robert, we've a run-down pub, no electricity, eighteen acres of pasture land, four acres of meadow, hardly any cash and I'm frightened to death. How's that for starters?'

He shook his head, but at least he smiled.

'C'mon,' she roused, 'I'll show you round as soon as the furniture's unloaded. Honestly, you'll love the place, it's got so much potential.'

CHAPTER 2

At last their few possessions were in place and they'd somewhere to lay their heads at the end of this day of days. They'd managed to get to grips with the vagaries of a temperamental Aga and successfully boiled the enormous kettle and fried bacon in an equally enormous pan.

Sylvia stared out of the kitchen window as another bout of rain dashed against the glass. Her nerves were on edge, not helped by the unforgiving weather. She just couldn't believe the rain. Somehow in that narrow valley it had an intensity not associated with the streets of Leeds. Perhaps it would put off any customers. Perhaps no one would turn up for their first night. What would they do then?

There were only a few hours left before opening time, too few for her liking. She'd swept the flagged floor in the bar, passage and cellar and was about to put the huge kettle onto the Aga for hot water to mop out, when to her delight they had an unexpected bonus. Robert discovered the small stove next to the Aga had a back-boiler which was piped to the cylinder in the bathroom airing-cupboard. They had hot water on tap!

'Aren't we just idiots? Fancy nobody noticing the cylinder in the bathroom and the two taps to the hand-basin and the bath. But what about down here, surely there's a tap in the kitchen?'

Investigating, Robert pulled aside a hinged strip of wood alongside shelving on the wall next to the sink. 'Well would you believe it?' he laughed. 'There's a tap here. It's got to be the hot water.'

'They must have hidden it to stop folk wasting the water,' said John thoughtfully.

Sylvia had no time for discussion, she had that tap filling her bucket to the brim. Before long mopping was completed, along

29

with gleaming rainbow trout and shining windows. Thrilled, but dissatisfied with the dismal light from the single gas mantle, she racked her brain as to how it could be improved. Then she remembered seeing a box of little lamps in the coach house.

'Where's the torch John? I need to go outside.'

'What on earth for? It's tippling down out there.'

She grabbed the instrument from his hesitant grasp and beetled off without a coat.

'The woman's mad,' sighed John.

The wind blew the rain nearly horizontal. It was all a bit eerie in the coach house. The piles of rubbish could be hiding all kinds of nasties, but she kept her nerve and quickly located the box of lamps under a pile of empty beer crates. Eagerly she carried her spoils back to the kitchen.

'Boys, look what I've got. They'll look lovely lit on the bar tables.'

'They could do with a clean. And you do realise they need filling with oil before you can light 'em?' Robert delivered the statement with an air of authority as he recognised the shortfall, something that hadn't crossed her mind. Feeling relieved that at last her brother seemed to be finding his feet, she had to grin to herself as he grabbed the torch from her and with a superior look marched to the door. Before she had chance to ask what he was up to, he was back.

'There you are.'

He dumped a rusty can of oil and a tin of Brasso on the table. 'I spotted them in the dairy when we looked around.'

John, looking rather disgruntled, in a half jocular way muttered, 'Eyes like a shit-house rat.'

Sylvia immediately abandoned her plans for more transformation. She recognised the grumbles of an empty tummy. Better feed the beast before trouble erupted.

'Enough boys, beans on toast time. There's a contraption in that cupboard, I think it's to make toast on the Aga.'

Robert delved in the depths and eventually produced what looked like a pair of tennis racquets joined together at the bottom.

'What the Hell's that?' John looked perplexed.

'This is how it works.' Sylvia cut a couple of slices of bread, sandwiched them between the metal-mesh circles and with aplomb, popped them under the Aga lid.

'How did you know that was what it was for?'

'Ah, I've got second sight,' she grinned. 'No, Anna's home had an Aga and her mum made toast with the same kind of thing. Look. It works.' She lifted the lid. 'Lo and behold. Toast!'

Soon they were tucking into a mountain of Heinz beans on special Aga toast.

'Only half an hour to opening time, its 6.30 already. You two better tidy yourselves ready for the fray. I'm going to clean the lamps and fill them with oil, then we can have them lit on the tables for the opening. That's, of course, if anybody comes in this foul weather.'

'For Heaven's sake sis, stop nattering. We're sure to have some customers. Remember the place hasn't really been used as a proper pub for yonks and folk will want to have a look.'

John added his two penn'orth. 'Don't worry Sylv, the locals have got wind there's an attractive landlady to gawp at.'

She was mortified. If there was one thing she hated, it was being the centre of attention. It was going to take a lot of effort for her to get behind the bar, despite ambition not being in short supply. Her intention was that most of the time she would be tied in the kitchen for, as far as she could see, every minute would be taken in looking after visitors. The men should run the pub side of things.

'Come on woman, I'm only teasing you. The locals are bound to be curious, they'll want to see how three townies will manage their first night. Especially when one's a bit of crumpet.'

He and Robert were convulsed with laughter as the 'landlady designate' flounced out of the kitchen and stamped up the stairs. Smiling at the repartee, she walked into the bathroom to have a wash in *warm* water and tidy herself, just in case she was forced to make an appearance.

The sound of a vehicle approaching sent her senses galloping. With some urgency she ran a comb through her hair, then dashed down the stairs to open the bar door for a final check on the room. It looked inviting. The little oil lamps, cleaned and polished, added a soft glow to the cold light of the gas mantle. The fire burned brightly, giving a warm welcome to any visitor.

Anthony the churchwarden was their first customer. He arrived in a back-draught of noisy splendour. His old grey Fergie tractor rorted down the road and juddered to a stop on the car park. It was driven by Anthony, but standing tall, perched on the back axle, was a replica of himself. In the dim light the figures bore a strong resemblance to deep sea fishermen. They clambered down from their steed, shook themselves and deposited great macs and sou'westers in the doorway at the foot of the stairs. They seemed to almost fill the small room, these giant farmers.

Sylvia glanced from the spreading puddle running from the pile of oilskins to their first customers. Anthony nodded to her as he smoothed back his water-slicked hair.

'Evnin' missus. This ere's mi brother, Thomas.' He looked the older of the two. His untidy greying hair flopped over beetle brows that seemed to protect deep eye sockets in a skeletal face, covered by a thin layer of gnarled skin.

'Pleased to meet you, Thomas.'

'An' thi'sen lass.'

Sylvia felt her eyes grow to the size of saucers as her gaze fixed on a large single tooth dominating a barren upper jaw. His smile was fearsome, yet comic.

' Sylv, love…' She heard John's quiet tone and turned to see him gesturing her towards the wall. 'Let our guests come through.'

She turned back to the two brothers still waiting patiently and realised her mistake. 'Oh, yes, sorry.' She backed into the doorway, feeling the squelching oilskins grip her ankles.

Thomas' tombstone smile grew wide. 'Thank ye kindly,' and with a nod from Anthony they passed in to the bar.

Sylvia looked after them. They may not have the education or the experience of city dwellers, but they had manners. And they were kind. She was definitely going to like it here.

'Landlord. A pint o'mild an wun o'bitter if ye please,' said Anthony.

She watched John, preening at being called landlord, go into the cellar, a small extension taken from the adjoining barn, no bigger than a good cupboard. There was just enough room to hold a stone gantry for the two barrels of beer taken over in the wet stock valuation, one of mild and one of bitter, the lifeline of the pub. The practice was to fill a large enamelled jug directly from the barrel, the customer being served from the jug. The barrel of bitter had been left spiled and tapped, all ready for use. John turned the tap and was proudly watching the stream of golden liquid fill the jug, obviously taking care not to lose the creamy froth, the mark of a good pint. Robert made her jump as he whispered in her ear.

'Oh good, he looks pleased he's got a good froth, but he's still got to tap the barrel of mild. I think he's a bit nervous. He's going to have to be brave and bash that tap through the bung before any beer can be drawn off.'

They watched as he confidently put the tap in position, then, with a whacking blow of the enormous wooden mallet, he struck it home.

'Thank God,' they heard him mutter.

The tap, though, had other ideas. It blew back, shooting to the wall, followed by a torrent of dark brown mild joyfully jetting in all directions.

'Oh my God!' gasped Robert. 'I bet that barrel's not been spiled to let off the pressure.'

'What do you mean?'

'We had the same thing happen in the navy. Someone had forgotten to knock the wooden peg into the cork-bung on the side of the barrel, so as to ease the pressure inside. The tap was blown out. We lost the lot.'

They peered down the passage as John, a dancing King Canute, struggled manfully with a brass tap, the wooden mallet and a brown waterfall, which was in danger of flooding the cellar.

'For God's sake, give me a hand,' rasped John between clenched teeth.

Galvanised into action, Robert dived at the barrel. 'That's our cash disappearing down the drain.'

He slapped his flattened hand over the gaping hole. At the same time John desperately aimed the tap and swung the mallet. Robert yelled and jumped feet in the air, clutching the hand that had quelled the flood. By some fluke the tap had hit home, but Robert's fingers had suffered some rearrangement in the process.

Sylvia rushed to the soaking pair, willing herself not to laugh at the farcical picture set out in the cellar.

'Both of you, dump your clothes in the bath and get changed as fast as you can. Quick, Robert, let's have a look at that hand.'

His fingers were swelling rapidly and she couldn't be certain what damage he'd done. Robert pulled his hand away in annoyance and marched down the passage into the kitchen, then round to the stairs, so avoiding the bar. John looked embarrassed and a trifle annoyed, but, as always, was ready to see the funny side and braved the customers, whose numbers had swelled during the fiasco. The laughter at the sight of a dripping landlord, set the mood for the rest of the evening.

In the chaos, Sylvia had forgotten her fears of being on display. She looked round the room at the sea of strange faces and felt her new found confidence slipping away. She was on her own. And they all needed serving. To make matters worse she hadn't the remotest idea of what was what, but Robert had had the foresight to put the prices of drinks on a card and pin it on the wall. Feeling apprehensive, she tried to look as though this was something she was well used to. As she stepped forward to serve her first customer, the door burst open and a gust of wind bore down a life-raft in the shape of Gerald, along with a nice looking fellow of similar age.

'Hi, darlin'. Tha looks luv'ly t'neet.'

The greeting and saucy grin made her laugh. 'Gerald, nice to see you. Robert and John have gone to change. They got drowned tapping the barrel of mild. If I get stuck, will you give me a hand?'

'A'll do that alright!'

On hearing the full story he guffawed loud enough to disturb the churchyard occupants. The ice was broken, she felt relaxed. Thankfully no one wanted draught beer and she soon came to terms with de-capping bottles, pouring into glasses, measuring shorts and coping with the till; a compartmented drawer on the window ledge in the passage. Finally, when all were served she was able to chat to Gerald.

'Meet Mark, Sylvia. Y' ll see 'im everyday. 'E brings thi' milk from 'farm across bridge.'

'Hello Mark.' She smiled at the tall, hawkish faced young man who, to her surprise, blushed.

'I..if th' tha tells us what milk th' tha' needs a'll bring it int' m..m..mornin."

She felt concerned over poor Mark's pronounced stutter. It seemed such a shame; no wonder he was shy. 'I think we'll just need enough for us tomorrow, there'll be no visitors.'

'Cum an' sit wi' us,' said Gerald, reaching for her. 'Tha can sit on mi knee if tha wants.' Sylvia sensed her eyes grow wide and the start of her own blush.

'S,steady, tha', tha'll upset 'lass.'

Sylvia liked this new-found champion. They chatted easily; it seemed to puzzle Gerald. She knew from her brief association with him that he considered himself irresistible. The conqueror of the whole female spectrum, he would expect her undivided attention. She felt comfortable in their company, so dared to ask about Thomas's gravestone of a tooth, thinking they must find it as peculiar as she did. But they were all too busy scratching a living in this unforgiving hill country to even consider such trivia. To them Thomas's tooth was as insignificant as a raindrop in the river.

'Why,' said Gerald thoughtfully, 'the man's never been out o'dale. The farthest e'll 'ave been 'll be about 10 miles from 'ome across tops 'an there ain't a dentist in that patch. Nay, alus pulled 'is own 'as Tom!'

Sylvia gaped at her companions. 'How on earth does he do it? Does he tie string round the door knob and bang it shut?'

Her thoughts harked back to childhood tortures for removing baby teeth. The two lads found her curiosity amusing; they'd never considered methods of tooth extraction and started being silly, as young men with one foot still in boyhood often did.

'Ee ties it t'auld cow's tail an' when she lets fly, out pops tooth.'

'Nay, ee t..t..teks pliers t..t..damned tooth.'

To her relief John reappeared, freshly kitted out and in a better humour. He smiled as he gazed round the well filled bar, though she saw his nostrils twitch as he met the earthy odour of steamy bodies tinged with alcohol fumes. It made her giggle, for John was extremely fastidious, he took forever to get ready. She was frequently driven to distraction by his attention to looking the part in contrast to her crash-bang wallop approach.

'What's the joke?'

Mark and Gerald looked sheepish. Sylvia, leaned against her husband and whispered, 'All's well. I'm going to the kitchen now. The customers want their landlord.' He grew an inch and beamed at his flock.

Turning down the bar-passage doorway she saw Robert standing by the Aga with his head bowed. 'Is that hand hurting?'

'The damn thing's throbbing, but I don't think there's anything broken. I just thought I'd have a cuppa before going in there.' He motioned to the bar.

'Sit down.' She brewed tea and poured him a cup, which he downed in great gulps.

'Is John ok in there? I'd better go and help.'

She watched him hesitate at the bar doorway and decided her brother was as nervous as she had been. Really, there wasn't enough room for the two men and the customers. 'Lord, what a stupid arrangement,' she muttered to Cassie, half asleep in her basket. That passage should be out and a nice little bar put in its place, there would be more room for them and the customers, she decided. But perhaps the ceiling would drop if they took the wall down....

Her plans were interrupted by the sight of John being backed into the passage by a chest-high little man talking rapidly.

'Tha'll be 'landlord, Charlie's mi'name. If there's 'owt tha' needs, me 'an our Fred, mi' brother,'ll gi' thee an 'and. Mi wife's built like a gert' whale, she's good fer 'ard graft when tha git's goin' wi' caterin' job.'

She recognised him as one of two brothers from Oughtershaw; Gerald had told her all about them earlier. They were stocky individuals. One had a round face with the cheekiest grin imaginable and an air of confidence that Sylvia did not associate with shy, sheep farmers. His brother, the elder of the two, was a different kettle of fish. He was much quieter, his thin pale face held ewe-like eyes and a sloppy mouth that seemed to have trouble keeping the saliva in check. These untidy fellows, Charlie and Fred Middlemas, apparently were very gifted musicians. Mark told John they had never been given any training, music seemed to come naturally to them. They could play any instrument, but specialised in the accordion and always played for the local dances. Charlie, with animal cunning, had sourced the main figure of the three.

John looked somewhat startled as he focussed on this untidy individual. Charlie's heavy stubble crinkled as he gave a saucy grin and looked unflinchingly back. His nondescript hair stood on end at a variety of angles as though the Inn's absent power supply had found its way to the little man's scalp. Sylvia, transfixed, watched the proceedings. Her smart husband contrasted sharply with these brothers. They both sported waistcoats, stiffened into creases by years of grime and sweat, some buttons stretched under the strain of a bit of belly thickening, some not there at all. Heavy cotton collarless shirts, top buttons undone, revealed once white, round-necked vests. Old suit jackets, which looked as though they would hold all bends and shapes when discarded, and brown cord trousers tied round the middle with twine, completed the ensemble. John, unusual for him, appeared uncomfortable, but she knew he wouldn't want to offend or risk losing a customer.

'Thank you both, we'll bear it in mind, but at the moment we don't know what we'll need. In fact, we don't even know what the Hell we're doing.'

A ripple of laughter ran round those nearest. Charlie, obviously pleased with the thought that he had opened the door to an easy touch, battled on.

'Thee an' thi missus 'as t'cum t' owr' next dance, it's in village 'all, 'bout five mile up'dale. Tha'll enjoy it, me an' Fred's playin' accordions, tha's got t'come.'

Sylvia's heart thumped as she heard John saying they would love to go. Oh God, I don't mind the work, but I do NOT want to be on show. Not just yet anyway, for pity's sake, can't we get acclimatised first? She tried hard to catch John's eye, but he knew her better than she realised, for all night he successfully avoided the chance to be buttonholed.

The evening went well, the atmosphere was cosy and convivial, so they were shocked when at about 10 o'clock their customers, in quick succession, drank up and bid their farewells. Only one remained, Mark from across the river. He didn't seem surprised at the exodus, but his eyes glinted mischievously at the concern of his new neighbours.

'D, d'na worry. Thiv' g'gone up t' Lord Markham's spot.'

'Who in Heaven's name is Lord Markham? I didn't know there were titled folk around.'

Sylvia couldn't imagine landed gentry living close by and even more, the idea of the locals descending on the country seat at that time of night was ludicrous. Mark surely must mean something else. Then she caught sight of a smile lurking round the corners of his mouth.

'Mark, what do you mean? Who is Lord Markham anyway?'

He had the good grace to look uncomfortable and blurted out, 'Lord, ain't a t..t.title. It's a f.f.first name, like Earl, M..M..Major and Duke. Lord Markham is't landlord o'pub at top o' n.next l'ille dale.'

'But why on earth have they gone there at this time of night?'

Mark shuffled his feet, hesitating before he replied.

'W.w.well e's a local and e'd mek 'em f.feel disloyal if they didn't go t.t''is place t'neet.'

'Why?' she demanded.

By this time Mark was backing towards the door, 'Cos it's thi op'nin neet. An' thee's, 'oft cummed uns.'

Sylvia had begun to get exasperated, but feeling sorry for Mark, who had been put squarely on the spot, she softened her tone.

'Just what, pray, is an 'oft cummed 'un?'

In one fast move, Mark turned and leapt for the door, sending a chair flying as he gasped, 'Folk t t.that ain't bred up 'ere.'

But his escape route was well and truly blocked as the door flung open, almost hitting him in the face. Filling the entrance was a town-smart lady with a dapper little man. She pushed forward in Mark's direction. 'You're not leaving Mark?'

Sylvia gaped, they were not the type of people she'd expected. Pulling herself together she smiled. 'Hello, I'm Sylvia. I'm so glad to meet another female. I've been outnumbered so far.'

'Oh no dear, it's a nice position to be in, surrounded by men.' She laughed, a harsh sound with the suspicion of a gin-voice.

Sylvia immediately felt immature and decided that this person would not be a friend. She was attractive in quite a hard way, her figure had been kept in good order, which she showed to best advantage. Small and slim, her tight black skirt was slit to the thigh, showing off a pair of good legs. Pale blue knitwear skimmed a curvaceous bust. Not a hair was out of place and she seemed totally alien in the gas-lit bar. Up close, her face had a crumpled look, as she continually screwed up her eyes to diminish the permanent cloud of fog from the cigarette she smoked greedily.

'Mark, come and sit next to me.'

Sylvia watched, mesmerised, as poor Mark was bulldozed into a corner with little room for escape. Suddenly, she became conscious of a presence at her side.

'Hello. I'm the local artist, Alfred Fewston. My wife and I live in Buckden.'

Sylvia immediately liked Alfred, though he seemed to have a bit of an ego and he certainly was a dresser. His fawn drill trousers were immaculate, as was the green sports jacket, cream shirt and Paisley cravat. He had a neat military moustache that twitched as he talked. The rain must have stopped, she thought.

'Have you been into Buckden yet? he asked.

'No not really. We just drove through.'

'We have the prettiest cottage in the village. I do all my painting there in a small studio and we take in B&B's during the summer months. Our visitors usually call here for coffee after church. If you are intending catering we'll send them for evening meals.' He smiled magnanimously.

She swallowed; the prospect of cooking dinners for strangers was suddenly imminent. 'Why, that's very kind of you, but I don't know quite when we'll be ready.'

Feeling vulnerable, she turned her attention to Alfred's wife, introduced as Carla. The lady bothered her. No secret would be safe with this one, she decided. Smiling to herself, she watched with amusement as she logged the lady's passion. Carla became coy, crossed her legs, revealing a frill of black lace and peeped up at Mark out of the corner of her eye. She flattered and teased the poor lad, who was about half her age.

'Now why were you running off? Surely there's all you want here.' She placed her hand on his knee.

Mark turned bright red. He tried to speak, but nothing came out.

'Why Mark, you're blushing. How sweet!'

This was all too much for him. He stood up, struggled with the table and Carla's well placed legs. His feet, on the large side, were an obstacle to contend with and seemed to get dreadfully tangled. In his haste to flee, he managed to knock his drink all over John, who for the second time that night suffered a soaking.

It wasn't long before Alfred and Carla decided to follow suit and also leave.

'They're probably dashing to the domain of the Lord of the Dale, Mr Markham,' said Robert with some bitterness.

'I bet he's telling the locals they should support him and not the townies. We could be up against it, you know.'

'It won't be easy these next few months, but until spring comes and brings out the tourists we'll all have to work to get this place ship-shape (he gave John a meaningful glance that said a thousand words) and hope we get some of the local trade.'

Sylvia realised that John was beginning to see that life wasn't going to be a bowl of cherries. And he didn't like it. Whilst Robert, in pain, hadn't tried to hide the slight animosity he felt.

Trying to lift the mood she joked, 'I don't know whether to laugh or cry. I wouldn't have thought it possible so much could happen in such a short space of time. Though to be honest, I'm absolutely knackered.'

'Same here. Though my worry is how we'll keep afloat.'

Robert glared at John and, his sister picking up the tension, thrust a mug of coffee, laced with rum into each ready fist.

'I think we'd better sit down and get a plan of action sorted.'

She'd already realised that the pub could not support them until the summer trade started. She'd mulled round the problem. There was nothing else for it, John would have to keep his job for as long as possible. The intention had been for him to give in his notice when they moved, but that, now, was not on. She and Robert could manage any trade that came their way together with the decorating and cleaning. Besides John would be there for the weekends. His employment probably wouldn't last long anyway for, to be fair he was well out of his designated area for selling office equipment. His reputation was that he never reigned long in a job, a stigma he'd lived up to in the two years she'd known him. She would have to tread carefully in suggesting her plan. The best way would be to make them think it was their idea, though John would probably welcome the freedom it would give him. Feeling happier that she had found a way out of the immediate worry, she sat at the table.

'Boys, I think we've been a bit naive in thinking this place will support us until the weather improves and the visitors start coming. Now that we know there's also strong competition close at hand for even the local trade, it's going to be more difficult. John love, your wages will help until you've worked your notice, but what then...?'

Her plan worked. John jumped to the rescue gleefully, but the speed he took the bait gave her a moment of concern. He was obviously pleased he would be able to get away from her and the shackles of the business. That hurt, even though she had got exactly what she wanted.

CHAPTER 3

Sylvia woke as dawn softly lit a dark sky. Startled by the unfamiliar surroundings, it was several minutes before she brought the events of the previous day into focus. She stared at the sickly, green distempered walls; they were quite ghastly, reminding her there was so much to be done. The depressing influence of the early hours sat with her, squashing her usually optimistic outlook. She solemnly reflected on the discussions of the previous night and the decision they had made.

Since the wedding, John had precariously hung on to his sales rep job, which he had intended to pack in when they took the pub. Now, necessity had reversed that decision. She hoped the plan for him to carry on would work, though uncertainty hovered round the edges of her thoughts. John would have a carte blanche to play, and she and Robert would be left holding the baby.

Oh, what the Hell! Count your blessings girl, just look out of that window.

The patch of sky, embraced by leaden hills, was a soft, grey lagoon of shimmering depths, softened by fingers of incredible pink. She craned her neck to include the stone-tiled roof of the vicarage and snatches of the busy river, fuelled by yesterday's deluge. How many could wake to a view like that? Certainly no one in Leeds. She smiled and with renewed optimism felt ready to take on whatever came their way.

Stretching lazily, she gave herself the brief luxury of gazing at her husband, fast asleep beside her. He could sleep on a clothes-line. She'd often been amazed at his ability to nod off as soon as he sat down, whether it be on a bus, sometimes even whilst driving the car, or in the middle of a conversation. It didn't matter, it was all part of his charm. His brown hair, now greying at the temples, curled untidily on the pillow. She leaned over and gently kissed the top of his head, before sliding out of the warmth. There were things to do, and she did want a good look at that dining room on her own.

Grateful for the warm water and the cosiness of the tiny bathroom she washed and dressed in comparative luxury. The change in air temperature as she opened the door made her shiver. A cold draft coming up the stairs from the front door seemed to be the culprit. Braving the chill, she tiptoed down to the warmth of the kitchen, thanks to the wood burning stove and the Aga combining to up the heat.

'Hey Cass, you've got the best spot in the house.' She bent down and picked up the eager animal, holding her close as she leaned against the cooker's rail, relieved that Robert had managed to keep both stoves lit. She knew from staying with Anna, that it was a difficult job if the Aga went out, for it involved starting up with charcoal. Ominously, there was a bag of the stuff under the stairs, and she couldn't help but wonder if they had inherited a temperamental beast. No good worrying, so, up with the Aga lid and on with the heavy kettle for tea. Leaving it to boil, she entered the room that she'd only been able to peep into yesterday. Surprisingly, it was filled with light. There were more windows than she had remembered. One overlooked the river, there was another at the side of the fireplace, and on the garden side stood a half-glazed door with a window at each side. Even the fireplace was acceptable, and the room was big enough to give ample space for a good few diners. Excited at the prospect of cleaning and decorating the place, she hummed softly as she made tea for the boys.

'Tea in bed! My goodness you're keen.' John shuffled up the bed to take the cup from her.

'I've been looking at the dining room. It's filthy, but it's perfect. I know exactly how it's going to be decorated. John, you're laughing at me.'

'No. I'm so happy you're happy. I thought yesterday you might be having doubts.'

Smiling, she left him to join Robert, already getting a refill.

'Fancy a walk up the road before breakfast?'

43

Robert nodded and swallowed down his tea. Looking out of the window, he hunched his shoulders as though to prepare for the cold and grabbed his duffle coat from the back of the door. In front, Sylvia pulled up the hood of her jacket as the cold hit, and he immediately followed suit.

'Crikey, it's cold. Thank God it's not raining, but just look at that river, it's fairly racing down to Buckden.'

The pair leaned over the bridge and watched the cream-topped brown waters boiling with raw power. 'I wouldn't like to fall into that cauldron, but you've got to admit it is glorious. You can see why visitors come here. Though the noise did keep me awake for ages. I suppose it's something we'll get used to.'

Sylvia shivered. 'I never noticed, went to sleep straight away. Let's move, this rawness is creeping into my bones.'

They left the crashing waters and walked past the church gate, then on towards Mark's farm. At the entrance a long, gangly figure walked towards them carrying a small milk churn. 'I'se j.j.just bringin' thi m.milk.'

'We'll take that for you,' said Robert.

Sylvia gave him a beaming smile and took the can from the shy farmer, who ducked his head as he muttered, 'T..thanks.'

'It's a good job it's stopped raining. Do you think it will be a nice day? The sky is glorious,' she said, trying to put him at his ease.

'Nay. R..r..red sky in't m.mornin' shepherds' w.w.warnin.'

He turned and without further comment left them standing there feeling somewhat deflated. They watched his long stride take him back home and then, they, too turned to walk back across the bridge.

'I bet he's feeling a bit uncomfortable after last night's episode with Carla. That'll be why he acted so strange.'

'Oh, I don't know,' said Robert, 'you're making excuses. He's probably the moody sort.'

Rather than reply, she raced home to cook breakfast. The kitchen was empty, no John. Her heart sank. She saw Robert cast his eyes round the room as he came in. Before he could say a word she filled the gap, 'Breakfast in a jiffy.' To her relief she heard a movement upstairs and making a beeline for the door called out, 'Breakfast's ready.'

John made his appearance, immaculate in grey worsted and gleaming, handmade shoes. She couldn't help making a comparison as they sat down to eat, the lord of the manor and his two skivvies. Feeling guilty she made cheerful conversation, but when he eagerly climbed in the car, full of confidence in his new role of saviour, she had misgivings. He waved happily. 'I don't know what time I'll be back.'

She watched the car go down the road until it was swallowed between those craggy stone walls. Anxiety tweaked in her subconscious and Robert, recognising the signs, put both hands on her shoulders. 'Come on sis, it's time for action. We've to start the big clean-up.'

That day and the ones that followed, blurred into a sentence of hard labour. Robert and Sylvia took on the role of muck shifters. They swept, scrubbed, sandpapered and whitewashed. In the dining room, ancient lace curtains were held captive to the windows by nests of dead flies, cocooned in webs laboriously woven by armies of spiders. The haze of dust and damp, tainted with the smell of disuse was blitzed away by gallons of soap suds and relentless elbow grease.

The kitchen clean-up was a different kettle of fish. Over the decades it had been wallpapered, wallpapered and wallpapered again. The only tools they could find to attack this half-inch thick wedge, were ancient kitchen knives. In places, much to Sylvia's delight, great chunks could be levered away, protesting as they were prised from the ancient horse hair and lime plaster. They worked steadily without stopping to eat, partly because it would be an effort to prepare food in the Hell-hole they had created and they were filled with enthusiasm to carry on. But Sylvia knew if her engine was starved of fuel she became decidedly bad-tempered, and hunger eventually began to bite. 'Robert, the dust from this plaster is starting to get to me. I feel as though my pipes are closing. I need food and a cuppa.'

Her brother turned and scowled. 'Don't moan sis, just get on with it, it'll soon be tea time.' She straightened her back, stretched and looked quizzically at him, then began to giggle.

'You look as though you've been dipped in a flour barrel. The little hairs in your nose are dusted white, and even your ears. Lordy, I didn't know you grew so much fuzz.'

Half in fun and half in annoyance, he picked up the wet floor cloth and slung it at her head. She ducked, grabbed the missile and flung it back.

'Stop it, sis. At least, let's get this wall finished.'

Grumbling, she returned to the job in hand. Some spots were so resistant to their knife blades that deep scores were left in the plaster. In one such spot, Robert exclaimed, 'Sylv, look here, there's something hidden behind the layers.'

They pulled away at the thick mass of paper to rescue a pretty, pearl-handled, silver buttonhook cocooned in the ancient wall-hangings.

'Oh Robert, it's so delicate. I wonder who it belonged to?'

'It must be quite old. Perhaps one of the locals might know. We'll ask them.'

Their find gave them renewed determination to return the room to virgin splendour and hopefully more treasure, but the only other thing to be resurrected was a bent darning needle.

In amongst the dust and debris, Cassie had slept peacefully in her basket next to the Aga. Sylvia kept glancing at the sleeping hound, amused by her running feet as she dreamed of chasing livestock. So it was with some shock when Sylvia noticed that the basket was empty.

'Robert. Cassie's gone!'

'She won't be far. She wouldn't leave you. Have a look upstairs. You know how she likes her comfort, and it is grotty in here. She's probably on your bed.'

Sylvia charged past him and galloped up the stairs. The door to Robert's room was ajar. She flung it open, and there, laid out on his bed like Lady Muck, was a defiant Cassie. The jaundiced expression on her face clearly stated, don't you dare move me, I've nowhere else to go and you've taken over my bed! Sylvia smiled and bending down, kissed her haughty soul-mate. 'Ok,' she whispered, 'just until we've cleared up and then you can have a walk, but don't let Robert see you here.'

Hurrying back downstairs, she was startled to bump into John coming through the door looking as fresh as when he'd left the house that morning.

'Hello, love, I've finished work early to help get ready for the weekend trade, but I could murder a sandwich or something.' His gaze rolled over her. 'Good grief, Sylv... What have you been doing?'

She looked at him, at his clean shirt, his manicured nails and she felt her jaw tighten. 'Eating cake and drinking sherry.'

He blinked at her response and she followed him into the builders' yard masquerading as a kitchen, and was rather pleased to see him blench. He soon recovered, though, turning to her with one of his charming smiles.

'Any chance of a sandwich? I'm famished.'

They both looked to Robert as he slammed his knife down on the Aga and stormed out the of the room.

Sylvia managed to restore some kind of order, and soon the effect of food and a good cuppa took over.

John sat back in his chair and made a show of viewing the room. 'I must say, I'm impressed. I never thought you would get so far in such a short space of time.' Sylvia watched her brother roll his eyes towards the ceiling. 'You have worked wonders, the pair...'

Insistent knocking on the front door cut John short, and as Sylvia glanced at the wall clock, to assure herself that it was not opening time, Robert heaved himself to his feet, glad of an excuse to leave.

The knocking had turned to a hammering by the time he reached the front door and opened it.

Filling the entrance was a presence that could only be described as a substantial and irate farmer. His walrus moustache bristled, his bulky frame and big, black boots announced trouble.

'Ave y' got a little yella whippet?' he rapped out.

Robert, taken aback, nodded. 'Yes, we've a whippet, silver fawn in colour.'

'Aye, yella. Look up there, on top o' yon fell.'

Robert's gaze followed the direction of the shaking finger. There on the skyline across the ridge of the hill was a reluctant, galloping flock of sheep followed in their wake by, indeed, an enthusiastic, little yella whippet.

'Cassie! Oh my God.' Robert turned, bent round the kitchen door and shouted, 'John...! Sylvia.!'

Outside they watched with abject horror at the display Sylvia's darling was putting on, having the time of her life rounding up the exhausted sheep. John began to whistle, as piercing and loud as he could manage. Robert bawled, 'Cassie! Cass!' Sylvia started to run up the garden steps towards the fell.

'Tha'll not catch 'er!' shouted the farmer.

To prove him wrong, Cassie stopped the chase, turned, and came gleefully down the fell into the eighteen acre pasture.

'Thank God,' muttered John as he turned to the farmer. 'Sir, I'm so dreadfully sorry, we all are. Will your sheep be alright? Is there anything we can do?' Already he had his arm around the man's shoulder. 'Please come inside and have a tot.'

Much to the man's delight, a treble whisky was thrust into his expectant hand. The pair settled comfortably in the bar, tucked up to the fire, John leaning forward in that easy way of his that always inspired a certain trust and cosiness.

'How long have you lived here then, Mr...er?'

'Me name's Albert.'

Another whisky was popped into the welcoming glass.

'Well Albert, it's good to meet you. I'm sorry we started on the wrong foot, but I assure you, it won't happen again.'

Cassie approached Robert and Sylvia hesitantly. Her mouth was drawn back in an almost death mask grimace, her dripping tongue hanging, eyes wide. Sylvia could see that the dog sensed that her exploits were not to be applauded, but she grabbed her anyway and fairly threw her into the kitchen shutting the door behind them.

'What on earth am I going to do with you? It's going to be trouble for you, my girl. Reckon you'll have to be tied up in the barn.'

'Sis, up here they shoot...'

'I don't want to hear that,' Sylvia snapped.

'I know, I know, but we've got to face it. That kind of carry on just won't be accepted. Sheep are their bread and butter.'

She felt sick inside, for deep down she knew this wouldn't be the end of Cassie's escapades. Robert patted her on the shoulder and left to slip quietly into the bar. His tension left him immediately. Farmer and landlord were chatting like old mates. John's command performance in charm, assisted by the hard stuff, had won the day. Robert drew himself a half pint in relief and settled into an adjoining chair. Fortunately, the exhausted sheep were not the 'in lamb' ewes, as these were in the bottoms waiting to produce. These were last year's lambs, which no doubt had now had enough exercise to last a lifetime. It also turned out that Albert had the farmland adjoining Lord Markham's pub. He had lived there all his life, scratching a living from his sheep and a few hill cows, and knew all about dogs.

'T'only way t'cure thi dog, is t' tie it to an auld tupp for a neet. That'll mek it mend its ways.'

John and Robert cast furtive glances at each other, both aghast at the prospect of approaching Sylvia with that particular remedy. Rams could be rather aggressive, especially if handcuffed to a lightweight precocious bitch. John plied more whisky.

Sylvia, now alone with Cassie, slid slowly onto the floor and sat beside her basket, the tears rolled down her cheeks, 'Oh Cass how could you?' A bleary eye opened, giving Sylvia a guilty glance and then feigned sleep. It was pointless to be cross with her, whippets had been bred to chase and kill. She wiped away the tears, rubbing her face vigorously with the bottom of her apron, as though to get rid of the unhappy event. Dragging herself to her feet by the Aga rail she heard the steady conversation of the men in the bar. Surreptitiously, she gently cracked open the door to the bar passage. She could hear the voices, they didn't seem annoyed, but she dare not think what fate could befall her pet. The noise of chair legs being scraped on the flagged floor, startled her. The farmer must be leaving. She closed the passage door as quickly and quietly as possible, then knelt to hold Cass close. The animal, too, seemed to recognise her anxiety, for its heartbeat wildly against the thumping of Sylvia's own.

The kitchen door knob turned and Robert came in, followed by John. They didn't say anything, just stood there looking down on her and Cass.

Sylvia looked from one to the other. 'Well? What did he say?'

She watched Robert glance at John and dip his gaze to the floor. Her stomach followed.

'What did he *say*?'

John cleared his throat. 'He said... he wants... to tie her to a ram for the night...'

'*What?!*' Sylvia was up from Cassie's basket and taking a fighting stance, while John made conciliatory gestures as he backed towards the kitchen door.

'Nobody – *nobody* – is going to tie my Cass to any ram!'

'They're not,' said Robert. 'Sis, they're not. We talked him out of it.' Sylvia felt herself deflate with relief. 'Well, we drank him out of it.'

John shrugged his shoulders and stepped forward to wag a finger in Cassie's direction. 'And how much profit you've just cost us doesn't bear thinking about. The man had hollow legs.'

Cass had the good grace to whine and duck down in her basket, making John turn instead on Sylvia. 'She'll have to be fastened in. We can't have a repeat of that incident.'

'I know,' Sylvia snapped back. She saw the two men exchange glances of resignation and knew it would have to be done. Without a word she bent low and tied her beloved hound to the Aga rail with a length of bailer twine. 'Don't worry pet. We'll sort this out.'

'Probably a case of bolting the door after the horse had flown,' said Robert phlegmatically.

She ignored the comment and began sweeping the floor so hard as to cause a dust cloud to rival a sandstorm in the Sahara. Amidst coughing and spluttering from the two men, she felt a degree of satisfaction at their discomfort. Served 'em right. They might have shown more concern for poor Cass, tied to a horrible tupp of all things.

50

Somehow the afternoon sneaked into evening and no customers appeared. The hamlet was silent. They had expected some custom for the start of the weekend, but hopes were shattered.

'Listen!' Robert held his hand up.

'Good Lord. Surely not customers now? It's just about closing time.' John opened the door. He stepped back a pace and shut it. 'Hell! It's the law!!'

The three of them looked at each other questioning the visit.

There was an authoritative knock and in burst a large, square, police sergeant, followed by his gangly sidekick. 'Good Evening. I'm Sergeant Watt and this is Constable Smith.'

John stepped forward and confidently introduced the three of them. He hesitantly asked if they would care for a drink, but when he saw Sergeant Watt's moustache bristle alarmingly, he hastily said, 'A coffee?'

'No thank you. We've called to make sure you understand the licensing laws. We do not tolerate after-time drinking. Periodically we will make calls upon you to ensure you are obeying the rules. If you do not, your licence will be in jeopardy. Now, I wish you goodnight.' They picked up their hats, and then they were gone.

'Well. That's what I call a perfect end to a night without one single bloody customer!'

John flopped in a chair. And Robert and Sylvia stood open-mouthed.

CHAPTER 4

'Sis... You haven't forgotten it's Saturday tomorrow have you?'

Sylvia was puzzled. What the dickens was the matter with Robert? Of course she knew it was Saturday. Saturday, the village dance night. How could she forget? 'No of course I haven't forgotten. Why?'

'Well,' he cleared his throat, 'we haven't cleaned the church yet. Remember, we were excused for the first weekend, but it's our responsibility now.'

'Oh, Robert. I had forgotten. I've been so preoccupied with the thoughts of this damned dance it completely left my mind.' She looked crestfallen. 'There was so much to do here, and still to do. Oh, I suppose I'd better do it now.'

Robert smiled, 'Ok, ok, I'll give you a hand until opening time. We'll lock up here. Be quick, it's 10 o'clock already.'

Swiftly they gathered dusters, Brasso and polish and set off across the bridge with Cassie at their heels. They trod the worn flagged path through the churchyard, a grassy compound, brimming with ancient, skewed tombstones.

'Robert, just look at this gravestone. The man's name is Ottiwell, I've never heard that one before.'

'Come on, sis. Time's passing.' He pushed open the blackened oak door. It gave an obligatory groan, causing them to exchange glances as they stepped inside. As their eyes became accustomed to the gloom, Sylvia started to look about her. 'Oh Robert, I hadn't realised the church was pretty.' Her gaze took in the rough-hewn, stone walls, the flagged floor, the alter with the giant brass cross and the blue prayer stools inviting worship. She let her hand travel over the back of one of the pews. 'Well, would you believe it. There's a tiny mouse carved on this one.' Her finger gently stroked the lifelike work of art.

'If you look closely, there's a mouse on every pew.'

Delighted with the find, Sylvia eagerly investigated. 'You're right. Just look at this one, it's climbing up the side.'

'Yes. The vicar told me that the craftsmen of Kilburn made them and a mouse is their trademark. They're fairly recent, a contrast to the lighting. Look up there.' He pointed to the medieval, round, iron candelabra hanging above their heads.

'Gosh. I hope we haven't to change the candles.'

'Nobody's mentioned it, so keep quiet,' said Robert with feeling.

'John says that centuries ago, the river flooded and hundreds of fish were washed into the church. There's supposed to be a mark on the wall somewhere showing the level it came up to.'

'That's one of the points of interest for visitors, but the main one is the rood-loft!' He pointed upwards to the heavy, wooden, ornate balcony that spanned the aisles. 'There's only one other like it in Yorkshire. I did a bit of reading up on the place when I knew we were coming here.'

'You swot! Why are there only two in the county?'

'Cos' the rest were destroyed in about 1570. The York diocese issued an edict that all rood-lofts had to go, but this place is so remote nobody bothered.'

'Yes, well, it's cleaning we're here for, not history. Let's find the cleaning tools.'

They located brushes, dust pans and mops in the boiler house and began to shift buckets full of powdered plaster and grit shed from the stone walls. It made their first clean-up a prolonged affair.

'I'm not polishing any woodwork this time. It's going to have to be on a rota system. One week polishing and no sweeping, the next a sweep and a quick flick with a duster. I'm damned... sorry God... if I'm going to mop, it would take forever.'

'Fair enough, but you do realise you've lost your ticket to Heaven. Blaspheming in church... tut, tut.'

Sylvia laughed. 'I don't suppose it'll help my case bringing a dog in as well!'

'You're wrong there. In the old days apparently, they used to have a whip hanging in the church. Farmers would bring in their sheepdogs and the whip was used to keep them in order. I suppose they'd have the dogs with them to cast an eye on their flocks whilst walking to church.'

'I wonder what it was like living up here then? It's remote enough now, but then it would be really isolated.'

'Stop daydreaming. We've still got the brasses to clean.'

'Bags I do the big cross on the alter.' She rushed towards it before Robert could stake a claim.

It seemed to take ages before they finally finished the job and were crossing the river back home. Looking at the kitchen clock they were horrified to discover it was already midday.

'Oh heck. Another black mark. We should have been open an hour ago. I hope nobody's called.'

'Don't worry Robert. I think we're safe. The vicar has just walked under the window. I'm sure he didn't see us. Put the kettle on, it's grub time.'

The rest of the day turned out to be fairly quiet with small spurts of custom between a few sharp showers.

Saturday, in contrast, was a surprisingly busy day. The weather decided a repeat of the Chinese water torture should be inflicted on the already sodden hamlet, but it had the advantage of drawing into the bar every Tom, Dick and Harry hardy enough to brave the elements, in exchange for raw beauty and increased blood flow. At one point, the bar was packed solid with enthusiastic walkers, exuding warm dampness as their wet apparel dried out. They hugged cups of coffee, relaxing stiff fingers with the heat of the steaming brew. Sylvia's hot scones, dripping with butter were in huge demand.

'Syl, more scones. I need lots more,' called John from the bar.

'There's none left. I'll have to make some.'

'It'll take ages, won't it?'

'Tell them they'll be ready in 15mins. If they want to wait.' By now she'd found all the short cuts to speedy production. The ingredients were thrown in, no weighing, and the permanently hot Aga baked them in no time.

She pulled out of the oven the tray of golden goodies, split them and slapped inside slices of butter that quickly melted to give a mouth-watering confection.

'They'll never go home if you keep giving 'em hot scones,' said Robert after he'd been asked for the umpteenth time if they could be bought for customers to take home.

'Shop's shut. It's the dance tonight and there's plenty of clearing away to do. Besides, I've baked about a stone of the things. Enough's enough.' She was feeling a bit mulish anyway for she had tried every ruse in the book to either dissuade John from going to Charlie's jig, or to cajole him into going on his own. Nothing had worked.

'You shall go to the ball' was the final command from 'her Prince Charming'.

What to wear? Cinderella didn't have such a problem, she'd known exactly what to expect, a frothy frock and a pair of glass slippers. Sylvia had no idea, and there was nobody to ask. After a great deal of mind-changing she settled on a plain skirt, cream silk shirt, flat shoes and pearl earrings. Finally ready, she hugged Cassie, popped her in the basket and waved to Robert. He was obviously more than eager to stay in the pub to serve any stragglers and to lock up for the night, rather than trip the light fantastic in a wooden hut, with glee he urged John and Sylvia off the premises to their night of carousing. 'You enjoy yourselves. I'll be fine in my warm bed. Don't make a noise when you come home.'

'You are absolutely rotten,' and at that moment she meant it.

Eventually, she and John set off on a drive into wet blackness and unknown territory. They twisted and turned, climbed and dropped. A couple of farmsteads, lost souls, clung together on a bend in the road. The headlights picked out a jumble of farm buildings and the plain-fronted houses. As they drew level, a stench came into the car, creeping in on its belly and surreptitiously filled all available spaces.

'What in God's name is that?' gasped Sylvia, hands over nostrils.

Between snorts John, managed, 'It's Tommy Smith.'

'Oh, come off it, John. One man can't make such a stink.'

John nearly choked with laughter and asphyxiation.

'No idiot, he makes his own silage to feed his cows. No one knows what secret extras he puts in other than grass and molasses, but he has the best milk yield in the area, or so I've been told. Obviously he's doing something right. He came into the bar earlier today for a packet of cigarettes and the smell came with him. Even worse, it stayed with us for a couple of hours afterwards.'

Sylvia opened the window. 'I bet if he bottled it he'd have a ready market.'

John slapped her knee in agreement.

Gradually the air sweetened and their senses returned to concentrate on the road as it wound and flirted with now, torrential waters of the river. Three or four houses snuggled on the side of the fell flanked this angry black snake of spitting white curling waves. Sylvia guessed this was where Anthony and Thomas lived. Before she could ask the question, twinkling lights from the dwellings disappeared. A sharp corner hid them, as though they'd never existed.

The darkness seemed more intense. No lights, only the beam of the headlights, which fixed on clumps of tall reeds in amongst the rough wild grass. The river encroached onto the road in places, so much so that Sylvia was alarmed.

'John, be careful. Slow down.'

A giant wave of spray covered the windscreen, blinding them for a moment. The engine coughed and spluttered on its forbidden intake of H_2O. They held their breath; thankfully the little workhorse pulled itself together and battled on.

'Shouldn't we go back?' whispered Sylvia hopefully.

'No, we'll have to appear. They'd take it as a snub if we didn't turn up.'

She didn't answer, but sank deeper into the seat and watched the angry river as it crashed over great flat-backed rocks that glistened like killer whales.

'Heavens, the river could easily cover this road. It's a good job the rain's stopped,' came the uncharacteristic comment from John. The headlights caught a glint of water in a dip in the road ahead. John slowed down. 'I think the road is completely under water here.'

He stopped the car at the edge of what looked like a lake. 'I can't tell how deep it is. It seems as though the stream coming down from the fell has built up so much volume that it's burst its bank. The drain has probably bunged up.'

'We can't go through that, surely. Even if we did it could be worse coming home. And who would know that we were stuck out here?'

With his usual carefree attitude, John's answer was to release the handbrake and aim the car straight into the abyss. Sylvia shut her eyes. She could hear the arc of water cascade over the windows as they chugged forward. She felt a surge of power beneath her feet and silently sent up a little prayer.

Thankfully, their brave steed pulled out of the water with a further bout of coughing, yet, somehow managed to keep going. They both heaved a sigh of relief as they began to climb, leaving the turbulent waters behind.

A Praying Mantis of a tree hung over the road at the start of the village, a straggly untidy place. A collection of higgledy piggledy dwellings half hid the dance hall. If it hadn't been for the cloud of noise coming from the direction of a broad shaft of yellow light, they would have missed it completely. John parked the car on a strip of rough grass on the roadside, close up to a dry stone wall, leaving Sylvia hardly enough room to open the door. She squeezed out, quietly cursing as her foot hit wet and soggy undergrowth.

'John, my feet are soaked.'

'You'll soon dry out when you start dancing.'

She had no answer, so followed him resignedly to the 'palace de dance'. The path degenerated from wet grass to mud. Supervising her feet, shod now in wet cream-leather, she desperately tried to avoid further deterioration to her favourite shoes. Each foot searched for the tiniest of dry patches in the bog leading up to the entrance. They stepped through the open door. A smoke haze lent an eerie backdrop to a scrum of unrecognisable bodies, intermingled with dancers of all ages in a variety of shapes and sizes. Sylvia was aghast. Even in her wildest dreams she had not imagined this totally uncontrolled gathering. As her senses came into focus she saw there were two men on a bit of a raised platform, playing colourful accordions as though there was no tomorrow. One she recognised as Cheeky Charlie, who enthusiastically gyrated with every squeeze of his instrument. No change in his apparel was evident and Sylvia wondered whether his clothes ever came off. Alongside him, eyes closed in admiration of his own musical prowess, was a slim, more serious version of the now familiar features of the 'up-daler', that look of native cunning, locked in a hungry, hunted face, inherited over the centuries from a desperate bid for survival. She had expected to see Fred, Charlie's brother playing but this man was a stranger to her.

A dour youth sat between the two musicians. He banged away in an hypnotic trance on a set of drums, not always with the beat, but it did nothing to spoil the jubilant and, to be fair, the tuneful rendering of the rousing Scot's dance tunes.

She turned her attention to the revellers, a sight to behold. Dress code for the men appeared to be wellington boots, with possibly a clean shirt thrown in. Children dived between the legs of the dancers, wild things, there to enjoy the victuals supplied by long suffering wives and mothers. One youngster was avidly devouring a whole sponge cake as he dived and rolled on the dance floor, jam streaked from ears to chin.

Sylvia's gaze swept round the room. She would have liked to have seen Gerald and Mark in amongst the sweaty melee of eager-eyed sheep men, but her two favourites were nowhere to be seen. Probably the delights of the upper dales hop didn't compare to the hot spots of Skipton. The female supporters merged into the background. No bright colours or special outfits were displayed. She felt dreadful. Her outfit, too plain and simple for Broadway Hall dances at home, was here a Dior ball gown. Embarrassed and annoyed, she fiercely yanked off her pearl earrings and plunged them into John's pocket.

'You might have told me overalls and boots would be the dress code.'

'Don't be silly you're fine.'

She had hardly time to collect her thoughts when she was roughly grabbed by some stranger in hob-nailed boots and dragged into the middle of the revellers. 'Play a Spanish Waltz Bert!' he shouted to the leader of the band. Before she knew what was happening, her hands were grasped, and she found herself in a circle, made up of most of the females in the room, only the old and very young sat out. They faced an inner circle of all the menfolk, thankfully including John. The music started. It was a waltz; Sylvia presumed the tune must be the Spanish waltz. The two circles rotated in opposite directions. She couldn't imagine what kind of a dance it was going to be. The music stopped dead, and she was faced with a shy, tubby youth. He flushed and his alcohol-laced breath blew over her. They stood awkwardly face to face.

'What do we do now?' she asked hesitantly.

'Tha' dances.'

There was a preparatory single chord, and out blasted a vibrant rendering of the Gay Gordons. The youth clutched her hand and marched her round the floor with the enthusiasm of the whole Gordon clan in full battle charge. Sylvia loved dancing, but this was more like being partnered by a Whirling Dervish, though she had to admit it was a damned good way to get everything going. She was just getting accustomed to the work-out when the tune changed and she found herself, once again in the circle.

This went on for what seemed an eternity. She had the strangest assortment of partners, most of them so worse for wear, that the drink must have been flowing freely from the moment the hall had been opened. John managed to grab her, but the moment was fleeting, almost as though the band changed the tune to cut down their time together. At one point the main accordion player left the dias and asked her to dance, leaving Charlie and the drummer to play alone. Sylvia was immediately apprehensive, she guessed what was coming. He was fairly tall and slim and he leered as he put his arm familiarly round her waist and drew her close. He was making no bones about his intentions. He held her far too tight and kept breathing in her ear, whispering words she couldn't decipher. Thankfully, at last, the music stopped.

'Tha' wa' good. W'll 'ave t'do it ag'in soon?'

She answered with a fleeting smile and rushed to John.

'Please, can we go home. Please!'

'Sorry love, I've promised we'll go back to Fred's. You know, Charlie's brother. He wants us to have a drink with him and his friends before we go home.'

'Oh no! Do we have to?'

John smiled. 'Won't be for long I promise.'

Things started to slow down, and tiredness, coupled with the significant intake of alcohol, seemed to magically hit the whole room and the party began to break up.

They left the village hall with Anthony, the churchwarden, three village lads, and the flirting accordion player, who turned out to be Gilbert Thorndike, a sheep farmer from higher up the dale. His wife Mary, helped at the Big House at the very top of the dale.

They hadn't far down the road to walk to Fred's home and soon were all seated round the kitchen fireplace with a drink. The roaring fire was welcoming as the night walk had been chilly. The room, quite dark in the glow of just the fire and a single oil lamp, was plain and simply furnished. There was no wife in sight. Apparently she had left the dance earlier and had gone to bed, much to Fred's disgust.

'She teks t'auld dog t'bed wi' 'er and if they git in fust t'auld dog w'ain't let me in. It growls and bares its teeth then 'av' t` sleep on t'floor.'

Everyone broke into peels of laughter. Sylvia watched the proceedings with amusement and was surprised when Anthony, looking serious, leaned over to John and whispered, 'Click thi' glass.'

John picked up his glass of beer, he seemed puzzled as he gazed around searching for the reason of Anthony's command. Sylvia more curious than ever, dug John in his ribs. 'He looked up at the ceiling.'

The ceiling was typical of dales houses, planks of wood butted together laid across the beams to make a plain wooden floor and a ceiling with no under-drawing. Immediately above John's drink on the table was a large ham with a skin like leather, hanging by an iron hook from the beam. Sylvia studied the ham. At first she couldn't see anything untoward, until, creeping down from the cracks in the floor above, she spied a slow trickle of amber liquid making its way down the leg of pig. The first drop about to be released, was going to be a direct hit into John's glass of beer. She saw his hand tighten round the glass, and he looked quizzically at Anthony.

'T'auld dog 'as a pee up there,' he grunted.

Sylvia got the giggles, those uncontrollable giggles, with tears rolling down her face. She just could not contain herself.

'I can't stop. We'll have to go home,' she gasped. 'They`ll never invite us again!'

She need not have worried, their companions seemed oblivious. Too much eating, too much drinking and too much dancing had obviously taken effect. A couple of lolling heads accompanied by sonorous breathing gave them the excuse they needed. John stood upright.

'Thank you all for a most enjoyable evening. We'll say goodnight now if you don't mind.'

His polite speech was greeted with a total lack of interest. John looked somewhat abashed and took Sylvia's hand as they left the heap of inebriated revellers to their slumbers by the fire.

Relieved to step into the cold night air, they exchanged rueful glances. Then they started to laugh helplessly as they made their way to the car. To Sylvia's relief the journey home was uneventful. The waters had subsided from the edge of the road. They drifted into silence and every so often one of them would burst into a bout of laughter as recollections of the evening returned. 'It was just like a comic film,' said John, 'I'll never forget it as long as I live.'

'Me neither. Our first experience of an up-dale bash. Never to be forgotten. These people have no inhibitions. They have very little money, yet, they love life and enjoy every moment. I feel humble in a way. I'm so glad we came to live here.' She smiled sleepily and laid her head on his shoulder.

CHAPTER 5

As the weeks went by, Sylvia became accustomed to the fluctuations in trade and the movements of the up-dalers. Sometimes there could be the odd variation when one of the locals would land in a panic, anxious to use the telephone for a call to the vet or doctor. On one occasion in early April, she was surprised by the appearance of an elderly man limping into the bar. He was small and thin, his clothes, though well worn, were clean and neat. He leaned heavily on a horn-handled stick.

'Can thee 'elp me, young lass. A' need's t' telephone doct'r'. Me' daughter's gon' int' labour.'

'Oh goodness me. The telephone's here in the passage. Have you got the number?'

Suddenly, she felt sick. Was this an omen? She watched the man fiddle in the pocket of the thinning cloth of his waistcoat and produce a scrap of paper. 'Ere's number. Will thee do t'call fer us?'

Sylvia hesitated then, realising the poor man was terrified of the phone, agreed. 'What name shall I say, and where does your daughter live?'

'It be Liz Smith, up a' Raisgill.'

'Ah. Is she Tommy Smith's wife?'

'Aye.'

Hastily, Sylvia made the call. She had never met Tommy's wife and was only aware of him from the strong smell of his silage. But, the doctor knew that Mrs Smith's birth was imminent, and after a relay of questions, promised he would start the 20 mile drive in the next few minutes. The little man looked relieved that his mission was over, and he sank gratefully onto the settle in the corner of the bar.

'Can thee let me 'ave a drink lassie?'

She glanced down the passage at the kitchen clock, 10.30! Well, that was near enough to opening time at 11o'clock, though she wished Robert would hurry back. He'd walked down to the Grange for eggs, but she guessed he'd be chewing the fat with Gerald.

'Alright. I'll let you have a quick half pint.' Teasingly she added, 'But you'll have to be as quiet as a mouse, and if the vicar comes in, hide your glass.' They both grinned as she poured his half of mild.

'Now then sir, I haven't seen you before. Do you live round here?'

'Me' name's Lodge Foster. Raisgill wa' me f'ather's farm. A' lived ther' as a lad, till wi up't sticks an' moved t'Awes. Now me' daughter lives in t'farm.'

'That's lovely, to think your family still has roots at Raisgill even though you live in Hawes. Did you enjoy living in this dale as a boy?'

'Aye lass, a' did. W'used t'cum 'ere, t'pub fer ale w'en we wus 'ay mekin. T'auld lass called Grace 'ad t'spot then. She wa' a queer 'un. Lived all 'er life at 'ubberolme, til' she wa' tay' auld t'keep pub. So did 'er fath'r an' granfath'r a'fore 'er.'

Sylvia was intrigued. She remembered the pretty pearl-handled buttonhook. Leaving Mr Foster sipping his beer, she went into the kitchen. Reaching up onto the top shelf, she retrieved the buttonhook.

'Do you think this might have belonged to Grace? We found it hidden behind layers of wallpaper in the kitchen.'

Lodge Foster, viewed the object with some apprehension and refused to take it in his hand. Sylvia was puzzled. 'It's only a buttonhook.'

'Aye, but a'remember i' well. A' can see 'er now, bendin' down t'fas'n buttons on t'lile black boots. She only weared 'em in t'bar. Durin' day, t'wa 'ob-nailed boots. In them days ther' wa' a farm wi' t'pub. Niver married did Grace, stayed 'ere till she couldna' manage n'more. Went t'live in Buckdin. She said ther' wa' t'be a big tea fer t'mourners w'en she d'eed, but wi' non 'o that blown up pastry stuff. Strange 'un our Grace, she 'ad t'power.'

Sylvia felt a shudder run through her. 'What do you mean, *the power?*'

'Well, she c'ud see things t'others c'ud na.' She told me fath'r we'd move out o' dale before 'e knew 'is'sen.'

'Good Heavens. Was he worried?'

He didn't answer, merely gave a quick jerk of his head. So Sylvia dared herself to ask. 'There's a big wardrobe in one of the bedrooms, would that have belonged to Grace?'

'Aye. T'wa' in t'room o'er t'bar. Only that an' 'er bed. Nay rug on t'floor just bare boards. Or so nurse sed' w'en Grace… w'poorly.'

Lodge Foster clammed shut. He stood up, grabbed his stick and hobbled to the door, 'A'l be off. A've sed t'much. Thank ye fer t'drink…'

Disturbed, Sylvia watched him go. He'd a long trek to Raisgill and she couldn't help, they'd no vehicle. Besides, neither she nor Robert could drive. She sat there for a couple of minutes reflecting on his words about Grace. Now she was certain it was her presence she'd felt in the room where the wardrobe stood.

Robert burst into the bar, 'I'm sorry I've been so long, but you know what Gerald is when he gets talking. I'd no idea you'd customers.'

'Not really a customer, Robert. He wanted to call the doctor for Tommy Smith's wife who's gone into labour. But he succeeded in scaring me to death!'

Robert listened to the tale and immediately pooh-poohed Sylvia's idea that Grace lingered in the Inn. Though she had the feeling that he was uneasy; his protestations were too loud.

'Why don't you take Cassie up the road for a little walk. It'll do you both good.'

Deciding a bit of peace and quiet was what she needed, she set off with Cass. Every time she stepped out of that well-trodden front entrance she thought she would never get used to the absolute joy that welled up inside her. The sky was still grey, but there was a hint of spring in the air and the valley nipped between the fells, with the river busy in the bottom, somehow seemed more alive. They were so lucky. But was that about to change?

She listened intently to her feet as they crunched the loose gravel. Then silence as they stepped onto the worn tarmac of the road leading to the top of the dale. Cassie trotted beside her on invisible springs and every so often leapt into the air, all four legs as one in a killer dive. Tail akimbo, she would pounce on a rustle of grass moved by some innocent creature about its business of survival. The charade made Sylvia smile, especially as no little timorous beastie had come to a sticky end.

Before long, she realised they'd walked as far as the Poor Pasture, a great lump of reedy grassland owned by the church and quite a distance from the pub. It was auctioned every year by the vicar on New Year's Day in the dining room of the Inn. An event covered by press and media alike. She had been told this Land Letting ceremony was good for business, but the downside was providing a free supper for everyone present. The proceeds from the auction were supposed to be distributed to the poor of the parish. She wondered wryly, if they would qualify, for the way things were going they could easily end in the mire.

'Oh Cassie,' she softly confided to the little dog still eager to get on with the hunt, which had now degenerated to hard backed beetles and scuttling spiders. 'I don't know what to do, I'm worried sick. We haven't even started with the business and now this. It's going to blow the lot.'

She fell silent again and walked with her head bowed. 'You won't like it either. What will the boys say? What will we do? I daren't tell them. It upsets everything. We're on the bones of our backsides already.'

Totally ignored by the busy whippet, she kicked a pebble and watched it catapult down the hill. That's what's going to happen, she thought, we'll go downhill. She lapsed into a cocoon of silence as the pair made their way home.

The narrow end of the Inn came into view. Sylvia made a mental note to get the boys to take down the oversized wooden sign that dominated that empty wall. She decided it should be repainted black with white lettering. There was a book on heraldry and sign writing somewhere around which would help. For a few moments her worries disappeared beneath the job of revamping the wall to a gleaming white with a bright sign advertising their Inn on the river.

A cheery, 'Mornin!' from Mark returned her to the uncertainties of the moment. They had built up quite a friendship over the weeks. He delighted in telling her of country lore and local customs, but this morning she did not want his company. Oblivious of her mood, Mark followed her into the kitchen.

'I've cum t'ask thee if it's ok t'go in t' eighteen-acres. Two o' me sheep 'ave gitten in there.'

Robert put down his cup. 'Of course it's alright, Mark. Cuppa?'

The three of them sat round the kitchen table chatting. When, to Sylvia's surprise, John's car drove up to the front door, she rushed out to meet him. 'What's wrong? Are you ok?'

John climbed out of the car and slammed the door shut. 'The damned thing's got a leak.'

Mark and Robert came out offering a variety of opinions as they peered under the bonnet. 'Looks like your radiator could be holed,' suggested Robert.

'Don't know what the Hell it is, but Jeff from the garage at Kettlewell said he'd come up this afternoon to have a look at it.' He dismissed any further discussion. 'I need a coffee.'

They sat for a while discussing the weather, until John stood up, his hand on Mark's shoulder.

'Come with me, Mark, and have a look at the changes we've made.'

Robert opened his mouth as though to protest, but shut it like a clam as his sister's foot kicked his shins. He followed her dutifully up the stairs and joined in the tour. Sylvia briefly touched his arm as they listened in silence to John's eulogy. She felt both amused and annoyed. How dare he imply he'd done some of the work. Though to be fair, he'd brought in a wage, so she supposed that made it ok. The place did look pretty. Gone was the darkness. Now their rooms and the landing were an all-white panorama, interspersed with colourful curtains and bedspreads and the odd tufted cotton rug which broke up the stained floorboards. She was rather pleased with the overall effect of cosy freshness, especially when she had managed to stretch the furniture from their bedrooms back home to furnish all four rooms.

'Well what do you think of our efforts. A transformation eh?'

Mark nodded in agreement.

John looked surprised, 'Well wait until you've seen the dining room.'

They followed John downstairs to the last room for viewing. Sylvia wondered how Mark would react to the colours. The job-lot of white emulsion paint had managed to finish the kitchen and bar, but had reached the point of exhaustion when it came to the dining room. This couldn't have worked out better for she wanted something special there. She had chosen dark green for the walls, echoing the stately fir tree at the end of the garden. The sharp contrast of the white woodwork, windows framed in curtains of pink and red roses on a white ground and the deep red carpet, gave the effect she had anticipated. Mark went very quiet. At first Sylvia thought he didn't approve, until she remembered how little money these sheep farmers seemed to have. Cash would not be wasted on home improvements, but used to buy stock. Or perhaps any spare would be stuffed under the mattress.

Finally he spoke as he stared directly at her. 'Tha's d..done a g.g.grand job.'

Without a goodbye, he turned and left them to round-up his roaming sheep.

Sylvia decided she must talk to John there and then. He seemed to sense there was something unpalatable in the offing, for every time she was alone with him he'd beetle off on some excuse or other. Finally, in frustration she got on with her jobs, starting with the bedrooms. She attacked the pillows with punches that would have been the envy of Henry Cooper, and didn't hear John come up behind her.

'Now what's up, Sylvie? I know there's something wrong.'

She folded like a wilted stem and sank onto the bed edge. Her bottom lip trembling with pent up emotion, half-afraid of the reaction she was about to get, her words tumbled out in a cascade of anxiety.

'I know the timing's all wrong. I don't know how we'll manage. We've not even started properly with meals and guests and what will Robert say...?'

'What the Hell are you on about? I can make neither moss nor sand of that lot.'

'I think I'm expecting!'

His face didn't change, not a word or gesture escaped from her beloved. She felt the colour drain from her face, even her body seemed to shrink. She was still somewhat in awe of her more sophisticated partner and just dare not speak.

Finally he cleared his throat. 'We'll get you to the doctor in the morning. Then I'll tell Robert if you are pregnant. There's no need to bother him unless we're certain. Hopefully they'll be able to fix the car this afternoon.'

He casually patted her head. She felt like a retriever who had brought back the wrong prey, and her heart sank even further. This wasn't the reaction she'd hoped for. She knew the timing was abysmal, but she'd hoped for some reassurance and comfort. Rising to full height, and in true Lady Macbeth fashion, she stalked past him to the bathroom.

The mechanic arrived. Sylvia kept out of the way, but was relieved when she heard good humoured banter in the bar. John came through to the kitchen.

'Guess what? The problem was a leaking hose and not a burst radiator. Fortunately, Jeff carries an assortment of spares. And he's a resourceful lad. He's managed a temporary fix until he can get the correct part.'

Sylvia was relieved, at least John was in a good mood and she would be driven to her appointment, instead of catching the once a-day bus to Skipton. After a fitful night's sleep, her thoughts fluctuating between the stories of Grace and the strong possibility that she was pregnant, she woke with a feeling of dread.

The twenty mile journey down the dale was made in relative silence. There was no mention of the impending bombshell. She decided John was an ostrich with his head buried deep in the sand. In an effort to drown her thoughts she scrutinised the scenery, logging its mood swings as they progressed. The river flanked by long parallel meadows, now held a hailstorm of sheep and lambs. The fertile riverside meadows, protected by tobacco grassed hills, reached high above. Gradually the meadow land widened and the hills sank, some sliced with a planting of trees. The villages became more affluent; flower-potted houses with a shiny car or two; ponds sporting ornamental ducks not intended for the pot. And soon the little town of Skipton began to erupt. A bevy of well-to-do dwellings in spacious gardens with mature trees, their boughs bent over the road, quickly gave way to ancient buildings. A muddle of shapes, low on one side of the road, high and precarious on the other. She caught a snapshot view as they passed the blacksmith's cottage, the yard open to the road. A handsome hunter waited patiently for new shoes. The blacksmith, grey and bent, wore a leather apron to protect him from sparks that spat from the hot metal shoe, ready to burn onto a horny hoof. She could imagine the acrid smell as he secured a perfect fit on that workmanlike foot. The fleeting picture came and went. Then the road bridged a stream, originally the castle moat. The castle, hidden by the blackened stone church, sat at the peak of the rise. She couldn't help but smile as she remembered her first visit there. What had intrigued her and set her imagination racing, was the 'long-drop' privy. A chimney-like structure at the top of the castle that spiralled down to the ground below into a pit. The most surprising thing was the continuous howling gale from top to bottom, a tornado that would certainly not encourage meditation or light reading. Heaven help the poor subject who dared sit on that vortex.

Her smiles turned to anxiety as they passed the war memorial onto the main street. It was market day. A higgledy-piggledy of colourful stalls, wares tumbling beyond the designated cobble area and creeping onto the road. Normally she would have been delighted, longing to rummage through the goods on offer. Crafts, local produce, fish fresh from the east coast and best of all, the fabric stalls. The rolls of colourful cloths always drew her, she could dream of making ball gowns or just yearn for the rich furnishing fabrics to grace their home.

Today was different. They turned sharply at the bottom of the main street and left the bright jumble behind. John drew to a stop outside the surgery.

'I'll meet you in a couple of hours back on the car park. I've a job to do first.'

'I thought you'd come with me,' she said lamely.

'Sorry love, business is business. I'll see you later.'

She watched the back of the little car disappear round the corner, swallowed the lump that had suddenly walked into her throat, and turned to climb the mountainside of steps leading to the front door. The waiting room, stiff and unwelcoming, didn't help to instil confidence. She nervously perched on the edge of a metal and leatherette chair. They must have made them by the million, for they seemed to be in every doctor and dentist's waiting room in the country. She picked up a two year old magazine and tried to occupy her thoughts. An article on childbirth caught her eye, but before she could read about Dr Spock's philosophy, the broad door, panelled with pebble-glass, swung open and she was bidden into the dreaded surgery.

After many minutes of interrogation, poking and prodding, she was told by the very gentlemanly doctor that she was about four months pregnant. Totally floored, she looked at him in disbelief. He didn't seem to notice her shocked silence.

'Well young lady, good news eh? I've only one immediate concern. How are you going to cope with a little one and a busy residential Inn?'

Silly man, she thought, but replied, 'That won't be a problem. The problem is... the baby is due before the summer season has finished and we've bookings through to October.'

He looked at her pityingly. 'We'll see. I'll arrange for the District nurse to keep an eye on you. She'll visit you every few weeks and will keep me informed. I hope all goes well and I'll see you later in the year.'

Then with the obligatory iron tablets put in her hand, the discussion was ended.

In a dream she walked up the main street, not heeding the persuasive chatter of the stall-holders. But for some ridiculous reason she bought herself a little luxury, a jar of body lotion. The defiant purchase clutched in her hand, she walked to the car park at the top of the main street. She caught sight of John waiting for her next to the fish and chip café. Walking slowly towards him, she wondered what his reaction was going to be.

'Well, what's the news?' was his stark greeting.

Rigidly in control, she quietly gave him the verdict. And to her surprise and delight he hugged her in full view of the chip-eaters and whispered, 'We'll manage.'

CHAPTER 6

It was washday. Sylvia hated washdays. The kitchen took on the roll of a Chinese laundry, with antediluvian equipment filling the floor space. There was the dolly-tub and posher, kindly donated by Gerald's mum, and her own mother's discarded hand-wringer on a stand, together with buckets and scrubbing brushes. There was little joy in the struggle to get their clothes and bedding clean, but every time washday came round she thanked the powers that be, for the luxury of hot water on tap. She just couldn't imagine how she would have managed without it. To make life easier, Robert had found a short length of hosepipe that fitted on the end of the hot tap and reached into the tub, dispensing with her hazardous bucketing that usually resulted in a puddle-dotted floor.

That morning, she happily watched the flow of hot water filling the dolly-tub as it stirred the soap flakes into mountains of froth. She heard Robert coming along the bar passage to the kitchen and gleefully reached into the tub, scooping a handful of foam. As he opened the door she blew the mass of bubbles at his left ear.

'Oh Lord, sis. It's not playtime, it's too early. I've come in to load up the stove so you'll have plenty of hot water.'

Sylvia looked crestfallen. 'Sorry.'

Robert ignored her and purposefully emptied the coke hod into the little stove, filling it to the gunnels and noisily forcing down its lid. He stood up, stretched his back, then cheekily grinned, 'I'll give you a hand if you like.'

She was grateful, for she knew that tiredness would creep in as the day wore on. 'Thanks love. If you could give the sheets a good poshing whilst I scrub the shirt collars.'

Robert, enthusiastically set about the task of coming to grips with the posher.

'Gosh Robert. There's no need to use it like a battering ram,' she smiled ruefully. 'I wonder how long it'll be before we get electricity. Lord knows how we'll cope when we're full of residents. It will mean...' She started counting 'a dozen sheets, two dozen pillow cases, at least a dozen towels. Robert, this isn't funny. Just imagine if we get umpteen changes of folk in a week. It doesn't bear thinking about.'

Robert looked suitably worried. 'Perhaps we ought to get up earlier and try to shift it before breakfast.'

She glanced at the clock. 'You mean earlier than 6.30!'

She scrubbed the clothes in the sink with unnecessary vigour.

'I'll turn the wringer handle for you,' Robert said helpfully.

She guessed he was thinking of her condition and a wave of fondness for her brother swept over her, especially as John was still in bed. Silently she hauled the sheets up to the rollers, cursing as her hands complained in the scalding water.

Robert dumped the last sheet from the wringer onto the draining-board. 'There, sis, that's the lot.'

'Afraid it's not. We've to empty the tub, fill her up with clean water for rinsing and then start the whole performance again.'

'Golly Moses,' uttered Robert. 'This is a nightmare.'

'Wait until we're fully booked! Thank goodness we've got mum's wringer. I couldn't have handled the sodden sheets. My muscles wouldn't cope.'

They struggled on until the last piece of washing was pegged out on the line in the garden, where a gentle breeze promised to dry the fluttering array of garments and bedding. Feeling quite satisfied with their efforts Sylvia began to relax, but before they had fully cleared the kitchen, a couple of hikers bowled into the bar wanting morning coffee.

'It's no good, sis. We'll have to have an earlier start on washday. Six o' clock at the latest. We can't expect to cope with customers as well. And, remember, when we've residents there'll be breakfasts to do.'

'You're right. It's nearly opening time and we're only just ready. Cassie hasn't had her walk yet. Would you take her whilst I bake a batch of scones?'

He readily agreed. 'I'll kill two birds with one stone and pick up that extra milk you need from Mark.'

Robert stepped out with Cass across the bridge. He stopped to peer into the now quiet waters of the Wharfe. He could see the bottom quite clearly. A lazy trout swam downstream and a dipper sat on a rock watching, its shirt front glistening white. The bird started to bob, then flexed its legs before diving into the crystal depths. It seemed to walk on the bed of the river facing upstream, gathering food as it went. Robert watched entranced until it surfaced, then reluctantly he dragged himself away calling Cassie to heel.

The entrance to Mark's family farm was spotless. There was no clutter, no trimmings with flowers or pots, and no one about. Robert hesitated, not quite knowing what to do, when the front door opened and a rather formidable woman stood on the threshold.

'What's tha' want?' she snapped.

'Sorry. I was looking for Mark. We need more milk.'

'Is thee from t'pub?'

'Yes. I'm Robert, brother of the landlord's wife.'

Her square face lit up. She was transformed from a gaunt unfriendly body, to a pleasant, homely one.

'Pleased t'meet thee lad. Mark's int' milk parlour round t'end o' buildin'.' She pointed to the side of the house. 'You'll find 'im in there.' With that she closed the door on him.

So that was Mark's mother! Robert hesitated, then remembering Cassie's liking to stray, took a length of twine from his pocket and tied it to her collar. 'We better have you safe, Madam.'

They found the milking parlour. It was clinically clean. Mark was hosing down the floor. At first he didn't hear Robert calling, but when he did, he jumped a mile and sent water in all directions, spraying Robert and Cass in the process.

'Tha g..gev' me a sh..shock. Does tha w..want sum' milk?'

'Please. We could do with a couple of pints, if that's ok.'

Mark plunged a metal can with a long, brass handle deep into a churn. 'Tha's lucky. M..milk wagon left p..p..part churn til' mornin'.' He poured two canfuls into a small lidded churn and handed it to Robert.

As Robert had watched the creamy liquid being poured, it dawned on him that their milk came straight from the cow, not pasteurised as they were used to in Leeds. The farm milk was beautiful, and full of cream and everyone seemed healthy. Did it matter?

'Ye' thinkin' o' pasturised? Cows 'ave a b..betta' w..watar supply than t'pub. Cum wi' me.'

Robert followed as he was bidden, through the big double doors to the back of the building where Mark proudly pointed to a concrete construction.

'There thee is. W..w..wata' treatment p..plant.'

At first Robert was lost. Then he realised the stream gurgling down from the hill above supplied water into the back of the unit. It looked a costly piece of equipment for livestock.

'Well that's a bugger. The cows are better looked after than the humans.'

Mark grinned, 'C..could na' sell t'milk if w..we 'adn't dun' it.'

Robert looked down the pristine milk parlour and the many empty cow stalls. The significance hit him forcibly. 'Mark. How do you manage to milk all the cows on your own?'

'Nay. Mm.mi bruther Tom 'elps me.'

'Oh. I didn't know you had a brother.' Though he did remember seeing a stocky fellow, wearing glasses, riding a bike near the farm.

'Aye. Tom d..dus' na' drink round 'ere. E.e.e goes int' next dale.'

That sort of explained him not being around, but Robert wondered why he had not seen Tom bringing in the cows or other such jobs.

'An' where d..d'ye go f..fer a neet out?'

Robert laughed. 'No time for such things Mark. We're too busy trying to get established.'

'Tha's welcum t.t' cum' wi' us t'Skipton on Sat'di neet if tha wants.'

'Why thank you, Mark. Perhaps one day!' He raised his arm in farewell and turned for home deep in thought, followed by a very bored and impatient whippet.

As he crossed the bridge he caught sight of a gleaming car coming slowly down the dale. To his surprise it was a Rolls Royce. He was even more surprised when it drove majestically onto the car park. Out stepped a smart individual, wearing, of all things, black riding breeches and long, shiny black, boots. Robert couldn't believe his eyes. The man's jacket looked almost military, and to top it all he sported tan leather, gauntlet gloves. A chauffeur, a full blooded chauffeur! Robert couldn't think he'd ever come across one before, except in the navy on ceremonial occasions, when personnel drove the top-brass. He watched, open-mouthed, as the man opened each door in turn, bending low to assist the occupants to alight. Three, crumpled, elderly ladies tottered out onto the gravel. Without ado, they proceeded to lift their skirts, cronk down around the car and relieve themselves, glancing to neither right nor left. The chauffeur stood rigidly to attention with his back to the performance. Filled with embarrassment and intense amusement, Robert stood as though carved from stone. Cassie, must have picked up his vibes, for she stood equally still, the pair hardly daring to breathe. At last, the three old dears were decent, and made their way towards the pub door. Robert couldn't follow straight away. He just had to laugh. He leaned over the bridge parapet as though looking in the river, to hide his guffaws.

As Sylvia was just about to pop the tray of scones into the oven there was a sharp knock at the kitchen door. She guessed it must be the two hikers wanting to settle up for their coffee. They'd hugged the fire as they'd downed several cups whilst studying their maps. She'd begun to think they were installed for the duration. To her surprise it was a sturdy, middle-aged man wearing some kind of uniform.

'Would it be possible to have an early lunch for four?'

'Yes, of course. Would ham and eggs be alright?'

The man nodded his approval, turned and marched towards the car park. Sylvia peeped round the door and watched him collect the rest of his party, three old-fashioned, elderly ladies. She waited at the door to greet them and led them through to the dining room, where they immediately sat in front of the fire. The man, Sylvia guessed must be the chauffeur, had installed himself in the bar.

Robert burst into the kitchen looking dishevelled. 'You've got customers?'

'Yes. They've ordered ham and eggs. They're a bit strange. They act like landed gentry.'

Robert hurriedly secured Cassie in her basket and began getting together the cutlery and crockery ready to set the table. 'You wait till I tell you what I saw,' he whispered.

Sylvia looked at him quizzically, but smiling he shook his head. 'Later.'

She started slicing the ham, popping each succulent lump in turn into the big frying pan on the Aga top. She wondered if the ladies would be able to manage the thick slices as they sizzled appetisingly.

'Do you think they'll be able to eat so much?'

'What they leave Cass will finish,' replied the practical Robert.

But there were no worries on that score! When collected the plates were absolutely spotless and even the plateful of scones had all disappeared.

'Gosh. Appetites like Irish navvies, and only small ladies. Where did they put it all?'

This set Robert into chuckles of laughter and she couldn't really understand why. They were interrupted by the chauffer, who came to ask for the bill and the visitors' book. Brother and sister looked at each other questioningly. Then Sylvia suddenly remembered she had seen a dog-eared book on a shelf under the stairs. She hastily went to retrieve it, wiping away the dust before handing it to the waiting chauffer.

'The ladies would like to sign the book. They came here years ago at the same time as J. B. Priestley was staying. He wrote a book on that visit. It had something to do with going into the future,' he stated authoritatively, and turned to march back to the ladies.

A few moments later they trundled through the kitchen. The chauffeur passed the book back to Sylvia. 'Thank you for a pleasant stay.'

She smiled and took a longer peek at their guests. The three of them looked fragile. Their clothes, though old-fashioned, appeared expensive. One of them was wearing an enormous square, emerald brooch surrounded by diamonds on her faded wool jacket. It caught the light as she passed the window, and a myriad of rainbows shot in all directions.

Sylvia escorted them to the door and was surprised to see them climb into a Rolls Royce. She watched in awe as it sailed down the road to Buckden. Turning to Robert, she smiled. He was still holding the book and looked decidedly shell-shocked.

'See if you can find JB's signature.' Without a word he passed it to her. Impatiently, she turned the pages.

'Oh look Robert. I've found it, right at the start of the book.' She pointed to the faded scrawl. 'There's some others' as well. One's a, Sir! How exciting. I wonder what was the title of his book?'

Robert looked over her shoulder, 'It looks as though a party of them stayed for a few days, so perhaps he could have had a story to tell.'

'Let's see what the three ladies have said.'

Curiously they searched to see what their visitors had written. The signatures were illegible, but they could just make out the scrawled word, Lady, in front of one of the names.

'Gosh, more titles! Listen to the comment Robert... A Heaven sent oasis.'

Sylvia smiled, it fitted the strange trio perfectly.

Hilarity reigned on John's return home, when Robert told them about the incident on the car park.

'Not, Three Old Ladies locked in a lavatory, but close,' laughed John. 'More a case of three old biddies loose on a car park.'

78

'I bet when they were here before they used the privy at the top of the garden and decided they just couldn't face it again,' gurgled Sylvia. 'I should have told them that lady customers have the use of our bathroom nowadays.'

'You've missed an important bit,' said John, suddenly more serious. 'Don't you realise J.B. Priestley has stayed here and has written a book based on his stay.'

'A fat lot of good that'll do us,' retorted Robert.

'I disagree. People will be interested to visit the setting for one of his books. I'll try to find its title when I'm out and about.'

Sylvia saw an argument coming and quickly changed the subject. 'Time for tea. Bar customers will be here before long.' And true enough, they were hauled from the food stakes early doors.

Gerald was the first to arrive with a sloppy individual close on his heels.

'This is Walter. He lives in Buckden.'

'Hello, Walter, I'm John.' He turned to Gerald, 'Nice to see you matey.'

Sylvia was just about to go into the bar to talk to Gerald, when in came Alfred, the artist, and his wife Carla. This time the lady appeared to have dressed down, her outfit simple and more countryfied. Sylvia wondered whether on her first visit she was out to impress. Guardedly she nodded to Carla, who hardly gave her a glance. She immediately felt uncomfortable. There was something about this woman that sent her senses awry. Could it be she was frightened of her extreme confidence where men were concerned, or was it she didn't trust any man to escape Carla's clutches? She watched her greet John with fluttering eyelashes. 'Hello John. We had a nice little chat this morning. Didn't we?'

Sylvia was agog. Had her husband been time-wasting in Buckden instead of working? The woman was trouble. She felt herself watching her every move, so much so, that Carla turned to face her, staring with cold blue eyes. 'Something wrong, dear?'

'No. Nothing.'

She felt stripped bare and dropped her gaze. Alfred came to her rescue. 'Would you like a drink?'

He fumbled in his pocket and produced a black leather pouch. His lips pursed as he counted out the coins for her glass of lemonade. Before he could hand it over, Walter sidled up to him. 'Buy 'us a pint will thee?'

Alfred stood tall, his moustache bristling. 'I most certainly will not!'

Walter endeavoured to look pathetic. 'Well 'arf then.'

Sylvia had to smile as she watched John struggle to keep a straight face. He came over to her in the doorway and whispered, 'The man deserves a medal for cheek.'

She turned her head away, still smarting from Carla's comment. Walter skulked to a chair and sat without a drink. She felt anxious for the man and wondered if he'd any money, or whether he was tight and would just sit there hoping somebody would take pity on him. But Walter's patience came up trumps.

'Walter. A pint o' mild?'

The voice belonged to a strong, stocky man. He wore no jacket. His shirt was opened to the waist revealing a grey, hairy chest. He was roughly shaven and had a receding mop of wild hair. His shirt sleeves were rolled up, exposing muscular, heavy forearms. He seemed like a man as one with nature. Sylvia watched him. She decided he was a nice person; he chatted easily to Robert and John, and they obviously thought the same. Alfred brought his chair and sat next to her. She bent towards him and quietly asked, 'Who is he?'

'That's Bob Drysdale. He's the local stone-waller. He recently married a widow from Bradford who retired up here. She bought a cottage in the village and, like us, runs a B&B. Poor Bob has to sleep in a shed at the bottom of the garden when she has visitors. I think she's ashamed of her husband's rough and ready ways – she's a bit snooty.'

'Oh dear. The poor man.'

'He doesn't seem to mind too much. He gets away regularly walling in other dales. He's always needed. Most farmers do their own wall repairs, but there's often the time when a gap appears, usually when they are busiest, at lambing, clipping, hay-making and the like. It's then that Bob is invaluable.'

She glanced across the room to see that Carla had settled down with Walter, Bob, Robert and John. She mildly flirted with whoever gave her any attention, taking no notice whatsoever of her husband. Sylvia found Alfred's company enjoyable. The man was intelligent and moreover knew Bradford and the wool trade well. He questioned her with interest. 'I didn't know you had a textile background. Did you work in Bradford?'

'No, I studied textile design and engineering there.'

'Oh indeed. And where did you go from there? If you don't mind me asking.'

'Of course I don't mind. I went to the Wool Research place in Leeds as a technical assistant in the cloth analysis section.'

'Well, I'll be damned. I knew the head of that department. He acted for us in a court case.'

'I hope you won.'

'We did.' He changed the subject. 'I'm curious, what made you come here?'

She glanced across at Carla, John and Robert, 'Love and a bit of common sense.' They laughed and continued with a nonstop dialogue until closing time.

As Robert, followed by John, climbed the stairs for bed, Sylvia hung back.

'I won't be long. Just want to do a couple of things before I come up.'

John was truculent. 'What in God's name are you doing now? Have you seen the time?'

She hesitated before replying, 'I won't be a minute, just need to list the groceries that are on the low side.'

He lost interest and didn't bother to answer. She reached up to the top shelf and took her half-written letter from behind the salt jar. Grabbing a pen she hastily finished writing home to arrange to meet her mother in Leeds the following week. She hadn't mentioned the idea to John or Robert, but had made up her mind to go. More than anything, she wanted to tell her mum face to face, that she was to become a grandmother.

The rest of the week seemed to last forever. She counted the days. Sunday dawned, only one to go before the big day. The weather had improved at last. It was wonderful to see a golden hue instead of the greyness that had seemed to surround them since they'd moved in. John whistled cheerfully as he stocked the shelves in the bar and she had to remind him it was nearly time for him to ring the church bell for morning service.

'Ok. I'll pop across now.'

Sylvia watched John make his way across the bridge to the church for the bell ringing operation. He certainly was taking his time walking through the churchyard. He seemed to be scrutinising the old gravestones. She turned away, too many jobs were waiting.

She was up to her elbows in dough when Robert came into the kitchen, 'Hey sis. Have you noticed the bells?'

'What?'

'Listen. There was one hell of a clanking and now it seems to be, sort of dying. Not like the normal cut off when the peel's finished.'

She went on with kneading the dough. 'I suppose it sounds a bit odd. We'll have to ask John when he gets back.'

The door opened. Sylvia glanced up, then did a double take. 'My God, John. What have you done?'

He looked a sorry sight. His shirt was torn, blood dripped down his arm, his cheek was grazed, and strangely, his left hand clutched a remnant of black cloth.

'Had a bit of an accident.'

Sylvia rushed to his side. 'Sit down. I'll make you a drink. Then you can tell us about it.' Robert was curious but waited patiently until John was able to recount his story. He sipped the hot sweet tea Sylvia thrust in his hand. 'As you know I went across to the church. The birds were singing and I felt at peace with the world and happy with my lot.'

Robert sniffed. John ignored him. 'I opened the oak door. The sun shone in through the windows and made those shafts of dusty light. Y'know what I mean. Well, the font had some flowers on its wooden cover, they looked like jewels with the sun on them.' He waited expectantly for a comment, but Sylvia and Robert just gazed at him. Shuffling in his chair, he coughed, 'I looked around at the pews and at the painted rood loft, and a feeling of calm came over me. But I had to get on.'

Robert looked Heavenward. Sylvia glared at him. How melodramatic was this story going to be?

'I went to the bell tower and got hold of the bell-rope. It was grubby, and looked threadbare and grey. Anyway, I got hold of it. At first I pulled the rope gently down towards me, letting it rise easily, then gradually increased the stroke. Before I realised, I'd crept into quite a vigorous rhythm.'

'Oh John. You didn't break it?'

'Wait a minute will you.' John put up the palm of his hand to Sylvia. 'The old bell rang out. Its chimes echoed round the foot of the tower. I bet they heard it in Buckden. The joyful peels made me a bit too enthusiastic, the poor old rope couldn't stand the pace… and it parted. I was shot airborne. Funnily enough, I was still clutching its furry end. I reached out, trying to grab anything in a desperate effort to save myself. As my arm scraped down the rough wall, I managed to clutch a bundle of cloth hanging on the wall. I clung to it like a drowning man to a piece of flotsam, but I'm afraid I was too heavy. There was a wailing, tearing noise… the cloth gave up the fight and deposited me in a knotted heap on the cold stone floor.'

'What will the vicar say?' Sylvia was now well and truly worried.

'That's priceless. Worried about what he might say, not how I might feel. I could have broken something.'

'But you haven't. Have you?' Robert was scathing.

'No. But I could have. Anyway, I'll go on. If that's ok? In a daze, I untangled myself from the heap of rope and a lump of fabric,' ruefully he rubbed his grazed elbow. 'The rope had broken at the top of the tower. It's just impossible to mend. Unless a monkey had been on hand.' He waited for the laugh, but none came. 'I looked around to see what was what, and there on a hook in the wall hung a lump of black cloth. Then the awful truth dawned on me. It was the remains of *the vicar's cassock!* The rest laid in rags at my feet–talk about incriminating evidence! I felt terrible. Thankfully, the bell had clanged down to a more gentle rhythm, then it gradually sighed to a stop. I'll have to tell the vicar. Won't I?'

Sylvia and Robert looked at each other, they could control themselves no longer and dissolved into unrestrained hysterics.

'Good God!' chortled Robert. 'You do realise it's only you who can tell the vicar.'

John looked uncomfortable. 'I was hoping you might think of something. Perhaps we could mend the rope?'

'No way out John. You'll have to face the music. Have you forgotten you tore his cassock?'

Sylvia guessed her brother was quite enjoying the prospect of John getting an ear-bashing from the vicar. She suddenly felt sorry for him, 'I'll come to the vicarage with you. He won't be too angry if there's a female present. He's too gentlemanly.'

Reverend Fullerton opened the door to a blood-stained, guilty-faced John and a demure Sylvia. Not much fazed the wily old vicar, who'd spent twenty odd years in the outback of Australia before coming to Hubberholme. He'd seen it all before.

'Now John, what's amiss? You're obviously perturbed.'

John tried to smile and turn on the old Bainbridge blarney, but his words melted into gibberish. Sylvia was surprised; she'd expected him to sail through the meeting with his usual panache.

'Come lad, it can't be so bad, surely.'

John managed to blurt out the embarrassing story. The Reverend was silent and looked sternly through those milk bottle spectacles of his. The culprit shifted his feet. 'I think I got carried away, probably a bit too enthusiastic, though the rope did look very worn.'

'Indeed!' was the noncommittal reply. 'I'll give it some thought.'

They were dismissed with a glare.

'I feel like a naughty school kid,' muttered a shame-faced John.

Sylvia felt uneasy. Had this opened a can-full of worms? Would the vicar use this incident to complain that they had never been to one of his services, or even demand more cleaning time in the church? She was more than aware that the cleaning needed at least double the time she spent if it was to be kept up to scratch. But, how could she possibly give more?

Silently they walked side by side, back along the couple of hundred yards skirting the river up to the Inn. Absent-mindedly, she noticed that already there were people about, taking advantage of the beautiful weather. Another busy day stretched before her. The well-to-do in their cars, the enthusiasts on their motorbikes and the hard core of walkers would soon be descending in force. She had to be ready.

'Come on John. There's work to do. The vicar won't sack us!'

CHAPTER 7

Sylvia was excited. At last she was going to see her mum. It seemed forever since they were together. This visit was special. The news of a baby on the way would thrill her to bits, and she adored babies. Up to now, Sylvia rather preferred the animal variety.

John had promised to run her to the village so she could catch the bus to Skipton, which gave her just enough time to get the Leeds train. However, it seemed he had other ideas, and surprised her as she cooked breakfast. Sneaking up behind her, he slid both arms round her waist. 'I'm taking you right to the station. I've moved my calls around to fit in. It will give you more time to get ready, you won't have to rush.'

Sylvia hesitated. Any excuse to change routine and possibly not do his job properly was typical but she didn't like to hurt his feelings. 'Are you sure it won't interfere with your work?'

'No worries on that score. Everything's fine.'

She'd no choice but to agree. 'Right. I'll pop up and change.'

She wanted to get away for fear of showing her displeasure. He just had to be in on her day, whereas she'd never any idea where he was or what he was doing. Reluctantly though, she had to admit it would be much easier having a lift to the station.

John's voice, chatting animatedly, met her as she came back down the stairs. He was obviously talking on the phone to Gerald, and that, she knew, meant a bit of a wait.

'Robert, will you tell John I'll be on the bridge. I'll give mum your love. See you later.'

'Tell her we're all fit and well. I'll look after Cass. There won't be any visitors today. Mondays are always dead, so don't worry.'

It was another lovely morning. There was a slight mist and drops of dew dangled on cobwebs slung between dead stems on the riverbank. As she looked over the bridge, a movement caught her eye. There, to her absolute delight, playing on the rocks and diving into the deep pool worn into the riverbed was an otter and her three kits. Sylvia watched with awe as they launched themselves into the peaty waters, throwing showers of crystal droplets that turned into tiny rainbow flashes. Effortlessly, the creatures leapt from their swim onto the flat rock, shaking the harsh fur on their tactile little bodies. It was such a treat to see these rare animals, but to be able to watch their antics in their natural setting was something that would stay with her forever.

The sound of John's voice calling her from the car park broke the spell. The otters disappeared in a flash and she was left feeling privileged, yet disappointed that the moment had gone. She turned away and walked to the car, ready for the journey to the city.

John always drove fast and this morning was no exception. He was capable, and never panicked, though his driving was not usually passenger-friendly. The near misses didn't particularly bother Sylvia, if your number's up...so be it. But now it was different, there was an unborn child to consider. To her consternation, when they reached Threshfield, instead of taking the road through to Skipton, he followed the Burnsall route.

'John. What on earth are you doing? I've to catch the train in Skipton.'

He turned to her and grinned. 'Ah, ah. I've a job to do in Ilkley. So you can catch the train to Leeds there. And I'll be able to pick you up. It will make your time in Leeds longer.'

She agreed, but somehow felt disgruntled.

The scenery lifted her mood. Burnsall, sitting next to the river, looked particularly beautiful in the morning light. The road climbed steeply out of the village. It was narrow and closed in by trees on the right. A precipice drop to the left was contained by an earth bank, strengthened with the roots of odd trees and bushes, giving vehicles some sort of protection from the sharp descent.

The view was spectacular. She caught a glimpse of the village of Appletreewick across the fields. And farther over, the rising ground was topped with a menacing rocky outcrop, Simon's Seat. Sylvia smiled to herself as she gazed across the valley. That was where she had walked with her first ever boyfriend, exploring the wild and rugged area.

'Christ!'

Her attention jumped back to the road. Coming towards them, round a blind corner, was a great black predator, a fast threatening beast of a car that almost filled the road. It had nowhere to go, a collision was inevitable. She shut her eyes and braced herself waiting for the crash. It didn't come. Instead, she was thrown in all directions. It felt as though they were driving over rocks. Opening her eyes, she was startled to see they had mounted the bank. Without any change in his demeanour, John had his foot rammed flat to the floor and was aiming the little car at a treeless section a few yards in front. They lunged and bounced but, with limpet like determination, they clung at a precarious angle to the ragged undergrowth. As the Bentley bore down, there was a brief coming together and a rather expensive sounding scrape. They had brushed its immaculate wing, causing them to crazily spiral yards down the road. John held the wheel in a fierce grasp, fighting to get back onto an even keel. Gradually the car came to heel and obediently sat square on all four wheels.

Shaken, Sylvia stared at John, who was smiling triumphantly.

'Bet they've stained their linen,' he said with glee as he looked in the rear-view mirror at the disappearing adversary.

Sylvia was surprised that the occupants hadn't stopped. But everything had happened so quickly, they probably hadn't had time to collect their wits. If John hadn't acted with such presence, there would have been a horrible crash and they would have come off worse. She breathed a sigh of relief. 'Good Lord. I don't know how you managed to miss it.'

She had to admit, his reactions were lightning and it had been a wonderful piece of driving. Secretly though, she half blamed him for driving too fast and was pleased when they continued at a more sedate pace and reached the railway station in one piece.

At last, safely installed on the train, she began to relax and was lulled by the singing clatter of the wheels as they ran on uneasy rails, protesting at every points' change. The open landscape gradually gave way to industry and rows of terraced houses, homes for workers, to feed the appetite of that twentieth century giant. Soon the city centre came into view: imposing buildings, punctuated with resting places for statues, immortalising the famous. The train groaned to a stop in the bustle of the station, and waiting to greet her on the platform stood her mother. She hurried forward to hug her daughter, then leaning back she gave Sylvia a searching gaze. 'You look a bit peaky, love. Are you alright?'

'I'm fine. Come on, let's get some lunch. I'm famished.'

The two of them sat and gossiped over lunch, until, out of the blue, Sylvia's mum, who had been scrutinising her every move said, 'I think you've some news for me, young lady.'

Sylvia was quite taken aback and gazed at her. 'You've guessed!'

'Of course. You don't think I wouldn't know my only daughter's secrets.'

'Mumsie,' she unwittingly returned to the childhood name for her mother, 'do you think Pops will be pleased?'

Her mother was silent for a moment and bit her bottom lip. 'Sylvia. You know how much he loves you, so he will be happy. But that will never stop him worrying about you. I'm afraid he just can't trust John. He's convinced that one day he'll let you down badly.'

Sylvia's eyes burned with unshed tears. 'Oh Mum. We'll be fine. He's got a job and Robert and me have made the Inn look lovely. Trade is starting to come and summer will get us on our feet. Honestly, everything is fine. Besides, I've got Robert.'

'Well dear, I'm thrilled and I'm sure it all will work out well. No more talking now. We're going baby shopping.'

They had a wonderful time buying presents galore for the forthcoming addition to the family until Sylvia remembered her mother's favourite haunt. 'We've plenty of time. Let's go to the covered-in market. You know how much you enjoy going round it.' She took her mum's arm and marched her down past the Corn Exchange and on to the portals of Leeds market hall.

They wandered through the different sections, enjoying the smells, noises, and the variety of goods, all making a vibrant and colourful scene that changed with every step. The sea-fresh smell of the fish market enticed them. Melting lumps of ice clattered onto the cobbles as crates of gleaming cod were spilled, slithering onto the stalls. Live clawing crabs, with awkward deliberation tried to escape the waiting coppers of boiling water. The fishmonger in his rubber boots and waterproof apron, plunged his bare, red hands into the bubbling cauldron, to grasp an elusive crustacean.

The meat hall was noisier, with more stalls, the stall-holders, shouting out their wares with gusto. Game birds hung in crowded lines, their beautiful feathers shown to full advantage, but Sylvia wished they were still browsing in the wild heather. She was mesmerised by the Aladdin's cave in the vegetable section, such a varied choice was strange to her. They purchased far too much, in reality more than they could easily carry, but her mother was happy, and that was important as the place held special memories for her. They stopped to view plump chickens inviting purchase on a poultry stall.

'Do you know that in the old days, late on a Saturday night, the stall-holders, like this one, would sell off unsold goods for next to nothing. There was no electricity then, so it was impossible to keep things fresh over the weekend.'

'Mother. Tell me about it!'

'Sorry dear. I'd forgotten for the moment that you are in the same boat,' she went on, unperturbed. 'My father would call as late as possible to pick up cheap food for us all. He would often take me with him as a treat. And, if he'd had a win on the horses he'd buy me a bunch of anemones.'

'He must have found things difficult. No wife and three children to look after?'

'He did. But we were never hungry. He was a good cook. Stew and dumplings was his speciality.'

'Mum, how old were you when your mother died?'

'Nine. Arthur was eleven and Gladys just a baby.'

Sylvia went quiet. Her mother never complained but, she guessed she must have had a hard time looking after a brother and sister when their father was at work, or the pub, for he did like a wee drop. Suddenly she noticed the big clock.

'Gosh Mum. Look at the time. We'd better get going or I'll miss the train. Besides, if we buy anything else we'll need a pack horse!'

Hastily, they shifted their purchases into manageable bags and made for the station.

The train for Ilkley was already waiting. Sylvia clambered aboard, her shopping trailing haphazardly behind her. She stood at the carriage door with her head hanging out of the window. The train started to move.

'Oh Mum, I wish you were coming back with me. I've only men around the place and they don't understand things. Even though they're really good.'

Her mother looked anxious. 'Try not to worry, dear. I'm coming up two weeks before the baby's due and I'll stay to help as long as you need me.' She touched her daughter's hand. 'Daddy will be fine for a few weeks. He'll be glad to be rid of me for a while.'

They laughed, choking back the tears. Sylvia knew her father would enjoy his own company and wouldn't mind in the least, and she so needed her mum around.

As the train pulled in to the station, Sylvia glanced at her watch wondering how long she would have to wait on the platform for John. It was one thing being dropped off and picked up from Ilkley, but if all else failed she could get the bus from Skipton; she certainly couldn't from Ilkley. She might be here hours and she was dying for a cup of tea.

So when she finally disgorged herself and her packages on to the platform it was a bit of a surprise to see John bustling through the throng towards her.

'How are you, love? Had a good day?'

Without waiting for a reply he gave her a peck on the cheek and relieved her of the bags to lead the way to the car.

'Lots of baby things, is it?' he threw over his shoulder.

'Yes. Mum went quite wild.'

He helped her into the car, and as he sat behind the wheel he stared through the windscreen. Sylvia had a shiver of apprehension. Something was wrong. Then, he blurted out, 'I've no job. They don't need me anymore.'

She felt sick, even though she'd realised at some stage it would happen. To be fair, the pub was well out of his sales area, but that didn't stop the cold hand clutching her inside. She wondered how Robert would take the news.

John looked so miserable, she felt she had to be supportive. 'Oh dear. Don't worry, you'll soon get another one. I know you will.'

He nodded and started the car. As Sylvia listened to the engine burst into life she had the most awful thought. He'd lost his job, *and* the car.

'This means we'll have no transport. How are we going to manage?'

He didn't answer and they made their way back in near silence, punctuated only by the odd irrelevant comment. As soon as they got home she rushed to break the news to Robert on his own. To her relief he appeared unperturbed.

'I've been expecting it. Even a totally dedicated man would have found it difficult to work from up here. It's no good worrying. Just wait and see what the gods turn up.'

He was right. After several secretive excursions John came back from one particular jaunt full of the joys of spring.

'I've got a job! Perhaps not the best in the world, but for us it's perfect. It's local. Gerald told me that the couple who run the general store in Hebden were in need of someone to deliver orders to outlying homes and farms. So I went over. And they gave me the job there and then.'

Sylvia rushed to him and threw her arms around his neck. 'Oh, congratulations.'

She knew it would suit him down to the ground, for there was nothing he liked better than hobnobbing. The weekly visit from the grocer would be a highlight for some of the customers. The outlying farms would see no one else for days on end. She only hoped he wouldn't get ensconced at some particularly welcoming household and forget his other deliveries.

'How are you going to get to there? The engine on my old bike won't cope with your weight up those hills to Hebden.' Robert didn't try to hide his sarcasm.

John gave him a withering glance. 'I'm getting a second-hand motorbike from a mate of Gerald's.'

'And how much will that cost?'

'Fair words and money, Robert.'

Recognising that the conversation was getting out of hand, Sylvia butted in. 'By the way. Reverent Fullerton called this morning. You've got the sack, John.' She knew she was being mischievous, but something had to be done to change the atmosphere.

John looked startled. 'What do you mean?'

'He's going to ring the church bell himself. He doesn't trust you with the new ropes.'

They all laughed, but John seemed to be still feeling a bit uncomfortable about the incident. 'For pity's sake you two, let it drop will you.'

As usual, Mark had got wind of the new job. When he delivered the milk the next morning, he casually let slip, 'John. Tha'll b..be g..gettin' to know them w..wild 'uns in them ther' 'ills.'

Sylvia threw the wet dish cloth at him. Laughing, he ducked out of the kitchen. A few seconds later his head sneaked back round the door.

'A' f..forgot t'.. t'.. tell y' latest gossip! Y' remembe' d...dry stone waller, Bob Drysdale? Well. 'E must 'a g..got sick t'death o' bein' t' turned out o' 'is b..bed f' visitors and roughin' it in't wooden 'ut.'

Sylvia and the two men looked questioningly at Mark.

'Well this mornin', 'e went. B..but 'afore 'e left, e'd writt'n a note, an' l.left it in t'kitchen'

'Where has he gone, what did the note say?' demanded Sylvia impatiently.

He paused. Then with a wide grin and obviously relishing the moment, he said,

'It said…Gone wi' t' wind !!'

They all dissolved into fits of laughter and agreed it didn't sound as though he was heart-broken.

Mark went on his way and a rather truculent John muttered, 'I'd like to know where he gets all his information.'

Sylvia smiled. 'It's the Dales' Grapevine. Anyway, we've no time to worry about that. Remember we're fully booked this weekend. We've the six ladies coming from Halifax.'

With that statement she bounded upstairs to set about moving her and John's clothes from their bedroom into Grace's wardrobe in Robert's room. She decided John and Robert should sleep there and she would make do in the kitchen to be ready for an early start. Besides, if the truth was known, she was nervous in that room. Grace's wardrobe always gave her the willies.

As she expected, there was opposition from the two men. But she was adamant, and they finally relented with the threat that tomorrow was another day!

The bus arrived in the village around six o'clock. Charlie had agreed to meet the six ladies in his old banger and bring them to the pub. He not only played the accordion, he also ran the school-taxi. It involved picking up children from the remote farms from the head of the dale, and all the way down until he reached the village school. Sylvia was pleased to be able to give him a little business, for she realised his earnings were minimal. Though she did wonder how long the car would hold together. They'd followed it down to Kettlewell one day. By the time it arrived at its destination, it had developed a bit of a list and bursts of colourful sparks escaped from the rusty exhaust whenever it hit a bump in the road. But as its maximum speed was twenty miles an hour, it gave them little cause for concern.

The taxi duly arrived. It trundled up the drive and hiccupped to a stop at the front door. Out clambered six, somewhat bemused ladies, followed by an eager, grinning Charlie.

'Wi'gona 'av a music neet t'morra,' he informed John and Robert, who had come out to meet their guests. The two looked enquiringly at Charlie.

'Aye, wi'll bring t'accordions and 'av a reet sing-song.'

Sylvia came out to join them, catching the tail-end of the conversation. The ladies seemed pleased and rather amused at the prospect of a music-night, whilst John and Robert looked decidedly bewildered. Sylvia didn't know what would be involved, but it sounded as though it might be good for trade, and for Charlie. He went on his way whistling and she took charge of the ladies and showed them to their rooms.

She had taken an instant liking to the visitors, but couldn't help noticing how very small they all were. They had told her they all worked in a woollen mill in Halifax and had been there since leaving school. It reminded Sylvia of the time she had visited a mill in Huddersfield. During the tour she had worried about two of the workers whose job was to inspect the fabric as it left the dye-bath and came up over rollers at the top of the machine. The trouble was, they had no headroom, as the roof was too low. The men were bent double, and had taken on a permanent, gnome like conformation. She wondered if perhaps the ladies had some similar restrictions in their mill.

Eventually they came back to the kitchen and drank tea, chatting amicably till dinner was ready. They were all thrilled with their bedrooms and the novelty of oil lamps and candles. But most of all, they were all looking forward to the promised musical evening the following night.

Dinner went well, and the bar was comfortably busy. The ladies enjoyed a drink and a joke with the locals until closing time. Fortunately there were no lingering customers on this occasion and everything was cleared away at a reasonable hour. Sylvia puzzled just where and how, she could make her downstairs-bed. The settee in the dining room was small, it would mean being curled up all night. Perhaps four or five of the big dining chairs could be better? Carefully, she arranged them in a line with the backs alternating, then gingerly laid out on the seats. Not too bad, was her first thought. She collected spare blankets and pillows and made up a very reasonable looking sleeping bench. It was exciting, almost like camping for the first time.

John and Robert came into the dining room together. 'Sylvia. This is ridiculous. You can't sleep down here. Get yourself upstairs, I'll sleep in here.'

'No Robert. You will not. I'm staying here. And that's that.'

'Come on Sylv. Be reasonable. Robert's right.'

'Disappear you two. I've made up my mind.'

Finally they gave in with Robert's parting shot of, 'Tomorrow's another day!'

When the ladies were safely tucked away in their rooms, the menfolk left Sylvia to wrestle with her sleeping arrangements. She looked doubtfully at the bed she had put together.

'Well I've made it, better lie on it!' she said ruefully to Cassie, who, was more than pleased to have the company of her beloved mistress. It wasn't too bad for the first hour. She managed to snatch some sleep, but awoke, so stiff and desperately uncomfortable, that the latest design in beds had to be abandoned. Besides, the chairs seemed to have walked in all directions, leaving gaps that nipped her bottom!

Her next choice was the small settee. It proved to be a little better, but had the added joy of Cassie deciding to share it with her. After another hour or so of disturbed sleep she had to find somewhere else to stretch out her aching limbs. Finally the pair ended on the kitchen floor, in front of the Aga, whose gentle warmth lulled them into a fitful sleep. Only Cassie found the situation to her liking.

'We'll have to do better than this tomorrow night,' she muttered to her companion as she dragged herself upright, thankful the night was over. She could now set about the daily tasks. But first, a mug of sweet tea. She sipped the hot energy-brew, and mulled over the fact, that very shortly there would be a new baby. Letting all the bedrooms then would become impossible. Radical changes were needed.

Sylvia wished the place in hell as she went about the morning tasks. She felt sick and ached all over. Better pull myself together before the boys see me like this, she admonished. They'll only say, told you so.

A beautiful morning helped her to feel better. At that time of the day there always seemed a certain peace about the place, which helped to quell some of the night's anxieties.

Robert was the first to arrive downstairs and was pleased to hear she had slept ok.

'Ah, but we'll still have to make other arrangements before we take another full booking. This carry on just won't do. Perhaps the best thing would be to divide the room I'm in. That would keep a place just for you and the baby.' Thoughtfully, he toddled off to clean the bar.

'That's a damned good idea,' she called after him.

After breakfast, the ladies decided it was such a lovely day they would take packed lunches and walk till teatime. Sylvia made up the lunch-boxes, and watched the little gang set off along the path at the back of the church, leading up to Paul Hartley's farm, known locally as the Quaker farm. The hike would take them past the farm, up and westwards to the Iron Age stone circle. She watched them disappear up the steep path, happy that the day was fine and they seemed to be enjoying themselves.

There were no lunches, but the afternoon made up for it. Ham and egg teas were demanded, one lot after another. In fact, there were so many Sylvia had to make another batch of scones in amongst cooking the meals. She cursed under her breath. Her back ached, she so wanted to sit down. No such luck. The ham she was preparing was getting too diminished for her to cut reasonable slices 'Robert. Could you get me another ham? This one's just about finished.'

He turned into the bar passage and grabbed one from its hook on the ceiling. 'There you go. I'll clear the table under the window.'

'And I'll get the damned thing boned.'

Using a sharp, thin-bladed knife she quickly got on with the job, but soon her fingers became greasy. As she struggled to extract the bone, the knife slipped from her grasp and dropped to the floor with a clatter. Hitching up her skirt to make room for the bump she lowered herself in a squat to retrieve it. Her arm caught the handle of the big slicing knife. It bounced from the worktop and twisted in mid-air. There was a moment's terrible premonition, but she couldn't get out of the way and it landed across her thighs. She heard Robert gasp and glanced to see him standing in the doorway, his hands full of crockery. Next, there was a clattering onto the table as he leapt forward to help her rise.

'Good God, sis. Are you alright?'

She hardly dare look down, for she was sure the blade must have cut through her legs. Thankfully, instead of gaping flesh, there was a thin scarlet line across both of her thighs.

'You've been so lucky. The blade's landed sharp side uppermost and the back of it has just broken the skin.'

She caught her breath, and hung onto Robert's arm. John dashed in from the bar, took in the scene and dashed out again, returning quickly with a poured brandy. 'There you go. That should do the trick.'

Everything had happened so fast, she felt no ill effects and was soon back to normal, feeding the hungry until late afternoon.

The ladies arrived back from their trek, desperate to get their boots off and have a cuppa. They were tired and chatted away about their day like a flock of noisy starlings. Sylvia smiled to herself as they drank their tea. They certainly were a jolly crowd with their quick movements and strong Halifax accents. They were obviously looking forward to meeting Charlie again and the musical entertainment.

After dinner, the ladies, along with four casual diners, made their way into the bar to await the promised entertainment. It wasn't long before Charlie arrived in his old banger, along with brother, Fred, *the* Gilbert Thorndike, Charlie's eldest son, and the estate manager Nobby with his wife Jenny. Soon, the bar was alive with chatter and the magic music of Middlemass and Thorndike. News of the 'do' must have spread down the dale, for it wasn't long before Alfred Fewston and Carla landed along with half a dozen of their bed and breakfast folk. Mark, and Paul Hartley from the Quaker farm, came in together. Mark didn't stay long, his call was just a warm up for his weekly visit to Skipton's Hot Spots.

The atmosphere was quite special. In the small, crowded bar, happy talk competed with the foot tapping music from Charlie's accordion. Sometimes the crowd sang along with a particularly well-known tune, or just sat and enjoyed the little man's gifted performance. Closing time came and went. Sylvia worried that they might have a visit from the police, who were rather keen on checking after-time drinking. With so many residents, they would be able to use the ruse that the locals were guests of the residents. A hard one to swallow, but pubs had used it before.

As the night wore on, some of the clientele were getting worse for wear. Particularly the quiet, gentle, Paul Hartley, and Charlie, who, in spite of playing most of the night, wasn't far behind him. On one of her trips to collect dirty glasses, Sylvia, stood mesmerised. Charlie, without any warning, had risen unsteadily on his bandy little legs and carefully placed the red and silver accordion, with its myriad of buttons, on his chair. In a strange gait, he made his way to the fireplace, stood on tiptoe and lifted the brass and copper hunting horn from its hanging place. In his drunken stupor he decided they would have a competition.

'Let's see if any 'o ye' can git a tune out o' this 'ere. Best 'un gits a pint!' He held the battered instrument on high.

There was the odd snigger and a giggle or two, then a few of the visitors had a go, turning blue in the face without even managing to get a noise out of the instrument. Then the locals stepped up. The sounds produced were quite unbelievable, ranging from a howling hyena to a strangled cat. Not one managed anything like a melody. Fred, Charlie's brother, decided to have a go. He had been sitting there, apparently oblivious of the goings on around him. His sheep-eyes were half shut, his mouth slack and dribbling from one corner, but at that moment, he came alive. Grabbing the horn, he stood to his full height, made sure all were watching, and he blew. The notes, as clear as a bell, trilled round the room, conjuring up a dawn start for an eager hunt. There was a moment's silence, then in unison everyone applauded. Fred sat down, quite pink from his exertions and the resounding praise. Not to be outdone, Charlie, grabbed the horn from his brother's hand, and promptly stood on the chair. Putting it to his lips, he made ready to show the audience his prowess. Then he hesitated, turning to Fred.

'Fred, lend us thi' teeth. I ain't gitten mine in, an a' need 'em t' blow a tune!'

Without blinking an eyelid, Fred opened his mouth and calmly removed his dentures, passing them to Charlie. Deftly, he popped the gruesome contraption in his mouth and proceeded to blow the horn.

The place was in uproar. The whole building rocked with laughter and poor Charlie's efforts to give a tune were lost in waves of noisy hilarity.

Sylvia laughed as she went back to the kitchen with her load of pint pots. These far flung neighbours of theirs certainly were characters. They were gifted, accepted their hard lives with little reward, lived each day as it came and had no modern day trappings. Yet, they were as happy as the flowers in May. She suddenly realised how privileged they were to be part of a community which couldn't stay as it was for much longer, but for the moment was locked in a time warp.

Gradually the throng broke up, though it was well into the small hours before all was quiet and Sylvia could curl up with Cassie in front of the Aga once more. They had a better night than the previous one, but she knew there would have to be some changes made fairly soon.

Next morning, Robert came down early to help his sister. She looked at his wan face and tousled hair. 'I'm making a cuppa Robert. Why don't you sit down for a minute until it's ready?'

Filling the kettle at the sink, she idly glanced through the window. 'It looks as though somebody has left a coat on the bridge.' Robert replied with a grumpy, 'Humph'.

'I tell you what would be a good idea. When you've finished your tea, you take Cassie for her walk. The fresh air will do you good.'

He scowled. 'Ok then.' Silently he clipped the lead to the dog's collar and tottered out of the kitchen.

She was grateful. A quiet time to get ready was just what she needed. A bath would have been nice, but the visitors would need the hot water. Through the bathroom window, she noticed the coat had gone from the bridge. But Paul was there laughing with Robert as they gazed into the river. Her curiosity began to

100

get the better of her. She hurried to get dressed and was soon scurrying outside to discover what the two men had seen in the water to give such amusement.

'What's going on here then?'

Robert looked a little uncomfortable, though he seemed to be hiding a grin.

'Poor Paul had a drop too much last night and was sick going home.'

Paul's face, white as driven snow, screwed into a grimace and he ducked his head.

'Are you alright Paul?' Sylvia felt concerned. He nodded at the same time as a strange gurgling sound came from his throat. Then, he expelled an almighty guffaw exposing an expanse of pink gums.

Sylvia looked away and down to the flowing Wharf, then back to that gaping mouth. Eyes met, and they all convulsed with howls of mirth.

Shaking her head she took hold of Cassie's lead and left the pair giggling like teenage schoolgirls. As she walked to the other side of the bridge, she sneaked a look over her shoulder and saw the two of them stumbling down the bank to the edge of the river. 'Oh Cass. Men! They never grow up.'

The rest of the day was fairly hectic. Late in the afternoon the ladies departed. A rather pale looking Charlie came to collect them to catch the teatime bus. They booked for another long weekend, a month ahead. They'd had a weekend 'as never' and couldn't wait for the next.

Glory be, thought Sylvia. We'll never top this weekend. I only hope next time they wont be too disappointed.

The three of them stood at the door and waved goodbye to their guests. As the somewhat dilapidated rear of the vehicle disappeared, Sylvia turned to her husband and brother and said in a business like manner, 'We've some alterations to do before their next visit!'

CHAPTER 8

Sylvia knew she could not have a repetition of her recent night's escapade. Swinging off trees and sleeping on branches, was ok for monkeys, but not pregnant females. The mental picture tickled her, though something had to be done before they had another full booking. Perhaps Robert was right, his bedroom would be the easiest to split. Eager to get a solution, she darted upstairs straight to Robert's room. It certainly was the biggest. It covered the bar and the bar-passage, with the extra bit over the stairs where Grace's wardrobe resided in solitary splendour. Even though they'd painted it pristine white, to Sylvia, it still remained Grace's property with that air of a...presence...still about it. She deliberately kept her back fixed in that direction whilst she measured. If the corridor was continued, and an L-shape taken off at the end, they could just squeeze in a set of bunk beds and a cot. There would still be enough room for a double bed and the drawers-cum-dressing table in Robert's room and, of course, Grace's wardrobe would stay put. Satisfied she had the solution for their sleeping arrangements, she anxiously wondered how they could afford it.

Over the evening meal she broached the subject but, to her disappointment, she was faced with a brick wall.

'Sorry love. We haven't got the cash. It's good thinking, but it will have to wait.' John helped himself to more pudding.

'Oh, I don't know,' said Robert thoughtfully. 'How about we have a go ourselves. Surely we've enough cash to buy some wood and plasterboard?'

'Is that all we'd need?'

'Yes. We already have the door. It would just need to be fitted into the false wall, which would be a wood frame with uprights and cross pieces to hold the plasterboard. If you hang on a minute I'll measure up so we can have an idea what materials would be needed.'

'Brilliant. I'll come up with you.' Sylvia grabbed the tape measure.

'Steady woman. What will you do if we get more bookings and you've a room less. It will take a good few days to finish and then there's the decorating. Remember, none of us have done anything like it before.'

'John, don't be such a stick-in-the-mud. Mark's mother said she would let out a couple of rooms for us. We wouldn't get as much profit, but we wouldn't have to turn anyone away.'

'Right. Let's get going.' Robert took the tape from her hand. 'Get some paper and a pencil and we'll start.'

The debate had made John's morning departure later than usual. 'It's a good job I'm only going to Skipton cattle market with my boss. He wants to buy some sheep. I'd better get off.'

Sylvia waved to John as he drove past the door, then rushed to join Robert in the bedroom. They had just finished measuring, when they were stopped in their tracks by a sharp knock at the door. Followed with another, this time, an impatient rap. Sylvia rushed down the stairs and reached the door, just as it burst open, to be greeted by a round little body wearing a tightly-belted, navy mac. A matching hat was perched on the back of a thatch of red hair streaked with grey. Her face, cherry pink, gave the impression she'd just finished a long distance hike.

'I've come up on my scooter.' She followed Sylvia into the kitchen and dumped her black bag on the kitchen worktop.

Damnation, thought Sylvia, she was hoping there would be no residents until they'd finished the alterations. But as her gaze swept from the black bag to the piping on the hat, she realised that this cheerful character must be the district nurse.

'Oh, you must be the district nurse.'

'Indeed. I'm Nurse Brown. And you, young lady, should have been seen before now. I was only told about you yesterday. Heaven knows what the powers-that-be have been playing at. You must be almost six months pregnant.'

Almost without taking a breath, she ordered her charge upstairs and continued talking at breakneck speed whilst she set about the routine examination.

'It's a good job you'll be having the baby before winter sets in. There'll be no trouble in getting to you in late August. I nearly didn't get to one lady in the thick of winter.'

Sylvia was curious. 'Why? What happened?'

The nurse needed no second bidding. 'One year the snow had been very heavy. A farmer's wife at the top of the dale, living in the bleakest of farm houses, was due to give birth. I got a message at midday that the mother to be had gone into labour. Their farm man had struggled through the blizzard wearing make- shift snow shoes. He managed to get to a farmstead a bit lower down the dale where they had a tractor fitted with a home-made snowplough. That got him as far as here, The George, where he telephoned me.

'The only way I could possibly reach that bleak outpost was on horseback. The snowplough would have taken a couple of days at least to get so far, and that would have been too late. I'd never even sat on a horse, never mind ridden one, but farmer Robson lent me his reliable grey mare, Dolly, who was bomb-proof. So, with my bag tied to the saddle, my knees knocking and my stomach in my boots, we set off into the unknown.'

Sylvia felt she was there with her. 'Good grief. What an ordeal.'

'Yes. The weather was atrocious. The wind blew the snow into a 'white-out' and we couldn't see a thing. My nose dripped and froze to an icicle and poor Dolly had stiff white eyelashes and great balls of snow on her feet. I don't know how she found her way. There were drifts, so deep we could have been buried. She was so brave. She put her head down and trudged through to Beckermonds, then on and upwards to the farmhouse. I was so stiff that I fell off at the gate. The farmer helped me into the house, gave me a stiff drink, and I went straight to his wife, to find the baby was well on its way. After an hour's wait, we had a healthy, 8lb baby girl. And I managed to dry out and have a good meal.'

'Oh. How wonderful. What a story. How did you get home?'

'The snowplough got through the following afternoon. I was so relieved to get back home, and I felt quite proud. Though I slept a full twenty hours the next day.'

'What happened to Dolly?'

'The family were so grateful, they kept her all winter and spoiled her to death. She came home in the spring looking beautiful.'

'Well nurse Brown, I think you and Dolly deserved a medal,' said Sylvia in awe.

'It's funny you should say that. I was awarded the MBE the following year.'

'How marvellous. I feel as though I should curtsy.' They laughed.

'Back to business, young lady. Considering you've been left, you're doing ok. Everything is spot on. I hope you're taking those iron tablets. From now on feet up for an hour in the afternoon.'

Sylvia nodded, knowing full well she hadn't a hope in hell of sitting down for even half an hour in the height of summer. They had to grab every opportunity to make a crust. Winter wasn't so far away.

'Would you like a drink before you go?' asked Sylvia, thinking in terms of tea or coffee. But the mid-morning answer surprised her.

'A large gin with a dash of pep would be lovely, thank you.'

A bit taken aback she obliged. An hour later, after another couple of doubles, and a list of do's and don'ts, a happy nurse mounted her scooter and went on her way.

Robert asked, with a note of concern in his voice, 'Are you doing the right thing having the baby at home. Wouldn't you be better going to hospital?'

Sylvia grinned at him. 'You old natter can. It might be a dammed sight worse trying to get to the hospital. Remember it's twenty miles away and there's no saying we'd get there in time. What then?'

'Suppose you're right,' was the taciturn reply. Then they had a giggle at Nurse Brown's liking for the gin bottle as they went about their daily jobs.

John arrived back earlier than expected, along with Mr Souter, his boss, and the livestock trailer. They drove past the pub and parked up the road next to the pasture gate. Sylvia was perplexed as she watched from the front door. To her consternation, John lowered the trailer ramp, and out tottered two black and white calves. He shouted, 'Give us a hand!'

Robert joined her on the step. 'What the Hell's going on?'

'It looks as though we've got some livestock.' She cast a concerned glance at her brother. 'We'd better go and help.'

'Bought these at the auction. Two heifers. They were going cheap, and we need to get stocked up. We've twenty odd acres to fill, remember!'

John looked at them defiantly. It was obvious he was on the defensive, he seemed to expect opposition from his partners but they were too surprised to argue. Obediently they helped to herd the tired animals through the two gates and into the little croft next to the garden. Sensing peace and safety, the pretty beasts gambolled round the lush half-acre, tails held aloft like banners in the wind.

Sylvia's mothering instinct came to the fore. 'What do we feed them on? We'll need some straw for bedding in the hut. What about hay? Shouldn't they be on milk?'

Mr Souter laughed at the barrage of questions. 'Nay lass. Steady on. Tha'll meet thi'sen cumin back'ards. There's a couple 'o bales o' straw int'trailer, an' a bale of 'ay, an' sum milk nuts. Tha'll be ok.'

He gave her a quick lesson in animal husbandry, recognising that she would be the one doing the job. Then as soon as the trailer was unloaded, he hastily drove off as though the devil was on his tail.

'He's taking his wife out tonight and he's late,' explained John as he waited for the seal of approval from his partners.

Sylvia was won over immediately. Robert, however, questioned the cost on their already tight budget. After a bit of arguing, they decided it should be possible to manage. And really John was right, they would have to start stocking up or they could lose the land and their tenancy might be in question. Their agreement with the church was that the land must be stocked

106

and well maintained. Now unanimous, they had an increase to the family, Daisy and Buttercup. Sylvia was delighted and designated herself as calf feeder.

'Oh my God, she's clucking already,' Robert sighed.

That evening was a strange one. Unusually, Sylvia sat in the bar with Cassie on her lap, chatting to Anthony and his brother. There were only half a dozen or so other customers, one was a stranger to the pub. He turned out to be a young farmhand from well down the dale. A chubby lad, moon-faced, slit-eyed, with a wide, near lipless mouth and straight brown hair that flopped from a flat head. She decided he must have to make up for his lack of visual attraction by being brash, and extremely vociferous.

'Young buck c'ud do wi' a lesson i' manners,' muttered Anthony under his breath.

At that moment in walked the shy Tommy Smith. The smell of his special brew of silage hung around him in a cloud. He ordered a drink and sat in the corner next to Sylvia and her companions, opposite the young buck. Sylvia immediately felt an antagonistic undercurrent. As though to confirm her thoughts, the youth leaned back indolently in his chair.

'By 'ell. There's a stink in 'ere. I'd be worried if I wa' thee, missus. It'll turn thi beer.'

Sylvia was embarrassed, realising the remark was directed at Tommy. She sprang to his defence, and tried to look haughty.

'I hadn't noticed a smell.'

He ignored her. 'Mucky boots I'll be bound. Hen shit stinks.'

Tommy looked away and thrust his wart covered hands, deep into his pockets. Sylvia had been told that he eked out his living with a small hen-unit. In summer the eggs were sold at his door to passing visitors. Rumour had it, that constantly handling eggs brought about the skin condition on his hands. The poor man was obviously embarrassed by his toad like extremities, but she suspected that anger was beginning to smoulder. The youth, too, possibly sensing warning signals, suddenly changed tactics and directed his attention to Sylvia and Cassie.

'Wy d' ye want a stupid dog like tha'un. It's n'gud fer owt, jus' sits i thi lap.'

With that, the now irate Tommy, made no more ado. He leapt across the room as though the chair seat had delivered a charge of electricity to his backside. With his fist clenched and drawn back to shoulder level, he released a blow as accurate as the first cannon on Nelson's flag ship. It was a direct hit, right on the nose-end of the flabbergasted youth.

'Tha'll leave missus 'an lile dog alone. They've dun nowt t'thee.'

Flushed, he turned on his heel and stormed to his tractor. Sylvia froze, but heard it cough a couple of times, and then angrily growl away up the dale seeming to reflect its driver's mood.

There was a heavy silence in the bar. The youth was half slumped across Anthony's knees. His flat nose dripped blood in a steady dribble down the front of his white shirt. John moved forward to help him, but Anthony gave the lad a shove. He scrambled to his feet, lurched past them both, almost giving himself further injuries as he wrestled with the door. All eyes gazed through the window, apprehensively watching as he unsteadily mounted his pushbike and launched himself down the drive, wobbling unsteadily out of sight.

Sylvia hibernated to the kitchen. She felt extremely uncomfortable, yet just a little flattered that Tommy had sprung to her defence. Though perhaps she had been an excuse for him to vent his obvious pent-up aggression. As she wondered what reason Tommy could have had to be so upset by the youth, Cassie leaned against her leg, 'Ok, you want a walk. Come on we'll go to see Daisy and Buttercup.'

The sun had dipped behind the tops, but the air was warm as the pair ambled through the garden up to the croft. At the gate, Sylvia turned to admire the Inn and pinch herself, that this, indeed, was her home. In the fading light, she spotted a figure at the front door that set her senses in disarray. It was Walter, the local who could wheedle a pint, or half, from any poor innocent victim. He was standing over the small stone trough at the side of the front door. She was right. His stance proved he was doing exactly what she had suspected for some time, peeing on her delicate clematis. No wonder the poor thing had struggled. She'd tended it with great care and couldn't understand why it failed to flourish. Well, now she knew for certain. 'Just you wait you horrible little man. I'll teach you.' She ran down the garden steps two at a time, across the drive and into the kitchen. Hurrying into the bar-passage she whispered to Robert, 'Let me know the minute Walter goes outside again.'

He was curious, but she would only say, 'I'm going to teach your disgusting customer a lesson.'

About an hour later, nature called and Walter moved. Sylvia ran upstairs where she had left a large jug of water at the open window. The bumbling culprit appeared below her. He positioned himself over the stone trough and performed his party piece. Gleefully, she balanced the jug on the sill and deliberately emptied the contents in a steady stream on the inviting target, the greasy terrain of his flat cap. Water bounced and flew to all points of the compass. It dripped from the peak of his cap in his direct line of vision, yet there was no acknowledgement. He remained unmoved. And finished his job without even registering that anything out of the ordinary had taken place. Her efforts were of no avail. She watched in disbelief. He shook himself like a wet retriever, banged his sodden cap against the wall, then plonked it back on his head and returned to his beer a damned sight wetter than when he'd left. Sylvia didn't know whether to laugh or cry. She was sure he would have looked up when he felt the deluge. Flattened, she sneaked back to the bar. 'Robert, what's Walter doing?'

'Why, what should he be doing? He's drinking his beer.'

She turned disconsolately back to the kitchen and in disgust brought out the ironing, a punishment, waiting in the laundry basket. She plonked a couple of flat irons on the Aga. Soon one was hot enough. Folding a cloth to grip the handle, she rubbed its flat bottom on a block of soap, finishing off with a polish to give easy ironing. The smell of the hot metal on the freshly dried cotton and the hypnotic motion of the task managed to dull her annoyance.

She stood back to admire the mountain of sweet-smelling, creaseless, articles piled high on the worktop. 'One of these days I'll hit the jackpot and actually touch the ceiling.' Cassie was unimpressed, which made her smile at the silly goal she had set herself and her thoughts returned to Walter and her clematis. She knew the damned thing would have to be moved; he wouldn't stop even if given an ultimatum. It had nothing to do with the gents urinal being a bit smelly, or any legitimate excuse. The man was just bone idle. She sighed, the doorway would look bare without the clematis. Perhaps what was really needed would be a colourful sign over the door. Something to denote the Inn's history or its connections.

Once she had an idea, it had to be actioned there and then. Even though darkness had fallen, she grabbed a torch and made her way to the coach house where she cautiously searched amongst the stored bits and pieces discarded over the years. Sure enough, a stout wooden frame, about four foot by three, leaned against the wall, half hidden by a couple of dilapidated doors. She yanked at the filthy object. It was heavy, but determination gave her muscles the strength to haul it into full view. Stepping back to assess its appearance, Sylvia was pleased. It looked as though it might have been the frame for a sign in the dim and distant past. Delighted with her prize, she excitedly ran back to tell John and Robert of her find.

They looked at her aghast. 'Where the Devil have you been. You look as though you've been down a coal mine.'

She ignored their comments. 'Come and see what I've found.'

Reluctantly, they followed her outside. In the light of the torch, they gazed unimpressed at the dilapidated apology of a frame.

'It's an old frame. What good is that?' questioned John.

'All it needs is a backing piece of wood and then we've got our sign for the George!'

'What would you paint on it?' Robert sounded doubtful.

'Oh, I don't know, something heraldic. I like rampant lions,' she joked.

John grinned knowingly at Robert. A grin that said there would be no peace until she had her way. They made a hasty retreat, leaving Sylvia lost to the world, with pencil, paper and an old book on heraldic signs.

CHAPTER 9

The task of designing a sign for the Inn took more time than Sylvia had realised. It came as a bit of a shock when she glanced at the kitchen clock to see it had run round to 2a.m.. Stiffly, dragging herself upright, she viewed her efforts. It didn't look too bad, in fact, it was rather pleasing. Now she could go to bed happy. Smiling with satisfaction, she quietly whispered goodnight to Cassie, turned off the calor gas lamp in the kitchen, and immediately wished she hadn't. The small hand lamp left to light her to bed had exhausted its oil supply during the hours she had been lost in artistic prowess. Darkness sneaked around her, and for a moment she was held captive in its clutches. Quickly gathering her thoughts, she stumbled to the shelf above the bar door where the candles were kept. In her uneasy haste, she managed to grab one of a few, the rest fell to the floor in a waxy clatter. Where was that blasted newspaper?

'You're no help, Cassie,' she whispered to the sonorous whippet as she located the daily rag. It was where Robert had left it, rolled and tucked in the top of the coke hod ready for laying the dining room fire in the morning. She tore a lump from a page and rolled it into a spill. Holding the Aga rail, she bent low and opened the ash door. The red embers of the slow-burning coals lent a cosy glow to the grate. Carefully, she stuck the spill into the hottest spot. It lit. Holding the flame to the wick of the candle, she anxiously watched it flicker hesitantly, then settle to give her light. It threw a golden glow into the room and made eerie shadows climb the walls, causing her to cast nervous glances in every wavering corner. She carefully dropped a soft circle of wax onto a saucer and stuck the candle in place.

Relieved to be able to see again, her nervousness subsided. She took a look at Cassie. 'Of course there's nothing there. Silly old me. What do you say Cass?' Sylvia was acknowledged with a one-eyed baleful glance from her pet, before returning to her musical snores. Quickly leaving the kitchen, Sylvia closed the door behind her and began to climb the stairs. She shivered. Perhaps the night was extra cold, or perhaps she'd become starved sitting in one position too long. No, the cold was a strange, creeping, clammy mist that seemed to invade her bones. Now rather frightened, she involuntarily pulled her blouse collar up around her neck. Something made her look to the top of the stairs. She went rigid. Her hands shook. She screamed! The shrill note surprised her, even more so, the shadowy figure that hovered there. Suddenly, it vanished and Robert stood in its place.

'What in God's name's the matter? Are you alright?'

'Robert... ' Sylvia clutched her chest. Her heart was beating so fast she could hardly breathe. '...Robert, I've just seen Grace. She was standing where you are now.' Her gaze followed the line of her outstretched arm. She was trembling. She had to calm down.

'Oh come on sis, there's no such thing as ghosts. It's been a trick of the light. Get yourself into bed and I'll bring you a warm drink.'

She stared at him. He didn't believe her. 'Honestly Robert, I saw her.'

'Sis, you've not so much as seen a photograph of her, so how could you possibly see her ghost?'

He opened the door and pushed her gently into the bedroom, where a sleepy John wanted to know, just what was amiss. He pulled back the covers for her to climb in beside him. 'Now, what's all this about?'

Dithering, she snuggled close to him. 'I saw Grace.'

'No. Never. You've dreamt it.'

Aggrieved, she sat up as Robert popped his head round the door. 'Your drink. It's all ok. See you in the morning,' then mischievously. 'Pleasant dreams.'

'Poor Robert, he's got to sleep in her room,' she mumbled before falling into a fitful sleep.

Next morning, Sylvia decided she must have imagined the whole nerve-shattering experience of the night before. Her mind must have played tricks because she was over-tired. Somehow, designing Inn signs didn't seem quite as exciting as the previous night. However, she tried to muster some interest and showed her work of art to the boys.

'Well, do you approve?'

'Mm, it looks ok, but does it mean anything?' questioned Robert.

'Of course it does. Mind you, I don't know whether it's correct from an heraldic point of view. That won't matter, will it? Surely, no one will go into such detail.'

Without waiting for an answer she went on to explain the design.

'I'm going to use a board divided into four quarters...'

'We can see that,' John interjected. She eyed him wondering if he was in one of his supercilious moods, but he gazed at her expectantly and so she carried on.

'One set of diagonally opposite squares will carry the red cross of St George on a white background, and the other a rampant white lion on a black background. This one is holding a shield with the Church Diocesan coat of arms – I thought would go down well with Rev. Fullerton – and the other the cross of St George.'

'And the pale blue diagonal with six white roses?' John asked.

'For Yorkshire. Besides, it looks pretty.'

She watched him nod and felt pleased with his approval.

'Six roses?' queried Robert.

She gave her brother a push, hoping he wasn't going to ruin the moment. 'They fitted!'

Smiling, he too, nodded. 'It's quite striking, I'll give you that. It'll look well above the front door against the white walls.'

She looked from one to the other of them and took a deep breath ready to strike while the iron was hot. 'I could do with a trip to Skipton to get some little pots of paint and some gold-leaf.'

'Gerald's going to market this morning on a flying visit.' John suggested. 'You could go with him, and get the things you want.'

'Do you think he'd mind?'

John picked up the phone. 'No sooner said than done.'

The arrangements were made, and Sylvia, feeling happy, was collected by Gerald. He spoke little on the way down. She guessed his visit involved some serious business, for the only thing he mentioned was that he mustn't be late for the bank manager. Luckily, they arrived in plenty of time, in spite of Gerald's somewhat erratic driving skills. She left him at the car park and made a beeline for Manby's hardware shop in the middle of the main street. Money was short, but she managed to buy all she needed, including the gold-leaf. Just two sheets, each one only two inches square. Mr Manby told her how to apply it. First, she had to use a glue on the bits to be covered, then the paper had to be pressed over it and gently pulled away leaving the gold in place. Fortunately, there were only tiny highlights to do, even so it would be a tight squeeze from two sheets, but that was all she could afford. Counting her change she was pleased to find there was enough for a coffee from the caravan-café on the car park.

It wasn't long before Gerald caught up with her, 'No time t'be supping. We've got t' get goin'.'

She was bundled to the waiting Land Rover. Before she had even closed the door, the vehicle leapt to a racing-start, and they were homeward-bound. She was fairly certain that he would make some kind of a pass at her before they reached Hubberholme, but she was totally unprepared for the nerve-jangling journey. They'd left Skipton behind, when Gerald turned his head a full ninety degrees, and stared deep into her eyes down the length of his bumpy, roman nose. 'How about we av' a bit o' scenic tourin'. Tha's niver seen 'idden dale. As tha?'

Normally, she would have laughed it off, but she daren't take her eyes off the road ahead. The Land Rover was gaily ploughing its own furrow, everywhere but to the left of centre. It bounced off the verges with gay abandon. Sliding all over the seat, she almost departed company on one enormous lurch. It crossed her mind that the baby would be having a bumpy ride. In spite of her philosophy to ignore her condition and carry on as normal, she felt concerned. Gerald seemed totally oblivious, and held his stare.

'*Gerald.* You're going to hit something. Look at the road, will you.'

'Does that mean yes?'

He grinned, and to her relief he focussed his eyes in the direction they were travelling. Sylvia regained her composure. 'No it does not. You are a so-and-so, Gerald.'

He laughed with full-blooded gusto, yet still carried on with the stare every time he spoke. It seemed forever before Buckden appeared. She breathed a sigh of relief at the sight of the village green. They turned left onto the Hubberholme road. As they approached Mr Fell's farm gate on the left of the road, Sylvia caught a movement of black and white heads over the top of the wall. 'Stop! Stop!'

Her scream broke Gerald's seductive gaze. He hadn't seen the farmer's milk cows beginning to cross the road to the riverside meadows. He came to his senses, and braked so hard that the vehicle nose-dived, making the back end jump in the air before coming to a screeching halt. Thank God, we're nearly home, thought Sylvia.

Her companion was quite unperturbed. 'That wa'close.'

As they passed Gerald's farm, he let it drop that John had arranged to buy two of his gilts, young female pigs.

'In a couple of weeks they'll be ready t'cum t' new boar. 'E's a rare animal. 'E'll git thi' good litters. Them gilts o' thine are out o' me best sow.'

He rambled on enthusiastically leaving Sylvia way behind.

Pigs! What were they going to do with pigs? What had possessed John, and to not even mention it? Pigs needed housing. That meant more cleaning and disinfecting. *Oh Lord!* More scrubbing and there's so little time before the baby's due, and so much to do. It was a good thing her mum would be with them in three weeks and after that there were no bookings. Thoughts charged around in her head as she tried to slot all the tasks waiting to be completed into some kind of order. Before she knew it, they were at the front door. Gerald followed her into the kitchen, giving her posterior a quick nip as he let out a devilish laugh. Sylvia giggled, she knew him so well, he always had to try his hand. If there was no response, he carried on cheerful and saucy as usual. She wondered just how many females had succumbed to his charms.

Robert greeted them with a welcome cuppa and they chatted happily, until the two pigs were mentioned. Sylvia winced as she saw Robert splutter over his tea.

'Pigs!'

'Piglets,' she said, and wished she hadn't. Robert looked fit to burst.

'Gilts are not piglets,' he snapped.

'Ah, 'e's right thar. Gilts be…'

Gerald's voice faded as he finally read the situation. Backing slowly into his chair and then settling down his cup, he rose and made a hasty retreat.

'Pigs!' thundered Robert. 'He's agreed to take pigs and not discuss it with us?'

'I'm sure John—'

'I'm sure John won't lift a finger caring for them, and certainly not mucking them out, not Mr High and Mighty, the Squire of Hubberholme!'

Sylvia tried to calm him, desperately trying to make it seem a non-event and suggested they'd better decide where the pigs should be housed.

'Robert, do you think the little stone sty in the corner of the 18 acres will be the easiest to clean for them? The deal's done, so we might as well make the best of it and get a place ready for them.'

'I suppose so.'

She grabbed his arm. 'Come on. Let's have a look.'

He followed her sulkily, up the garden steps and through the croft where Buttercup and Daisy were grazing. She struggled to open the metal gate, her bump seemed to get in the way, but Robert didn't help. Standing aside, she let him through before her and made a face at his back as he passed. He yanked at the door of the low stone building, an extension on the rear of the privy.

'Crikey sis. It's filthy in here.'

'It's only surface muck, cobwebs and such.' She pushed past him and opened the door wider, ducking her head to get under the lintel. On a pile of old muck, something moved.

'Robert! I think…'

She screamed as a body shot through the air over her shoulder, and her head hit the top of the doorway. Rubbing the sore spot, she became aware that behind her Robert was laughing like a drain. 'What's so funny then?'

'Your face. The rat nearly landed on your shoulder.'

'*Rat?*'

'Aye. A big bugger as well.'

Feeling a bit weak at the knees, she nervously cast her eyes round the sty. She'd never seen a rat before. 'You are mean. That was a shock and I've a big lump coming up on my head. There won't be anymore, will there?'

'Mind out of the way. I'll make sure.'

Robert's six feet had to bend nearly double under the low roof. He kicked at the pile of muck, hesitantly at first, then with more vigour when no more livestock appeared.

'All clear in here. You can come in.'

She lowered her head and cautiously joined her brother. 'It won't take much cleaning. A good brush down and a lick of whitewash should do the job. Let's get going. We can be finished by teatime.

'Fit for a king,' said Robert, as he finished whitening the last wall. He was jovial, his upset seemed forgotten.

'Well, two princesses. Genevieve and Ariane, names fit for royalty.'

Robert raised his eyes heavenwards and laughed. 'We better get cleaned up. I'm covered in whitewash and you've got cobwebs in your hair. Then we can sort out the plan for the weeks up to mum coming.'

Sylvia went quiet. She knew what he really meant was, to get organised before the baby came. Suddenly the nearness of the birth hit her hard. Her hand went involuntary to the bump, which thankfully had kept small and neat below her waist. She didn't want to let him see her anxiety, so slapped his backside. 'Off you go. We'll look at everything when you're clean.'

She followed him upstairs and went quietly into the bedroom closing the door behind her. Sitting on the bed she absent-mindedly brushed her hair wondering why she felt like crying.

Robert clattered down the stairs and she joined him at the kitchen table with the list of bookings.

'We've got people in for the next three weekends. That brings us up to the eleventh of August. After that there's just a coach party of W.I. ladies for lunch on Wednesday the fourteenth. The baby's due two weeks after and mum comes up the Sunday before. Things seem to have worked out hunky-dory.'

'And, the timber for the partition's arrived,' Robert chimed in. 'That needs to be erected as soon as possible. You want the sign to be painted, and there are three busy weekends to get through.'

'I know, but the partition won't take long. We won't be able to plaster it, we've neither time or money, so I'll just size the wall, then wallpaper over the joints. There, we're done and dusted.'

Robert looked doubtful.

The days of that week flew by. Genevieve and Ariane were ensconced in their little house, as happy as pigs in the proverbial. Daisy and Buttercup were settled and growing. The partition was halfway to completion, and the Inn sign looked good.

'We've a foursome from the East Riding this weekend and a Mr Jones from somewhere near Kirkstall Abbey,' mused Sylvia, more to herself than anyone else. 'We've got to get the partition finished so we can get upstairs looking presentable. A good thing we've only five residents, otherwise we would have to board out.'

At that precise moment the telephone rang, and a couple from Leicester wanted to book for the weekend in question. They were more than willing to be farmed out for sleeping, so the booking was taken.

'You've taken the booking without checking that it's ok with Mark's mother.'

118

'Well, she did say, anytime.' Sylvia felt uncomfortable, realising it was only polite to ask.

'I'll walk across the bridge to the farm, to ask Mrs Hollins if she would care to let a double room for the weekend.'

'Oh, listen to you,' Sylvia taunted.

Robert ignored her and went on his way, but he was away ages, and Sylvia wondered if something had gone wrong. When he returned, he had an air of superiority about him. Proudly, he showed her half a dozen beautiful, russet eggs flecked with deep brown.

'These are eggs from Mrs Hollins special hens. They're dark grey, speckled with black and white. They really are striking, and they're her pride and joy. We're favoured!' He grinned. 'She also said they'd be killing a pig next week, and she's going to let us have some of her black puddings. Apparently she makes the best in the dale.'

'Gosh, you're in her good books, clever-clogs that you are. I thought she scared you to death on your last encounter.'

'Perhaps she likes me!'

'Oh my, oh my. Don't you think it might be something to do with the bit of extra she'll be making by letting her rooms?'

'Sylvia, you're being cynical. It doesn't suit you.'

'No, just realistic.'

He ignored her. 'Actually, the lady's quite dry. She got talking about the war years. One story in particular tickled me, it was about killing a pig.'

'Oh no. I don't want to hear it if it's gory.' She hated the thought of her pigs meeting the same fate.

'No, it's ok. In wartime it was illegal for farmers to keep any slaughtered animal for their own use, obviously because of rationing. But most of them managed to keep something back for themselves. The authorities were well aware of what went on, and periodically carried out raids. On one occasion, the landlord from here, his wife and a neighbouring farmer, were in the act of cutting up one such rogue carcass when they had a warning telephone call from lower down the dale. The Inspectors, were on their way!'

'This happened here?'

'Yes. Listen will you. They were panic stricken. The joints of meat were suddenly red-hot loot. Not one of the blacklegging threesome could think what to do. After what seemed an eternity, the landlady had the bright idea to hide it in the church, thinking the officials would never think to look across there. In a panic, each picked up a piece of pig and raced across the bridge, dumping their precious cargo at the foot of the belfry tower. Dashing back, they stumbled in a heap at the church gate in their haste to get back to the kitchen and remove all the evidence. Panting from effort and nerves, they nursed sore shins and elbows, but managed to clear away before the anticipated raid.'

'I bet they were in a right state.'

'Yes. They must have managed to look reasonably innocent when the inspectors arrived. It was obvious there had been a tip off. Someone, perhaps feeling thwarted at not being in on the deal, must have shopped them. Anyway, the two pen pushers from officialdom searched with the determination of alley cats. Nothing could be found. They looked into every nook and cranny, even the outside privy wasn't spared. They searched for well over an hour before admitting defeat. Finally they reluctantly departed, two decidedly perplexed and deflated pussy cats.

'When all was clear, the three pirates charged back over the bridge into the church and returned, jubilantly carrying their spoils of victory!'

'Oh, what a tale. I can hardly believe it. I must tell John when he comes home. It'll tickle him.'

But later, when she recounted the story to John, she didn't get the reaction she'd expected.

'I suppose they would be better off up here for food during the war. They would have the chance to have the odd joint or two and they could grow a few vegetables. Not like people in the towns, who had no chance.'

John's rather bitter reply made her think one of his tirades on injustice was coming on. He'd experienced the war first hand in the Fleet-Air arm, so was acutely aware of the hardship of others. But she didn't want a full-blown lecture, so gently ushered them out of the kitchen. 'Sorry boys, I must shift you. This sign has got to be over that front door for the weekend.'

The weekend arrived and the sign was in place. Sylvia kept having a quick dash out of the door to admire her handiwork. It looked well, and seemed to finish off the front of the building. The gold highlights glinted in the sun. She was pleased, at last everything was falling into place. They'd managed to finish the partition in Robert's bedroom, with the help of choice language from all three. Her trick to avoid plastering by sizing the plasterboard and papering on top had worked. Though she hadn't enjoyed working in there, alongside Grace's wardrobe. It reminded her repeatedly of the apparition she had seen, or thought she had seen, at the top of the stairs. Apprehension wrapped around her every time she went into the room, so she was more than relieved when all was finished. It gave them a small place to house the bunk beds and the baby's cot, as well as an extra room for letting.

The first visitor to arrive was Mr Jones from Kirkstall, a slow moving, square man, with grey hair cut in a hedgehog crop, and a neck almost as wide as his huge shoulders. He portrayed someone who had pushed his body to the limits all of his working life. He was extremely quiet, but smiled in pleasure at the pot of tea and plateful of scones put before him. When Sylvia came to collect the tray, it looked as though a swarm of locusts had passed through. There wasn't a crumb in sight, even the milk jug was empty. Good, a healthy appetite; that she liked. When she mentioned it to John, he couldn't believe the man had shifted five, hot buttered scones in one go.

Two young couples from the Hull area were the next to arrive. Mr Guy had made the booking. He was tall, dark, and good looking. He had a deep voice and spoke well, public school, Sylvia guessed. His wife was slim, with shoulder length dark hair and was absolutely beautiful. She had a sweet smile and such a kind expression. Sylvia was mesmerised; what a gorgeous couple. She realised she was staring, and quickly turned to the other two, Hal Dexter and his wife, equally as nice, but a little more homely. He was not as tall as his male companion and his hair and skin were fair. He had a naive, boyish charm and seemed to be half a step behind in the conversation, but he laughed readily and came across as a kind, genuine person. His wife, Jo, was dark and pretty and just as sweet. She was obviously expecting a baby and had that air around her of serenity. Unlike herself; she felt more reminiscent of a fully charged workhorse. Sylvia couldn't help the sigh that escaped from her lips: oh to be more ladylike. With that hopeless dream, she showed them to their rooms. They were delighted, as had so many before them. It was fun to have candles and oil lamps when there was the luxury of returning home to modern creature comforts. Wistfully, she longed for the day when they'd get electricity. Smiling, she wondered just what she'd do to celebrate the event.

Dinner was almost ready before the people from Leicester landed: a tall, thin, morose man with a small, nondescript wife and a hefty bull-terrier with a severe slobber. They were quickly settled in at the farm, then hurried back for their meal. It was enjoyed by all, especially Mr Jones. He was left alone in the dining room after the others had gone into the bar. When Sylvia came to clear the tables, she was filled with admiration and amusement. The decks had been, not just cleared, but vacuumed. It looked as though a minesweeper had cut anchor in the room. Cheese and biscuits left on the other tables had disappeared. Nothing edible remained, not even a solitary little white mint or a knob of butter. What an appetite! She could hardly credit what the old bull had shifted, and then to top it all, his beer consumption could have floated the minesweeper! As she stacked the empty plates Peter ambled in looking a bit perplexed.

'I think I've put my car keys down somewhere. I could have sworn I left the bloody things on the table,' he boomed.

Sylvia tried not to laugh. She turned to the fireplace where something had caught her eye. 'Here you are Peter. They're sitting on the mantel-shelf, safe and sound.'

'You're a star. I'd have been up shit-creek without a paddle if they'd gone missing. There would have been all Hell to pay.' He gave her a grimace and went off tutting under his breath.

That night a family from Leeds appeared in the bar, a mother and two daughters, all quite large ladies, their relationship, strikingly obvious. One of the girls, Jocelyn, was unusually attractive. Her brown velvet eyes dominated a round honey-coloured face, edged with locks of inky black. Her sister, Edwina, not nearly as eye-catching, seemed shy and withdrawn. Gerald, who had been in the bar, followed Sylvia as she returned to the kitchen with a tray of dirty glasses. 'Thought a'd just see 'ow tha' wa' keepin'.'

He came up close behind her. She sidestepped and threw him a tea towel. 'You can dry if you're staying in here.'

His ready laugh rang round the kitchen, 'Ok, ok.'

Sylvia was curious about the family in the bar. 'Gerald, who are the three ladies sitting in the corner?'

'They're from Leeds. They come up every summer, they rent a cottage next to Anthony's farm.' Then, almost as a punch line, he smirked. 'It gives 'em' chance t'see brother. 'E's farm'and, fer' big 'ouse at top o' dale.'

She realised a bit of gossip was on the way, 'Oh?'

'Rumour 'as it, 'es 'avin' it off wi' owner's wife. Mrs Victor Smythe.'

Sylvia giggled and sneaked another peep at the newcomers. As she studied them from the doorway Anthony came in. Always cognizant of body language and quick to pick up feelings, she realised the moment he walked into the room that he had fallen for Jocelyn, who gazed straight at him with those enormous dark eyes, fringed with long, black lashes. Oh, jolly good, thought Sylvia, a romance in the offing. How lovely for Anthony. He deserved a bit of affection. Sylvia nudged John, 'I think Anthony's fallen in love.'

'Don't be daft. He's a confirmed bachelor. Anyway, I've a customer waiting to be served.'

At that point, Mark ambled into the bar, chortling before he could even begin to tell his latest bit of news.

'Y' y'yu'll never guess, W' Walter, w'went 'ome from 'ere l' las' neet an' got an'an' earful from wife f' f' bein' drunk. Anyroad, 'e must 'ave decided t't' teach 'er a lesson, 'f' durin' neet, 'e set f'f'ire t' bed!! It's ok the're both f'ffine, though bed an' carpet's knackered.'

There were looks of consternation from the visitors, but when John explained Walter's goings-on, they saw the funny side. Hilarity became the mood for the night.

Sunday morning brought more fun. Mr Guy, Peter, had walked into the bar whilst Rev. Fullerton was making his normal Sunday purchase of a bottle of whisky. He always popped in after the morning service and paid for the bottle with the church collection. His line of patter never varied. 'Here you are, John, your small change for the till. It should keep you going for a while. I'll square up with a cheque as soon as I get home.'

John was watching Peter's open-mouthed surprise, and when he caught his eye he gave him a huge wink. Peter seemed to be tickled pink at the little transaction and couldn't wait to tell the tale to his wife, Bernadette. John and Robert overheard the conversation and were hard put not to laugh out loud. Peter's vocabulary was colourful to say the least. Swear words by the dozen punctuated the story, delivered in a public school accent. A docker would have been proud at the extent and variation of the expletives, not one was repeated. He endeared himself to the boys. They were full of admiration and immediately felt a bond with this flamboyant character, though they didn't want him to get the wrong impression of Rev. Fullerton, for over the months all of them had come to respect the little clergyman. They had found him kind and understanding, and his enjoyment of a drop of the 'hard stuff' had made him seem more human. John explained this to Peter who was immediately contrite and declared that the reverend was a man after his own heart. He even pronounced that on his next visit he would attend the morning service. However, his wife's glance made a mockery of that promise.

The day flowed smoothly. It was busy, there were plenty of teas, but no extra lunches or dinners, which gave a steady work-load. After dinner, Mr Jones, as before, stayed behind and cleared up all remnants of food from the other tables. Then wheezed his way to the bar to enjoy more beer.

That night, he snored fit to wake the dead. Sylvia heard him quite clearly and wondered how Robert was faring on a makeshift bed in the new cubby hole with only the partition wall between them. The noise was deafening, but not rhythmic, which made it seem so much worse. There were moments after a huge exhale when absolute silence reigned, and it seemed to go on for ever.

Oh God, he's died, she thought anxiously.

To her great relief there was another noisy inhale, followed by a howl like a banshee in distress. She didn't sleep much for worrying that Mr Jones might breathe his last. She was sure there would be complaints by the cartload from the other guests. But worst of all, what if they had a corpse to deal with?

She was wrong on both counts. No one commented and Mr Jones entered the dining room for breakfast with a smile on his granite face.

CHAPTER 10

It all began when the post arrived on Monday morning. Postie, cheerful as usual, knocked at the door and rushed through to the kitchen clutching a large, brown paper parcel.

'It's for you Mrs Bainbridge.'

He reverently laid the object of his undoubted curiosity on the kitchen table. Sylvia couldn't imagine who would be sending her a parcel, let alone such a sizable one. Excitedly, she tore open the outer wrappings and delved into sheaves of tissue paper.

'Oh, look at these John. It's a baby paradise.'

She held up little garments, causing her to giggle with delight, then silence as she discovered a divine, gossamer web of a shawl. Perplexed, she read a card tucked in the folds, 'Sorry we had to cancel our weekend, but we look forward to seeing you and the new baby on our next visit. We've all had a hand in making the enclosed. Best Wishes, the Halifax Six.'

Sylvia was quite overcome. John put his arm round her shoulders, 'My word, they must have enjoyed their visit!'

'No. I think they're quite looking forward to a baby they can coo over.'

John gave a secretive smile. 'There's another surprise on the way for you.'

He delivered this piece of news with an air of one-upmanship. She begged and cajoled, but he wouldn't even give her a clue. 'You'll just have to wait. Perhaps tomorrow.'

The following evening Sylvia was surprised to see Mr. Souter's Land Rover roll onto the car park with John at the wheel.

'Robert. John's in his boss's Land Rover. Do you think the motor bike has broken down?'

Robert's face was like thunder. 'It better not have done. He pinched my motorised-cycle as a deposit for the bloody thing. No by your leave or explanation. Bugger all in fact.'

Sylvia wished she hadn't opened her mouth. She assumed everything had been cleared between them before the deal was made. A brief shudder of unease passed through her. Didn't John realise it wasn't on to take someone else's property. Or did he think the deed was justified as he needed transport to get to work to bring in much needed cash?

She was interrupted by John's eager calls. 'C'mon you two. I need a hand with this.'

Reluctantly, Robert followed Sylvia to the car park where John stood to attention at the back of the vehicle. As they approached he flung open the back door with a theatrical flourish.

'There! What do you think of that then?'

Sylvia peered round the edge of the door and gasped. There, in pristine glory, sat a stunning coach-built pram.

'Oh, my godfathers. This is gorgeous – my dream pram! But we can't afford it. Can we? Where's it from?'

Anxiety began to creep through her veins. It was exactly what she had dreamed about for her baby, even to the colour, navy blue with a cream inside. She recognised it as a Silver Cross pram. A top of the range carriage that seemed to float on its large chrome wheels. Fearful that John had done one of his deals without thinking of the cost, she held back her excitement, expecting the dream machine would have to be returned.

'Don't panic, it's not new. One of my wealthy customers has finished with babies and she's let me have it for a song.'

Sylvia could hardly believe her ears. Just how lucky could she be? She guessed John must have worked his charm on this unknown fairy godmother. Hardly believing her luck she hugged him. 'All I have to do now is to finish the cot.'

They laughed, but she noticed that Robert looked quite stern.

The excitement of getting the pram made her want to have everything finished and ready for the baby. So that evening she started on the crib, or rather a large wicker clothes basket. A proper cot would have to come later. She worked on the basket until her fingers were sore. Finally padded and frilled with white spotted voile and finished off with a huge white satin bow, it made a fairy tale picture to sit beside their bed. At last everything was ready, and she was able to relax, happy to settle into the daily grind.

That weekend the Inn was full. Peter and Bernadette Guy had booked three double rooms. They were bringing with them another two friends, along with Hal and Jo. The fourth bedroom was taken by a couple from Leicester. A last minute telephone booking by a keen fisherman from Bradford, who was more than willing to sleep out at the farm, brought the total of residents to ten.

The angler was the first to arrive, a cheerful, enthusiastic little fellow, whose only thought was how quickly he could get to the river to reel in those jewelled swimmers. He promised any trout he caught would be given to Sylvia to cook for breakfast. Apparently, he worked in a large hospital as an assistant pathologist, and he delighted in telling her gory stories about his job. It was the last straw when he went into great detail on stomach linings. He bragged that he knew whether any of his unfortunate victims had been an habitual imbiber of a famous brand of liver salts. 'It's the degree of gut-rot. You see.' He proudly went into the pros and cons of gullet erosion.

Sylvia cornered Robert. 'Please keep that mortuary ghoul away from me. He really is upsetting my inside.'

Smiling, Robert tweaked her hair. 'Getting squeamish? ...Ok, ok. I'll keep him at bay.'

'Thank you. Hey-up, our visitors are here.' Hardly pausing, she rushed out to meet them. It was good to have Peter, Bernadette, Hal and Jo staying again. They were nice, and she had enjoyed their company during their last visit, but her delight was immediately overshadowed when she was introduced to the third couple. For some unknown reason she felt wary. They seemed ill at ease and obviously upset at the hostelry chosen for them. When they were shown to their room the rat-faced husband looked down his snooty nose. 'What? Not even a hand basin in the room. This isn't our usual standard, dear. Will you be able to manage?'

He took his wife's hand as though helping her to be brave. In acute embarrassment, Sylvia made a hasty retreat leaving the pair to face their inadequate sleeping quarters. It was obvious they were not going to treat the experience as a bit of an adventure, as did the other four. They all had their feet firmly on the ground and had no delusions of grandeur, but these other two were a different proposition. Sylvia felt upset. She knew she shouldn't let it worry her, yet it did. Poor Robert received the brunt of her concern.

'For Heaven's sake, don't bother, they're not worth it. You know damned well everyone who's stayed here has loved it. If they don't like it they can bog off.' He banged the worktop with his fist to emphasize his annoyance.

'I'll show the snotty-nosed pair. They'll have a dinner as good as any posh hotel they've stayed in,' she said with defiance.

That night, Sylvia made an extra special effort. A meal to be remembered, hopefully. She knew the soup was especially good, for the stock had been made from marrow bones and best ends of beef. The wild local ducks were plump and young, served with orange salad, fresh vegetables and garnished with watercress. They looked fit for a king. A light-as-air apple charlotte topped with Mark's wonderful thick cream, and a good Wensleydale cheese completed the meal. She felt satisfied that she had done the best possible and if it didn't suit the new visitors, well, so be it!

After dinner, Peter, Hal and their wives thanked her for an excellent meal, but their two friends said very little. Sylvia felt somewhat mollified, though annoyed the twosome hadn't had the decency to comment.

The following morning Peter Guy broke the news to John that their friends would not be staying. They were going on to the Lakes to stay at one of the upmarket hotels. It was obvious that Peter was rather upset at having to give the tidings. Sylvia was unhappy. It put a dampener on her spirits. But as the day was especially busy, the slight soon evaporated in hard labour.

The fisherman spent his time casting under the bridge. Sylvia watched him through the kitchen window as she washed mountains of dirty dishes. He was enjoying himself in the beautiful dale. A pity that snobby pair couldn't take a leaf out of his book. They were too much in love with themselves to be aware of real beauty. New rich, she decided, without values. She felt satisfied now they were categorised. Turning her attention to the angler, she smiled as he grinned with pleasure when his line flew and alighted in the water alongside an innocent swimmer, soon to grab the tempting bait. Then a twisting, writhing fish, fighting against its inevitable fate was deftly hauled ashore. The man was in his element. She couldn't help but smile at his dedication; he was totally absorbed in his sport. At the end of his stint he marched into the kitchen and proudly presented her with ten, evenly sized, slithery trout. Delighted, she promised them for Sunday morning breakfast. He seemed to have mellowed after his day under the bridge. He didn't annoy her at all, in fact she quite warmed to the fishy mortician.

Saturday night in the bar turned out to be quite lively. Cheeky Charlie, not one to miss the chance of getting accolades from a party of visitors, not to mention free ale, brought his accordion and had everyone entranced with his old tunes. Anthony Holdsworth sat in a corner with Jocelyn and her sister. It was obvious they were more than just good friends now, and sister Evelyn was certainly playing gooseberry. Sylvia was sure there would be a wedding in the offing, though Robert and John disagreed. They considered the different backgrounds of the pair would finish off any such notions.

Alfred Fewston, Carla, and their weekend residents were in the throng. Their guests turned out to be young potholers, intending to explore the 'pot' above Kettlewell the next day. Sylvia hated the thought of going underground, especially in the conditions prevailing in the local warrens, for if there was a sudden bout of rain they could be flooded without warning.

The room was full of such a variety of folk from widely different backgrounds and experiences. The hum of conversation when Charlie stopped playing to drink his pint was as loud as the little man's music.

Sylvia washed glasses and provided hot ham sandwiches. She was delighted with the happy atmosphere, evident every time she popped her head round the bar door. The merriment went on until well after midnight and by the time the visitors had made their way to bed, all customers on their routes home, the bar and kitchen cleared, it was getting towards 2a.m.. But there was one consolation, she and John had their own bedroom, thanks to the couple who had gone off to the Lakes.

They had just settled down for the night when the peace was shattered. A jeep snarled up the drive, its horn blasting out, sharp in the still air. Doors opened and slammed shut followed by a peppering of gravel thrown at their bedroom window.

'Hey, landlord! Open up. We want a drink, tha's got t' b' neighbourly. I'm Lord Markham from next pub t' thine.'

The voice guffawed, helped along by girlish giggles from his companions. Sylvia shot upright, 'What on earth is happening?'

John got out of bed and went to the window. 'I don't recognise 'em. Though I think one is Charlie's brother. I'd better go down.'

'John. They're drunk. Don't go down to them, please, not at two in the morning. For pity's sake.'

At first he was noncommittal. Then, as though coming to an instant decision, he pulled on some clothes.

'It's no good, we've residents to think about. This noise would waken the dead.' He purposely walked out of the bedroom and closed the door quietly behind him.

Sylvia seethed as she looked out of the window. This Markham fellow was large. Not bad looking, probably about fifty-ish, but it was obvious he was out for trouble. Mark had told her that morning when he delivered the milk that the Lord's pub had no residents for the weekend. She guessed the rival landlord was out for revenge in the best way possible, to upset her sleeping guests. It was a sneaky ruse. 'The no good lout,' she muttered with venom. She watched the unwelcome callers tumble through the front door. Gradually all went relatively quiet, apart from the odd laugh and the chink of glasses. Eventually, she fell asleep and knew no more till morning.

She woke to find John snoring rhythmically beside her. He was pale with a tinge of yellow around his mouth and eyes. He definitely didn't look as though he'd be any use for work. She decided it was a good job it was the weekend and he didn't have to drive to Hebden to the shop. Better still, he could sleep off the hangover in their own bed.

Quietly she stole out of the room. Robert had already started cleaning the bar.

'Just look at this lot. The bar's reminiscent of a shipwreck. They've drunk two and a half bottles of whisky. It'll be thick heads all round this morning. I hope they suffer.' Robert spat out the words.

Sylvia gently asked, 'What would you have done Robert? That man, Lord Markham, meant business. He was determined to cause a rumpus and disturb our residents.'

Robert turned his back on her and she began cooking.

The Sunday breakfast turned out to be a happy affair. The trout, dipped in oatmeal and fried in bacon fat, were a huge success. The fisher fellow enjoyed lavish praise. He returned to the river as soon as his belly was filled. Hal, Jo and Bernadette decided to have a stroll at the other side of the river, and Peter stayed behind in the kitchen chatting to Robert and John.

Over the fireplace, at the nonworking end of the kitchen, John had put up a rack to hold their three guns; a twelve bore, a .22 rifle, and a .410 shotgun. They were out of the way and gave a form of decoration to the fireplace wall. The .22 had been used by all three of them for competition target shooting before they moved to Hubberholme. The twelve bore was John's, supposedly for rabbit shooting, and the .410, had been one of his swop deals. The guns had sat there untouched since they'd moved to The George until recently, when one of the locals asked to borrow the rifle to attack an influx of rats in his farm buildings. It had been returned promptly and put back in its place on the rack.

Peter appeared quite interested in the little 'armoury' and asked John if he could take them down for a closer look. Naturally John agreed, and Peter took each one for a close inspection. The last one to receive his scrutiny was the .22 rifle, a

Remington five shot. He cradled the stock in his shoulder and pointed the barrel at the open window. 'This is a nice piece John.'

That precise moment Jo walked into view, framed in the open window. Jokingly, Peter pointed the rifle barrel at her.

'Hi, Jo, Bang!'

He lifted the gun out of range and pulled the trigger.

The noise was deafening in the small kitchen, then an eerie silence enveloped the room. The stillness was broken by a gentle flutter of plaster drifting down from the ceiling from where the bullet had penetrated.

Peter turned a ghastly white and half collapsed into a chair. John rushed to his aid. Sylvia charged outside to see how Jo had fared. Robert snatched the rifle from the floor, carefully checking that the magazine was empty, and forcibly placed it back on the rack as though to wipe out the incident.

Jo had not registered precisely what had happened. She had heard the shot, but the noise outside was not as deafening as in the confined area of the kitchen. She seemed fine, but later, when everyone realised just how close she had been to be badly injured, or even killed, they all descended into a subdued cloud of depression.

When things settled it was plain that a bullet had been left in the breach of the offending weapon.

'Well. That's it. We'll never lend out the bloody things again,' John vowed.

'And we better secure them now. Anybody could take one off the rack. I think we'll have to chain them in place.' Robert scuttled outside.

'Where's he gone? Blow it, I'm going to give Jack Inman a call.'

Sylvia felt concerned. 'You can't go and blame him, John. It's as much our fault as his. We should have checked it before putting it back.'

Robert came in with a length of chain and a padlock he'd found in the toolbox. He caught the tail end of the conversation.

'Couldn't agree more. But we'll have no more accidents.' He firmly secured the guns in the rack. 'Even though it's legal to have them on display as they were, it would be an open invitation for anyone to take one. Not anymore.' Stepping back, he admired his handiwork.

The incident quietened everyone for the rest of the day. Sylvia couldn't shake off a nasty sick feeling and longed for the weekend to be over. The day dragged and the visitors left after an early tea. They all wanted to get home and have some quiet time before the Monday morning workload.

'Thank Heaven, there's only one weekend to go with visitors to look after. Then a couple of free weeks before the baby arrives. And mum will be here next Sunday. Roll on!' Sylvia said with feeling. She had begun to get very tired and a little depressed.

However, the trials of the last few days paled into insignificance when they heard the news in the bar that night. One of the potholers leading the fun with the merrymakers on the previous evening, had had an accident whilst exploring the underground system. The Rescue Team eventually managed to get him to the surface, but he was already dead.

As the customers absorbed the news they went silent, and a pall descended over the room. It wasn't long before the company broke up, leaving in dribs and drabs until the place was empty.

Robert sat heavily on a chair. 'Well. That's finished our trade off for the night.'

'How can you be so insensitive?' Sylvia was aghast. 'A grand young man has lost his life.'

'Aye. Doing what he wanted. He knew the risk. And we're still here struggling to make a living.'

Sylvia could see his point, but couldn't help feeling sad. She walked out of the room, turning her back on the dirty glasses. 'I'm off to bed.'

CHAPTER 11

'Hey sis. You do realise this is your last weekend in bondage?'

Sylvia rubbed her cheek with a floured hand. 'What are you talking about Robert?'

'Well, when Monday comes we've no more bookings until after the baby arrives. You'll have a couple of weeks to take it easy.'

She vigorously rolled out the pastry. 'I suppose. Remember we've a coach load of Women Institute members for tea on Wednesday. And mum comes on Sunday. Yippee!'

Robert grinned. 'Hope you haven't forgotten that this weekend's visitors want the piano in working order. I'd better dust it and give it a tinkle!'

'Listen to you! You've no idea whether it's any good or not. And I certainly haven't. We aren't exactly musically minded are we? I do hope it's ok. They want to practise their Gilbert and Sullivan songs for a performance at the Bradford Alhambra. I think they're an amateur operatic society.'

She felt quite proud they would be having stage-folk as residents. Thankfully Gerald's mother had offloaded her old upright piano to make room for a new settee. At the time Sylvia didn't want it but, not liking to offend, gave it a home. Fortunately, it seemed to be in reasonable condition and all they could do was to hope it would meet the needs of the concert party.

Sylvia awaited their arrival with eager anticipation. But, when they finally landed, she was disappointed. She had imagined there would be some evidence of glamour and greasepaint. Instead, the three couples were probably in their forties and looked like thousands of other successful business people. The most bumptious of them was a dead ringer for a vociferous Punch. In a rich, dark brown voice, he very quickly made everyone aware that he was Clerk of the Courts at Leeds Assizes. His wife, quiet and mouse like, hardly uttered a word, but clung to the attractive partner of the best looking male in the party. He was tall and well proportioned with a sculpted mop of dark hair, strategically peppered with grey. A striking untidy face, rather self-opinionated, but there was a glint of mischief there, making Sylvia think he could laugh at himself. She guessed he would be the one most likely to play the hero in any of their productions. The third couple were two little barrels of fun, both so similar it was uncanny.

After the greetings, Sylvia herded them to the foot of the stairs intending to escort them to their rooms. They would have none of it. 'Can we try the piano first?'

Surprised, she guessed this Clerk of the Court would not accept any excuses. In fact, he rather rudely pushed past her back into the kitchen. Cursing to herself, she led them through to the dining room and lifted the piano lid praying it would come up to scratch. She needn't have worried. Nimble fingers ran deftly over the keys rending clear notes of a pretty melody. 'This will do fine,' the pianist sang out to her. 'We'll stay here a while if you don't mind.'

Her heart sank. She didn't want her busy schedule to be interrupted. The attractive lady of the party seemed to sense Sylvia's desperation.

'I'll come upstairs with you and see the bedrooms. Then I'll be able to have first choice.' Laughing she linked arms, and they climbed the stairs together. 'This is the one for me.' She had decided that John and Sylvia's room was hers. Sylvia had to hide a grin when Grace's room was chosen for the bumptious clerk.

Returning to the kitchen she found the group singing happily round the piano. Whilst she enjoyed the music she hoped they wouldn't hold up dinner. They did. Evening meal was an hour late. And as soon as it was over they were back on the piano. Robert wasn't pleased. Their prolonged stay in the dining room had made it difficult for him to clear away. He eventually managed to collect a load of dishes and noisily clattered them down. 'I hope they'll get sore throats.'

'Robert, the customer is always right and always comes first.'

'Yes. But there's a limit. What about the casual diners? They didn't like the racket. They left before coffee!'

She decided the best policy was to keep mum. So, taking advantage of the lull in the workload she picked up a book that some kind soul had given her about natural childbirth, by a Dr Spock. The man's name tickled her, but he seemed to talk sense.

'Robert. This man says childbirth isn't painful, it's the most natural thing in the world. It's what you expect that matters. That's the key, I think. Mind over matter.'

'Mm…' Robert cocked an ear. 'At last they've shut up. Now I can clear away.'

Even so, it was midnight before the singers climbed the stairs to bed.

Lovely weather heralded Saturday. Sylvia rose early. She hadn't slept well even though she was dog-tired. It was already quite hot and in the bright sunshine the dale looked particularly beautiful. The fells in differing shades of green showed off cascading waterfalls, highlighted with crystal wings, tumbling into the peaty waters of the Wharfe. The church nestling at the foot of the hill seemed to reflect the bright light, making the ancient stone walls glisten and contrast sharply with the dark green of the two yew trees at the door. A magical day. With Cassie at her heels she prepared buckets of feed for the calves and pigs. As she struggled up the garden steps, two buckets on each arm, she began to feel queasy and broke into a cold sweat.

'Gosh Cass, I just ain't as fit as I was. Roll on the next two weeks when I won't have this bump to carry around. This damned humidity doesn't help either.'

She stayed with the calves a bit longer than usual watching them chew their food whilst she gently rubbed their heads. Now feeling a bit better she made her way to the pigs. They complained loudly and pushed at the door in annoyance at being kept waiting. She was always wary of going into their little house, memories of the rat episode usually surfaced. Eager squeaks greeted her as she opened the door and two hungry noses dived into the trough as the wet mix was poured in. 'You greedy girls... I can't stay long I'm running late today.'

Smiling at their antics she reluctantly left and hurried back down the garden steps onto the drive. To her surprise a motorbike and sidecar pulled onto the car park. The rider and his passenger alighted. Sylvia wanted to laugh. The men were wearing leather helmets and white silky scarves which seemed to be wrapped twice round their necks, leaving long trailing ends hanging down their backs. Oh my God, she thought, those magnificent men in their flying machines!

The thinner of the two walked towards her. 'Can ye do 'owt fer us?' he questioned.

'Pardon?'

'Aye. Wi' want'a book a meal. 'Am an' eggs f'one o' clock. Mi name's Todd.'

Before she could manage to say that it would be fine, he was mounting the bike, closely followed by the plumper pillion rider. They were off fishing. The sidecar was filled to the gunnels with rods, nets and baskets. It protested with a clatter as the machine burst into life, almost disembarking its cargo, and the Biggles twosome roared up the dale with scarf ends flying wildly behind them.

Sylvia couldn't wait to tell the men folk of the early morning booking. Half past six was an all-time record!

Robert had hoped he would be able to see the object of his sister's amusement when the bikers came back for lunch but that was not to be. No sooner had they cleared the dining room after breakfast than it started. There was no demarcation line between morning coffees, snacks, lunches, afternoon teas and high teas. The kitchen floor was a hazardous obstacle course. They just couldn't get it clear of dirty pots. As soon as they made some headway it filled up again. There was no time to get a bite for themselves. Robert periodically grabbed a slice of bread as he served and cleared, and John in the bar made do with the odd bag of crisps. Sylvia's appetite had flown.

The day became hotter. At one stage the thermometer near the Aga read one hundred degrees. Sylvia thought she would pass out. It was unbearable cooking. Her loose shift dress stuck to her legs, beads of sweat dropped from her chin leaving a dark mark down her front. 'I wish it would rain and get rid of this humidity,' she muttered to Robert as he passed in an air of melting desperation.

At about five-thirty there was a lull, giving them all a chance to get reasonably clear and drop the Aga lids ready to build up heat in time to cook dinner. The residents were warned that the evening meal would be a bit late. They seemed quite happy. Sylvia guessed they'd enjoy the extra time for another drink.

Somehow they managed to get through dinner, but even before the coffee cups had been emptied the room echoed to an enthusiastic rendering of songs from 'Yeomen of the Guard'. The music rang out and could be heard in the bar where everyone appeared to enjoy the performance. Somehow, it lifted Sylvia's flagging body and spirits, especially when one of them sang 'Take a pair of sparkling eyes'.

The day had been terribly long, and when all customers evaporated at midnight, Sylvia almost collapsed. The concert party folk were great fun and it was brilliant to listen to the music, but, oh dear, how they could eat.

John pontificated. 'It isn't the same as Mr Jones. He needed large quantities three times a day. This lot never stop wanting. To ask for bread and cheese and more coffee two hours after an enormous dinner is downright cheek. Especially when everything is all inclusive. We've no chance of getting paid.'

Robert joined in. 'And then the others who hadn't wanted extras decided they wanted the same an hour later. We've been at their beck-and-call all night.'

Sylvia was too weary to comment. Her back was in half and the only way she could get any relief was to lie on the floor with her legs up the wall. When at last they crashed into bed she was almost asleep before pulling the covers over herself.

The heat continued through Sunday, but it was even more humid. The flagged floor in the bar would not dry after its daily scrub and every movement seemed an effort. Robert insisted on feeding the animals. 'You look awful. What about this afternoon?

John has to go to Skipton to pick up mum off the Leeds train. He'll be gone at least two hours, and if we're busy...?'

John walked in on the tail end off the conversation. He cast a quick glance at Sylvia. 'I'll tell you what we'll do. I'll ask Gerald if he can pick up your mum. He was going down with me anyway. He's a job to do in Skipton. I'm sure he won't mind.'

Sylvia half wondered what the pair had been planning. But it was a relief when John rang Gerald and he readily agreed to go on his own. She knew they would have found it hard to manage with just the two of them if the day had turned out to be like Saturday.

Sure enough, the pattern repeated itself. It was chaos. They had to refuse some parties for lunch, though most agreed to have ham and eggs later on. They were in the thick of these late lunches, together with washing up from the set meals, when a brand new white Rolls Royce, sailed majestically to the front door.

'Who on earth is that?' John questioned as he peered curiously out of the window.

Sylvia peeped beside him. The doors of the beautiful car were flung open and out scrambled a strange collection of folk. The driver was a stocky fellow, his face round and ruddy. He wore a pale, lightweight suit, open-necked shirt with a red-spotted kerchief knotted at his neck. But, by far the most startling, on his head was the biggest white Stetson she had ever seen. Two colourful ladies followed him. They were short-skirted with high heels and dazzled with bright tops and red lips. They hung on the cowboy's arm possessively. One was blonde and the other smirked under an auburn frizz of shoulder length hair. The men, two of them, had the look of travelling people. They seemed startlingly alien as they clambered from the luxurious leather seating. The white hat led his group into the bar and it wasn't long before he was the centre of attention. He bought drinks all round, entrancing the locals and some late diners. Naturally, John was all ears. After a while he came excitedly into the kitchen. 'You'll never guess who it is in there! It's Percy Shaw. You know, the man who invented 'cats eyes'.

'What?' Sylvia asked, rather befuddled.

'Oh, come on. You know, the cats eyes on the road.'

Enlightened, she and Robert were impressed. 'No wonder he can afford a Roller.'

Sylvia wasn't listening. She suddenly dashed out of the kitchen calling, 'Mum's here, mum's here!' She had spied Gerald's Land Rover pull in behind the Rolls Royce at the front door.

Gerald escorted the eagerly awaited visitor into the kitchen and her daughter's open arms.

'You don't look too good, Sylvia, love.'

'Oh Mum, I'm fine, and even better now you're here.'

Any further exchanges were cut short by another influx of meals.

Percy Shaw and his party stayed drinking in the bar until nearly dinner time. They had enjoyed their afternoon and came into the kitchen to say goodbye. Then they climbed unceremoniously into the beautiful chariot. The doors slammed and it majestically drove away.

Somehow, Robert and Sylvia managed to clear the kitchen and get dinner out of the way. The concert party left the piano alone. Instead, they popped into the bar for a quick snifter before setting off on their journey to Bradford. By this time Cheeky Charlie and his pals were already installed. When they realised the visitors were about to depart, Charlie decided to natter them for a final song. There was some argy-bargy, but finally they agreed to give just one before they set off back home.

There was a good deal of whispering. Then the three men of the party took on the pose of mincing, little girls. They pulled the edges of their eyes into slits and began to sing, 'Three Little Girls from school are we', from the Mikado. The picture was hilarious. The tall, the short tubby, and Punch. In squeaky falsetto they enthusiastically mimicked the three pretty, kimono clad schoolgirls. The bar was in an uproar when they came to the end of the recital. In amongst the applause the three bowed, waved and with typical theatrical aplomb left their audience in a rush to their cars and away.

Everyone had really enjoyed the cameo performance, especially the strangers in the room, who were entranced by the music and the locals. At ten o'clock, Sunday closing time, they decided to keep the party going and ordered ham and egg suppers. Sylvia's heart sank. She had been getting a niggling pain in her side, and her back ached nonstop. The last thing in the world she wanted was to be cooking at that time of night. However, not one to turn away business, she cooked until midnight. Her mother was concerned and did her best to help with the extra load.

She said softly, 'This is no life for my daughter. Especially when you're due shortly. You should be pampered.' Sylvia answered with a smile.

Finally, the evening came to an end at half past one. They couldn't get to bed fast enough and Sylvia was more than happy to collapse and drift into welcome oblivion.

Her sleep was short lived. At three o'clock she woke John, 'Call mum and ring Nurse Brown. The baby's on its way.'

Poor John half fell downstairs as he shouted frantically to Robert, 'Call Nurse Brown! The baby's coming!'

The good nurse arrived on her scooter in less than half an hour after the call. She must have moved like greased lightning. In she marched and took over, carrying out the necessary tasks as she rapped out quick commands. Sylvia was so relieved, for now the contractions couldn't be ignored.

The following few hours were a shock to her. She hadn't expected so much pain. She had been convinced it was all in the mind. She swore loud and often.

'Bloody Dr Spock! And that's no damned use either.' She flung the gas and air mouthpiece across the room. Her mother held her hand tightly.

'Shush Love. You don't want to frighten John and Robert, now do you?' They had been booted out of the room and were probably waiting at the door. Sylvia was thankful they were out there. She wanted privacy!

Nurse Brown took everything in her stride, frequently giving the command, 'Push.'

Finally, at 6.10 a.m., the sun threw shafts of early brightness into the room and a baby boy with a shock of black hair, took his first breath.

Thomas Ottiwell, Otti, slept peacefully in his pretty frilled cot. The proud mum, her mother, brother, husband and the good nurse, sat round the bed drinking tea. Nurse Brown decided she needed something stronger. John promptly obliged with a treble gin. They all felt so grateful to her, especially Sylvia, who would have given her anything she desired. As they talked there was a little whining noise at the bedroom door.

'Oh, my poor little Cassie, let her in. Please,' begged Sylvia. Nurse frowned, but relented. Cassie bounded in and without any hesitation jumped on the bed and happily settled in a tight ball.

When Sylvia was left to have a sleep, Cassie took it upon herself to creep under the covers and curl up next to her mistress's feet. Gently, they both drifted off into a light sleep, but were awakened by a knock at the door. In came the doctor.

Oh my God Cass. For pity's sake don't move. Sylvia sat up, praying the whippet would stay quiet. Trying to hold a sensible conversation with the doctor was almost impossible, her mind was not in gear. Thankfully, Cassie was either too happy and contented, or had sensed Sylvia's fears, for she lay rock still all the while he was there.

It seemed an eternity before he at last said his goodbyes. He wished her well. 'You and Nurse Brown have done an excellent job. The little boy is a smasher!'

As soon as he was out of the door a tired looking nurse gave Sylvia a big hug. 'You'll get me hung. Dogs, indeed. I'll be back early evening and I hope to find no animals in here!'

Later it dawned on Sylvia that a wish she had made weeks ago, but had seemed so unlikely, had come true. She couldn't wait to tell her mother. The bedroom door quietly opened and Sylvia called, 'Mum. Do you realise you've got a very special grandson?'

'Of course I do. Is everything alright?'

'Of course it is, Mum.'

Before she could continue, her mum, looking very pleased with herself, gabbled, 'Daddy's been on the phone. He was so surprised to find he was already a grandfather. He sends you his love.'

Sylvia grinned. 'Today is your wedding anniversary. Otti has come two weeks early to give you both a surprise present, and it couldn't be better now that Poppa knows.'

She felt near to tears. Her father still loved her. Her day was full to overflowing. Raising her empty cup she gave a wide grin.' 'I think we ought to celebrate with rum and coffees all round. I could murder one. Please?'

John came in the room. 'What's all the noise about?'

'Oh John, I want a rum and coffee to toast Otti arriving on mum's wedding anniversary.'

'I hadn't realised. I suppose we can let you have a small one.'

Then the phone rang. John dashed downstairs to answer, returning later with a tray of boosy coffees and the news that the Otterhound Hunt was on its way up the dale.

'They'll be calling in for beer and sandwiches.'

Sylvia started to panic. 'We've a decent sized piece of beef left from Sunday. We'll need more bread from the post office. There's plenty of eggs and some home-made mayonnaise, we can add chopped chives...' Her words tailed off and tears started to roll down her cheeks. 'I don't want them to kill those lovely little otters.'

John and his mother-in-law exchanged glances. She bent over her daughter. 'Snuggle down dear and have a little nap. We're perfectly capable of making a few sandwiches. Stop worrying, everything will be fine.'

Sylvia was awakened by the boisterous arrival of the unwelcome visitors. There was noisy chatter, punctuated by short, sharp blasts of their hunting horns. She sat up, took a peep at her tiny son fast asleep in his pretty basket, and whispered to Cassie, 'You'll soon have a playmate.' At that moment the bedroom door burst open. Startled, she didn't know what to say to the very large, bespectacled man standing framed in the doorway. His pot belly adorned with a bright yellow, brass buttoned waistcoat preceded him over the threshold. He, just as surprised, backed out of the door, muttering 'Sorry, sorry,' something about looking for the toilet.

There were a couple more disturbances, but not as intrusive as the first. John popped in to see her during a quiet moment in

144

the bar, and was aghast when she told him of her unannounced callers. 'The trouble is, they're well oiled, and rowdy. It's going to be difficult to get any sense through their pickled layers. But I'll have a go.'

He must have worked the oracle, for she had no more interruptions. Her mind wandered and she suddenly remembered the booking for Wednesday and the W.I. coach party for tea. In all fairness, she couldn't expect her mother to take that responsibility. Sandwiches were one thing, but teas another. 'I'll be ok, I will definitely be ok by Wednesday,' she determinedly told Cassie, who was far too happy with the current arrangements to even open her eyes.

Mondays were usually quiet, though sometimes visitors made the weekend a bit longer by leaving the home journey till first thing that morning, but generally there was little movement. This gave Sylvia and her mum the opportunity to catch up on all the news and admire the new baby. John had dashed off as soon as the Otter hunters departed to make the odd call, though his boss had told him not to bother under the circumstances.

Next day, they settled into a new semblance of order. Sylvia had asked her mother to bath Otti, as she felt too nervous to do the job, fearful she might let her precious charge slip. They laughed about it. Her mother teased her, but gave comfort. 'You'll be alright next time, don't worry, it's a normal reaction.'

'Mum, a car's pulled up at the front door. See if you can see who it is.'

Her mother leaned out of the window, then turned to her daughter. 'It's a smart green van, with an equally smart driver. He's wearing dark green overalls with a gold badge on his pocket. It's a delivery for you, dear.'

'What is it?'

'I don't know, but you'll find out in a minute. Robert's bringing it in now.'

He flung open the door smiling and handed Sylvia a long, transparent box tied with an enormous, pink bow. She gasped as she took it. 'Oh, Lordy, this is film star stuff!! Who on earth, can they be from?' She secretly thought it must be John, but when she untied the bow and lifted the lid, on top of a dozen, pink, long stemmed roses was a card.

'It's from the Master of Otterhounds apologising for the noise and disturbance yesterday. They hadn't realised that Otti had only arrived that morning. I feel like a star! Though I hope it's true what you said about the otters. They didn't catch any, did they?'

Robert put her mind at rest again, but she wasn't certain he was telling the truth. She occupied her mind on the local well-wishers, all bringing gifts for the newborn. It turned out to be a day to keep locked away, to remember for years to come.

Wednesday dawned, the day of the WI. Sylvia dressed quietly leaving John snoring and Otti sleeping like an angel. She sneaked downstairs and began baking for the afternoon's onslaught. She had managed to disturb no one. Pleased with herself, she made everyone a cup of tea before giving them a call. Robert was furious with her. She giggled and told him she'd been good and hadn't fed the stock! He stomped out of the house cursing at her crass stupidity, but he had a smile on his face when he returned after attending to the animals. John and her mother didn't comment. Sylvia guessed they had more sense. She glanced up as a black form passed the window. 'Oh heck. It's the vicar. What can he want?'

John quickly went to the kitchen door. 'Don't worry. I'll see him in the bar.'

A full quarter of an hour went by, and then, the Reverend Fullerton popped into the kitchen. 'Congratulations, Sylvia. I won't delay you. I'll see you this afternoon.'

Sylvia stared at the closing door. 'What does he mean, this afternoon?'

John came into the kitchen down the bar-passage. 'He's giving the W.I. party a talk on Hubberholme, the pub and the church.' Hesitating, John seemed to have to pluck up courage to go on. 'He did mention something I've never heard of before.'

'About what?' Sylvia questioned.

'Well, he said that you couldn't go into the church for six weeks. Apparently, after a birth a mother is considered – unclean – for that length of time.'

'Unclean!' Sylvia gasped.

Her mother full of righteous indignation rasped. 'I've never heard such nonsense. Where on earth does that come from? It's archaic.'

Robert chimed in. 'Well, sis. Since none of us hardly ever go to church, there's only the cleaning to consider, and I'll do that.'

'I tell you what. I don't want to enter the place ever again.' She felt scalding tears. *Unclean!* How awful. The status bothered her until it settled to the back of her mind with the arrival of the coach load of thirty-eight W.I. ladies. They tumbled out of the vehicle, an assortment of all shapes and sizes, scattering themselves throughout the pub.

They were a jolly crowd, and were thrilled to be in time to meet a brand new baby, introduced to them by the vicar. He soon was in full voice on the history of the hamlet. Sylvia listened in, and was surprised to learn how much he had studied the past of Hubberholme. Apparently, the pub site dated back to about 700AD and would have been, as well as a vicarage, a hostelry to befriend travellers on the pack horse route from Newcastle to Lancaster. The name, Hubberholme, was given by the Norsemen. As he finished the lesson, he puffed out his chest and told his audience that little Otti was very special. 'He's really quite famous. This morning he made the front page of the daily paper. He's the only child ever to be born at the George Inn. And of course, he'll be christened at the church by myself, the parish vicar.'

Sylvia raised her eyebrows to Robert. The Reverend wasn't her favourite person.

CHAPTER 12

Sylvia was upset. She had been selfish keeping her mum away from home for so long. Why on earth hadn't she realised how the time had flown since the birth of Otti. Her poor father all alone for more than six weeks and she hadn't given it a thought. Worst of all, she had had to be reminded by her mum, who diplomatically suggested that it was time for her to be heading home. Secretly, Sylvia didn't relish the idea of losing her mother. They had enjoyed their time together with the new baby. There had been many a laugh in those weeks, in spite of some hectic weekends and latterly some atrocious weather. But the time had come for them to part.

The Inn was full to bursting for the coming weekend. John and Robert were banished to the bunk beds in the passage room. Sylvia, her mother and baby had the luxury of their own bedroom. The six Halifax ladies were incumbent at the Inn, a couple from Hull in Gerald's home and three from Blackpool at the farm across the river. The action was nonstop and mum's extra pair of hands was more than a blessing. She seemed to be a permanent fixture at the sink washing hundreds of dirty dishes and pans throughout the day. A day that rapidly deteriorated into a comedy of errors.

The first mishap was lunch. Sylvia always prided herself on keeping a good stock pot, the basis for her now quite well-known soups. There were so many meals that the soup ran out and she was forced to do a quickie by using stock and a Swiss dried soup mix. The container of strained chicken stock sat next to an identical one of pear juice, intended for the next day's fruit jellies. In haste Robert grabbed a container. Sylvia made up the dish, but in the rush forgot to taste it before serving it to the waiting customers. Clean dishes were returned but, something niggled her. She sniffed the empty container dubiously. 'Oh, My God, I've used pear juice instead of stock!' She couldn't believe the mistake and couldn't understand why no one had complained.

Robert laughed. 'No problem, sis. Someone even said they'd enjoyed the soup. So there you are, you've invented a new dish.'

Unconvinced, she could hardly look the diners in the eye when they came to pay and still felt guilty when told they intended to come again.

The trend continued. In an attempt to attract more custom Sylvia had introduced steak and chips to the tea menu, much against the better judgement of her brother. The constant cooking dropped the Aga temperature and to get another heat source they resorted to stoking up the coke boiler. Its flat top became hot enough to take the chip pan. Robert had done a good job in getting the fire roaring, but neither of them realised the intensity of the rapid build up of heat. They had used the boiler before to keep a pan of soup hot but, now, with all vents open, it thundered power and seemed to develop an all-over glow.

Sylvia struggled to cook steak, ham and eggs on the flagging Aga, whilst keeping an eye on the chips. Her attention was diverted by the couple from Hull pushing into the cooking area.

'You've got to help,' said the woman with a demanding shriek.

'We're terribly busy at the minute. Is something wrong?'

The pair had seemed a bit odd to Sylvia and she hadn't warmed to them at all, though she gave them points for being animal lovers. They had arrived in an old Austin car with the unique number plate PAT 2. Disconcertingly, they kept addressing the vehicle as, Girl Pat. To add to the jumble, a middle-aged ginger moggy tagged along with them, who was named Pattie. Sylvia decided that Freud could have a birthday with this pair.

'Pattie is stuck up one of your trees and she can't get down. She's crying.'

Robert cast his sister a look of caution. He must have guessed she wanted to say that it wasn't their fault there was a tree in the garden that the stupid cat had chosen to climb.

Controlling her emotions, she smiled politely. 'We'll be out just as soon as these meals are served.' Then under her breath muttered. 'What the Hell can we do about it? Can't you see we're up to our necks?'

Momentarily, their attention had strayed from the job in hand. They were totally unprepared for the deafening, explosive roar that reverberated round the kitchen. Sylvia's eyes, wide with horror, darted to the source. The pan of chips had ignited and was snarling with the ferocity of the devil's cauldron. Angry flames leapt up the wall. Far reaching scarlet fingers tried to grasp the yellow and white checked frill she had proudly hung across the alcove. A pretty bit of nonsense, now an invitation to trigger an inferno.

Her head felt in danger of bursting. Some of the residents had planted themselves in the kitchen, a regular occurrence of customers on their way to or from the dining room. They would home in like bees to the honey pot and chat, enjoying the familiarity with the cooking scene. Sylvia usually managed to cope but, this was something else! She had to draw on hidden resources to keep her cool, yet foolishly carried on a conversation with the Blackpool lot. In desperation she threw a towel over the ball of fire that was once the chip pan. Outwardly a Joan of Arc, inside a screaming virago but, too late, the leaping flames grabbed the frill. Robert, in one single movement, pushed down the kitchen window at the sink, grabbed the flaming pan, and threw it onto the tarmac below. As luck would have it, there was no one around at that moment. The fireball bounced across the road, then settled spluttering in the long grass on the riverbank. He turned back to the scene of devastation. Sylvia frantically tried to catch the black, floating, bits of fabric, remnants of the brightly coloured frill. The flames from that piece of frivolity had burnt themselves out, and the only damage was to the white gloss paint above the cooker, now sporting streaks of black and grey. The acrid smell of burning fat crept on its belly out of the open door.

Sylvia furiously washed up the mess then started on the teas still to be served. The customers readily agreed to abandon the idea of chips!

In amongst the melee the pair from Hull had continued to anxiously hop around on the edge of the disaster zone. As the dust settled, one of them grabbed Robert's sleeve.

'Can you come now. Pattie is terrified.'

Robert impatiently followed the man outside with Sylvia bringing up the rear. They all stood under the offending tree, heads craned, looking up at the crabby cat precariously clinging to a lateral branch. Every few minutes the owners called to the cat.

'Patty, Patty, come down to mummy. Patty, Patty, daddy's upset. Come down, darling.'

They periodically danced and chanted at the base. Sylvia watched Robert. He seemed to be caught between emotions of fully charged annoyance, anxiety and absolute hilarity. She guessed he didn't quite know what to do. Guardedly, he went to the foot of the tree. Was he thinking to try and climb out onto the branch and grab the cat? But, a little 'yella' whippet had other ideas. The sheep chaser, to all intents and purpose, was cured of that desire. She had even left Gerald's hens alone since trying to make them dance until they almost died of exhaustion. But, cats were a different proposition. Cass flew to the foot of the tree, barked and stretched her lithesome body as far as she could reach. Patty apparently thought whippets could climb trees and launched herself into oblivion. They all watched in horror as the ginger missile sped through the air, her aim the ample bosom of her 'mummy'. The lady staggered as she received the onslaught of a direct hit, gasped and fell into her husband's arms. The force of the landing sent his legs from under him. And the pair, plus a squawking cat, ended in a squirming heap on the lawn.

'Thank the Lord,' sighed a relieved Robert.

Giggling, they returned to the kitchen just as the Heavens decided to release another downpour. Waiting for them was a clutch of hungry folk wanting to be fed. Sylvia quelled the desire to scream. Otti, too, decided he needed a fill-up and demanded immediate attention in his usual fashion, a full blooded wail. The strength left her body, disappearing in a slow exhale of breath. She felt tears brim and slide down the side of her nose. Her tongue flicked lizard-like and tasted salty lips. She was being weak and stupid, she must pull herself together, but how could she find a moment to feed her son. The dribble of tears turned into a silent flood.

'Oh sis. What is it? Are you ill?'

Through the snuffles she managed to blurt out, 'Otti needs feeding.'

Robert immediately took charge and sent her upstairs.

'Off with you. Give Otti his feed, then he can be put back in his pram, and then, and only then, we'll get on with the waiting meals. John is looking after the bar but he can give me a hand if things hot up.'

For once in her life she obeyed, leaving her brother to explain to the waiting customers there would be a slight delay.

On her return Sylvia had become calmer but, little Otti would not settle. Every time she laid him in his pram he opened his mouth and yelled. She was guilt-ridden. Her son needed a cuddle and some of her time. How was she to manage? There was only one thing to do, drag her mum from the back of the bar. John would be able to manage on his own for a while. She picked up the crying baby and opened the door to the bar-passage. She stopped in her tracks. In less than a week there would be no doting nana to save the day, she would be on her own. Closing the kitchen door she looked at the leg of ham ominously waiting to be sliced. Young Otti would have to be put down. Then she spotted Cassie snoozing contentedly in her comfy basket next to the Aga. Tucking the shawl closely round her son, she gently laid him beside the oblivious Cassie. Sylvia knew her little friend would guard the precious bundle, and her warmth would comfort him. She was right. Cassie moved herself to give more room to her charge, laid a paw across him, and the pair were asleep in a matter of minutes. Now smiling, Sylvia looked down at her adored twosome. How lucky she was. Turning quickly to the job in hand she almost sent her mother flying as she came into the kitchen from her stint in the bar. Her first thought was to take a peep at Otti in his pram. Startled at the emptiness, she looked at her daughter.

'Where is he, is anything wrong?'

152

She followed Robert's gaze. 'Oh, no. Sylvia, how could you! You just don't know what he could catch!'

On the defensive, Sylvia put on a haughty look, turned her back, and dismissed the statement by furiously chopping parsley for the fish pie. Her mother kept quiet as they briefly grabbed a bite to eat before preparing the residents' dinners. The mood was a little strained but, Sylvia was more than pleased when Otti slept on peacefully with his unusual bedfellow.

Thankfully the rest of the evening seemed to float by on oiled wheels and Sylvia silently thanked the gods as they climbed the stairs to bed.

Sunday brought the foulest of weather. It rained and the skies were heavy. The visitors would be under her feet all day and Sylvia cursed, her patience was running thin. There was one consolation, it just might be possible for all of them to sit down together for a meal.

Sure enough casual trade was nonexistent and Sylvia was able to make a slap-up lunch for the family. They had just finished eating when a Mackintosh-clad male with a scout's hat pulled well down over his ears stood dripping in the kitchen doorway. In a voice close to desperation he asked hesitantly, 'Would it be possible for my troop of scouts to camp in that field next to the river. I've been told it belongs to you. We've had a mix up with our booking at a farm lower down the dale. I know it's last minute but we don't know where else to go.'

Robert explained, 'We only rent the field. It's owned by the church.'

The man looked so pathetic Sylvia felt sorry for his plight.

'John, would you ring the vicar and ask him if it's ok for them to camp in the meadow?' John obliged and returned giving the thumbs up sign. 'C'mon, I'll show you where to go.'

The scout master fairly skipped on the spot as though a ten ton weight had been lifted from his shoulders.

'Could I ask another favour please? Would it be possible to order some food for the lads?'

'How about fried egg sandwiches?' Sylvia suggested, guessing they would want a cheap snack before setting up their site. 'I'll make them now. The boys will have to be out of the bar before opening time.'

She quickly buttered warm bread cakes, whilst golden yoked eggs spat cheerfully in the hot fat. The boys greedily downed the treat watched by Sylvia. She whispered to John. 'The poor things are soaked to the skin. They do smell though. It's like hot mildew!'

Later, when the rain had eased she walked onto the bridge to get a breath of air and peep at the boy scout's camp. A group of white tents was pitched on the level part of the meadow close to the river. Hope nobody sleepwalks into the river she thought as she gazed at the busy scene. Looking down into the full flowing waters, she was startled by Mark creeping up behind her.

'Nah then. W..w'at's thee up to?'

'Just watching those poor lads. I bet they're in for a rough night.'

'Aye. River c..c'ud flood.'

Hoping he was wrong, she walked with him back across the bridge and couldn't help noticing he didn't seem his normal self, somehow more subdued. Then he began casually.

'D'd' ye' know M' m'missis V'victor Smythe 'as run off't wi' Ant 'oldsworth's, girl f'f' friend's brother. Y'know, 'ired 'and!'

Sylvia could hardly believe her ears, though it did explain the reluctance of the up-dalers to talk about the Victor Smythe family.

'What an unlikely match. It's like Lady Chatterley.' She laughed, but as she peered into the swirling waters she wondered what Jocelyn and her sister Edwina would think, and what about poor Mr Victor Smythe? How would he react?

'Aye, an 'ee ain't t'only 'un t' stray.'

Sylvia looked up quickly. Mark took a step back, his usual easy gait held rigid, his face flushing. He blinked at her, his lips a pale horizontal line, and she felt apprehension clamp her chest.

'What do you mean?'

'Nowt, nowt.'

He wouldn't hold her gaze. 'Mark…'

But he'd turned and was striding towards the farm. He had been on his way to the pub, so what was the matter? She ran after him. 'Mark. What's wrong?'

He carried on walking, his face averted.

'Shun't 'ave s..s..said 'owt. It w'ain't be t..true any'ow.'

Now she was worried. His words whizzed round her head. She had to know.

'It's John. Isn't it?'

His eyes confirmed her misgivings. He didn't answer and hurried away leaving her standing there, her head bowed. She thought hard. Had there been any clues she had missed? Cheeky Charlie had once mentioned that John must like Jenny's cooking, cos' he was always in there. Sylvia had only met the estate manager's wife a couple of times but she had quite liked the bright woman. Surely she wouldn't ensnare her John! But had Charlie been trying to tell her something? She bit her lip. Her turmoil would have to be shelved. Work was waiting.

Naturally, the conversation in the bar that night was all about the runaway couple. No one knew where they had gone. When the farm manager came in, all were agog. He was tight-lipped, and all he said was, 'Maister ain't 'aving 'er back.'

Significantly, his wife, the fair Jenny, Jocelyn and Anthony didn't make an appearance.

Sylvia watched John. His behaviour towards the husband of this rumoured lady-friend, seemed perfectly normal. He was his usual likeable self. Perhaps it was all imagination after all.

What a night it turned out to be. It started to rain again, quite gently at first, then a persistent curtain of water built up to a torrential downpour. Next morning it had eased back to a steady flow, blown by the wind, into those marching, ghostly, soldiers, and alas, showed no sign of relenting.

Sylvia didn't immediately think of the scouts, her thoughts were on Mark's fleeting words. But when the important jobs of baby and breakfasts were finished the boys came to mind. They must be in a mess after all that rain. She grabbed her mac and made her way to the meadow gate. What a sight. She had never seen anything like it. Overnight the field appeared to have developed umpteen little springs, scattered haphazardly over the level area where the tents were pitched. Small pumping fountains of crystal water bubbled out of the ground like determined young geysers. The angry waters of the river lapped the guy ropes of some of the tents. Miserable dripping scouts desperately tried to take them down to move onto the higher, sloping ground.

When the scoutmaster saw her, he rushed up and hung onto her arm like a drowning man.

'Is there anything you can do? Have you anywhere we could dry out? These poor lads will get pneumonia if we don't do something.'

Sylvia racked her brain. The barn adjacent to the bar was dry and fairly clean. They could go in there. She gave him instructions. His face crumpled and she expected him to burst into tears. Embarrassed, she rushed back up the track to tell Robert and John. They were in full agreement with her decision and John gave them the big Tilly lamp, sternly warning the troops to be vigilant as the Inn would go up like a tinder box if there was a fire.

The river developed into an angry, roaring, brown monster with white frilled, leaping waves at its throat. The level rose by the minute.

'It looks as though it could get as high as when the church was flooded years ago,' said John as he reminded them of the mark in the church recording the level of the big flood. 'The church and Hollin's farm are on lower ground than us. So presumably the Inn didn't suffer the same fate.' John put his arm round Sylvia. 'Not to worry. We'll be high and dry.'

She felt herself stiffen and before she could help herself had twisted from his embrace. He looked hurt and guiltily she wondered if she had got things all wrong.

The scouts settled in the barn and really enjoyed the adventure. So much so, the scoutmaster asked if they could stay in the barn for the rest of their holiday. The six ladies from Halifax were somewhat perturbed by the ferocity of the rising waters of the river and seemed relieved to give their goodbyes. It certainly didn't seem to bother the scout troops who were having a rip-roaring time. Their scout songs rang out loud and joyful, they could even be heard in the bar when the conversation lulled. Full round faces were a contrast to the drowned rats she had seen earlier. She was sure they had put on weight.

The hurly-burley of the wet spell came to an end. Sylvia was pleased when her mother decided to take a little walk with Otti in his pram, as she hadn't seen much of the surroundings since her arrival. So Sylvia was surprised when shortly after they had left, her mum burst into the kitchen, wind blown and breathless.

'Robert. I've just heard a funny noise in the barn where the scouts were.'

'What kind of a noise?'

'I don't know, but when I opened the door...there was a white thing in the corner. It was cowering.'

'I'll go and look.'

Sylvia grabbed a tea towel to wipe her hands. 'I'm coming as well.'

They entered the building cautiously, not knowing what to expect.

'Oh Mother! It's a kitten. I thought from the way you were going on it was at least a tiger.'

Robert bent to pick up the helpless mite, and handed the tiny white kitten to his sister. 'I expect that's another addition to the family.'

As they turned to walk back Robert jumped behind his mother and with hands raised like claws gave an ear-splitting roar. She grabbed Sylvia's arm. 'I'll wring your neck Robert. It was dark in there and I didn't know what it was.'

Robert hugged her, 'Only joking Mum.'

Needless to say, the kitten made itself at home and took on the role of Cassie's playmate. On her mum's last evening, she and Sylvia were chatting over a coffee when white puss jumped up to join them. It saucily popped into the empty plant holder in the middle of the table. Two little paws hooked over the edge and the prettiest of faces with fluffy, pointed ears and the bluest of eyes gazed innocently out at them.

'I wish I'd a camera. That is a gorgeous picture,' Sylvia whispered, not wanting to break the spell.

The kitten had a blissful look and remained motionless for a little longer. Then, as though off on a mission, it bounded out of the pot, off the table and straight onto Cassie asleep in the basket.

'That's what you call a rude awakening,' laughed Sylvia.

'Look. She's left wet paw marks on the table.'

They followed the footprints to the pot.

'Mum. You'll never believe it. The kitten's peed in the pot.'

Tears of laughter ran down her mother's face. 'Oh dear me. What stories I'm going to tell your father when I get home. They'll keep him entertained for hours.'

Sylvia hugged her mum tight. Tomorrow she would be going back home.

'Are you alright dear?'

'Yes, of course. It's just that I'll miss you, though I've got dribble-drawers to remind me of your visit.'

She smiled. Her mother mustn't guess that all was not well.

CHAPTER 13

Summer gradually changed to autumn. Golds and browns crept into the green of the fells. The early morning air became crisp and exhilarating and darkness dropped her veil earlier. The hectic rush of visitors subsided, which made life easier but gave Sylvia more time to think, and it did have the serious downside of reducing the cashflow.

Since Mark had put doubt in her mind about John's visits to the top of the dale she felt the need to talk to someone. But who? Robert would only say, what did you expect? Look at the women he's had. He even ditched the girl he was engaged to. She sighed. It was such a pity Anna wasn't nearer. Newly married, she and her husband had bought an hotel in Langdale, over in the Lakes. Thinking about it, Sylvia decided to telephone her friend. She might not mention the fears that filled her thoughts, it would just be good just to hear Anna's voice again.

The call went well. Anna guessed Sylvia was unhappy and persuaded her to bring Otti and stay for a few days with her in Langdale. Sylvia felt easier than she had for ages. Mark's faux-pas had made her doubt John, even though she had always known that he much preferred the company of females to the company of men. She hated herself for not trusting him. Perhaps she had got it all wrong. A trip to the Lakes would do her good, and John might miss her. She decided to broach the subject later that day. First, though, she had to do something to improve her and her son's sleepless nights before she could consider going anywhere.

Little Otti had adjusted fairly well to the hectic lifestyle but was proving difficult to settle in bed. He seemed to have a built-in clock that brought him into the land of the living at two hourly intervals, announced by an alarm call expelled from a Town

Crier's lungs. Sylvia rushed to his side at each rude awakening fearful the battle cries might upset her visitors. Reluctantly she decided to have a word with the doctor. He held a surgery a couple of times a week in Grassington, ten miles lower down the dale. Otti was due to go for his jabs, so she could discuss the problem then.

The trouble with a visit to the doctor, or any trip down the dale for that matter, was that it meant a whole day wasted. The once-a-day bus left Buckden at 9.30 a.m. and returned at 5.30 p.m., a round trip of eight hours for a half an hour appointment. Sylvia knew she would have to make the journey, but what could she do in that length of time with a pushchair and a whippet in tow? John came to the rescue by manoeuvring his deliveries so that he could drop her off at the surgery in time for the appointment.

The doctor was pleased with Otti's progress though he was concerned about his sleeping habits.

'The young scally-wag just might have got you taped Mrs. Bainbridge. I think he's cottoned on to the fact, that every time he yells you appear.'

Sylvia opened her mouth to protest. She was overruled.

'Yes. That is the problem. I'll give you something to calm him down and you will have to try to break the habit.'

Feeling rather aggrieved she walked aimlessly down the square. The medicine tucked in her bag looked like pink custard, she hoped it would work. But what now? She had four hours to occupy before the bus arrived and she'd only enough money for the fare home.

She could hardly walk about for that length of time. Gazing in the shop windows whiled away some time, though that was irksome for without money shopping was out of the question. There was only one thing to do, she'd walk back. They'd all enjoy the journey and really ten miles wasn't a great distance. Besides she could flag down the bus when it reached them.

They set off jubilantly on the back road out of the village. Cassie trotted beside the small pushchair holding a peaceful baby. Otti was always good in the open air. A decent walk out of the village the open fields changed to a wooded area, far reaching

160

and climbing up on her right. The land on the other side of the road dropped away to the river. She admired the ribbon of water as it glistened through the trees. It was quite wide and curved in a graceful arc. A lone fisherman on a flat stony bend cast his line onto the rippling surface. She wondered if his catch would be as good as the ten trout the fishing pathologist had caught. They should be, she mused, for a licence to fish in this particular stretch of river was reported to be exorbitantly expensive. The sun broke through the cloud. Brilliant shafts of gold lit up the rich autumn colours, turning a grey day into a picture of intense beauty. It was no wonder it cost an arm and a leg to fish in such a glorious setting.

Soon the river was hidden and the ubiquitous stone walls hemmed them in as the road narrowed in places, almost too close if they were to meet a vehicle. No one crossed their path. This back road was mainly frequented by farmers and the odd rogue sheep or lamb searching for pastures new.

The great crag of rock on the far side of the river came into view as they descended towards a cluster of homesteads. She always marvelled at Kilnsey Cragg, the huge overhanging lump of limestone that defied gravity. Enthusiastic climbers would cling like bats on the under-hang, and brave cross-country souls raced round its boundaries at the annual agricultural show. How they had the strength and willpower for this marathon made Sylvia marvel.

Cassie had started to hang on her lead and was now seriously trailing. She was tired, nearing the point of giving up altogether. Whippets were not designed for long distance trekking; short sharp bursts of speed were their forte. Feeling guilty, and rather worried, she picked up her exhausted pet.

'It's no good, Cass you'll have to ride in the pram. Sorry, Otti, love, you'll have to squeeze up a bit for the rest of the journey.'

She manoeuvred them into the best possible position and covered them with the blue woollen rug her mother had bought. In a blink, the pair were asleep. The folding push chair wasn't ideal. It was really designed for an older child, but it was perfect for travelling on the bus.

With renewed resolve, Sylvia decided she was going to beat the bus back to Buckden. Perhaps a stupid idea but, she had passed the halfway mark so there was the chance to win her self-inflicted challenge. Besides, she could save the bus fare. Her stride quickened into a lengthy, rhythmic gait and strangely, she felt good. The fields encased in their dry stone walls drifted past. Silence seemed to envelope them. The light started to fade, and the pace began to tell.

The road from Starbottom to Buckden felt as though it had stretched beyond its elastic limits. Her legs didn't belong to her. Cassie was shuffling and Otti was showing signs of the onset of a bawl. He had downed the remnants of his bottle, kept warm in the little thermos case, at Kettlewell, where she had sat on the seat at the school gates. Now the poor mite would be wanting another feed and a change. Her step moved up a gear, her goal had come into view.

About a mile ahead a few lights twinkled at the base of Buckden Pike. Thank God, she was nearly home. She wearily pushed her load up the slight rise into the village, when she suddenly became aware of a light behind them and the whirr of an engine. The bus. All red and well lit, it drove triumphantly past them in a determined dash to the winning post. She was beaten in the last 100 yards. Pipped at the post by a mechanical relic! Somehow the defeat allowed exhaustion to take over. Her feet took on gravestone proportions, her legs, leaden, almost refused to take another step, and she had another mile to drag her exhausted body and push her precious charges. That last mile, now in velvet darkness, was a marathon slog. By the time they reached the Inn she was almost crawling.

John and Robert were aghast. She knew they wanted to give her a lecture on her stupidity, but they were concerned at the state she was in. Before she could defend her actions a mug of hot sweet tea and a doorstep of a sandwich was thrust at her. She ate slowly and watched helplessly whilst Robert made Otti a supplement feed and John gave Cass her meal. Fortunately there were no diners that night, the visitors had gone to Appleby for the day. It was early to bed for the travelling threesome.

Morning brought problems for Sylvia. Her body had taken on the role of Frankenstein. Legs had become solid, and joints rusted to the point of seizure. She tried to make light of her plight but physical pain took over mental attitude, and she was forced to succumb. A good job it was midweek. They had only the one couple staying, the two from Leicester, who were a puzzle. Normal and ordinary on the face of things but, obviously not happy with their lot. They both had worked all their lives for the same knitwear manufacturers. Knitwear filled their lives and they could talk about little else. At first, Sylvia thought work was their love and it had become their replacement family. They had no children, only a substantial Staffordshire bull terrier. Her enforced day of rest was a boon to the pair. They homed in on her with glee and talked constantly, pouring out their troubles. To Sylvia it all seemed so trivial and was made worse by the dog wanting similar attention. She wished them in Hell, she had enough worries of her own. The conversation with Mark kept leaping into her thoughts and she couldn't make up her mind whether to confront John or leave well alone. She became quite desperate with their whining and had the ridiculous desire to run out of the room screaming. She had come to the conclusion that she could have gone to Leicester and efficiently run the knitting machines herself after listening to every detail of their daily grind. Why they stayed in the job if they were so unhappy was a mystery.

There was a knock on the door. She was saved by the local joiner, an avid breeder of game birds. Sylvia had been impressed when she and John had called at his workshop. He had proudly shown her his prize winning silver-spangled Hamburg bantams. They were so pretty. He was delighted when she had shown interest in his birds and promised he would give her a cockerel and two hens from his next sitting of eggs.

'Ther' thee is. Three birds as promised.'

He deposited the gift on the doorstep. Sylvia eagerly opened the lid and out swaggered the most handsome, conceited bird. His feathers gleamed black and silver. He held the scarlet comb on his head high, as though to say, look at me!

'Oh. He's gorgeous.'

Her praise was rewarded with a sharp peck on her wrist as she held out her hand in friendship.

'That 'un's git plenty 'o spark,' proudly announced its breeder.

'Mm. I reckon.' Sylvia dabbed the blood with a corner of her apron. 'Why aren't the hens coming out?'

With that the cockerel fluttered onto the drive and marched smartly round in a circle. His ladies, all clucking and obedient, followed him.

'They're a lovely trio, Mr Horner. Thank you so much. You're so clever to breed such beauties.'

Mr Horner dumped a bag of seed at Sylvia's feet. He seemed embarrassed by her thanks and hastily beat a retreat to his van.

It was plain from the start that Egbert, the cockerel, was trouble. The first few days at his new home, he was charm itself, but Sylvia began to have her doubts. One morning she found him standing on her dressing table, preening himself, whilst he gazed in adoration at his reflection in the mirror. The ever open front door had been an invitation to climb the stairs to explore and no way did he intend to be removed from his new found perch. She tried to shoo him onto the landing but he was having none of that. He dodged, fluttered and dived. The bed, the window seat, Otti's cot, then back to the dressing table. He defiantly glared at her, wings half spread, head held high. She grabbed a cot blanket to throw over him in an attempt to bundle him out. Egbert was in battle mode, and without hesitation he flew straight at her body. Landing feet first, he ran up onto her head, aggressively pecking and pulling at her hair. Squeaking, she dived out of the room and down the stairs, chased by a Battle of Britain fighter. At last he was outside with his harem and Sylvia sank into a chair laughing nervously. How silly to let a small bird get the better of her.

That wasn't the end of Egbert's battles. Later in the week they had to cater for a funeral, a small affair, with only a dozen or so mourners. After the service they came, Indian file, from the church, over the bridge and onto the car park. Egbert lay in wait. This was his patch and that meant no intruders, so into the attack went proud Egbert. His ploy was to run up the back of anyone who came near, and endeavour to peck the first bit of available flesh. Neck or ear, but for preference, a bald head. The Indian file of serious mourners very quickly forgot the dead and concerned themselves with the living. The women screamed. The men of the party tried to lash out at the bundle of feathers as it twisted and turned in the mad melee. All were desperate to bolt through the front door and, somehow, they managed sanctuary in the bar. Dishevelled and blowing, they eased their own ruffled feathers with a drop of the hard stuff. When fed and watered, they turned the incident full circle into an amusing adventure. A funeral not to be forgotten.

Egbert's bravado had been pardoned twice, but the third time had to be the last. Otti, fast asleep in his pram, hood raised and apron fastened down, was awakened by the king of cockerels as he dived at the tender flesh of a delicate ear lobe. Sylvia heard the bird screech and then her baby's cries. She flew to the pram, arms flaying to rescue her son. The ear bled, and to everyone's horror it was pierced right through to the other side.

'That creature is going. If Otti had been awake it would have gone for his eyes. Ring Mr Horner now, Robert. It's got to go today before he does any more damage.'

So, the feathered lionheart, together with his two ladies, returned from whence they came.

The colourful carry on delighted the Leicester couple. Another dimension was brought into their apparently humdrum lives. Towards the end of their two week stay, the weather changed. It was still bright during the day but a cold chill came with early evening. So much so, Sylvia decided hot water bottles had to be introduced. They had no heating in the bedrooms, so she hit on the idea of popping a hot water bottle in the beds before dinner, then another as the residents retired. She climbed the stairs with two bottles tucked under her arm to take to the twin bedded, blue room, where the knitwear couple were resident. Not thinking anyone would be around at five o'clock, she almost dropped her cosy parcels as she opened their door. One of the single beds was occupied. There sitting upright, backs pillowed against the headboard, blankets tucked under their chins, cuddled Mr & Mrs Knitwear. Not particularly strange in itself, but sandwiched between the pair was a head peeping over the taut blanket, a broad, flat head with a sleepy eye at either side, topped by small folded ears. The bull terrier! He gazed belligerently at the intruder. Sylvia froze. Her reactions went into slow motion; she managed a weak smile.

'Hot water bottles for you. I'll bring fresh ones at bedtime.'

She nearly fell down the stairs in her haste to get out of ear shot and share the scene with Robert and John.

'Poor things they must be frozen. Why on earth don't they come down to the fires in the bar or dining room?'

Robert grinned sweeping his arm theatrically, 'Perhaps, they 'vant to be alone!!!'

CHAPTER 14

John stared at her open-mouthed. Sylvia felt somewhat abashed, she hadn't expected this reaction. It was quite apparent he didn't approve of her wish to take Otti over to Langdale to stay with Anna for a couple of days. Trade had slowed to a trickle, and a few days away didn't seem too much to ask. Probably John thought he should be included, but that would defeat the object of the visit. She needed to get away from him and the pub to clear her mind. A push was needed, so Sylvia played her trump card. He would look mean if he refused now.

'It will only be overnight. Anna rang this morning to say her father would pick me up on Tuesday and bring me back the next day. Surely that would be ok?'

She still felt tired and sore after the ten mile tramp from Grassington. A short break would be Heaven. An arm came round her shoulder. 'You go. It will be a nice change,' then bravely, 'We'll manage.'

Robert caught her eye and gave a sly wink. She tried to hide a grin and put on a suitably serious face. 'Well that's settled then.'

Anna's father, as arranged, arrived on the dot of 9.30 a.m.. Sylvia walked up to the black Bentley to greet Mr Birch. He always made her smile, and this morning was no exception. The door of the car opened and out stretched a pair of sock-less, thin, white legs, ending in brown sheepskin slippers. His trousers, at half mast, were baggy and well worn. Sylvia liked the man. He was a bit eccentric but wealthy enough to get away with it. He greeted her warmly. 'Well Sylvia, so this is The George. Very attractive it is too. I rather like the sign over the door.'

She gave him a hug. 'I'm so glad. I painted it. Now then, how about some breakfast?'

'No, thank you, my dear. Nothing at all. I'd like to get off straight away, if that's alright?'

She readily agreed, eager to leave her troubles behind.

They loaded the carrycot and an assortment of bags, mainly Otti's necessities, into the boot and said their goodbyes. Before she had time to think, they were on their way.

The journey was a delight. Over the tops, a band of mist had settled giving an eerie effect to reedy grasses where sheep snuggled in twos and threes. The atmosphere cleared as they descended down to Hawes. They passed the remote Moorcock Inn where Cheeky Charlie occasionally fled for wild carousing. The swell of moorland dominated by the monumental viaduct gave way to the village of Kirby Stephen. Then on to pretty Appleby where they had a brief stop for refreshment. This place stuck in Sylvia's mind. It was where the gypsies held their annual horse-fair. Secretly, she hoped one day to visit, and if the gods were good, buy a horse.

The scenery changed to a glorious rugged sky line. Young mountains reached proudly to the clouds. Sweeping tracks of grey shale gave way to bracken swirls, and pockets of green, where snowy sheep stood out sharply. Soon the slate waters of lake Windermere came into view; a small brave boat bobbed with the wind. There were quite a few visitors in Windermere itself wandering in and out of the tourist-trap shops. The season obviously lasted longer, there was so much more to do in wet weather than in lonely Hubberholme. Sylvia preferred the lovely village of Ambleside, but there was no time to stop and stare, Mr Birch was eager to see his daughter.

The Langdale Hotel gave her a shock. It was bigger and more impressive than she had imagined. Anna was there to greet them, full of the joys of spring. No wonder, Sylvia decided, there must be cash aplenty flowing. She was even more sure when her friend told her that she and her husband were having a house built in the grounds to give them privacy. Sylvia recalled some of her own sleeping arrangements, and could fully understand where they were coming from, but she couldn't help but feel a wee bit envious.

After a tour of the hotel and a view of the house plans she and Anna settled by the open fire in the enormous kitchen. It was lined with wooden cupboards and shelving holding all manner of huge utensils. The comfort of an old rocking chair and the warmth of the fire relaxed Sylvia, and Otti slept. The ambience gave her the opportunity to pour out her troubles. Anna was alarmed, and begged her not to take any action but to wait until she was certain, one way or the other, if her fears were correct about John. Then she could decide what to do.

'You'll know when it comes to it, Sylvia. It's no good worrying about what may be.'

They chatted until dinner time when they were joined by the menfolk.

Later, Sylvia struggled with Otti. He grizzled when she put him to bed. Eventually he settled into a deep sleep; the long day must have tired him. She rejoined Anna in the kitchen and they chin-wagged about college.

'Do you remember Ken Watson?'

'Do not remind me, Anna.' Sylvia stared to laugh. 'You horror. You know very well he took me out.'

'And you never told me what happened.'

'It was a disaster. We went to the theatre. He picked me up from my aunt's in his open topped sports car. I was so excited.'

'I bet you were. He was gorgeous. I was very jealous at the time. But what went wrong?'

'Well, I borrowed cousin Shirley's pink dress, it looked lovely on her, but it turned me into a ball of candyfloss. And to make matters worse he drove like the wind and succeeded in blowing my hair into a bird's nest.'

'Oh, poor you. I bet he never even noticed.'

'You are so wrong. Next to his sleek sophisticated friends I was a wretched schoolgirl.'

'Surely not,' Anna smiled. 'Did he take you straight home?'

'Couldn't get back quick enough.' Sylvia flushed as she recalled her embarrassment. 'And to put the tin hat on it, he damned well made *a pass* at my aunt.'

The two of them fell about laughing, tears rolling down their cheeks.

'What happened?'

'Aunty Glad slapped his face!'

The two friends laughter became uncontrollable.

'Oh, for pity's sake. Stop! I hurt all over.'

They awakened to a mist of rain. The promise of a walk on the fells that morning rapidly evaporated and they had to be content with a brief visit to Ambleside. Mr. Birch treated them to a slap-up lunch, then announced. 'We'll set off back if you don't mind, Anna. This rain will make driving difficult. And I'm not as young as I was.'

It didn't seem five minutes since they had arrived and now they were heading home. The drive back wasn't as pleasant as the previous day. Mr Birch was unusually quiet and Sylvia felt quite concerned. She tried once or twice to start a conversation, but failed. The miles sped by and she gave thanks that once again her son had behaved. The last thing she wanted was to upset the driver.

Hubberholme came into their sights. John and Robert appeared on the car park. She was home. Anna's father refused to stay for a meal, no matter how hard they all tried to persuade him.

'It won't take me long to get back to Ilkley. Peggy will have something ready for me, and I'd like an early bed.'

'If you're sure. Drive carefully, and give my love to Peggy.'

Sylvia was fond of Anna's mother. She had always made her welcome on weekends spent with the family, and really rather spoiled her.

John, Robert and Sylvia waved Mr Birch goodbye, watching the car till it was out of sight. She sighed, it was good to be home with the folk she loved. She decided to take Anna's advice and let sleeping dogs lie. John was pleased to see her, that was clear, so why rock the boat? She took his arm and they went into the kitchen together. Cassie had been asleep in her basket, but as soon as she heard Sylvia she almost went berserk.

'What a reception, Cassie. I've missed you, too.' She picked up her jubilant pet and sat with her cuddled tight on her lap.

'Well Robert, has anything happened whist I've been away?'

'Sis. You'll never guess what's gone on.'

'C'mon then. Let's be hearing.'

'You remember the scandal at the top of the dale? Well poor Mr Victor Smythe is giving up the family seat to escape, to God knows where. His wayward wife and the hired hand have disappeared. Even his sisters, Jocelyn and Edwina, seem to have no idea of their whereabouts.'

'So is the estate going to be sold?' Sylvia thought about the place. There it was, isolated in hundreds of acres. Only fit for sheep, and then limited to one woolly creature an acre. Who would buy it?

'There's a lot of speculation amongst the locals. They're wondering who's going to be the next lord of the manor.'

'Gosh. I never thought it would come to this. I've only been away one night.'

'Whoever gets it will have to be special. The place is in the back of beyond. I reckon they'll have to have plenty of cash and be weird enough to like the lonesome life.'

John listened to Robert pontificate, then shrugged his shoulders. 'Time will tell.'

'He'll come down to earth with a bang. Just wait until he's been snowed in for six weeks.' Robert grunted.

Sylvia heard a vehicle coming down the dale as she crossed the drive from the dairy. A brand new, state of the art Land Rover skidded to a stop on the car park, throwing up sprays of gravel. The door flung open and out stepped the most arrogant looking male Sylvia had ever encountered. Her immediate reaction was one of intense dislike. Not only was he arrogance personified, she decided the gods must have run out of the best bits when they threw him together. Even if he had the millions that gossip allocated him, it would be hard to compensate for the pudding face with the protruding teeth. They reminded her of the orange peel Dracula teeth her father would make to frighten her as a child. The splayed legs and the flabber-footed expensive shoes stood almost defiantly on the gravel drive.

'I'm Mr Boyd. I've bought the estate at the top of the dale. I gather yours is the nearest telephone. Where is it?'

Sylvia was aghast. The ignoramus. Should she refuse him?

He seemed to sense her displeasure and immediately turned on the charm. 'What a pretty place you have here, Sylvia. It is Sylvia isn't it? I've heard all about your cooking. I'll be bringing my wife to sample it as soon as we're settled.'

Sylvia gave a weak smile and reluctantly led him to the phone under the stairs.

When his call was finished he came into the kitchen, chest out and hands in his pockets.

'I've got the cost of the call from the operator. So we'll have no problem with the charges.'

He started to count out onto the table the exact amount due down to the last penny.

This routine became a regular occurrence. The only difference was that somehow he inveigled himself to be included in the morning coffee break. One particular morning, he asked for the vet's telephone number. His horse had colic and a visit was needed urgently. Thinking to save a call, Robert gave him the number, and politely asked, 'Mr Boyd. When you speak to the vet would you mention that we need wormers for Daisy and Buttercup. Perhaps they could be dropped off when he passes through.'

'Yes, I'll do that for you. We can split the cost of the telephone call.'

Sylvia was astounded. The audacity of the man. He used the kitchen and phone as his own, drank their coffee, sought their advice and expected bottles of whisky and gin at cost. No wonder he's a blasted millionaire she fumed. Her annoyance subsided as her concern for the man's horse took over. She'd no idea he was a horseman. She felt quite jealous. To ride was something she had wished for all her life, she loved horses. Even as a toddler, her parents, much to their concern, had discovered her sitting on the road under the milkman's pony with her arms wrapped round a hairy leg. All she had ever managed to do to fulfil the dream was the odd holiday hack on downtrodden, bored ponies, their only thought to end the day and get back to the stables. The man must have read her mind, for out of the blue he invited her to the house and have a ride. 'Of course, you'll have to wait until the animal has recovered.'

Uncharitably, she suspected the invite would be a ticket for more favours, though she graciously accepted the offer.

More important things were in the offing. Sylvia had to prepare for their big event, the christening, fixed for the following weekend. Both her parents, Anna, cousin Shirley with her fiancé, and John's mother and aunt were expected. Excited at the prospect of having her nearest and dearest around, especially her father, gave rise to a surfeit of energy. Robert did his best to bring her down to earth, but failed miserably.

'For God's sake, sis. It's not the Admiral of the Fleet visiting. It's family. You don't have to spring clean at 100 miles an hour. In fact you don't even have to spring clean.'

As was her wont, she totally ignored her brother and continued her quest to have all round perfection for the big event. She was anxious to make a good impression on her father, to show him that his fears on her marriage were unfounded. Woe betide her if he suspected all was not well between her and John.

There wasn't long to wait for the arrival of her parents. John had driven over to Pontefract that morning to bring them to Hubberholme in time for dinner. Sylvia had hoped they would come a few days earlier, but her father would only allow two nights away from home. She realised his antipathy towards John must have been a factor, but hoped he would have buried the hatchet for the sake of his grandchild. Still, he was coming to the christening.

The noise of a car coming up the drive made her heart pound. She gripped the edge of the sink, it was John's vehicle. They were here!

'They're here, sis!' Robert called from somewhere down the passage.

'I know. I know.' Sylvia threw off her apron and charged to the door and out to the car. 'Mum. It's lovely to see you.' Hugging her mother she peered over her shoulder to get a glimpse of her father. He had climbed out at the other side and was standing with arms folded gazing up at the fells beyond the garden.

'Poppa?'

He turned. She walked towards him, hands outstretched. 'Oh. It's so good to see you.' She leaned forward and gently kissed his cheek. He gave the slightest of smiles and in a low voice said, 'Thank you.'

Robert broke the moment. 'Come on in. I'll show you around.'

Sylvia stood alone on the drive. Her brother had taken control; she was too dazed to really notice.

The day of the christening dawned crisp and bright and brought along with it the ubiquitous round of morning coffees. John had put a notice in the bar: 'Sorry. No lunches today.' And as it happened no one asked to book, which was a relief to Sylvia for she hated to turn away custom. This lull she had been given was an opportunity not to be missed. There was just enough time to take her father round the church before the service. It would give her a chance to spend some time alone with him.

'Poppa. How would you like a little walk with me over the bridge to the church?'

He hesitated. Then to her delight, he agreed.

They stopped on the bridge to look at trout foraging for food, then, slowly made their way to the church. Inside, the stillness made Sylvia feel rather vulnerable, she didn't know quite what to say. Her father stopped in front of the font and faced her. 'You are happy, Sylvia?'

'Yes Poppa. Of course I am. I feel as though I belong here. Perhaps it comes from you being born in Swaledale. The place is similar.'

She knew her reference of the connection to his birthplace would please him. He smiled and patted her hand. And that was an unusual gesture of affection, for he was not a demonstrative man. She was more than happy.

When they returned, Robert was curious. 'Where have you been? Is father ok with everything?'

'We've just been to see the church. Everything is fine. I think Anna and her husband have arrived.'

'The Leeds lot have as well.'

Sylvia was thrilled to see them all. Especially her cousin Shirley, they'd grown up together and were more like sisters. They wanted to chat, but that would have to be later. All the guests had managed to land together. It couldn't have worked out better. The christening would be on time.

The little twelfth century church looked a picture with huge bunches of Michaelmas daises adorning the font and vestibule. The visitors were spellbound as they gazed at the rood loft, a rarity in itself, the mouse man's pews and a wooden altar, once banished across to the Inn to be used as an ale bench! When everyone had finished viewing, they settled to wait for the vicar. He was late, and to Sylvia's concern he seemed a trifle unsteady walking up the aisle.

The service was simple and beautiful. Otti behaved angelically until they all gathered round the font. Reverend Fullerton was calmness itself, but when it came to the moment he had to take hold of the baby things changed. Shirley and Anna started to giggle. Sylvia couldn't believe it, then she realised the object of their amusement was the vicar. He was refusing, point blank, to hold the whimpering baby over the font.

'What's up with the old lad?' whispered John to Robert.

'I think he's under the influence!' replied a smiling uncle as he gently took the now, wide awake offspring, from the arms of the slightly inebriated vicar. Carefully he handed the Kashmir wrapped bundle across to John to hold for the rest of the ritual. From then on everything went according to plan. It wasn't long before the amused party ambled back to the Inn to drink the health of the star of the show and enjoy a late buffet lunch.

Sylvia buzzed around, eager to ply her guests with food, whilst Robert and John topped up the glasses. She was not immediately aware of the ripple of subdued laughter at the far end of the kitchen, but gradually it dawned on her the object of the amusement was again, the Rev. Fullerton, who, feeling the need to rest his rather unsteady body, had decided to find a seat. To her amusement and concern, the seat he had chosen was a low, rather squashy pouffe, placed in the middle of the floor. She realised that he had lowered himself, not knowing that it would give way to his weight. Unfortunately, he found himself planted on his bottom at a point of no return. Manfully, he tried to keep his balance, but with legs akimbo and knees level with his nose, he had no chance. He rocked back and forth, a round bottomed cleric, valiantly endeavouring to hold an even keel.

Sylvia watched in horror. Too far away to be of assistance, she was sure he would fall backwards and feel disgraced and defrocked. To her relief he made a supreme effort. Forcing his shoulders forward, he managed to get himself untidily upright. He looked dazed, yet amazingly he still clutched his glass of whisky. John helped him to his feet. The vicar whispered in John's ear. He smiled mischievously, and cleared his throat.

'Reverend Fullerton wishes to thank everyone. And, as he feels a bit under the weather, he would like to say goodbye.'

The company applauded the little man as he left on John's arm.

Robert grinned as he rocked his nephew. 'Well, not only is young Otti special in being the only baby to be born here but not many will have been christened with such panache.'

The bar that night was packed. The locals turned up in full force to give their good wishes and to take advantage of the free drink on offer. The merrymaking went on until the small hours. Otti had certainly been given a great start to his little life.

Next morning there were quite a few delicate souls. Sylvia had to smile as she served her visitors breakfast. Fry-ups were hastily turned down in preference for, 'just a slice of toast'. Even John looked a bit jaundiced as he set off for work and Robert seemed rather quiet going about his daily jobs. Midmorning, he came through to the kitchen.

'Sis, what do you think about giving the pigs these barrel bottoms. It seems a shame to ditch them, and surely it shouldn't do any harm.'

Normally the residue left in the empty beer barrels was thrown away. Sylvia felt doubtful, though really her brother was right. It was only grain and hops.

'Ok, give it a try. Don't give them too much. I'd hate to upset their tums.'

Robert later reported that the two pigs, Genevieve and Ariane, had enjoyed their boozy snack. Sylvia forgot all about the incident as she prepared lunch for her family and friends, who were all to depart after the meal. She was just about to pop the Yorkshire puddings into the oven when, to her surprise her father came into the kitchen looking a little anxious. 'Sylvia, I think one of your pigs is ill. I don't quite know what to think but, it looks peculiar. You better come and have a look.'

She and Robert dashed to the door, crossing the drive to make their way down the alley and up the steps to the croft. They were stopped dead in their tracks. There in the passage at the foot of the steps was Ariane. She staggered towards them, front legs crossing as she wobbled with each awkward step. Her eyes were glazed and she seemed to be frothing at the mouth.

'Oh my God, it's swine fever!'

Sylvia moaned out the name of the only pig disease she had ever heard as she sank to her knees, her arms cradling the nodding head of her favourite porker. She could hardly believe her ears when her misery was broken by a raucous guffaw from Robert. It sounded like a hyena who had just killed his latest meal.

'What the Hell's wrong with you? My poor girl's dying and all you can do is laugh. Go and ring the vet instead of standing there cackling like a damned donkey.'

'Oh sis,' he gasped, tears rolled down his cheeks, 'your precious pig is as drunk as a skunk!'

Sylvia carefully raised herself upright, gazed down at her fat friend, and slowly realised her brother was right.

'That's how she got down the steps. Dutch courage! I thought she'd fallen and really hurt herself.'

Robert subdued his mirth. 'Don't worry love. We'll put some straw under her and she can sleep it off down here in the passage. When she's recovered we can take her round through the pasture gate back to Genevieve, who's also a bit under the influence but not nearly as bad as this one.'

No sooner was the straw laid out, than the greedy Ariane had the sense to collapse on the comfy bed. She buried her head and began to snore. And how she snored. It certainly wasn't a ladylike noise expelling from the paralytic porker, more like a volcano ready to blow.

The christening party had watched the proceedings, first full of concern, then gradually turning to uncontrolled amusement. Some bright spark commented, 'God. It's like Casey's court at this place. You couldn't make it up if you tried.'

CHAPTER 15

It was difficult settling down to the mundane after the excitement of the christening. Christmas was too far away to start any planning and the tourist trade had trailed off into a last wisp of smoke from a burnt out bonfire. Otti's sleep pattern was improving, but he seemed unable to manage any longer than a good catnap. Sylvia needed a new challenge. Deep down she knew they all could do with a winding down spell after the hard labour of summer, but that last building yet to be cleared, called.

Galvanised, she rushed through the morning routine, feeding baby, animals and men-folk in quick succession. John was fairly bundled out of the door.

'Hey, what goes on? Are you trying to get rid of me?'

'Would I? No, I just want to get on with some cleaning.'

Robert looked askance, 'What cleaning?' She ignored him, and made great play of waving goodbye to John. As soon as he was off the premises she hurried towards the building that haunted her.

In the corner of the car park, squeezed between the old coach house and the small coppice, sat the stable. This place had been left untouched, the last in her line of priorities, but now, fired by the promise of a ride on Mr Boyd's horse, she wanted it empty. Secretly the thought of a clean stable was one step nearer to having a horse of her own standing there. Besides, it really did need sorting. She marched up to the doorway, full of optimism, but that feeling rapidly evaporated. The sight was daunting. Once the building must have housed several horses for transport and farm work, now it was relegated to a stewing dung heap. The floor was invisible, buried knee-deep under a compacted mattress of calf muck and straw. 'Oh God,' she muttered to the Heavens, 'I don't think Robert's going to like this idea.'

She knew she couldn't possibly clear the place on her own and decided that it would be best to ask him to help later in the morning when he'd warmed up a bit. But she couldn't wait. She marched back to the kitchen, and passing the bar window, she saw her brother's tall frame bent over the fireplace laying the fire ready to add a warm glow for the evening drinkers. Dumping her wellies outside she gently opened the door.

'Robert...'

He straightened slowly and without turning uttered, 'What now?'

His rigid back sent out a warning, but she ignored the signal. 'Robert, I just wondered if it might be a good idea for us to clear the stable? It's packed knee-high with calf muck. It's a breeding ground for rats if you ask me.'

'Oh no. Do we have to do it today?'

She'd hoped the threat of long tails invading the building might just persuade him. He turned to her, the tiredness in his face gave her a twinge of guilt, but she pushed it to one side.

'There's no time like the present. We've no customers, it's a lovely day and Otti's asleep.'

Sylvia felt disgruntled, he should be more enthusiastic. After all the business was one third his.

'Sis, don't you think we deserve a bit of a break. Frankly, I'm knackered. Remember, I'm not sailing down the dale every day on some jolly, supposedly delivering groceries.' He turned back to the fire, giving a definite finish to the conversation.

'Robert, are you implying that John's not working?'

There was a long silence.

'You know as well as I do he only makes three or four calls a day. I know the farms are far apart, but honestly, it's a doddle.'

She took a step back, her breath escaped in ragged gasps. She felt naked. To have her secret fears exposed was a shock.

'I know he's hopeless at sticking to a routine and easily gets sidetracked, but remember we'd be in queer street without his pay packet. Where will we be this winter if there's no extra money coming in?'

'It's not about keeping a roof over our heads. Haven't you got it through your thick head that he's no consideration for you at all. What man would let his wife work like an Irish navvy up to six hours before giving birth, then let her cater for a coach load three days later? Tell me, who?'

'Oh Robert, please don't get cross. We've got to pull together or we'll sink.' Her eyes began to sting, she didn't want to cry, especially with Robert in this mood, but the welling tears slipped free. Through blurred vision she saw his shoulders slump and his hand raise in a dismissive gesture.

'Oh sis...'

She didn't wait to hear the rest and turned blindly to the kitchen, furiously searching her pockets for an elusive hanky. He caught up with her at the Aga as she dabbed her face with a tea towel, laying a comforting hand on her shoulder.

'We're both tired out, you've got to accept that. We've been working full pelt. I'm crabby, you're exhausted, though you won't admit it. How about we have a rum and coffee and then take a look. What do you say?'

She nodded, glad they had made a truce and relieved that John wouldn't be back until late. It would give her time to recover before he came home. She didn't want to give him any hint that things weren't running smoothly. 'I'll put the kettle on.'

After breakfast, they donned wellies and walked to the stable. Robert was first through the door.

'Crikey sis, the muck's at least two feet deep. It's one Hell of an acreage. Why don't we clear part of it today and do the rest tomorrow? The place was used for tying four horses at some time. There's tons to shift.'

'Oh come on, we'll soon get it moved. I'll throw out onto the car park if you fork it into the barrow and tip it in the meadow.'

He sighed, and picked up his fork. Sylvia, intent on emptying the building before nightfall started rapidly swinging out layers of the compacted muck and straw.

'Slow down. If you keep going like a bull at a gate you'll suffer tomorrow. You won't be able to move.'

Sylvia ignored her brother, whose steady approach to the workload annoyed her. As though to cock-a-snook at his comments she increased the pace, sending layers soaring through the door onto the steaming pile outside.

It wasn't too long before her efforts began to let her body know it wanted a rest. Her shoulders began to ache, a dull nag that heralded trouble. Perhaps they should have a break.

'Robert, let's have a cuppa and a sandwich. Otti needs a feed and changing, he's been so good, I'm amazed.'

She put down her fork and eased her back with a huge stretch, 'I think you're right, I'm beginning to ache a bit.'

Walking over to the pram, where her son lay cocooned in a nest of soft blankets, she smiled. He was awake, his bright blue eyes gazing at the sky where a hawk hovered over the croft. He seemed to be watching its antics.

'Hey Robert, look at Otti. I reckon we've a budding bird watcher here.'

He laughed. 'Idiot, come on, I'm hungry.'

Several bacon sandwiches later, Sylvia decided they'd better return to the backbreaking shovelling. She cuddled Otti for another moment before popping him back in his cosy chariot and to her delight he laid there quietly content. 'I wish he'd do this at bedtime, he seems to prefer the outdoors to his bedroom.'

Robert ruefully replied. 'I wouldn't mind swopping places. Let's get started on that muck mountain.'

Surprisingly, it didn't seem long before their efforts were rewarded; they had sight of the stable floor. Robert grabbed the yard brush and furiously attacked the last remnants of bedding to reveal perfect, old-style flooring. It was a smooth concrete base, formed by grooves into small squares for good drainage and a non-slip finish. There was a channel at the foot of what would have been the standing for four horses, which ran to an outside drain. 'What a super floor. Perfect for when we can have a horse,' beamed a delighted Sylvia.

'You'll have a long wait for that one,' grunted Robert, as he filled the umpteenth barrow load to tip in the four acre meadow alongside the river.

When he returned she had swept clean most of the floor, but she had to admit that she'd had enough. In a no nonsense voice Robert announced, 'I'm going to make this the last barrow load of the day. The rest can wait till tomorrow.'

'It's getting cooler and Otti's starting to grizzle. I'll walk him up to the gate with you.'

She pushed the pram alongside her brother for the last trek of the day. They reached the gateway on the roadside, the path into the field dropped steeply down to the meadow bottom. Robert turned to her grinning. 'Watch this for speed.'

He set off with whoops of laughter and began to run down the path. Sylvia, smiled to herself, boys will be boys, but as she watched apprehension took over. The heaviest load of the day was getting the better of him and she spotted a half-hidden boulder waiting to cause mischief. The wheelbarrow seemed to develop a mind of its own and Robert desperately tried to keep pace with the runaway load.

'Let go of it. Let go.'

In awe Sylvia watched as the wheel contacted the immovable object. There was a moment of total inaction, the barrow stopped dead, then her brother sailed over the top in graceful, slow motion, his hands still grasping the handles. His feet sliced the sky on his way to a crash landing full length in the grass. A shower of calf muck, descended on him in a delayed barrage, that seemed to go on forever.

Oh God, his back, was the only thought in her head as she watched all 6ft 2in of him land in a muddle of limbs. She stumbled down the path, fearful of what she might discover. Robert lay there, not a muscle moved. Heart in her mouth, she knelt beside him. 'Robert, Robert are you alright?'

She touched the white face, spotted in calf muck. To her relief, one eyelid blinked, semi-glued by the shower of brown stuff. He painfully raised himself and spat out invading bits of tainted straw. 'After that I think I deserve a cuppa.'

'Oh Robert, you're alright. You said I'd hurt tomorrow, so will you. And by the way, you stink. I'll hose you down when we get back'

'Like Hell you will.'

Laughing with relief and amusement they trudged up the path, collected Otti at the gate and made their way back to that life-saver, a cup of hot sweet tea.

183

After their evening meal, Sylvia had to admit that perhaps she'd overcooked herself on the muck-shifting front. Even putting Otti to bed seemed a mammoth task and she found her senses slipping into Never-Never Land as she rocked his cot.

'Gosh Otti, that's a first. I just don't drop off willy nilly. If we haven't many customers tonight, it's early bed for your mum. That will please Robert. It'll be... I told you so.' She smiled at the now peaceful baby and gently touched his cheek with a caressing finger.

Reluctantly, she returned to the kitchen, hoping any folk who might venture out would depart at a reasonable hour. As luck would have it, only Charlie and Anthony appeared and they left early. She couldn't help but feel relieved.

'Boys, do you mind if I pop off to bed?'

Robert seemed unable to wipe the self-satisfied smile off his face. 'You wait till tomorrow. You feel bad tonight, but I bet you're as stiff as a board in the morning.'

He did have the good grace not to gloat too much and for that she forgave him for the taunts. Deciding silence was the best ploy, she gave him a slight wave of her hand, then briefly kissed her husband on her way out of the kitchen.

Climbing the stairs she mulled over John's attitude. She wished he had shown just a bit of concern at her plight. Surely, he must have known how hard it had been shifting all that muck, tons of the stuff. It seemed as long as he was dressed up and driving about the countryside he was happy, blow everybody else. Probably it would have been better if they'd spread the work over a few days as Robert had suggested. Perhaps John thought the same. Even so, he might have said the stable looked well and they'd done a good job.

Opening the bathroom door she knew a bath was out of the question, getting clothes off and teeth cleaned was all she could manage. Bed beckoned.

As soon as the blankets were tucked round her chin she was swallowed into another world. Otti surprisingly woke only once and then slept peacefully till his feed time.

The greyness of morning crept through the blackness of night and the alarm trilled its warning. Sylvia knew she was in trouble; her robust attack on the stables had left its mark. She raised herself on an elbow in a futile effort to get up, but her bones had other ideas. Unbelievably, her normally obedient body refused to follow any instructions. Overnight she had turned into Lot's wife, a solid block. Startled, she yelped as pain seared through her shoulders and chest bone, 'John I can't move.'

An incumbent bear, grunted as he entered the wakening world. 'Don't be silly. Course you can move; you're sitting up. Besides you fed Otti earlier and you were mobile then.'

Confused and still annoyed with him, she adopted the silent treatment, and instead called out to her brother. In seconds he knocked on the door and popped a woolly head into the room.

'What's the matter? Oh Lord, what have you done?'

Sylvia cringed as she caught the anxiety in his voice, even that hurt.

'You've seized up. It's all that mucking out yesterday. Your joints have dried out!'

'Oh thank you. What are you saying, I'm decrepit?'

Robert half smiled. 'No silly, but you better get to the doctor this morning.'

John now compos mentis took over the reins, 'I'll ring and make an appointment, then let Mr Souter know that I'll be late in today. You'll need taking down and bringing back.'

Sylvia had to admit he looked concerned. She'd never been ill since they'd been together, and one of them out of action would be a problem. Damn, she thought, pride comes before a fall. Serves me right for being pig-headed and cocky yesterday.

Somehow she managed to get her son fed, changed and settled in his pram but she had to dress with John's help, which didn't please.

The journey to the surgery held none of the usual delights; not once did she register the changing countryside. Her only thought was to prepare her body for every corner and bump in the road and that road seemed never-ending. When they arrived at the surgery door, she could hardly clamber out of the car. Fortunately, once upright her unfettered legs took over.

'What, Mrs Bainbridge, have you been doing?'

It wasn't so much a question as an accusation, and Sylvia couldn't hold his gaze as she briefly told him.

'Good God, woman, you've just had a baby. What on earth were you thinking?'

She didn't attempt a reply, but tried to look contrite in the hope he would stop talking and give her something to ease the pain.

When he mentioned a cortisone injection, and went to the glass-fronted cabinet, she felt relief flood through her...until she saw the size of the needle and heard where he was going to inject her.

'My *breastbone!?'*

She was sure he inflicted more pain than was necessary as he plunged the thick needle into her body. Determined not to let him see her pain and discomfort, she blinked away the tears that threatened to run unannounced down her cheeks. Finally, with a bottle of pain killers clutched in a damp hand, she joined her husband in the waiting room. 'Let's go John. I want to go home.'

John kept his arm round her waist till they got back to the car. He made sure she was comfortable and drove, for him, carefully back home. Happily, the return journey wasn't nearly as bad as the trip down the dale.

It took a couple of days before she was able to move with some ease. Gradually, over the rest of the week her skeleton returned to its former self, which turned out to be a blessing. They received an unexpected booking for a birthday dinner on the Friday, something she loved, a grand occasion, when she could go to town on with the menu and not be crippled by keeping the cost down.

'I'm going to give them rack of lamb. John will you be going to market on Friday?'

'Yes, all things being equal.'

'Good. Will you be able to bring back a catering pack of frozen peas? Then I can give them onions in white sauce, peas and mint sauce, mash and roast potatoes, and carrots for colour. Mum's recipe for chicken liver pate and toast for starters, then finish off with a hazelnut meringue. How does that sound?' She

186

smiled as she watched both men drool at the prospect of tasty leftovers.

Friday dawned, John went off with strict instructions not to forget the peas, and she and Robert rushed through the everyday chores, leaving plenty of time to prepare for the special meal. It was a day without hitches. Even Otti obliged and dropped off in good time. The dining room gave a warm welcome in the flickering firelight. The table glittered. Sylvia had put a candle at each place setting, and a huge bowl of spent hydrangea flowers, highlighted with silver paint sat in the centre. Everything seemed perfect.

Time slipped away as quietly as a soft-shoe shuffle and Sylvia began to nag. 'Robert, where on earth is John? He's not going to be here in time for the main course. No peas! What the Hell am I going to do?'

Robert shrugged. 'Have we any other vegetables?'

'No. Anyway, peas are right for the meal. I suppose we'll have to use those quick dried things. They'll just have to do. Where the devil is he. I could kill him.'

She found herself talking to fresh air. Her brother had disappeared into the bar to greet the revellers, who had boisterously entered the front door. Her anger subsided in deep concentration as she put the final touches to the tempting dinner.

The birthday guests were in high spirits when they eventually settled down to the meal, which they consumed in record time. Their celebrating continued till well past closing time, yet there was still no sign of the wayward John. Midnight came and the happy visitors, in varying degrees of alcoholic influence, departed.

Sylvia's anger turned to panic. 'What if he's had a crash on the tops and there's no one around to help him?'

'Don't worry sis', he'll be fine. He'll be talking somewhere, or something. He'll have forgotten we're waiting.'

She glared at him, ready to challenge the innuendo, but as he uttered the words, they heard the Land Rover pull onto the car park.

'He's here.'

Her anxiety, with the alacrity of a lightening flash, switched back to black anger, but she found her voice refused to make a sound and she could only glare at her errant husband as he sheepishly came through the door.

'Sorry love, I fell asleep at the farm gate on my last call.'

Robert looked away and under his breath spat. 'That takes some bloody swallowing.'

Sylvia, too tired and weary, long past any discussion, stomped off to bed.

She woke with anger still on her shoulder. Before feeding the hungry animals, she decided the first job was to check if John had actually remembered to buy the peas. Not knowing whether she would be more annoyed if he'd forgotten altogether, she quietly made her way outside.

The Land Rover, covered in mud, invited her to open the door. Warily she looked inside. On the passenger seat, in pristine glory, two packets of soggy, green spheres smiled up at her. All they were good for now was a feed for the birds. Oh for electricity and a fridge. She fumed, and her anger returned in a crescendo of demented rage. She tore open the wrappings and triumphantly scattered the innocent peas far and wide, in every cranny of the vehicle that alone knew the secrets of her husband's escapades.

'That'll teach him. It won't be a five minute job clearing up that little lot!'

At first she felt quite elated, but revenge wasn't as sweet as expected and returning to the kitchen her father's words sighed in her ears, 'Leopard's don't change their spots.'

CHAPTER 16

It was Monday, and Sylvia had more or less forgotten the incident with the frozen peas. But she could not forget that her husband may have been unfaithful. Unfaithful. She hated that word, it portrayed something devious, a broken contract. Pulling herself together she watched John cleaning the Land Rover. He had looked decidedly dejected, a subdued cockerel pecking at each sad and flattened pea scattered throughout his dream machine. Even she in her frenzy, couldn't have guessed that two packs of frozen peas would spread so far, and find so many crevices in which to hide. She fought the urge to help him with his penance but, amusement and satisfaction won the day.

It was to be a good day for her, she had been invited to ride Mr Boyd's horse. He had suggested she should get a lift up the dale with the postman but, John, eager to make amends had scotched that idea.

'I'll take you and wait while you have your ride. There's one or two things I need to discuss with the farm manager. Then you can come with me on a couple of calls to Dale head. We'll only be a few hours, Otti will be ok with Robert; there's no visitors, and everything's quiet.'

The idea appealed, though the thought of John dealing with Jenny's husband gave her an empty black hole inside. Except, if he was with Nobby Todd he could hardly be alone with Jenny. The saying, not on your own doorstep, crossed her mind.

Partly worried about leaving her son, yet excited at the prospect of a ride, she set off for her big treat. The only other time she had been up the dale for any distance was in the dark. She smiled as the memories flicked past in rapid snapshots, however, there had been no concept on that journey of the wild beauty that enthralled her now. They passed a tranquil stretch of river where great flat stones, dropped there by some friendly giant, glistened invitingly in the autumn sun. She imagined they'd made a playground for children and picnic seats for parents in the summertime. The mood changed as they climbed higher. Grasses touched by a rusty hand blew in chorus with puffs of smoking clouds, and white pompoms of cotton-like reeds waved cheerfully as they left the road that climbed on to Oughtershaw, where they had danced the night away. The little road they took was not much more than a track. It wended its way through wind-torn moorland to their destination, the imposing stone manor house, the home of Mr Boyd.

Sylvia recognised the ill-shaped master of the estate standing at the front door of the surprisingly plain house. At his side was a typical horsey girl, her fair hair tied in bunches with rather sad-looking tartan ribbons. She wore smart riding breeches and her brown leather boots shone, but her oversized navy sweater seemed at loggerheads with the rest of the outfit.

Mr Boyd stepped forward as Sylvia opened the car door.

'Now then, young woman. This is Angela, my groom. She is very capable and has been with us for years.' He put an arm round her shoulders. 'Angela, will you take Sylvia to the stables. You both can enjoy a bit of a gallop. You do know how to ride? Nimbus isn't everyone's cup of tea.'

He turned to John inviting him into the house.

Angela led Sylvia to the stables. At the sight of the waiting Nimbus she took a sharp breathe: 16 hands of golden muscle with blonde hair pieces and attitude, muscles rippling, nostrils flared. Her excitement began to wane. This beast looked fighting fit and held no comparison to her few riding school ambles on plodders.

Nimbus glared at her with an aristocratic expression, the white of his eye evident. Her father had told her that was a bad sign. Now, more nervous than she cared to admit, she mounted the volcano of horse flesh, adjusted the stirrups and gathered the reins, tentatively following her companion out of the yard. Angela's mount, a cob, seemed far more docile than Nimbus, and Sylvia couldn't help wishing that it had been given to her, though gradually her confidence grew and soon both horse and rider started to relax. She began to enjoy herself and view the scenery and decided this was a good time to quiz the stable girl. The opportunity couldn't be missed.

'Angela, you must find it lonely up here after the busy south?'

'No, I like it. Besides, I love the horses. I couldn't bear to be parted from them.'

Sylvia was quiet for a moment. 'You'll only have Mrs Boyd for company. And, er... doesn't Mrs Todd – Jenny – live nearby?' Her mouth went dry as she waited for the reply.

'I don't see much of Mrs Boyd; she's not interested in horses. As for Mrs Todd, I only met her once before she left.'

'*Left!*' Sylvia's inside made an almighty somersault.

'Yes. I believe she had a nervous breakdown and has gone away for a spell. To Lancaster, I think.'

Sylvia couldn't answer. She couldn't even pretend to act normal, she felt dreadful. What had happened? Did John know?

An enormous buck from Nimbus brought her back on track with a jolt. The narrow path they were following petered out alongside a gurgling stream. It happily made its way through a low gap in the wall, then ran triumphantly into the field beyond. Angela bounced off her piebald cob and opened a gate a few yards farther on. 'Come on, Sylvia. We can have a gallop on this stretch.'

In a turmoil, Sylvia followed the round backside of Angela's mount through the gate. To her consternation, a strip of short, greener grass ran beside the stream in a long curve, for what seemed an eternity. Oh God, it's like a blasted race course! And I've never galloped. Her pride wouldn't let her say a word to the girl, but before she had time to even think, Nimbus took over. This was where he had fun and fun he was going to have. He tensed his muscles into concentrated power, his body dropped to add boost, and he propelled forward with the acceleration of a bat out of Hell. His hooves threw clods of soft earth, pelting his stable mate, as though taunting him to give chase.

Sylvia grabbed the slack reins and pulled for all she was worth, desperately trying to slow down the half ton of charging horse flesh. She might as well have whispered sweet nothings in his ear for all the notice he took. In the struggle, she lost both stirrups. They became flying objects of torture, determined not to be caught, but to strike any part of her legs that came into the firing line. They evaded any connection with her searching feet, but periodically kicked Nimbus in his belly, igniting him to gallop faster. Somehow, she managed to keep her seat, though slipped precariously from side to side as her flying mount spooked at clumps of reeds, or anything else to give him an excuse to wind up his hapless jockey. To her horror the end of the fast track came into view. A twelve foot wooden gate in a boundary wall marked its limit. God, he'll jump it. Please, please stop, she prayed as the Grand National fence loomed nearer. The gods heard, and hastily plucked her from the saddle. Nimbus had decided discretion was the better part of valour. The sack of potatoes on his back would be no help to jump the gate, so evasive action was needed. A rapid left hand full stop, worked the oracle. His uncomfortable load was successfully dislodged and dumped in the mud at his feet. Sylvia, for whatever reason, had kept hold of the reins. At least a loose horse galloping home and meeting all kinds of hazards had been avoided.

Angela trotted up. 'I thought you could ride!' she rapped out at her muddied, shame-faced companion, and she grabbed the reins from Sylvia's hands. 'You better get on the gate to remount. It's too far to walk back.'

Sylvia felt like a chastised dung beetle as she gingerly placed her wet rear onto the rich brown leather of the brand new saddle. The pair set off, a heavy silence hanging over the little posse that did not lift throughout the journey back to base. To her consternation as they approached the house, John and Mr Boyd were waiting. She guessed they must have seen the horses from one of the windows. Her heart was in her boots. She felt a fool.

'What's happened then?' Mr Boyd took hold of Nimbus and cast his eyes over his precious animal. 'He looks alright. Thank your lucky stars, madam.' Then, as an after thought, 'Are you?'

Sylvia nodded. 'I'm sorry.'

He looked straight into her eyes. She shrivelled. His gaze seemed to pierce into her very soul.

'You should have said you couldn't ride. My horse, or even yourself, could have been badly damaged.'

He helped her dismount. And to add insult to injury, he had to support her as her knees buckled from the exertion.

She watched Angela take Nimbus back to the stable and thought she'd better offer to help. 'I'll help get his tack off and brush him down.'

'No need. The girl's paid to do that.'

John came to Sylvia's side. 'I think we'd better get off,' he said quietly.

Turning to the owner he muttered some kind of apology about his wife's lack of horsemanship. Sylvia spluttered. The rat. Surely he could have put it better? Feeling like a reprimanded schoolgirl, she thanked her host and climbed into the car, anxious to escape as quickly as possible.

The trip to Dale Head was fortunately short and sweet, for all she wanted to do was to get back to her son and the safety of home. All thoughts of Jenny Todd and her husband were put on the back burner.

Robert was waiting for her with news of a booking for that night for two separate doubles. 'Crikey, I'll have to get a move on. They'll want dinner.' She grabbed Otti close to her and ran up the stairs to see to his needs.

Sylvia had caught up with all preparations: bedrooms were ready, fires blazing, and food organised. John had gone back to the Hebden shop and Robert took the two pigs, Genevieve and Ariane, down the road to Gerald's new boar. She had laughed watching the threesome head towards the love nest. Robert, armed with a long stick, herded the chubby reluctant ladies towards their fate. Fortunately the stone walls, close in to the road on both sides, helped to contain the disgruntled pair, who vociferously let it be known they resented being taken away from home. Sylvia made sure Robert and his charges were well on their way before turning back up the drive. As she walked she noticed a small car heading towards the Inn. By the time she reached the front door it had drawn onto the car park: the first of the residents had arrived.

They were a quiet twosome, normal enough, but rather shy. Sylvia tried to make polite conversation as she showed them to their room. Her efforts were ignored and feeling rather disgruntled, she left them with the parting shot: 'Dinner is 7.30 prompt. Tea and scones will be waiting for you when you come down.'

Stamping downstairs she noticed the fire in the bar had burned low. She went in and picked up the poker, bending over the grate to stir the embers, unaware that anyone was close by, let alone in the room. She heard nothing until, without warning, she felt two arms shoot round her body and a pair of clutching hands grabbed her bosom. Shock and alarm shooting through her, she twisted from the searching grasp, to realise this creature was their guest. Common sense and reason galloped out of the window, then with instinctive reaction, she spun round and thrust the poker into the man's hand.

'You poke the fire!' And she fled, down the bar-passage, on into the kitchen, slamming both doors behind her. Breathing heavily, she collapsed against the Aga and bear hugged a surprised Cassie. Oh God. Was the fellow mad? The kitchen door burst open. She daren't look.

'Sis. What the dickens are you doing?'

'Oh Robert. Oh Robert!'

'What's the matter? What is it?'

Between gasps, she poured her tale of woe.

'Sit down. I'll make you a cup of tea, then I'll have a word with *him*.'

'Robert. You can't. He's a customer.'

'Customer or not. He can't get away with that kind of behaviour. Ok, I'll wait until John gets back, and then we'll see.'

When John returned, he and Robert mulled over the incident. Finally they decided to watch the molester's every move and say nothing, rather than upsetting his wife. To Sylvia's annoyance they found her reaction to the man's advances hilarious.

'You actually gave him a weapon!' John was incredulous. 'What would you have done if he'd threatened you with it? There was nobody to help you.'

Sylvia felt hurt and a bit let down. They did need the business, so she kept her thoughts to herself in spite of feeling shell-shocked.

The arrival of the second couple pushed the escapade away. They were absolute opposites to the other two. The husband seemed a force to be reckoned with, a powerful individual, who turned out to be a top-dog in the armed forces. He was an amusing, literate, self-opinionated extrovert. His wife, a bishop's daughter, was quiet and gentle, perhaps a trifle prim. Both of them were psychiatrists. John got on with the Commander like a house on fire and stories galore flowed after dinner. Sylvia was aghast as she earwigged, especially when she heard the way he interviewed raw-recruits. She watched him lean indolently back in the chair, legs akimbo, head on one side.

'I'd sit at my desk, an enormous one, right at the end of a long empty room. The poor unfortunates, still wet behind the ears, must have died a thousand deaths as they opened the door. The long walk facing them must have felt like the slog to the gallows.' He laughed, a deep rumbling sound. 'When they were halfway down the room, I'd bawl, "Boy. When did you last pee the bed?" A good way to differentiate the men from the boys, eh?'

John laughed, but Sylvia felt perturbed. The method sounded cruel and she couldn't help wondering just how successful it had been. Turning her back, she left them to carry on with their navy yarns, helped along with swigs of whisky.

She was rather concerned when, well after closing time she noticed the whisky bottle, shared only by John and his new pal, had dropped at an alarming rate. She tried in vain to entice John to bed but he was so under the influence, that any of her signals were, either ignored or unseen. Angrily she stormed to the kitchen.

'Robert, I suggest we go to bed and leave those two degenerates to their own devices. They're both stinking drunk.'

They climbed the stairs together and Sylvia plucked up her courage. 'Robert, have you heard anything about Jenny Todd lately?'

'Like what?'

'Oh, I don't know. Somebody said she'd gone away. I just wondered.'

'No. I haven't heard a thing. Goodnight.'

She slept, peacefully enough, for a couple of hours until Otti woke her. Still no John by her side. The rotter, he'll be legless, she fumed, not fit for work. That shrink is a bad influence. She debated whether to go down to the bar, then decided against it, not wanting the visitor to think she was a nagging wife. Besides, they were both old enough to know what they were doing. With that thought, she picked up her fitful baby and the pair snuggled down together in the big bed till morning.

On waking she was alarmed to find there was no inebriated husband sharing the bed. She threw on her clothes and scrambled downstairs. Not knowing what to expect she opened the bar door. The room was empty, the birds had flown. Silently, she crept back up the stairs to Robert's room. 'Robert, John and the Commander have disappeared. John didn't come to bed. I don't know about the other one. What shall we do?'

'Nothing,' grunted her none too happy brother. 'For Heaven's sake, they're both big enough and old enough to know what they're doing. Is his car still here?'

Sylvia dashed outside. No car. Where had they gone?

Robert emerged as his sister came in from feeding the animals, and her anxiety.

'I wonder if they're both missing. Perhaps our visitor is in his bed.' Sylvia glanced up the stairs.

'No,' said Robert, 'you can't wake them, or her. Just calm down and wait until breakfast. We should know more by then.'

Before any residents appeared, the grocery Land Rover returned. Two, grubby specimens, still influenced by the hard stuff, trundled into the kitchen. They both sported the same silly grin. 'We've been potholing.'

Sylvia glared in disbelief. 'You did what?'

The two men, schoolboys caught stealing apples, had the decency to look shamefaced. 'Well, we got talking about pot-holing and thought it would be great to go down one. It didn't matter that it was dark, cos' it's dark underground. Anyway, we had a torch.'

The two men looked at each other. John lamely went on, 'So we drove to the nearest pot and went down and when we got to an easy bit we sat down and... sort of fell asleep...'

They both knew they were skating on thin ice. Sylvia could hardly believe her ears. How could adult men, and one of high rank in a responsible position, be such fools? No doubt the influence of Mr Whisky had more than a little to do with the stupidity. In total exasperation, she turned her back on the pair and viciously stabbed the sausages, minding their own business, as they browned gently in the frying pan.

The molester and his wife left after breakfast. Sylvia kept well out of sight and heaved a sigh of relief as they departed. The mad commander and his indulgent wife decided to stay a few days longer. Happily there were no more hazardous exploits, though their whisky stock was somewhat depleted.

CHAPTER 17

Winter approached and the weather turned cold. It was time to add to the church chores: the antique boiler needed lighting each weekend. Rev. Fullerton had hung on as long as he dared but, the weather had got the better of him. And, as he informed Robert, new skills had to be learned to make sure the temperamental creature turned out sufficient heat to warm the toes of the sparse congregation.

With the change in temperature came bad news. Mr Souter decided to retire and the new owners of the business didn't need a handsome deliveryman. Sylvia was in despair. John had no job. It couldn't have happened at a worse time. The tourist trade was almost negligible, and general running costs began to pinch. She always knew her beloved could wield his charm to the best advantage, if he so desired, but even she hadn't bargained for the speed he landed his next post. A top animal feed merchant had advertised for a representative to cover the upper Wharfedale area, and John decided to apply. Surprisingly he was invited for an interview even though he had no animal husbandry experience.

The day of the interview Sylvia couldn't settle and when she heard John's footsteps on the drive her heart pounded. The door flung open and in bounded a bullish, jubilant husband.

'Guess what!'

Sylvia could feel the warm glow of pride emitting from him. She hardly dare utter the words. 'You've got the job?'

He seemed to grow in stature. 'Yes. And there's a car provided!'

'Oh John, How wonderful.'

She was over the moon. What had looked to be a bleak Christmas and winter, had disappeared; instead she was filled with renewed hope.

John appeared to enjoy his new job. He had an empathy with the local farmers which stood him in good stead. In no time at all he became the number one salesman in the north for the sale of calf-milk powder. Sylvia was proud. Perhaps this was his niche, and now that he had found it, hopefully, he would stay focussed and not meander off course.

She was delighted when one morning he suggested she should go with him to Hawes.

'I'll drop you in the main street. You can do a bit of shopping and have a look around whilst I go to the auction mart to pick up some business.' He turned to Robert. 'Will you come to the rescue and be babysitter for the morning?'

Robert nodded. Sylvia felt uncomfortable. Was it asking too much of him to look after Otti and the pub? He must have read her mind. 'Don't worry sis. I'll be fine. I can handle any trade there might be with my eyes shut.'

She smiled fondly at her brother. 'Thank you,' she said and left the room to get ready and make sure all eventualities were covered for Otti.

John was quite used to the freedom of leaving the pub responsibilities behind, but she was exhilarated. It was a joy to escape the silken threads of the workhouse web for a short spell. It seemed a long while since her last outing, her disastrous ride on Mr Boyd's horse. As they drove she greedily absorbed the changes in scenery. Each area had its own special beauty. High in the upper reaches of the dale there had been a light flurry of snow giving startling contrasts against a turquoise sky. Reedy grass held crusty, white powder puffs, high on dark green stalks. Sheep shook fingers of ice from their thick, greased overcoats and the sharp, clarity of the streams heralded the oncoming of winter.

They reached the topmost point of the dale. Here winter's warning was repeated, this time advertised by man. The recently erected snow posts stood stark, freshly painted with a mark at one foot intervals showing the depth of drift for any traveller desperate enough to cross that wild top. Sylvia gave a shiver, even the snow barrier fences were in place, ready to drift the white stuff away from the road. The view down the dale was breathtaking. The road, a black snake on a silver bed, followed the contours of the undulating hills, and swept majestically down to Hawes.

They began the descent, a nosedive into oblivion. The car seemed to have lost traction and Sylvia suddenly realised John had turned off the engine.

'John, what are you doing. It's awfully steep, we'll tip over.'

He laughed. 'Don't be daft. We've got brakes. Besides we save petrol. And it's fun.'

'*Fun!*'

Sylvia gasped as she took a grab at anything that came to hand. She was out of control, her body bouncing out of the seat with every bump. Not only was the road steep, but it closely resembled Blackpool's Big Dipper. There were frequent humps, each one hurling her like a rag doll. She knocked her knees on the dashboard, her head on the roof and even her shoe gave up the ghost and flew to the back of the car. There was no way she could stop herself. John had the steering wheel for restraint, but she continued to be thrown into the air. At one particular mountainous bump she defied gravity and was slung so high that her hip touched the roof of the runaway Morris. The louder she screamed, begging him to stop, the more he laughed and crouched over to the windscreen as though urging his charge to fly.

It seemed an eternity before the road calmed down to more gentle contours and then turned to cross the little waterfall at Gayle.

'God, that was hilarious! I thought you were going to bounce forever!'

Sylvia glared at her tormentor, still convulsed with laughter. 'No wonder folk don't like driving with you. Even Cheeky Charlie wouldn't drive back with you last week. Now I know why.'

John looked surprised. 'I'm a good driver.'

Sylvia, feeling exceedingly fraught, snapped. 'You may be fearless and have rapid reactions, but that doesn't mean you're a good driver. Stop here, I'll see you in two hours.' She slammed the door and made for the little café to collect her wits over a steaming mug of hot sweet tea. Gradually her blood flow subsided and her lost sense of humour clambered out of the chasm. She supposed she must have looked a bit of a comedy act, an uncontrolled puppet defying gravity. Even so, a husband shouldn't put his wife through all that. Should he?

Probably he wanted a laugh, though she had the uncomfortable feeling that he wouldn't have treated the fair Jenny that way. Sylvia had a twang of jealously, then quickly buried it. The shops and market stalls beckoned and soon she was absorbed, thoroughly enjoying the rare opportunity to browse and buy.

When John tracked her down, she was loaded with fresh vegetables, special sausages, local cheese and a colourful mobile for Otti's cot.

'Come on, we'll get back home. I've some calls to make in the next dale this afternoon and time's running away.'

She was surprised, she had never known him so keen to get to work and silently sent up a little prayer...Long may it continue, please God.

The journey back was a big improvement, though her racing driver again freewheeled the descent. Fortunately the return drop was not as steep and the switchbacks were absent.

Robert greeted them on the car park. 'I'm glad you're back. Rev. Fullerton's decided that the church boiler has to be fired up a day early. He says the building needs a boost to lift it out of the igloo category. Though the damned thing can't make up its mind whether to explode or die complaining. It could take most of the afternoon to woo it into submission. By the way, your son and heir has devoured a gigantic helping of that turnip and potato mash you left him. Talk about a gannet!'

Sylvia laughed. Thank goodness she had no problems on the feeding front. She tried to tempt Robert to have a sandwich. He refused and went off with a martyred air to meet his argumentative adversary.

It was a couple of hours before he triumphantly marched into the kitchen, well dusted with coke residue. 'She's burning like a good 'un, though it's been a struggle to keep her going. I'll have to pop back at closing time to stoke her up for the night.'

That evening the crowded bar was jumping. Locals from all ends of the dale seemed to home in on the little watering hole, with an early spirit of Christmas in their blood. Time flew and the closing-hour went by unnoticed. The customers had reached that more than happy state when the phone rang. John struggled through the throng to answer the demanding ring. He was so quick replacing the receiver that Sylvia, watching from the kitchen, thought he must have missed the call, then to her consternation, he flew down the passage into the bar calling, 'The police are heading this way. It looks as though we're about to get a lightning raid!'

Robert nearly knocked her over as he bounded into the kitchen frantically grabbing a tray and loading it with cups. 'Quick sis. Make some coffee, we'll put everybody on shorts and coffee.'

'You sneaky thing you. Don't you think the police will smell a rat?'

'I don't know, but it's better than doing nothing. Remember, they've nearly caught us out already and we haven't a hope in Hell of getting rid of everybody quickly.'

She needed no second bidding and soon giggling customers were nursing pale blue cups, quarter coffee topped to the brim with any spirit to hand. They hadn't long to wait before Sergeant Watt's square torso, towering over his sidekick, squeezed through the doorway.

'Now then, what's all this?'

His walrus moustache twitched as he suspiciously viewed the scene before him.

Sylvia swallowed anxiously, but John, all smiles, stood up to greet the local constabulary.

'Good evening Sergeant. You're just in time to join us for a cup of coffee before everyone heads for home.'

Somewhat taken aback, the Sergeant glared at the guilty congregation. If he suspected things weren't what they seemed, he said not a word.

Sylvia, who when nervous developed a bout of verbal diarrhoea, could feel her thoughts bubbling up, until they gushed out in a torrent. 'Sergeant, surely you'll have a coffee. Perhaps you'd care for something in it, you and the constable. I know it's past closing time but...' John kicked her ankle with some force.

She stopped herself from yelping, but still managed to look as guilty as sin. Thankfully, Robert calling her from the kitchen doorway saved her further embarrassment. 'Sis, you've let the milk boil over!'

The excuse let her flee the courtroom with alacrity.

'Oh, thanks, I couldn't stop talking. I didn't leave the pan on the Aga did I?'

Her brother grinned. 'No you idiot, I had to think of some way to get you out before you told the law we'd got booze in the coffee.'

He ducked as a flying missile whizzed past his ear.

'For Heaven's sake sis, keep quiet. We don't want the Sergeant in here. Wait a minute though, I think they're off.'

Sure enough, the suspicious duo were leaving the premises, and as their vehicle started up, the whole room in unison let out an enormous cheer.

Robert let out a wail. 'Oh Lord. I'd forgotten all about the boiler.'

With that he was out of the door, Tilley lamp in his hand. Sylvia watched the bobbing light as he crossed the bridge. The darkness was broken by brief appearances of a shy moon veiled in wisps of cloud. She knew he didn't look forward to going into the church at that time of night and half wondered whether she should join him. Cowardly she decided not to.

She and John washed all the glasses and ashtrays, wiped the tables and put out the lights in the bar before Robert returned.

'You've been ages. Had the boiler gone out?' Sylvia questioned.

'No. But you wouldn't believe what happened.'

She scrutinised her brother. 'You look awful. You're all white and funny.'

Robert gave a snort. 'If you shut up I'll tell you.'

He filled his lungs and let out the air in a blow as though to gather up his slack. John dropped the tea towel on the table and gave his full attention.

'Well. I pushed open the church door and y' know that musty smell of hymn book and damp there is? Well, add in the fumes from the smouldering coke and you get the idea. But at least I knew the boiler was still burning. So I walked to the foot of the tower, down the step, and into the boiler house. There was a lovely bed of glowing coals,' he spread his hands in front of him by way of illustration, 'just enough to take a full load of coke. Was I relieved! I bent for the shovel and...'

'...there wasn't any,' John finished, and he grinned.

'Don't get ahead of me.'

'Oh no,' Sylvia said, looking him up and down for sign of injury, 'you'd have to walk to the outside store through the grave-yard.'

Robert pointed a finger at her. 'In one, but I had the Tilley lamp so how dangerous could it be? Ha! Like a drunken pack of cards, those gravestones were all fighting to trip me up. My shins will be black and blue tomorrow. But I got there, put the lamp on the wall top and grabbed the barrow. I tell you, hearing an owl screeching from in here is nothing compared to hearing one screeching in a bloody yew tree overhead.' Sylvia heard the catch in his voice and she began to feel nervous. John was chuckling now and Robert played to him, waving his arms about. 'Even the Tilley lamp spluttered. I've never filled a barrow so fast in my entire life and wheeled it round to the loading hatch. Job done, I reached for the lamp. But instead of grasping its handle...'

All Robert's movement froze, his hand reaching across the space towards Sylvia, his fingers clawed.

'What Robert? What? You're scaring me half to death.'

Slowly Robert withdrew his arm, turning the still clawed hand in such slow, precise movements that when he brought it up to cover his face, Sylvia brought up her own hand to her mouth and held her breath.

'...my fingers touched... a *thing*,' Robert's body crunched. He waited a moment. 'I thought, good God, it's an alien being. It felt slimy and seemed to be dripping some kind of jelly stuff. I couldn't move. I was struck with terror.'

John stood up. 'You're taking the piss Robert.'

'Be quiet John!' Sylvia said, fearful, yet morbidly eager to find out just what had appeared in the churchyard.

Robert ignored them both. 'My heart was racing so fast I thought I was going to choke. An icy fear crawled through me and my joints seized up.'

'Are you alright now?'

'Yes,' he said impatiently. 'I managed to get enough strength together to pick up the lamp and lift it up high. It threw shadows on the rough stones of the wall top and from behind a jagged lump of limestone came the hiss of...a breathing monster!'

'Oh Robert. What was it?' Sylvia's thoughts immediately turned to Grace and she understood her brother's fear.'

'Shush Syl. Let him finish.'

'Its breath, like white smoke, showed up sharply in the cold night air. I was just about to turn and run when common sense saved me. I thought, the *thing*, has got to be alive, ghosts don't breath. So, with one finger I carefully felt around where the blast of air was coming from. A warmth seemed to be about the apparition. It was alive and very much so.'

'How brave Robert. What was it?'

He gave a rueful grin. 'I suddenly realised what it was. I laughed. It sounded like an hysterical guffaw rattling around the tin hut and bouncing through the night air. I think I frightened the creature to death, for it gave out an ear-splitting wail.'

Sylvia's gaped, awestruck. 'What did it sound like? Tell me. Please Robert.'

'Moo, moo, ooh.'

'No. Oh no. Not one of Mark's heifers!'

'Indeed!'

John, chimed in.

'I'll say one thing for you Robert. You tell a bloody good tale.'

CHAPTER 18

Robert's unnerving experience in the churchyard made Sylvia decide not to clean the holy-of-holies at her usual time of early evening. It was getting darker much earlier and no way did she want to get caught in total blackness. She had told herself not to be foolish, there had been no ghouls when Robert had stoked up the boiler. Nevertheless, a fear had been embedded.

'Robert. I'm going to clean the church this morning.'

'Why? It's only Thursday. Oh. I forgot. There's a funeral tomorrow.'

She too had completely forgotten. The vicar had told her the service would be at two o'clock on Friday. At the time she thought it was a gentle reminder for her to have the place spotless. Now she felt guilty.

'Who's died? It's not one of the locals is it?'

'All I know is that it's someone who used to live in Buckden and then moved away. He wanted to be buried back in the dale. We won't get any trade from it. Apparently, they're going to Skipton for the meal.'

'Well. I better get on with the clean-up. We don't want a scruffy church. Do we?'

Robert started to grin, 'You'd better be careful over there. Henry's digging the grave.'

She was going to say, who's Henry? Then she remembered he was the jack-of-all-trades, for Buckden as well as being the church sexton. She didn't fancy bumping into Henry, the grave digger.

'I just won't look!' She picked up her son. 'Mum's popping out for a while. Let's get you wrapped up warm and outside in your pram. You can watch the sky and the birds.'

She took the white, fur-fabric suit she had made and held it against him, then began to giggle.

'What's up?' Robert leaned over the back of the chair to inspect.

'I think I must have made this for a bloody giraffe. It's far too long. His little feet are miles from the bottom.'

She struggled to dress her wriggling first-born into the ambitious attempt at Eskimo clothing. Pulling the hood this way and that to fit around his ears, then rucking the spare material up his legs, she determinedly zipped him in securely.

'Crikey sis. It's Nanook of the North lost in six feet of fluff.'

'You are so mean, Robert. At least he's warm and cosy.'

'With room to grow!'

Putting on an exaggerated haughty air, she laid the snow prince in his pram. 'I'll leave him just outside the front door. Will you keep an eye on him? He'll be asleep in no time. I'd better get off.'

Collecting her bag of cleaning materials, she left the kitchen with Cassie at her heels. The damp air of early December made her shiver and she pulled her collar up high. A grey mist had descended close to the river, it hovered at knee height giving a ghostly picture. A slight gust of wind came unannounced making the empty stems of nettle and thistle appear as dancing skeletons. She gave a wry smile as the eerie music of Saint Sans, Dance Macabre, came into her mind. Shaking her head, she blamed her mood on Robert and his grave-digging innuendos. There was one thing certain, she had no intention of even glancing at that hole in the ground. John had once told her that it was one Hell of a job digging in the churchyard because the top soil was sparse, and the limestone rocks below were aplenty. Consequently, the old graves were full to capacity with coffins squashed one on top of another.

Reaching the church gate she opened it gingerly. The first thing she saw laid out on the path was a length of sacking piled high with soil. It could only mean one thing, she wouldn't be able to avoid Henry and the eruption on the sheep-nibbled grass. Sure enough, he was digging about a foot from the path. She supposed his task was about finished as only his head and shoulders were visible above the ground. The gate opening must have disturbed him, for he levered himself upright by hanging onto the grassy edge of the excavation. Ah, she thought, he's got an aching back. No wonder if he's been heaving rock.

Unsuspecting, she approached the workings with averted eyes. The sound of his guttural voice startled her.

'Hey missus. Catch!'

Her sixth sense came to the rescue. She dodged, sidestepping the anticipated flying missile. To her relief, Henry had not thrown whatever he'd intended to throw.

'Tha' wa' fooled then. Wa'nt tha'.'

She did feel a little foolish. Obviously, he found her antics highly amusing, by the chortling from the bowels of the earth. His delight had no bounds; he seemed to be gleefully hopping from one foot to the other. Lord above. Was the man on the verge of lunacy? Worried, she wondered whether he might possibly be a bit unhinged. He bent over and started to fumble in the bottom of the hole. Then, standing tall, he held aloft the intended missile. Sylvia couldn't believe her eyes.

On the end of a bent twig balanced a grimy, grinning skull. Her strength left her, this was so wrong. The man held no reverence for the dead.

She was just about to give him a piece of her mind when Cass decided to join in the fun. She launched herself at this strange creature in a hole, and desperately tried to snatch the grisly object from his grasp.

'Cass. Come here. Now!'

Henry acted speedily. In an endeavour to foil Cassie's attack and to appease her horrified owner, he bent low and laid poor 'Yorik' back in the hole. Lifting his face above the parapet he growled, 'Di' na' fret. It'll 'av bin' 'ere two 'undred years or more.'

This did not please the whippet on a mission. In the wink of an eye, she dived smartly into the grave to retrieve the coveted prize, startling Henry, who fell backwards and disappeared. Sylvia could only imagine what was happening in the depths. Muck flew and the grave diggers language became extremely colourful. To

208

her dismay, Cassie was shot airborne and landed on the path in a scrabble looking rather chaste.

Henry's hilarity was quashed. He struggled to get himself upright, turned his back on them both and started to dig.

Sylvia made a supreme effort to pull herself together. Holding her pet's collar tightly she deftly skirted the pile of soil on the path and tried not to look at the gravestones flanking her way. Slowly pushing the church door, she cursed as it squeaked on its hinges in typical thriller fashion. Swallowing, she wished the task facing her could be abandoned. Determined to blank out her fears, she squared her shoulders and marched to the boiler room for the brush and shovel. The brush head was substantial, it was suited to far bigger muscles than hers. Nevertheless, she worked like a demon from Hell. Dust flew to the Heavens. Never had Hubberholme church been licked into shape with such vivacity.

Finally the job was done. She threw the awkward brush into the boiler room, slammed the door and grabbing Cassie by the collar muttered, 'C'mon Cass. Let's get out of here!'

The ancient flags seemed to echo their running footsteps as they made their escape into the open air. Relieved, she took a deep breath, the church was finished with for another week. She hesitated on the stone step, there was still the grave to pass. The thought of the skull, and probably more laid in the rocky bed was not a pleasant picture. Death and its associates had worried her since she was a child. The fear of losing her parents hung in the back of her mind as a half submerged nightmare. As luck would have it, Cassie caused a diversion. She took it into her head to take exception to Henry. He had finished his ghoulish job of work and was busy sweeping the path clean. It was the energetic brushing with a nearly bald yard brush that aggravated Sylvia's pet. With staccato leaps the whippet ferociously attacked the sparse bristles, and quickly succeeded in grabbing a bunch between her teeth. Backside in the air and shoulders low, she shook the implement with such vigour that Henry let go of the handle, blaspheming loudly. In one swift movement, Sylvia seized the brush in one hand and Cassie's collar in the other.

'Sorry.' Her apology was careless and without meaning. She wanted to say, 'It damned well serves you right.'

Handing him his war-torn utensil she frog marched her canine friend out through the gate and across the bridge back home.

Otti's pram wasn't at the door, she guessed he must have woken. She peeped through into the kitchen and was happy to see him laid in the carrycot on the bed settee.

'Has everything been ok Robert?'

'Yes. No customers and Otti has been as good as gold – just hungry.'

'Thanks,' she gave a groan and flopped beside her son. 'Robert, that man, Henry!'

'What now?'

He sounded fed up, but she made no comment. Instead, she launched into the tale of Henry and Yorik.

Robert started to laugh. 'God, sis. You're a super target. You're so bloody gullible.'

'Oh. Charming. I'm sure!'

She strode out of the kitchen and up the stairs with the intention of washing the bedroom windows, starting with Grace's room. Determined not to think about ghosts and the like, she marched in with wash-leather at the ready. Passing Grace's wardrobe, her glance strayed to the long mirror in its door. She saw her own reflection but...behind her she could have sworn she caught a movement!

Not waiting to look, she almost fell out of the room in her haste. Flinging open the kitchen door she called out to her brother, who was on his knees emptying the ash from the Aga. 'That's it! I've had it. Be damned to the windows. I am not going into that bedroom again.'

'What on earth is the matter with you?'

She looked down at her brother. 'It's Grace!'

CHAPTER 19

The tiny Inn was booked to overflowing for the Christmas holiday. Sylvia enjoyed herself immensely in the preparations on the run up to the festive season. She collected unusually shaped branches on her daily walk with Cassie and even resorted to relieving the church yew trees of a few nicely shaped stems, later embellished to adorn the bar and the dining room. The old favourite, remnants of tins of white emulsion, turned winter worn branches into snow-white festoons touched with silver glitter and adorned with glass balls. Dark green fir branches held silver ornaments and the small alcove, under the cases of trout, became the stable for the nativity scene. A Christmas tree decorated with all her childhood trinkets and masses of tinsel reflecting the crackling fire seemed to light up the dining room. She was pleased with the welcoming aura her efforts had given to the place, and eagerly set her sights on the food stakes.

'Robert, I think we should do a Christmas menu for both lunch and dinner over the holidays.'

'Crikey, that's pushing it a bit isn't it? Christmas Eve, Christmas Day and Boxing Day, five full Christmas dinners!'

She ignored his apprehension. 'Christmas Eve we'll have Chicken, bacon, sausage, forcemeat. Christmas Day, Turkey, chestnut stuffing, bread sauce, then Pork, sage and onion stuffing, apple sauce. Boxing Day, Rabbit pie for lunch, and dinner, Goose, potato stuffing, gooseberry sauce. With all the extras of course.'

Robert lifted his eyes to the Heavens. 'Surely you're giving yourself an awful lot of work. All that stuffing, sauces and the rest. Is it going to leave any profit?'

'Oh Robert. Of course it will. Don't be such a misery. It's Christmas!'

'I'll shut up then.'

'Listen. John's back and…he's whistling.'

A smiling John came into the kitchen. 'What's tickled you?' questioned Sylvia.

He started to laugh. 'At long last. I've got one up on Mark. Wait till you hear the story about his exploits on Saturday night.'

Sylvia was all agog. She knew that it really bothered her husband when Mark seemed to know everything John had done, or was in the process of doing, nearly before he did, whilst she and Robert found Mark's gossip prowess a bit of a giggle. She guessed her husband must have some gossip on Mark.

'Well, come on. Spill the beans.'

In between bursts of raucous laughter he managed to spit out his story.

'You know how Mark goes to town every Saturday night to have a drink before he goes on to the dance hall? Well, last weekend he met up with this girl he's been seeing for the past few weeks. After the dance he asked to take her home.'

Sylvia impatiently rushed him on. 'Come on, get to the point.'

'Wait a minute. I'm enjoying this. Anyway, they got to the car park and Mark and the girl climbed into the back of the car and he started to get amorous. What exactly happened is anyone's guess. But, it ended with them both in a compromising position… Mark's foot got well and truly stuck fast under the front seat!'

Robert howled with laughter. But Sylvia's amusement was tinged with concern for her friend. 'Poor Mark. How absolutely awful. How do you know all this? How did he get free?' By this time John had dissolved in a heap on the chair. Tears rolled down his face and he rocked to and fro as laughter tightened his gut.

'Apparently, he managed to wind down the window and shout for help.'

'Oh dear, how embarrassing. Were they stuck there for a while? I feel so sorry for them. They must have felt dreadful.'

John sharply interrupted. 'Couldn't have happened to a better man. He shouldn't have such big feet! Luckily one of his

212

friends heard him shouting and ran to the rescue. I don't know how long it took to free him. But just wait till he brings the milk in the morning!'

Sylvia ventured a small plea, 'Don't you think he's suffered enough humiliation already?'

John grew a couple of inches. 'Blow that for a kettle of fish. He's given me plenty of hassle. Let's see if he can take it.'

The following morning Sylvia made herself scarce. No way did she want to witness Mark's ordeal of being taunted by John. Besides, she told herself, it's a man thing. Deciding the bedrooms needed a blitz gave her the opportunity to take a peek at her friend as he left his tormentors. She heard the goading voice of her better half, and Robert's laughter, but nothing from Mark. Anxiously she waited. Then Mark's hunched shoulders came into view. He didn't look very happy. She always felt a bit sorry for him. That stutter of his and his terrible shyness brought out her protective instinct when he was around. She dashed down the stairs at breakneck speed. 'You've upset him!'

Robert had the grace to look a bit shifty. 'He was ok, sis. He took it well, though he closely resembled a boiled beetroot.'

John stood up to full height. 'Serves him right. Anyway, I'm off.'

Sylvia smiled to herself as the picture of Mark and his girlfriend appeared in her mind. Two sardines in a tin, their moment of romance on view to the world. Sylvia's philosophy in times of stress was that all ills could be cured with food or drink. So a special coffee with a tot of rum would be on offer for Mark the next day. Satisfied, she returned to the Christmas preparations.

The long awaited eve of Noel arrived, along with a cartload of visitors. The six Halifax ladies and the odd two from Leicester were to sleep in the Inn and the couple of unknown doubles were to be farmed out. A nice round dozen of residents plus extra meals booked for each day. Sylvia was anxious until the first Christmas dinner was safely under her belt. Compliments came thick and fast to renew her momentarily flagging confidence. The bar custom swelled, and before they had time to clear the decks in the kitchen, a surfeit of customers spread throughout the downstairs rooms like a measles epidemic. Nowhere was sacred. Young potholers, staying in the next village packed into the kitchen along with a couple of attractive girl students working as waitresses over the holiday. One, a tall Audrey Hepburn look-alike, chatted to Sylvia whilst she made sandwiches, needed by some to mop up gallons of booze. The girl astounded her; the number of sweet sherries she knocked back must have approached double figures, but her conversation never faltered. They were in the middle of discussing the attributes of one particular potholer, who had shown an interest in the girl, when halfway through a sentence she stopped dead. There was no warning flutter or stumbling, she just dropped like a tree pole-axed in its prime. Sylvia gaped. One moment she was talking to a rather beautiful lucid girl, then in a heartbeat, she was gone. Sylvia dashed to where the girl had been standing to find her laid out rigid on the floor.

'Can somebody give me a hand. I don't know what's wrong,' she pleaded to the room in general.

One of the potholers came to the rescue. He bent over the prostrate girl. 'She's just had too much to drink. Far too quickly if you ask me, and probably on an empty stomach. If we get her on the settee she can sleep it off.'

Sylvia wasn't sure about him. What if he was wrong and it was more serious.

'Don't worry I'm training to be a doctor. She'll be ok.'

Feeling a little better Sylvia returned to the sandwiches. She couldn't help wondering how long the girl would be laid out on the bed-settee, her bed. She could see herself having nowhere to lay her aching bones. The boys were to sleep in the bunk beds in the passage room along with Otti's cot and of course, ever other bed was let.

The evening went on with drunken frolicking. There was outrageous flirting from repressed females, released from their inhibitions by the Svengali, alcohol, and the continual nag for food and more food. The ladies that didn't chase the men fell into a category of self-pity. Their tears flowed copiously between frequent slurps of port and lemon. A fog of inebriation allowed a brief admittance that their lives of hard labour held little glitter. The potholers chatted around the horizontal Ophelia as though she didn't exist. And Sylvia watched in sober amusement until the scene was interrupted by Cheeky Charlie's brother, Fred. He pushed his way through the kitchen throng towards her. His normally slack mouth appeared to have lost all control and drooled from either corner in a steady dribble. 'Na then missus, 'as thi 'owt f'or us t'eat?'

She hesitated. 'I'll make you a sandwich, if you like.'

Fred ignored the offer. He'd spied a feast. Sylvia was aghast as it dawned on her just what he was contemplating. At his feet was Cassie's food bowl. During the evening scrapings from the dinner plates had been dumped there in an unappetising heap, topped with a jaundiced fried egg. Fred's eyes shone bright. He sank unsteadily to his knees and grabbed the bowl as though it was manna from Heaven. Clutching his prize close to his chest, he beetled to a corner and eagerly began to devour his Cordon Bleu appetiser. Sylvia tried in vain to explain to him what he was eating, but hunger, greed and a saturation of Youngers best bitter, gave him a barrier he was not about to break. She gave up the fight, mirth took over, and she was quickly accompanied by those sober enough to grasp the situation.

Robert came in from the bar.

'Robert. Look what Fred's eating.'

'Well?'

He appeared to accept Fred's need for food, whatever the source, as quite logical. Sylvia couldn't believe his reaction. She watched him unsteadily roll towards the young crowd in the kitchen, then stutter to a halt as his eyes settled on Ophelia laid out on the sofa-bed. Turning to Sylvia, he shot her an enquiring glance, shrugged, and began dancing a jig. He was obviously ready for any bit of tom foolery that came along. Before she realised what they were about, a competition was under way.

'Who can touch both toes in mid air and land upright?' shouted one of the potholers.

To her horror, the first to step forward was her six-foot-plus brother. Sylvia stepped forward in an attempt to stop him, but too late. She watched in disbelief. He drew in a great breath, squared his shoulders, and with an enormous effort jumped in the air. Two long shanks manfully shot forward, horizontal to the kitchen floor. A pair of flaying arms desperately tried to reach his beer-soaked shoes. He missed by a mile. Sylvia watched in abject horror waiting for the broken bones. He seemed to hang in mid-air, then with a sickening thud he landed on his backside on the stone flags. An assortment of limbs seemed to fill the small space on the floor. She hardly dare look for fear of what she'd see, but surprisingly her stuntman of a brother looked up ruefully and giggled. Thankfully the amount of liquor he must have consumed had given him total relaxation. She sighed with relief. They could do without a lame duck at this stage in the proceedings. Casting a glance round the room she had to smile, there was her brother, Superman's trainee; Fred, Jack Horner in his corner; and Ophelia, still laid out on her bed, yet no one took the least bit of notice.

Bending down to Cassie in her basket, she gently stroked her silken ears. Sylvia smiled, her pet was pretending to be asleep, perhaps a ruse to avoid any contact with the crazy beings in her space. 'I know Cass. They've all gone mad. We're the only sober ones. God knows how on earth I'm to get rid of 'em,' she whispered. But Cassie curled in an even tighter ball and blew her breath out in gentle puffs making her jowls flap. Sylvia sighed, how long would it be before they could clear away the bomb damage the night's merrymakers had inflicted?

A couple of hours passed before everyone was off the premises, including the sleeping angel, who had regained consciousness with a decidedly vacant air. Sylvia couldn't crawl into her bed quick enough, eager to fall into the folds of sleep's insidious shawl.

It seemed only minutes before she awoke to the excitement of Christmas Day, Otti's first Christmas. He wouldn't know much about it, but she was determined to make enough time to be with him to open his presents. All was quiet upstairs, which gave her a worry-free spell to give the calves and pregnant pigs a special breakfast to celebrate the day.

Mark came early with the big order of milk and cream, his romantic ordeal, on the face of it, forgotten.

'Mornin' m m merry Christmas, av' c c cum early, afore y ye get busy.'

She returned the greeting with a quick peck on his cheek. The effect it had on him made her feel embarrassed, and she turned quickly to the Aga. He had blushed a bright crimson.

Busying herself heating the milk and grinding the coffee beans, she managed to avoid looking in his direction until the steaming beverage was ready.

'Happy Christmas Mark. Not only do you get a kiss, but a big mug of rum and coffee as well.'

John, and Robert carrying Otti, came in at that moment. And Sylvia, to put Mark at his ease, carried out the same ritual, a kiss and a rum and coffee for both. She took Otti in her arms, and with Cass at her feet, they all sat round the kitchen table to enjoy a happy few minutes before the onslaught of the festivities began.

CHAPTER 20

Flushed with the success of the Christmas festivities and a swelling of the coffers, Sylvia eagerly awaited the New Year holiday. Admittedly, only New Year's Eve was fully booked, there were no residents for New Year's Day. Perhaps it was a good thing for they had no idea what the Land Letting ceremony would bring. Reverend Fullerton was due that morning to explain the procedure they'd have to follow. Sylvia nattered. 'Robert, what do you think we'll have to do?'

'I'm not sure, but I've asked a few of the locals what goes on and they say we've to put on a free supper.'

'I'd heard the same. I suppose it'll be sandwiches and sausage rolls. It can't really be much else, cos' we won't know how many will turn up.'

'Shut up, sis. The vicar's here.'

Robert stepped forward to open the door. 'Come in, vicar. Would you care for a coffee?'

'Thank you, Robert. That would be very nice.'

He settled himself on the bed-settee and waited until the steaming mug was clasped in his hands. He took a deliberate drink then, in a church-pulpit voice, began the diatribe. 'The dining room has to be kept private for myself and the church wardens. It is given the status of the House of Lords. The public bar becomes the House of Commons. The routine is…during the evening I periodically enter the Commons and take bids for one year's tenancy of the Poor Pasture. On each visit more bids are taken until I am satisfied that we have reached the maximum. Distribution of the rent is for the poor of this parish.'

Robert and Sylvia nodded.

The vicar went on resolutely. 'On completion of the auction, the new tenant of the pasture comes into the House of Lords to sign the necessary papers and produce the money. In case you are interested yourselves in bidding, prompt payment is a requisite.'

Sylvia was annoyed. What was he getting at? They always paid the rent on time.

Robert butted in. 'No thank you. We've got more than enough land for our needs.'

The little man cast a glance at Robert. 'I thought so. Anyhow, at this point in the proceedings a free supper for everyone is supplied by your good selves.'

Sylvia tentatively suggested that sausage rolls and sandwiches would be best. He smiled pityingly and shook his head. 'No. Something substantial dear.'

She was nonplussed. What on earth could she make that would stretch if there were more customers than expected. One thing was certain, she didn't want to have huge leftovers.

Rev. Fullerton studied her puzzled look. 'Now then, Sylvia. I know you'll make a good job of the supper. You'll have a busy night. All good for profit, eh?'

She was about to challenge him when he rose and rapidly left the room with just a brief goodbye.

As his rotund little body waddled down the drive Sylvia stuck out her tongue at the self-satisfied square back. Substantial, eh!

'Sis. You are too bad. What if he'd caught you?'

'It's all very well but what can I make that won't give us waste and cost the earth?'

'You'll think of something!'

That didn't help. Feeling rather hopeless she walked into the outside dairy. There inspiration came to the rescue. On the top shelf sat six, large stone jars of pickled red cabbage. She had forgotten her efforts not to waste the rock hard cabbages Gerald's mum had given her. She'd shredded, salted and spread it out on every available tray and flat dish to start the process. It had seemed as though the red stuff had taken over. She had frequently cursed in a most unladylike fashion until the jars were packed tight, covered with spiced vinegar and sealed. There was certainly enough there to feed an army, and red cabbage went very well with shepherd's pie. That should be substantial enough!

It was amazing how her spirits lifted once the menu had been fixed, but her worries were not completely wiped away. They had been told that the BBC, together with the dailies, were to cover the ancient Land Letting ceremony, and that did trouble her. Never one to be on the front row, she wondered how she could manage to keep a low profile on the day. Both John and Robert seemed to be looking forward to the coverage and she realised it would be good for business, but it didn't stop the butterflies fluttering at frequent intervals. However, they were momentarily quelled with the arrival of the residents; six couples, four in the Inn and the rest farmed out. Some of them had friends in the locality who were to join them for dinner. Sylvia had eagerly accepted the extra meals without much thought, until Robert pointed out that she had taken bookings for twenty-six dinners. 'How on earth can we fit that lot in the dining room?'

'Oh, stop worrying. We'll sort it out. That small settee in there will have to be moved. C'mon Robert, give me a hand.'

They shifted furniture and rearranged tables umpteen times before Sylvia was satisfied. The small settee was unceremoniously dragged out and a folding garden table plonked in its place.

'The settee'll be ok in the barn for tonight. Besides they'll all go into the bar after dinner. Remember, Cheeky Charlie has promised to play his accordion,' soothed Robert. 'I know you hate disarray in your scheme of things. But I'll cover it with an old sheet.'

'That's fine, Robert. I'm more worried about in here. It might look better when the table cloths are in place.'

Quickly they shook out the snowy cloths and set the tables. Sylvia added bowls of fruit decorated with strands of silvered ivy.

'Well, it looks pretty, but it's a bit cramped. Isn't it?'

'It's ok. It's going to have to be. There's no time left, I've dinner to get ready.'

A happy atmosphere bathed the Inn. There was cheerful chatter and banter in the bar, the Aga behaved and kept up its temperature, and dinner was to expectation, the diners filed through the kitchen, eager to tuck into the New Year's dinner. Robert anxiously watched the ever growing number trying to sit in the ever shrinking room. 'Sis, they're awfully short of space in there!'

Sylvia grinned. 'Don't worry, they'll be fine when they start grubbing.'

Robert looked unconvinced, but dutifully marched to and fro with bowls of home-made tomato soup, swirled with cream, accompanied by hunks of warm crusty bread.

'Sis, they're not happy. Honestly they've no room.'

She smiled pityingly at him. 'Don't be silly. They'll be ok. If there's any complaints I'll pop in when the main course is ready.'

Robert presented succulent turkey with all the trimmings, dishes of fresh vegetables and roast potatoes with crispy edges to the waiting flock, but the feast did not seem to work the oracle. 'Sylvia. They haven't room to eat. They are really not happy. I'm not going in there again!'

She was shocked. He had never refused to do the job, no matter what it was. And he only called her Sylvia when he was cross. Quietly she decided she better have a peep and review the situation herself. Standing in the doorway she absorbed the scene. Her guests had become trussed chickens. Packed too tight to lift their wings, they sat viewing the tempting, out of reach feast before them, all, apparently too polite to push and jostle. Their faces were grim, hunger was growling under spotless napkins.

Sylvia gazed. The picture of her diners as farmyard fowl wouldn't go away. The comic scene was too much. She began to gurgle, then outright laughter had its way. 'Oh, I'm so sorry,' she gasped. In unison, there was a shocked intake of breath. The chickens looked aghast. Then slowly a mouth twitched, and gradually the whole room was brought to life in waves of mirth. Each in turn, saw the funny side and joined Sylvia in good humoured joviality. Between her giggles she managed to blurt out. 'Now, you can all enjoy a cuddle with your meal.'

Robert was still anxious when she returned to the kitchen. 'Is everything alright?'

'Don't worry. I reckon they won't forget this New Year's dinner in a long time.' Thankfully the happiness carried on well into the small hours. Drink flowed, Charlie's magic music lifted the spirits and the young year was let through the door with laughter and bonhomie.

New Year's Day was a different kettle of fish. It began with a plethora of thick heads. Sylvia kept very quiet and carried the day through on well-oiled wheels. Her husband and brother were grumpiness personified, performing their tasks at half throttle. She tiptoed round the pair, keeping them clear of the residents, who were also in a somewhat fragile state. They eventually departed after insisting on booking for next New Year. Sylvia was delighted. No one else had ever booked a year in advance.

John and Robert's mood appeared to improve after she had served them with large helpings of bacon and eggs. She hoped they would be on top form in time for *the* ceremony, which she awaited with a certain amount of trepidation. To control the hornets that had taken up residence in her stomach she immersed herself in building a mountain of shepherds' pies.

'Why, there's enough there to feed the five thousand,' marvelled John.

'Aye,' said Robert. 'And if it doesn't we'll be eating shepherd's pie for a week!'

'Look at it this way. If this lot disappears, we'll have had one Hell of a night!'

By seven o'clock the place was heaving. The BBC transit van was parked at the front door. It regurgitated miles of cables, strange futuristic pieces of equipment and isolated young men, their well-modulated tones lapsing as they struggled with the pub dimensions. Sylvia took on the mantle of the invisible man and merged with the pie mountain and baking bowls of crisp, red pickle. She stiffened as Robert called her, fearful of being dragged out of the dark into the limelight.

'For Heaven's sake sis, anyone would think you were off to the gallows. Stop worrying. They can't get their equipment through the door, so all they're doing is commentating on the proceedings. No interviews.'

She felt elated, now she could enjoy the evening. Humming, she popped up to the bunk room to make sure Otti was ok and that Cassie was still in place on the bottom bunk. It was her job for the evening to play guard and be out of the way of the impending chaos. Returning to the kitchen she had to clamber over cables and pieces of apparatus at the foot of the stairs. The bar door was propped open, revealing a smoke-filled heaving cavern that was once a cosy little room. She guessed the multitudes would soon be overflowing into the kitchen. Sure enough, as she opened the kitchen door new arrivals followed in her wake.

Rev. Fullerton and the churchwardens reigned supreme in isolated splendour. The three of them had the luxury of a crackling fire, stacks of space, comfortable seating and waitress service. It seemed incongruous that they had the biggest room when every square inch of the bar, the minuscule entrance, and half the kitchen held a multitude of steaming, jovial bodies with hardly room to lift a glass to quench their festive thirst. The poor vicar had a tortuous journey each time he braved the throng to thread his way to the Commons to take bids. As the evening progressed, his intake of his favourite whisky began to take effect. At one stage, John had to rescue him from the foot of the stairs where he had been surrounded by an army of drunken jokers, backed up by the BBC recording armaments. Slumped on the bottom stair, his cassock bunched round his knees, with his wellpolished army boots set in a retreat mode, he looked as though he was about to escape up the stairs. His spectacles had surrendered, they swung desperately on one ear, the milk bottle lenses magnified the grey stubble on the God-fearing chin.

'Oh dear,' whispered John as he raised the reluctant cleric to his feet, 'I think it might be an idea if you made this the last call for bids. Agreed?'

Rev. Fullerton manfully dragged himself into the land of the living, straightened his spectacles, smoothed the black cloth over his rotund belly and nodded in agreement. John helped him to the doorway supporting his wilting frame whilst he took the final bid. It was made by a local farmer nicknamed Pudding, from close to Lord Markham's place. A small, wiry, silent man, his hands were plunged deep in his pockets, and with head bent he followed John and the vicar into the House of Lords to pay his dues.

223

This was the wake up call for Sylvia. Drinking was forgotten. Food became the number one priority and she, along with John and Robert, girded their loins and began feeding the five thousand. The pace was nonstop. It seemed an eternity until all were appeased. They were just about to take a breather when a couple of fellows pushed their way to the Aga. 'Missus, tis hungry we are, is there any more?'

At first Sylvia was puzzled. She couldn't quite recognise the lilt in the man's voice and they had a different look about them. Then it dawned on her, it was an Irish accent. They wore the ubiquitous collarless flannel shirts and the well-worn navy waistcoats, but their flat caps, still in place, sat at a jaunty angle with the peak at the back. She felt sorry for them. They had that hunted look of souls who had long been deprived of sustenance and succour. Silently, she scraped out a couple of dishes and managed two reasonable helpings. The men, spoons at the ready, attacked the potage with the desperation of the inmates of Newgate Prison. Sylvia had never seen the like of it. John, watching the scene, smiled. 'Close your mouth Sylvia. It's rude to stare.' He squeezed past her and began to talk to the pair.

The night wore on. Midnight came and went. Robert absent-mindedly counted the assortment of empty plates as he loaded them for washing. 'Do you realise we've served more than eighty meals, and that's not counting sandwiches.'

'Gosh. Eighty odd helpings of shepherds' pie and not a spoonful left. Now, that's what I call a good guess,' Sylvia said with relish.

'Yes. And everyone's full and happy. Especially the vicar,' laughed John.

'I'd better see the old lad home. He won't be in a fit state to get back on his own.' Robert left the kitchen to quickly return. 'Gerald's father has beaten me to it. He and the vicar apparently sneaked out of the dining room door. There's only Anthony in there and he's ready for off.'

John came in from the bar. 'I'm worried over the state of Cheeky Charlie. He couldn't find his car on the car park and it was the only one left! Other than Anthony's tractor!'

He returned, dragging the somewhat awkward musician into the kitchen. 'He'd better have a black coffee. Though I doubt it'll have much effect.'

Charlie stumbled over anything and everything in his path before dropping like a rag doll on the kitchen floor. John shook him and forced the strong black drink down him in protesting gulps.

Sylvia was worried that the lure of the river where it flirted with the twisting road would draw him into the swirling waters. 'Charlie, don't you think you should stay here tonight?'

'Di'na worrit thi 'sen. Mi' fa'ther gits in wi' mi an' sees mi 'ome.'

She felt a bit easier. Perhaps his father lived in the next hamlet. After another mugful of the brew, they somehow managed to get him upright, nearly carried him to the car park where they lodged him behind the wheel of his ancient car. Standing in the cold night air they watched the car's meandering progress until it was out of sight, then reluctantly returned to the battleground waiting to be attacked. Chatting, the three of them cleaned the decks, still on a high from the successful night.

'I didn't know Charlie's father lived near here,' Sylvia murmured.

'Where have you got that idea from? He's six feet under across in the churchyard. Been there for years.'

'Oh, but Charlie said he got in the car with him to help him home when he'd had too much to drink!'

Robert gleefully teased her. 'It must be his ghost!'

She bit her lip. Ghosts were not often far from her thoughts these days. There was Grace and now Charlie's father. John sensing his wife's unease, rapidly changed the subject. 'You remember the two fellows who had second helpings at supper? Well they came over from Ireland to get work here at the hiring-day in the market. Pudding took them on for hay-time, but he's kept them on, though the poor things have to sleep in a barn! You'll never guess what he gives them for breakfast? One hard boiled egg between the two. Half an egg each!!'

Sylvia was astounded. 'Oh deary me. No wonder they did an Oliver Twist on us. This Pudding fellow must be a greedy so and so. Isn't it odd, most of the locals would give you their last crust.'

'You always get one rotten apple in a barrel. C'mon it's time for bed.'

In spite of being dog-tired Sylvia couldn't sleep. When she finally succumbed it was just one hour before the alarm clock stepped into action. She woke feeling strangely disturbed. Frightening dreams had plagued her slumbers. But, worst of all, in one of the nightmares, Mr Birch, Anna's father, had died.

A depressed feeling hung over her as she rose and the heaviness wouldn't lift as the morning wore on.

Robert called her to come for a coffee. Leaving her duster and polish in the dining room she joined him in the kitchen just as the phone rang.

'Drat it. The damned thing always rings when you don't want it to.' He picked up the receiver and answered the call in monosyllables. Something was wrong. Sylvia felt cold.

Robert, slowly and carefully put down the instrument.

'Sorry sis. I'm sorry, but that was Peggy. Mr Birch died early this morning.'

Chapter 21

The contrast between the happy mayhem of the Christmas festivities and the bleak absence of any custom in the raw weeks of late January was the most sobering blow the three of them had yet received. Any caller was an event in itself. Some days not one being crossed the threshold. Sylvia regularly sent thanks to the gods that John was employed and seemed to be holding down the job quite happily. Without his regular contribution they would certainly be tramping down queer street. To make things appear even more Dickensian, the snow came. It started after a mournful drizzle of a day that held no warning of what was to come. Evening prepared for night with a strange quietness. The damp air was slowly driven out by the long fingers of Sir Frost, leaving a steel blue sky to show off brilliant stars that glittered in competition. The first few snowflakes were hardly noticeable, they lazily floated to earth and nonchalantly settled on the waiting hamlet.

Sylvia stepped out into the night air to check Ariane, who was close to producing her first litter of piglets, when she noticed the flutter of snow. Smiling to herself, snow always gave her bubbles, she reached round the door to grab her jacket just in case her visit might take longer than a quick peep. They had moved her favourite sow into the barn adjoining the house to be handy for when she gave birth. Her sister, Genevieve, was due at a later date, so remained in the little sty next to the dairy across the drive. Sylvia happily opened the barn door eager to give Ariane a cuddle and the apple she had popped into her apron pocket from the bowlful on the kitchen table. She hesitated at the entrance. Something was wrong. There was a strange atmosphere, it was cold, unusually cold. She listened, soft moans were coming from the pile of straw in the corner, punctuated by the tiniest of squeaks. The yellow beam from the powerful torch clutched tight in her hand swept round the area. Sylvia gasped. She couldn't believe her eyes. The place looked more akin to the battle of the Somme rather than an innocent baby unit. She had difficulty taking in what had happened, then realisation crept in. 'Oh my poor girl. Nobody told you what to expect. I know. I know.' Dropping to her knees, she closed her arms round the great head of Ariane, whose eyes were dimmed and unseeing. Urgently tucking more straw round her charge, she soothed her with gentle promises of a nice warm feed. Her heart raced and panic almost won the battle over self-control as she viewed the scene of devastation. Shot haphazardly all over the cold stone floor, were still, pitiful, little piglets, their tiny bodies tinged with blue. It was obvious the poor pig had no idea what was happening to her as she began to give birth. She must have charged round the barn in a frenzy of fear, dropping her babies willy-nilly.

Sylvia's emotions were in chaos. She related to the sow's experience. It wasn't so long since she was in the same situation, but she had a mother and nurse Brown to ease the way. Anxiously, she rushed round the barn gathering up the corpse-like babies in her apron, holding the corners in a steel grip to keep them safe in the dash back to the kitchen.

'Robert! John! Get me a clean towel and open that bottom Aga door.'

Without explanation she bunched the towel with one hand into the bottom of the oven and reverently laid the apparently dead litter in the gentle heat of the slow cooker.

'Robert, pass me a bucket, quick!'

'Sis, for God's sake slow down. Is Ari' ok?'

Sylvia gabbled her tale of woe as she half filled the bucket with hot water and a packet of Scott's porridge oats. 'Father always gave this to tired horses, I'm going to give it to Ari.' The sentence disappeared with her through the door.

She held the tempting gruel under the traumatised sow's nose. There was a weak grunt, then, to Sylvia's joy the reluctant mum began to slurp. With her nose well immersed in the sloppy feed she slowly emptied the bucket in noisy relish. Thank the

Lord, breathed Sylvia as she tucked more straw between Ariane's back and the wall. She gently stroked, the now more peaceful animal, then hurried back to the kitchen. There to her delight, seven of the eight offsprings had recovered.

'It's terribly cold in the barn, I don't think they'll survive in there.'

Robert looked askance at his sister. 'You can't keep them in here, they'll need a feed. They've got to go to their mum. I tell you what. We'll light the Tilley lamp and hang it from the beam. It should be safe and it does give off a little bit of heat as well as light.'

No sooner said than done. John worked the oracle on the tricky lamp and led the way to the barn with Sylvia and Robert carrying seven hungry piglets. Ariane was not renown for her liking of men, and she made this abundantly clear as they approached. She let out sharp grunts of anger and threatened to charge. Sylvia stepped towards her. 'Ari. Ari. Look here's your babies.'

The new mum made soft noises and dropped on her side in the bed of fresh straw. The sound of her babies and the feel of the small bodies on her giant belly settled her. Soon eager mouths found the milk bar and Ariane accepted motherhood gracefully. The rescuers stood watching the rewarding scene until cold began to strike through their bones.

'It's so cold in here.' Sylvia was worried the piglets might not make it through the night after all her efforts.

'There's a couple of old doors at the back of the coach house. I'll get 'em. We can enclose them in a bit tighter. It should make things warmer.' Robert was out of the building in a flash.

'Help him, John,' Sylvia snapped, anxiety uppermost.

It wasn't long before a temporary sty was rigged across the corner of the barn, ingeniously held together with baler-twine.

'We'd better flatten the straw in front of Ari so the babies don't get lost.'

'No sooner said than done sis.' Robert, on hands and knees pressed the golden bed flat as he manoeuvred the sleeping piglets close to Ariane's rosy belly. 'There. They should be fine now. I'll pop back in an hour to make sure all's well.'

The three of them were surprised when they stepped outside. The drive was covered in more than an inch of snow. That wonderful eerie silence, the partner of first snow, cocooned the little hamlet. Sylvia skipped to the doorway, kicking a fluff of snow in fairy showers before her, ecstatic that all had turned out well. The snow had come as icing on the cake.

A couple of hours later Sylvia and her brother checked the piggy family. All was quiet. 'We better turn off the Tilley lamp. If it blows out, the fumes are pretty horrid. We won't take any risks. Eh?'

'Will the babies be warm enough?'

'Course they will. C'mon.'

They tiptoed outside, it was still snowing.

'Perhaps it will snow all night. Perhaps we'll get snowed in.'

'Not very funny, sis.'

Morning brought Lapland to the dale. Sylvia, first to rise, marvelled at the total whiteness broken only by the top of the grey stone walls and the odd blackened tree nursing pillows of frosted snow. The bridge parapets were cushioned with thick soft marshmallow. Below, the busy waters had taken on a hint of glacier green and icy edges adorned the dark rocks. She absorbed the stark beauty until her delight was shattered... they were snowed in! The road was impassable... no customers... no deliveries of provisions for the pub, themselves, or the animals. Concerned, she set off like a jackrabbit, snow flying over the tops of her wellies as she bounded into the dairy where they kept the sacks of provender for the pigs and calves. She hastily scanned the shelves and the floor space where the proven was kept. They'd just had a delivery, so the animals were ok. Food for the family was a bit sparse. The first shortage would be meat, but that wasn't too bad, there were a few tins of corned beef on the top shelf. A couple of hams hung from the beam. They would be a last resort, the customer came first, even though it appeared extremely unlikely there would be any knocking at the door for a while. Both bottled gas and coke for the Aga was well in hand. She breathed a sigh of relief. Little Otti's food was no problem, he had refused, with the stubbornness of a planted mule, ever to eat any of the specialised baby foods. He much preferred mashed vegetables, potato and gravy. Luckily, potatoes and carrots were in plentiful supply.

Robert called her from the doorway. 'Sis, what are you doing?'

'Only checking our food store. We're snowed in. I think we'll be alright for a good few days on the food front.'

'Is the road blocked then?'

'The snow is nearly as high as the wall tops. If it's a drift it looks to extend well past the vicarage.'

She looked anxiously at the sky. It looked full of snow and there was a hint of a wind brewing.

'Listen.' Robert straightened to full height, his ear cocked to catch the sound. 'It's the snow plough. We're going to be opened up!'

Looking down the drive they saw a grey Fergie tractor, with a V-plough mounted on its nose coming slowly towards them. It banked the powder snow on either side of a narrow passageway to give a way through to the Inn, the church, and Mark's farm. Henry was driving. As the hero of the moment Sylvia forgave him for his churchyard antics. 'Would you like a cuppa Henry?'

The dour, grizzled face broke into a rare smile. He raised his hand in thanks, parked his steed and was soon installed in front of the Aga with a large rum and coffee. He spoke quietly to Robert. Sylvia kept out of the way. He didn't stay long and was soon forging a path over the bridge to let the milk lorry pick up the daily supply waiting in churns at the farm gate.

As soon as Henry was out of ear shot, Robert let out a great whoop. 'Guess what? I've got a job!'

'What?'

He grinned, a Cheshire cat cheesy grin. 'Henry wants me to be with him on the tractor during the snow spell. Apparently two men are needed and the fellow who usually does the job is working full-time. I've said, yes. You'll be ok. Won't you? There'll hardly be any custom as long as we've got snow. And when it goes the job finishes.'

Sylvia felt a great surge of relief. They so needed extra cash and she'd be fine on her own. She couldn't help wondering how

John would react to the news. Would he be worried about her being alone?

John surfaced as Henry was making his return path back to Buckden to ensure the road was kept open. Sylvia had to smile, her beloved, always one to dress for the occasion, was wearing thick white, sea-boot stockings pulled up high and neatly turned over at his knees. An Aran sweater of oiled wool with a deep rolled, polo neck completed the Scott of the Arctic ensemble.

'You look ready to face the elements, John,' said Robert, with just a hint of a smirk.

'Yes, Robert. Be prepared. That's what I say.'

'Are you intending going to work?'

'Of course. It's Skipton market day. I heard the snowplough, and the road seems passable. The other ploughs will have been out lower down the dale. So it should be clear to Skipton.'

Sylvia, unable to keep quiet any longer, butted in. 'John, Robert's got a job.'

John listened. He readily agreed they could do with some extra income to make up for the lack of trade, especially with the weather as it was. But there was no concern for the prospect of Sylvia being alone with Otti, the pub and the livestock. She was flattened. A skivvy, that was what she had become.

The days that followed were lost in snows of blizzard proportions. The plough, manned by the two Sherpas, spent all their time keeping the road open as far as the Inn and Mark's gateway. Higher up the dale had to be left. It had been known for the topmost farms to be snowed in for six weeks at a time, and it looked as though history could be repeated. Then, unannounced, there was a break in the weather. The snow stopped falling, the temperature increased a few degrees, the sky cleared and a welcome glow from a weak, but determined sun, lit the whitewashed landscape. It gave the opportunity for the grey Fergie and its handlers to endeavour to make a way through to Yockenthwaite where Anthony and Thomas lived. Sylvia watched them set off. The wall of snow just beyond the car park was reluctant to succumb to the advances of the plough. But the determination of the old tractor, and with the persistence of its occupants, the wall of white relented. They moved in fits and starts. Sylvia couldn't believe they would succeed, but they seemed to make steady progress.

With Otti in her arms, she decided to take a quick peep at Ariane. Both mum and babies looked as happy as pigs in the proverbial. For no reason, she thought it would be a good idea to have a look at Genevieve. To her surprise, as she peeped over the half door into the sty, she saw her second porker was in labour. There was no panic this time. Genevieve appeared to be handling things really well; perhaps Ari' had sent over a few hints from across the drive. Sylvia popped Otti into his pram wrapped up warm and returned to help the new mum-to-be. An hour and a half and six piglets later she was puzzled. The little piglets seemed distressed and were not feeding as they should. Warily, she knelt beside her charge and gently tried to extract milk from several of the teats. Nothing came. Oh Lord. I don't think you've any milk for your babies! Uncertain of what to do, she wondered if Mark or Gerald might help. Mark was the nearest, it wouldn't take him a minute to come over. Closing the sty door, and with a quick check on Otti, she hurriedly crossed the bridge to find Mark. He was hosing down the milking parlour when she found him. ' nah then, w what's up?'

She poured out her troubles. Instead of ridiculing her for being a clucking hen, he sympathetically told her to go back and ring the vet. 'E'll be able t t' tell thi what's amiss.' She obeyed and rushed back across the bridge. The snow squeaked under her feet, the sound seeming to add to the urgency. Reaching for the telephone she noticed her hand was shaking. Fortunately, Tally, the vet, answered; more often than not it was his wife who was on the other end of the line. In a gabble she gave him the details. He calmed her down in his soft Scottish accent of the lowlands.

'There'll be nay trouble to get the sow to give milk, but there is a problem in getting the drugs across to ye. The road is well and truly blocked.'

Tally's practise was based in Wensleydale. He would have to come through Bishopdale and over the top to Cray.

'I'm sure I can get most of the way, but Kidstones is where it gets impassable.'

Sylvia was silent, not really knowing how to answer. She held him in high esteem; he was so kind and capable and put up with her worries.

'I tell you what we can try. I'll drive as far as I can on this side, then if at all possible, I'll climb up to the top. If Robert or John can do the same on your side, we should meet somewhere up there. Can you get one of them and we'll arrange a plan?'

Her mind worked at top speed. 'John isn't here at the minute, but Robert can do it. I'll take the details to him, he's over the road just now.'

Tally seemed uncertain, then agreed to leave things for her to arrange. They fixed an approximate time to hopefully meet, she thanked him and gently replaced the phone. Her mind raced. Perhaps Gerald's mother would look after Otti. The pub could be locked up. The piglets would die if she didn't do the job herself. Her hand reached out to lift the receiver when a sound filled her with hope. Could it be? It was. The throaty growl of Henry's tractor announced its coming with a huge back-blast as it slowed to a crawl to give Robert time to jump off safely. Sylvia waved as it passed under the kitchen window.

'Hi sis. We can't get through the dip near the poor pasture, it's drifted too deep. The tractor won't take it, so we've had to knock off for the day.'

She hugged him. 'I'm so glad to see you.'

He stepped back in surprise at his sister's explosion of affection. 'Now what have you done?'

She frantically told him of Genevieve's family's plight.

'Damnation. Henry's gone. I could have ridden with him to Buckden. The road's been cleared from there to Cray.'

'How about Gerald? He might give you a lift in the Land Rover as far as Cray.' Sylvia was beginning to worry, time was disappearing and Tally would be on his way.

'I'll get going. Pass me a bar of chocolate, Sylv. I don't know how long it's going to take.'

Sylvia watched her brother stride out down the road, then urgently rang Gerald's number. His mother answered. Apparently Gerald was cleaning out the hen-hut in the front paddock next to the road. Hopefully, he would see Robert when he reached the Grange. Sylvia wished John would come home. Waiting alone seemed endless. It was difficult to concentrate on any job, however mundane.

It was almost dark when she heard Gerald's vehicle draw up to the door. The time had dragged and her imagination was in overdrive. At worst, she'd had both Robert and Tally dead in snowdrifts or lost in a white wilderness. Her fears had been exaggerated by John's absence. As usual, he was late. Relief flooded through her at the sight of her brother's tousled head appearing through the door. 'Oh Robert. Thank God you're back safe and sound. Did you manage to meet Tally? Is Gerald coming in?'

'No. Gerald's gone home, and, yes, I met Tally. And here's the stuff for the pig.'

Sylvia noticed he was too tired to even say Genevieve. 'Sit down. I'll make you a drink while the soup's warming through. It's an injection for Genevieve?'

'Yes, and I'd better do it now before you feed me.'

'I'll have a go,' she said feebly, hating the thought of plunging the needle into the sow.

'Give it here. We all know you're squeamish when it comes to inflicting pain.' He grabbed the syringe and wobbled through the kitchen and out of the door. Sylvia followed feeling decidedly inadequate and waited at his side until the job was done. Robert groaned as he straightened from his crouch. 'Tally said that it would work straight away.'

'You get back inside Robert. I'll hang on a minute until they start to feed.'

She made sure that the milk had begun to flow, and marvelling at modern science, she flew back to the kitchen to feed her weary brother.

He was sitting up close to the Aga, his wet clothes in a heap beside him. He looked awfully pale. She filled a bowl full to the brim of the soup she had prepared during the long wait. 'Get this down you. You'll feel a lot better with something inside.' Cautiously she asked. 'Did you find each other easily?'

'If you wait while I've finished this I'll tell you.'

She plied him with more bread and soup and somehow managed to keep schtum.

Robert stretched his legs. 'I bet I'm stiff tomorrow.'

'Have a hot bath…when you've told me how you went on!'

'Ok. Ok.' He smiled. 'Well. I was worried. I knew I'd be up against it if Gerald wasn't around. But, as luck would have it, he was cleaning the hen-hut in roadside meadow. He came to the wall to have a chat. But when I told him what was going on he was full of concern. He seemed to think he had a kind of responsibility for the sow.'

Sylvia butted in. 'Why?'

'He did breed the damned thing, remember?'

He went on. 'Gerald got the Land Rover out and we drove down the narrow alley the snow plough had made to Buckden. The climb up to Lord Markham's spot proved a bit of a hazard. The road was well rutted. The view up there looked like the North Pole.'

'You could have done with a sled and a team of dogs.'

'Aye. The old lass coughed and skidded, but managed to get up that really steep bit. When we got to the pub at Cray, I thought I'd die. From thereon it was as though there had never been a road. A ferocious icy wind nearly took the car door off its hinges and snatched the breath from my mouth. I could hardly breathe and I felt as though I'd no clothes on. It found every minute gap, even blew in at the zip on my bomber jacket under my duffle coat!'

'Good God. It's a wonder you're here at all.' Sylvia leaned forward and touched his shoulder. 'Thank Heaven.'

He patted her hand. The gesture was her father's, and for some unexplainable reason her eyes filled with tears.

'You wouldn't have believed it, sis. The horizon and sky merged into one. The only way you could tell where the land ended and the sky began was where odd outcrops of limestone broke out. They looked as though they had been sculptured into strange forms. I tell you it was an alien panorama, totally unrecognisable to the view we had in the spring last year.'

'It was beautiful then.'

'I was just thinking that it was degrees colder up there and likely to drift like mad when Gerald made my day.'

'What did he say. He didn't leave you?'

'No. No. He said, 'Tha'd better git a move on. Thee an' vit'nary could be in trouble if tha's not quick. I'll wait in t'pub for thee'.'

Sylvia laughed as Robert mimicked his friend.

'Stop it sis. I won't go on if you're going to laugh.' He took a deep drink from his mug. 'I began the climb towards the topmost point, hopefully following the general direction of the road somewhere beneath several feet of snow. My nose dripped and froze, my eyes smarted. It was not funny. I was glad to be still wearing my work outfit. That Norwegian woollen hat you bought me was pulled well down over my ears. It did give some protection and I swear, if I hadn't been wearing the sheepskin gloves, I'd have got frostbite. The main problem was the drifting snow. In some places it was already deeper than my wellies and the snow melted and soaked down into my socks.'

'You'll get king-cough, Robert. Have you changed your socks?'

'Course I have.' He bent down and picked up a scruffy pair of sea-boot, foot-warmers and hung them haphazardly over the Aga rail. Sylvia wanted to chastise, they needed washing but she kept her mouth tight shut.

His words began to slur a little. 'The climb was hard. My breath came in short gasps and it seemed to freeze in a cloud. I struggled, by Hell, I struggled. My legs went to lead. At one stage I stumbled over a hidden rock and slithered down a glass-like precipice. Guess what it was?'

'Oh, Hell Robert. Not the waterfall?'

'Exactly. The waterfall. I'd left the road entirely. Fear gave me strength. No way did I want to slip down a half solid, long drop into the deep pool waiting at the bottom. I fairly clawed at the rock, dug my boots into the crust of snow and ice and drawing on every ounce of strength, managed to drag myself to safety.'

Sylvia gazed open-mouthed. 'You've been so lucky. Do you realise you could be dead?'

237

'Don't be so melodramatic. You would have laughed. There I was on all fours, with just enough breath to curse, when to my amazement a voice called out. "Robert, is that you?" I lifted my head and there, unbelievably striding towards me was a figure walking with a strange gait. It was Tally!'

'Gosh. He'd made good progress, hadn't he?'

'He was wearing snowshoes. Admittedly, fairly ancient ones, but they'd done a good job. He'd travelled at twice my speed. We met and hugged each other, laughing noisily. He had a hip flask. By Hell it was strong stuff, it certainly warmed the cockles. We both had a couple of swigs. He gave me the injections then we said our goodbyes.'

'Shouldn't we give him a call to make sure he got back alright?'

'I'll do it now.'

Robert returned smiling. 'He's fine. He was just about to sit down to a meal. I tell you what, sis. There's not many men would have done what he did. Especially for a measly sow.'

'We'll give him a bottle of whisky when he comes over next. And Gerald. It was good of him to wait for you. Ariane is not a measly sow.'

CHAPTER 22

There was no more snow that week, much to the relief of the threesome. Henry and Robert had managed to get the plough through as far as Mr Boyd's Manor house, and he lost no time driving to the Inn for his phone calls. John had been able to call on most of his customers, though some in the higher more remote spots were still held captive by the drifts. Sylvia worried for these families in their snowbound capsules. It had been only a few years earlier when a child had died of pneumonia after several weeks of being stranded. She was concerned about the sheep, often buried in deep drifts, and the dogs and shepherds who risked all to search for their desperate flock. Mark had carried an old ewe across his shoulders from the top of the fell behind the farm. The poor creature was near to death's door, but was saved by the warmth of a cosy barn. As Sylvia had watched Mark stumble through the deep snow she realised how dangerous this deceptive white beauty could be.

She was particularly relieved that the road had been kept open as a funeral for a lady from away, an Elizabeth Robins, had been booked and deliveries of stores were needed to cater for the fifty or so expected mourners. A light buffet was requested, which she would be able to manage on her own, though the bar side could end up as a bit of a problem if it turned out to be an up-dale style wake.

She was in the midst of baking sausage rolls, meat pies and an assortment of cakes, whilst a ham simmered on the Aga top and a great sirloin of beef sang and spat in the oven. The air was full of provocative aromas.

'My, there's some good smells in here.' The voice from the doorway was as welcome as a fox in a hen coup.

'Mr Boyd. You gave me a jolt. Do you want to use the telephone?' She looked at him with some impatience; he was interrupting her busy workload, and besides she didn't like the man.

'I will use the phone, but my main reason for calling is to invite you and John to dinner tonight.'

Her mind went into overdrive. The last thing in the world she wanted was to trail to the top of the dale and dine with him! 'Oh dear. I'm so sorry, but we've a funeral tomorrow lunchtime and I haven't finished preparing.'

Undeterred, he ignored her excuse. He would have none of it, and put her in the position of feeling rude if she made any more protests. No wonder he had been a captain of industry if he used these bulldozing tactics to get his own way. His poor clients wouldn't stand a chance. She felt aggrieved. All that way to dinner, especially after putting Otti to bed. She had, though, told a fib. The preparations were just about finished for the day, no more could be done until morning. At last he departed, fat and smug; he'd got what he wanted.

When John came home he was delighted with the invitation and Sylvia, perhaps unkindly, decided her better-half secretly enjoyed to hob-nob with the so called top-drawer lot. She reluctantly went through all the necessary motions to prepare for the visit, ending as a grumpy companion to her jocular husband on a journey through a snow-shrouded dale.

The half moon sat on its back in a ring of mist, suspended in a troubled sky. Its light reflected the whiteness of the hills and valleys climbing relentlessly before them. Walls and rocks cast soft shadows in the moonlight, giving a ghostly aura to the beautifully dressed landscape.

They left the main road to twist and climb over the top to Hawes and turned off onto the gated road to the manor. Sylvia was concerned, the track was just wide enough to allow the car through a narrow channel cut by the snowplough. A wall of snow, nearly as high as the window top, encased them on both sides. A white, gun barrel of a run stretched ahead in the yellow headlights. It finally opened out to a flat moonscape, broken only by a snow-crusted wall and a drunken gate. She stepped out, at this first, and hopefully only, closed gate, thankful she had put on her short wellies. They reached to mid-calf, but at least her shoes were kept dry in the car. It was difficult to open the gate, snow had bunched in front of the bottom bar and left behind a pristine arc of white iced cake. She would have liked to have left the gate open ready for their return, but country code won the battle. A hook dangled at the end of a bit of frozen chain, a rusted apology for a fastening, stuck to her quickly freezing fingers as she struggled to secure the gate. Quietly cursing, she turned into the breeze and felt soft spots of moisture on her face. Oh Heavens, surely it wasn't snowing. Perhaps it was just blowing in the wind... but no, the sky was a backdrop to floating spots of lace. 'John, it's started to snow.' She tried to rub warmth back into her numbed fingers. 'Will we be alright?'

John spoke before she could ask whether they should turn back. 'Don't be silly. Course we will.' And drove on.

Sylvia, hunched into the seat, wondered if this man beside her really cared about her well-being. Surely, they were dicing with danger going on in these conditions? The place wasn't exactly hospitable, or even safe. People had been lost in better weather than they were experiencing. She started to feel uneasy, especially when they passed Jenny's home. No lights were visible; she must still be away in Lancaster, or wherever. Her husband, Nobby, would probably be busy with the Mr Boyd's sheep. In contrast, lights blazed at the big house.

Puzzled, Sylvia asked, 'There's no electricity up here. So how come they've got so much light?'

'Because, my dear girl. There's a generator out-back that supplies all the power they need.'

Alex Boyd, bathed in the luxury of electric light, stood in the doorway waiting for them.

'Come in. Come in.' He bustled them through the wide front door, hung their coats on the ugly hallstand and placed their wellies in the boot room. 'Through the second door John, we'll go straight in to dinner.'

Sylvia popped on her shoes and dutifully followed, with the lord of the manor hard on her heels. She almost fell over in shock. Her walk down the passage was assisted by a handful of her left buttock clutched in his meaningful grasp! A rapid half-turn released the stranglehold. She entered the dining room stiff-backed and decidedly unbalanced to greet the man's wife. Silently, she gave thanks for her ability to hide her true feelings and managed to put on an unconcerned face for the sake of Marian Boyd. No wonder the little mouse of a woman looked so downtrodden if this was what she had to endure. With false gaiety Sylvia managed to get through the mediocre meal and somewhat disturbing conversation that sent everything else into oblivion. It continued when they moved to the sitting room for coffee. Mr Boyd gleefully told the tale of escapades at his tennis club before he left the London area. Apparently, over the latter years, a cult had developed with a taste for wife-swopping on a regular basis. 'We'd throw our car keys on the table at the end of our monthly club dinner,' he boomed in anticipation, 'and the 'ladies' would chose a set. And then...'

John was smiling. Sylvia wasn't, she'd an idea what came next. She glanced at Marian, who had kept very quiet, but she flushed, pushed back her chair, and escaped to the kitchen on some pretext or other. Her husband seemed to grow wider and higher. The port he had consumed, in significant quantities, gave him a burgundy hue and he laughed loud with forced humour.

'You'll never believe it. Out of the twenty couples involved, at least four marriages broke up. Stupid people! They should have kept it as it was meant to be, a game.'

Sylvia was aghast. Did people behave like this and more to the point what was coming next? His rude grasp at her posterior when they arrived didn't ease her anxiety. Her life had been very sheltered. A Victorian type father, an all girls' school, then three years at college where she was the only girl with all men who protected their 'schoolgirl'. She felt nervous. John appeared to be enjoying himself and he certainly had taken far too much drink on board. She wished Marian would come back. A clatter outside made Sylvia look up to see the poor woman struggling to carry a basket of logs for the fire. John glancing at his wife as she half rose in her chair said gallantly. 'Stay there. I'll help Marian.'

'Doing a Walter Raleigh job, John?' Alex Boyd laughed louder than ever, ignoring his wife a few yards from him. She didn't smile and didn't lift her gaze from her tightly gripped hands.

In desperation Sylvia piped up, 'I wonder if it's snowed anymore? There were a few flakes on our way up.'

The dutiful wife, eager to please, jumped from her chair and pulled back the curtain. 'Oh dear, it's coming down quite heavily.'

Sylvia, seized the moment. 'What a pity. We'd better get moving or we could be in trouble.'

Hardly had the words fallen from her lips, than 'Boyd' slapped John on his shoulder. 'No problem, you must stay here.'

Sylvia's heart sank and fear crept round the fringes of her soul, every sense in her being jangling at the possibility of what might happen. She gripped her husband's hand in an endeavour to communicate her fears.

'We've a funeral tomorrow, I must get back tonight.'

Fortunately, that statement, delivered in a don't mess with me voice, just had to be accepted and they were reluctantly escorted to the front door. But Sylvia's relief was short lived, the breeze had more force than when they'd arrived and the snow was falling with a determination that heralded a nonstop performance. For once, she was pleased John had over-imbibed on the red wine. He good-humouredly ignored nature's warning signals and clambered happily into the driving seat. Her face, smiling, her inside churning, Sylvia waved goodbye, and they set off into the nothingness before them. The Heavens continued to drop abundant frozen tears onto the welcoming white covering that smoothed the rough moorland of the upper dale. The little car struggled as the snow did its utmost to bring it to a halt, but somehow they reached the gate she had had trouble opening on the way up. Already the bottom rung had disappeared. She doubted whether it could be opened. Would they manage to get home?

Stepping out from the warmth, her short wellies almost disappeared in the embrace of the soft white blanket. Gingerly, one foot after the other with stilted steps, she avoided the snow sneaking over her boot-tops. The gate had no intention of moving. With every fibre of her body tensed, it only shifted a couple of inches, and that was probably the wood breaking. She turned back to the car intending to ask John to lend a hand but John was standing at its nose gazing blankly under the bonnet.

'What's wrong?'

Her bleary eyed partner, in quite a matter of fact tone, replied, 'The bloody thing's conked out!'

Her heart sank. She knew nothing about engines. But there might not be anything wrong with it. John could have just forgotten to fill up with petrol. It was a nasty habit of his to forget to feed or even water the beast. There was no use worrying about that at this juncture. She silently juggled her choices. If they went back to the manor they would be facing a battle in one of the most exposed areas of the dale which was already feeling the effect of the weather. There were no land marks in that area, just miles of desolate moorland, one sheep to an acre country, with no protection from the wind. Enormous drifts soon built up and judging by the stronger wind it wouldn't be long before the whole scene changed and that meant the possibility of losing their way. To go forward seemed a better idea. They would hit the main road, such as it was, down the dale to home. The danger of losing their way was less likely as they could follow the river all the way. There were stories of folk perishing in these conditions and all she could think about was getting home.

'John, I think we better get walking. We'll soon be home if we step on it. Come on. Remember I've the funeral tomorrow.' She hoped her decisive manner would avoid any discussion and that her inebriated better-half would fall in line.

Without a word he got back in the car and slammed the door shut. Oh Lord, she breathed, he would decide to be awkward now. Determinedly, she went to the passenger door with the intention of sheltering next to her husband whilst she talked him into walking back. To her surprise, in the short time they had been there, snow was already banked up against the car door. The seriousness of the situation hit home. She bounded round the back of the car to the driver's side and yanked open the door.

'Get out John. Now! We can't stay in the car. It'll be covered in a couple of hours, or even less. We could be dead by morning.'

She pulled his arm with the grip of a starving alligator. Under such mental and physical force, he dragged his semi-conscious body upright, 'For God's sake Sylv, we can't walk home in this!'

'We can't do anything else. Come on!'

They trudged through the white eiderdown touched only by the freezing wind already building banks at every obstacle in its path. They religiously kept the turbulent river at arm's length on the left. The snow eased, but the wind persisted, an icy blast that found its way with uncanny precision straight through to their stiffening joints. Sylvia vaguely noticed her nylon clad legs had left her, though they must be still attached to her feet, for they walked on with clockwork determination. As she puzzled at this lack of feeling she failed to notice she was striding out alone. Panic took over. She whizzed round, 'John! John!'

Her voice was lost in the blast. At first, all she could see was a white world with a dark sky broken by airborne flurries carried on a bitter wind. Where was he? Then she spotted her errant husband. He was sitting, quite comfortably, on a snow capped lump of limestone, his head bowed. Her fatigue vanished as she rushed to him. 'Deary me, John. What on earth are you doing?'

He lifted his head. 'Need a rest. Let's hang on a few minutes.'

She knew if he didn't move he would rapidly succumb to the cold, of that she was certain, for she was fighting an inner battle herself. 'Come on, not much farther. Our warm bed's waiting.'

Somehow or other, she got him to his feet and they continued the tortuous trip. She pushed, cajoled and swore. Eventually, a familiar rise in the ground heralded the edge of their 18 acre pasture. Thank God, we're nearly home. Her feet and legs didn't belong to her body, but she forced them to move into a half jog and pulled her now very silent husband along in her wake.

The end of the Inn came into view. It was the most welcome sight she had ever seen. They were safe!

The pair dragged their numb bodies through the front door and into the kitchen. Cass, joyfully came to greet Sylvia causing John to stumble awkwardly against a chair sending it clattering to the floor.

'Shush. Don't make such a noise, you'll wake Otti.' That was the last thing she wanted to happen. She turned up the gas on the single mantle that Robert had left on low to give them some light when they got home. Lifting the Aga lid, she put the kettle on the welcoming hot hob with the intention of filling the hot-water bottles, but to her surprise, they weren't where she had left them. She could have cried with joy as she realised that Robert must have filled them and put them in their bed. Peeling off her coat, she helped John out of his big, unwieldy duffle, then grabbed a couple of mugs. She poured two drinks and handed one to John. 'Drink this.'

'It's water!'

'I know. Drink it.' She sipped the hot liquid letting it slide slowly down her cold, cold pipes. She could swear that she felt it journey down to her very stomach, healing as it flowed. Even so, her flesh and bones felt as though they would never be warm again. The last drop drained, she tucked Cassie back in her basket, who immediately settled in spite of her rude awakening.

'John! Bed!' She had to smile. He had collapsed over the Aga with his upper body slumped on top of the lids. 'John! Now! You can't stay there.' She pushed his resisting bulk through the kitchen and up the stairs to bed and they fell into the embrace of warm sheets.

Next morning as she opened her eyes the whole room appeared to be bathed in white. Leaning on her elbow she peered at the window. It seemed to have shrunk. Snow had covered half the glass. Snow filled every available space; there was so much of the stuff coming down hardly any sky was visible. Stretching, she realised her joints had taken a bit of a hammer from last night's escapade, but no way had she bargained for the sight of those legs. She viewed the swollen, bright red appendages stuck out before her. 'John, wake up, what's wrong with my legs? Are yours the same?'

She pulled back the bed clothes, much to his annoyance. 'Come off it, Sylv, don't be such a pain.' Then he caught sight of the object of his wife's concern.

His strong legs reluctantly emerged from the warmth of their cosy nest. They were normal, perhaps a bit pink, but nothing like the two scarlet trunks standing in front of him. 'Hell, I think you've got frostbite. My thick trousers and socks must have saved me. If you look, you're sort of ok up to the top of your little wellies. Above them where you only had nylons, it's bad. We'd better get you to the doctor.'

She raised her eyebrows. 'Don't be silly, I've the funeral this lunchtime.'

At that moment the phone rang. They heard Robert's voice answering the call. Then a moments silence. 'Hell sis. The coffin's snowed in three miles away. The funeral's off!'

Sylvia's inside dropped. 'Robert, how long before they'll be able to get through?'

He was quiet, then finally replied. 'It could be a week or more. The snow has completely covered the wall tops.'

'What about all the food?'

'I don't know. I suppose I can take some for my packing up.'

'A drop in the bloody ocean!'

Robert tried to soothe her. 'Henry is walking from his cottage in his snowshoes. He says there's a frozen crust on top which will help. If he gets here ok, we'll pick up the plough over at Mark's farm and try to get the road open.'

She felt flattened. 'All that hard work and all that food. Will we get some payment towards the cost, do you think? What a waste.'

In the week that followed the three of them ate as much as they could of the funeral buffet, helped along by the two pig families. Poor Robert said he never wanted to see another sausage roll as long as he lived. Sylvia had suffered during the chaos and without the doctor's help, her legs had been quite painful for a couple of days and then they started to violently itch. She hardly knew which was worse, but by the end of the week they had subsided to almost normal. Then, they had the phone message, the funeral was to take place the next day. A sledge had been located to carry the coffin and it was to be dragged to the church. Sylvia had the inane desire to giggle, until she realized food would be needed. After umpteen telephone calls they finally got some idea how many would make the journey with the coffin.

'Heaven be praised,' said a relieved Robert. 'They're only expecting a dozen or so. It's a long and difficult walk. Only the able bodied will be able to manage.'

Sylvia felt disgruntled. 'That's all very well, but we'll have lost a packet on this job. Besides there's not much left to give them to eat.'

She had to use her ingenuity to provide something reasonable. Fortunately the tins of corned beef, stored for such emergencies, together with onions and potatoes would supply a tasty filling for pasties and there was plenty of stock for soup. That settled, her thoughts strayed to the actual mode of transport for the coffin. 'Robert. How on earth will they manage? It's a good stretch from Buckden to the church just walking in normal conditions, but pulling a sledge?'

'We'll no doubt find out tomorrow.'

The morning was clear. There had been no more snow so the path through to the church had not worsened. Sylvia eagerly watched for the approach of the entourage as the pasties baked and the soup bubbled. She kept popping into the dining room where the view from the window looking down the dale would give the first sighting.

'Robert. They're coming!'

He joined her at the window which kept steaming up as they peered down the road.

'How many are there? Can you see?' She rubbed the side of her hand against the pane to get a better view.

'About half-a-dozen following and then there's the four fellows pulling the sledge.

Sylvia's shoulders drooped. 'I was hoping for a few more. Still, there won't be as much left as last time.'

Robert gave a wry grin. 'I won't mind eating the odd pasty. It'll be a change from sausage rolls!'

'Do you think I ought to offer them a bowl of soup before they go into church?'

'No!...Oops! They nearly lost the coffin then.'

Sylvia wiped the window again to see what had happened. The four black clothed, wellington booted, men were wrestling to right the sledge as it slithered on a bit of sloping ground. 'Good grief. If it hadn't been roped they'd have lost the coffin just there. Elizabeth would have gone sledging on her own!'

'Sis. That's not very nice. By the way, you can't ask them in for soup, the vicar's waiting at the church. He went past about half an hour ago.'

She moved to the other window and watched the strange procession pass below. 'Well. I suppose not many will have had two funerals.'

Robert corrected her. 'Almost two. But not many will have arrived on a sledge!'

CHAPTER 23

The dale seemed eerily quiet after Sylvia had waved goodbye to John and Robert. There had been little movement that morning other than the snowplough, followed by the milk lorry to collect Mark's churns waiting at his gate. She guessed Paul from the Quaker farm up behind the church would soon be appearing. Ever since the snow came he had been a regular caller, making the journey on foot, as his ex-army jeep had continued to refuse the challenge of an alpine decent. Luckily he had no milk to be collected; his cows were kept to suckle calves. Sylvia thought it was one Hell of a struggle to make the trip just for a coffee and a couple of pints of Guiness, especially before ten o'clock in a morning, though she supposed he timed his visits to coincide with Mark delivering the milk. They both seemed to enjoy a chin-wag. This morning was no exception. She watched Paul cross the bridge in a flurry of snow. He burst into the kitchen in a draught of cool fresh air, his apple cheeks rosy from the exertion. Smiling shyly, he hesitated in the doorway.

'Would you like a coffee, Paul? I think Mark's on his way across.' She'd caught sight of him as she filled the kettle. It was a relief. She would be able to leave the pair of them chatting whilst she carried on with her jobs. A short tap at the door heralded the milkman. He grinned with appreciation as Sylvia thrust a large mug of coffee in his hand. 'Th.. Thanks.'

She had to smile as he picked up a stool in his free hand and plonked it in front of the Aga, beckoning Paul to do likewise. The pair of them hugged the warm stove like a couple of wily tomcats. They were rather in her way, but she enjoyed listening to them prattle on. Besides, she could start making the bread. It seemed pointless bothering to light the bar fire just for them, as it was extremely unlikely there would be any other callers, even though the road down to the village was now open some of the time. No one in their right mind would risk the one and a half miles in such uncertain weather. Custom was so sparse and she felt thankful that Robert was working on the snowplough. His earnings, small though they be, together with John's contribution, was keeping the wolf from the door.

Paul stood up. 'Look at that weather! I better get moving it's coming down with a vengeance.'

Sylvia and Mark joined him at the window.

'The gods are having a pillow-fight.' She marvelled at the feather-like flakes descending on the place.

'Aye. And a w..wind's springin' up.' Mark pulled up his collar, slapped his cap firmly on his head and made for the door with Paul at his heels.

The weather certainly appeared to be worsening and she wondered how Robert and Henry were faring. The snowplough had no protection from the elements and she doubted whether they would be able to even see in these conditions. They certainly would be desperately cold. She gave a shiver and bent to give her son a hug. She hoisted him from the floor where he was busy taking coal from the bucket and dropping it in Cassie's feed-bowl.

'Now then young man. We're going stocktaking. First to the bar and then outside, brrr!'

She had decided to take advantage of the quiet spell and have another look at their cash situation. Her last attempt had shown an adverse discrepancy and she could not find the reason. She had no experience in book-keeping, neither had Robert, but John had been an auditor for a clothing company when she first met him. Admittedly, he hadn't reigned long. Perhaps that was why he offered her no help. With Otti on her arm she started the slog in the bar. The quantities were similar to her original findings, which wasn't surprising as there had been so little trade. Wrapped warm, she stepped out into the cold for a rapid skirmish round the dairy and coach-house of the coal, gas, proven and food stocks. There were no differences there, and she'd no need to count the animals, for she fed them twice a day.

Disappointed, she couldn't face costing her list, it would have to wait.

To ease her concerns out came the stock-pot and in minutes soup was underway. Tears rolled down her cheeks as she peeled and chopped Gerald's mum's onions. They were wonderful, but she wished that whatever had been put in the soil to make them taste so good didn't have the effect of giving her Hell when they were peeled. Grabbing a tea towel she buried her face and failed to hear the door open.

'Sis. A cuppa for pity's sake.'

'Gosh, you gave me a shock. I didn't hear you come in.' Rubbing her eyes she viewed her brother through an onion haze. 'You look frozen to death. Here, sit down!' She pushed forward the stool that Mark had been sitting on. He stretched to pull it towards him, but his fingers refused to close round the leg. 'My God, sis, I'm pretty well frozen!'

Sylvia helped him take off his boots and coat, then throwing her cardigan round his shoulders she took the largest mug on the shelf and filled it to the brim with scalding hot tea. 'There, wrap your hands round that. I'll get your slippers.' She was up and down the stairs in a trice and, quickly kneeling beside him, thrust his stiffened feet into the furry linings.

It was several minutes before Robert began to thaw and a normal colour replaced the dead white of his hands and feet. Sylvia couldn't help noticing that his face remained blotched in shades of bright pink and scarlet and hoped he wouldn't have the same problems as she had had with her legs. 'Are you feeling a bit better?'

'Yes thanks. God, it was awful up there. It blew a blizzard. The snow came at us horizontally, like knives striking. D'you know, it hurt my eyeballs. It was like being pierced with hundreds of needles. We tried to hide behind our snow shovels, holding them a couple of inches from our faces. Even our eyebrows froze!'

'You poor things. Is Henry ok? He's much older than you.'

'He's as tough as old boots. He desperately tried to keep going, but Mother Nature must have had a particularly bad turn. It got even fouler.' He swung his arm in an arc for effect. 'The wind swept down the dale with the force of a jet-engine, driving the snow before it. We couldn't see a thing. A complete white-out. I thought about nurse Brown struggling in similar weather on a bloody horse.'

Sylvia smiled fondly at her son crawling at the far end of the kitchen with Cass close by. The mention of nurse Brown brought home to her just how lucky she had been. Since seeing the struggle that the pigs and sheep had experienced in giving birth she realised that it was all too easy for something to go wrong.

'Mm. No wonder she got a medal.'

'Aye, and she deserved one! Even breathing was a battle, it was like being suffocated. In the end we had to give up or we might not have been able to get back.'

'Oh Robert, you would have perished.'

He allowed a smile to surface, and as quick as it came it was gone. Sylvia realised he wouldn't feel himself until he'd had a good night's sleep. 'I think you better have an early night.'

'Never mind that. What's for dinner?'

She laughed, 'Thank goodness! Meat pie if you behave.'

The sound of a vehicle shattered the peace. Sylvia peered out of the misted window. 'It's Gerald's Land Rover. What's he doing? He's got his trailer on the back. Surely he's not carting stock in this weather?'

She went to the door just as John drove onto the car park. Gerald and John together spelled trouble. What was he up to now?

Gerald, with his usual exuberance, shouted, 'Where do you want these sheep?'

Sylvia exchanged glances with Robert who had joined her at the door. John came towards them looking a trifle uncomfortable.

'John, what have you done? You haven't bought some sheep?' He nodded. 'No. You know we've no money. Oh, John.'

'They were going dirt cheap at the auction. There were hardly any buyers because of the weather. Honestly they were just too good to miss. Besides I got a little bonus this month.'

She knew it was no good arguing. 'Where do you intend to put them? How many are there?'

He hesitated. 'Sixteen and a tupp.'

'Sixteen!!' Robert was incredulous. 'And who'll be looking after them?'

Sylvia, anxious to avoid a scene piped in. 'I will. Let's get them in the croft. They're squashed in there.'

'Nay, Sylvia. Th'll b' fine in t'eighteen acres. They ain't pets y'know. Y'll mek 'em soft.'

She gave him a look that would have withered a full grown oak. 'Gerald. If I am given stock to look after, I will do just that. The weather is foul. There's nothing to eat...and they're going in the croft where I can feed them twice a day. OK?'

Gerald looked uncomfortable and hunched his shoulders.

John gave Gerald the nod to shut up, and before there was any further discussion, the motley crew were deposited in the croft beyond the garden.

The small flock scrambled into the safety of the walled patch, watched by their brand-new shepherdess. 'That one. The pretty one with only one horn, she's Lucy. And the tupp... oh, he's got no horns, he's Sydney.'

The three men looked pityingly at their landlady-cum-sheep expert. 'For God's sake, sis, they've only just got here, why the names?'

She looked coy, grinned mischievously, and wiggled her bottom as she minced back to the front door. 'They told me what to call them as they passed!'

In unison, the three men raised their eyes heavenward. John was visibly relieved. 'Well I suppose that means we've got the seal of approval.'

The days that followed developed into nightmare proportions. Lucy, the one-horned ewe, decided she would go into training for the Grand National. Her woolly backside, bald tail held high, and scrawny legs tucked neatly under her belly, was a regular sight as she launched effortlessly over the craggy walls to escape the confines of the little croft. No wall was too big, no gate too high for her gymnastic prowess. She sailed over every obstacle with the grace of a stag. Her fluid jumping and her cavalier outlook would have been the envy of any would-be steeplechaser. She roamed the upper stretches of the riverside, snow, ice and boundaries no barrier to her, nothing seemed to curb her wanton wanderings. She was brought back on three occasions by non-too-pleased neighbouring farmers, and a couple of times she was rounded up by John and Robert. Eventually, Lucy, who was always partial to her grub, settled into the routine of being fed morning and evening in the croft and roamed round the eighteen acres in between. However, she must have given Sydney an insight into the trailing game, for one morning he, too, went walkabout.

It was one of those crisp days. The sky, cloudless and cobalt, held a golden ball of sunshine and the snow-wrapped dale glittered. A good to be alive day, Sylvia decided as she climbed the steps up to the croft. She carried the two buckets full to the brim with sheep fodder, to load into the troughs. The flock were waiting! So far, she had beaten them, but not today. No way had she bargained for the force of sixteen woollies, more than eager for their breakfast. They charged and bunched around her. She was lifted off her feet, and like a wisp of straw, helplessly carried several yards before being dropped in amongst soft, greasy overcoats. Then, to add to the indignity, she was trampled by what seemed like hundreds of stiletto clad feet. The buckets of food were scattered far and wide, and before the contents could settle, they were greedily devoured by eager jaws. Struggling to her feet, cursing at her infant bruises, she noticed that Sydney was missing. There was no sign of him in the immediate view. Sighing, she returned to the kitchen and called up the stairs. 'Wellies on Robert! We've lost Sydney.'

She half hoped that John would come down to sit with Otti, who was now needing more attention, but there wasn't a movement. Picking him out of his pram, she carried him upstairs into their bedroom. Pulling back the covers from his sleeping father, she placed the grumbling child beside him. 'You'll have to look after *your son*. I'm off to find Syd. He's gone walkabout. By the way, he's just filled his nappy!'

John let out a groan and she had to hide her mirth as she closed the bedroom door.

Robert was climbing into his big duffle coat when she came down the stairs. 'I won't be a sec. Just need my scarf. Still in bed is he? Give me pigs any day. Pigs are no trouble. Just muck out, feed, and stay put. And why is it, why is it always me and you who have to go out in all weathers when he bought the bloody sheep?'

'John is looking after Otti.'

'Well put out the flags! There's a first. What did you do? Hold a gun to his head?'

She dare not look at her brother for fear of showing her disappointment in John; it would only invite another diatribe from him. Turning away, she stepped outside pulling her collar high to hide her face. 'C'mon. The longer we are the farther he'll get.'

The pair of them set off up the steep climb of the eighteen acres. They crossed diagonally, hoping to see most of the terrain in the shortest time possible. The snow nearly reached their boot tops. Each step broke through the crisp topping, their feet sinking into soft cotton wool. In places, odd clumps of reeds pierced the icy crust, in others, hillocks hid lumps of limestone. Their attempts to find the best route was not the easiest. Their breathing shortened and it wasn't long before they were puffing and blowing. Without snow it was a hell of a pull, but with the added handicap it became a Herculean ordeal. In between gasps Robert pointed to a gap in the boundary wall. A few iced, moss-covered stones had fallen and sunk in the snow below, leaving dark holes in the virgin whiteness. Sure enough, the runaway's footprints were evident over in the next pasture.

'Look at the gap Sylv. Sydney must have had a bit of a struggle to hoist his ageing carcass over the wall. He's knocked off umpteen stones. Another job waiting!'

They began the chase, their quarry couldn't be too far ahead. Bounding through the snow, they gleefully followed the runaway's tracks. At first there was no sign of him. Then Sylvia spotted the errant tupp. 'Oh look Robert! Poor Sydney!'

There, at the bottom of the hill in a drift reaching to the wall top, was a pathetic looking Sydney, well and truly stuck halfway up his belly.

'We've got him!' yelled a jubilant Robert as he ran, stumbling down the hill, in a cascade of soft snow. Sylvia followed at a more sedate pace, pleased that the escapee was at the end of his flight of freedom. With some amusement, she watched Robert launch himself on the substantial back-end of the erstwhile ram. But that creature had other ideas. With a supreme effort he leapt forward, taking his handler by complete surprise.

They were quite a distance from her, and surely, by the time she could get down to them Robert would have won the battle. She stood with the warm sun on her back, partly mesmerised as she watched the struggle. From the higher vantage point, Sylvia had a first class view. There seemed to be umpteen legs working like overcharged pistons as the pair were catapulted into deeper snow in an explosion of powder. Robert, a red-faced snowman, was determinedly hanging on to the thick fleece and Sydney was equally determined to escape. The action seemed to go on forever. Sylvia started to laugh. Sydney was galloping like a train but moving nowhere. Robert, clutching great handfuls of wool, performed a nonstop gyrating exercise. Having no horns, made the tupp's capture exceedingly difficult, and the exhibition showed no sign of stopping. She knew she should dash down and help, but she couldn't move. Laughter shook her whole being. And then she missed her footing and fell sideways, rolling around in the snow as her tears fell and her ribs ached.

'*Sis!*'

The word conveyed exactly what her brother thought of her antics. Not one for accepting the role of fool, he endeavoured to appear nonchalant and in full control. Sydney sensed the change and seized the opportunity to engage every muscle for a surprise escape. There was a moment of fierce panic, a volcanic eruption, but somehow Robert managed to regain control. Stony-faced, he glared in her direction, managing to bring her back to some level of control. Still chuckling, she made her way to the gyrating couple. The advent of another pair of hands decided the now, rather tired animal, to surrender. Fortunately, they were fairly close to the field gate leading onto the road. They managed to herd Syd calmly through, and back in the right direction. The journey followed without further mishap, other than aching backs and Sylvia's confession…

'It was so funny, Robert, I wet my knickers!'

'Serves you right!' was the jaundiced reply.

CHAPTER 24

The snows slowly left the valley. Spring girded her loins and pushed the brown grass aside to let the delicate green shoots take over. Lucy decided her roaming antics should cease and acknowledged her imminent role of motherhood, spending her days along with the rest of the flock devouring the new grass. Even Sydney changed, and acted out the role of father figure to his sixteen pregnant ladies. He should have been separated from them, but as he was getting on in years and the only male, he was left where he was. Most of the time he would stand on guard watching for imaginary foes.

Sylvia was happy. The promise of Spring's outburst filled her with hope, and relief that they had managed to survive a hard winter with very little trade. She was excited at the prospect of having their own little band of white-fleeced lambs who always seemed to wear black and white football socks. Otti, now crawling, enjoyed watching the animals and Sylvia looked forward to the time when he could see the lambs frolicking in the croft.

The promise of an improvement in the weather brought out a few hardy souls over the weekend. Saturday was never as busy as Sunday, but this one proved an exception. Sylvia decided that the sunny, though cold Friday, must have made all and sundry want to shake off winter's blues. A stream of cars blitzed the hamlet before twelve o'clock, the occupants desiring anything from liquid refreshment, to sandwiches, to full blown luncheon. The sudden onslaught threw the threesome into a frenzy of work.

'Gosh, I'm out of condition,' Sylvia blew, as she cooked ham and eggs at the same time as baking scones.

'You wait till Easter. This is just small fry. You've built up a reputation for good grub.' Robert was all smiles, happy to have some trade after winter's starvation.

'Is John ok in the bar?'

'He's fine. I wish we'd more room to keep him going with sandwiches!'

Sylvia started to worry. 'I wish we'd seen this lot coming. I've just about run out of bread, so sandwiches will soon be finished, and we're down to the last ham. If it's like this tomorrow we're in trouble.'

But Mother Nature stepped in and did her usual early spring turnabout. The clouds began to roll in, bringing with them the threat of rain and, as if by magic, the hamlet emptied. Top coats were donned, cars sprang to life and sprinted away like rats up the veritable drainpipe.

John came in from the bar looking rather deflated. 'Well. That was a bit quick!'

But Sylvia had had enough. 'Let's have a scone and a cuppa before we clear away.'

They settled round the kitchen table surrounded by dirty pots and the remnants of a scavenged ham when their moment of self-indulgence was shattered by the most dreadful squealing, an ear-splitting sound with the intensity of a howling banshee. The clan, in a befuddled haze, stood up in unison. Sylvia sent her chair flying and made a beeline to the barn where the growing litters of young pigs, now at almost Porker stage, were housed.

Peering over the half door she could see nothing untoward. Quickly lifting the latch she pushed the door open. The clean straw smelled sweet but was overpowered by the stench of fear and diarrhoea. The noise stopped. Her first thought was that the young pigs had been fighting amongst themselves and her interruption had ended the squabble. They were all bunched together in a corner. Then she spotted the problem.

'Robert! John! One's got his head stuck in the trough.'

The cross pieces, supporting the long galvanised troughs, had acted as a trap for one of the youngsters who was held tight by its neck in an iron grip under one of the bars. The poor creature's legs thrashed in an attempt to get purchase on the floor to release itself, but to no avail. Sylvia guessed it must have nosed sideways under the bar, pushing its head and ears past the point of no return, and when it tried to escape, it found itself well and truly clamped.

The two men charged into the barn. Robert, first to be aware of the situation, groaned. 'Oh my God. It's as fast as a thief. Its neck is swollen, that's why it's stuck fast. We'll have to saw through the bar.' He turned to get the implement.

'Stop! The poor thing's dying. That will just finish it off. It'll panic!'

Sylvia's mind was working overtime. She remembered once soaping her swelling fingers to free her wedding ring after wrenching her hand in a stumble. Frantically, she pushed past the onlookers, flung open the dairy door and grabbed the catering pack of lard sitting on the top shelf. Armed with the seven pounds of blubber she knelt beside the trapped animal, whose head was rapidly developing elephantine proportions with eyes that rolled back in an alarming fashion. Madly, she plastered handfuls of the lubricant on every bit of visible flesh. The animal had the sense to have one last try to free itself. It made a valiant effort, there was a violent pull, another scream, and the porker freed itself, albeit with a fat head blathered in lard.

Relief ran through Sylvia, leaving her feeling weak and rather dithery. An animal in distress was one of her worst nightmares. John put his arm round her shoulders. 'They'll be gone at the end of the week. I'm taking them to Gisburn market. We should see some profit, Porkers are doing quite well just now.'

She was startled and not very happy at the thought of losing their first-ever litter, especially when she knew their fate. To hide her sickening anxiety from her men she marched back to the kitchen throwing over her shoulder, 'Who's going to take them then?' But she didn't wait for an answer.

The morning of the Porkers' departure arrived. Sylvia gave them double rations for breakfast and silently watched Ariane's offsprings messily devour their last meal. She couldn't help but feel proud of the seven. Their skin gleamed under a fuzz of soft white bristles, mobile pink ears twitched as they ate, and bright eyes watched every spare crumb. When the trough was empty they ran together round the pen, woofing, as they charged in play, scattering straw in every direction.

John broke the moment. 'Come on, let's get this lot loaded.'

She peeped through the doorway, expecting to see Gerald's trailer, but all she could see was John's company car. 'What are they going in?'

'They're going in the car.'

She couldn't believe her ears. What in Heaven's name were they thinking? She strode out of the barn to the Morris Minor, innocently waiting. The back seats had been taken out and a straw bed stretched from behind the front seats to the boot lock. Shaking her head in disbelief she confronted the pair.

'You can't get seven pigs in there. You'll wreck the car, or kill the pigs, or both. Remember, it's not your car, John, and you've had one near squeak leaving it overnight in a blizzard. You...' She broke off, too astounded at the plan to continue.

Robert had the grace to look rather sheepish, but John merely shrugged.

'What on earth are you both thinking of. It's a Hell of a way to Gisburn. The pigs will suffocate. What then?'

'We've no choice. Gerald's Land Rover's bust and this car couldn't pull a trailer. Besides it hasn't a tow hitch. We've got to go. We need the cash. Anyway, the pigs are entered at the auction.'

He turned his back on her and the two men proceeded to load the vociferous litter into their cramped conveyance. The windows immediately steamed over and had to be fully opened so the driver and his mate could see. In spite of being unhappy with the situation, Sylvia couldn't help but laugh out loud as the little car set off down the road, obviously under severe strain. 'Oh Cassie, I hope they'll be alright.' She bent low and hugged the slim body.

The sun shone and it felt quite warm in the spring air. Young Otti opened up his lungs to action his mother's attention. She casually wondered when he would start to talk, so far he hadn't even tried to utter a word.

His protest continued through morning coffees and when she had taken orders for six ham and egg lunches and his cries persisted, she knew a plan of action was needed. He had a full belly, a clean posterior and warm clothing, there was no wind, so his behaviour had to be just cussedness. To make matters worse, Ariane escaped from the croft and had taken refuge in the garden. Sylvia was at her wits end, then she had an idea. Like a woman conquering Everest, she hauled the playpen onto the lawn, laid out a thick blanket and plonked Otti in the middle. She waited. Ariane lumbered up to the bars of the pen, grunted, and calmly began devouring the fairly substantial covering of lawn. Otti happily viewed this new, fat friend through his prison cell, crawling round the perimeter to view her, until tiredness took over and he fell sound asleep in the sun. He slept and Ariane decided that was the best thing to do. She dropped her bulk as close as she could get to the blanket and proceeded to snore in the gentle warmth.

Sylvia was able to carry on with the lunches and kept having a peep at the charade on the lawn, which gave many an, *aah*! and much amusement to the customers. She managed to get through the rest of the day without a hitch. Ariane obediently followed the 'bucket' back to her sty and Otti downed his tea with gusto. But no word from her menfolk. In truth she would have been too busy to take a phone call, but it would have been nice to hear how their trip to market had gone. Then she heard the sound of a rather tired Morris under the kitchen window and she ran out to meet them, thankful they had returned safely.

Robert was already dragging out the stinking straw bed from the boot of the car. She came up behind him. 'How will you ever get that floor clean again?'

He lifted his head. 'Sis. That ain't my problem. I'll get rid of this stuff and give the floor a brushing over, then it's up to John!' He glared at the pub door that John had just walked through.

Oh, she thought, had they been falling out? 'I'm making tea, so don't be long.' She left her brother and went into the kitchen to interrogate her husband. He was fairly blathering the butter onto one of the freshly made scones.

'Hungry?'

He nodded with cheeks bulging. 'When you've emptied your mouth would you mind telling me how you went on?' She popped the shepherd's pie into the oven. 'Dinner won't be long, so go easy on the scones.'

Smiling he gave her a peck on the cheek. 'Yes luv. The litter sold very well indeed. I reckon we'll have made a decent profit.'

She half resented the term 'we' but felt thrilled that their first skirmish into the farming game had paid off. 'Are you going to tell me the full story then?'

Teasingly he replied, 'When Robert comes in and when we've eaten. I'm ravenous!'

She was consumed with curiosity. They must have had a job with the piggy cargo and she wanted to know. But it wasn't until they had almost finished their meal before her tormentors began to recount the events of the day.

'There's one thing certain, sis. I'll never forget selling our first litter!'

John started to laugh. 'I've never had to smell so much shit for so long. We had the windows fully open as well to get rid of the stench and to keep the pigs cool.'

'Didn't they try to jump out?'

There was more laughter. 'No. They were wedged in too tight.'

Sylvia wanted to cry. Losing her babies was bad enough, but the thought of them going to meet their fate squashed and frightened really troubled her. Robert seemed to guess her thoughts. 'Don't worry sis. They were fine. They didn't make any noise. In fact, I think they went a bit sleepy.'

'Rob, do you remember that policeman's face when we drove up to the entrance for wagons and trailers?'

Robert hated his name being shortened and he gave John a withering look, but he began to smile as he recalled their meeting with the law. 'It was so funny. The policeman was directing the traffic. When we approached he stepped forward with his hand held high to stop us going through the gate. "Turn back please," he said, all officious like, "This way is for animals entered to be auctioned." He even glared at us.

'His face!' John dissolved into howls of laughter.

'Stop it! You two. Get on with the tale.'

Choking, Robert carried on, waving his arm theatrically. 'He glanced into the back of the car and had to do a double take. Oh sis, the look on his face. Slowly it glazed over, his mouth slackened and he took another look at the load as though he just couldn't believe what he was seeing. "What the Hell is this then?" he blurted out. When we told him we'd travelled from Hubberholme he started to laugh. "I think you'd better get to the ring as quick as you can. I can't stand the stink, so I think you two lads must have had more than enough."'

'Gosh. You were lucky. He might have turned you back.'

'I think it rather tickled him. Besides, John talked himself out of any trouble. In fact, in the end, we were escorted to the unloading area by the policeman himself.'

John chipped in. 'Yes, and the stockmen in the unloading area were incredulous. They'd never seen anything like it. I do believe we had such a good sale because of the bit of notoriety. We probably attracted more buyers.'

Sylvia had listened with mixed emotions, but now she intended putting her foot down. 'All very funny boys. I'm pleased we did so well with our first sale. But, I tell you now, no way are you ever carrying stock in that car again. Next time it's Gerald's trailer or not at all.'

The two men said not a word.

CHAPTER 25

Only a couple of weeks to Easter and Sylvia hadn't taken into account that the first bank holiday of the year would fall bang in the middle of lambing-time. She spent every spare moment spring-cleaning, to be ready for the anticipated mayhem. They were already fully booked, so any extra visitors would have to be farmed out. Hopefully the weather would be kind, but that seemed a pretty vague wish as she viewed the decidedly grey day. The air was heavy. There was no movement. Even the delicate stems of the clump of daffodils she had planted drooped in sympathy. She began to think the mood heralded inclement weather, but re-hanging the freshly laundered bedroom curtains, patterned with yellow and orange flowers, a shaft of sunlight transported them to a brilliance which lit up the whole room. All that she had left to do was to bring the clean bedding from downstairs. Standing back to admire her handiwork she heard the phone ring. Damn. Robert was mucking out the top sty; she'd have to fly to catch the call. She dashed down and through the kitchen to answer its strident command.

The voice was well educated. 'Good Morning. Mr Priestley's secretary here. Could I book lunch for two at twelve noon, today, please.'

Sylvia mentally checked the food stakes before confirming the booking. She replaced the receiver. A shaft of recognition sifted through her grey-matter. Could it be? The woman had said she was the secretary. What if it was the great man?

Panic jumped to the fore. She rushed to meet Robert as he came into the kitchen for his midmorning cuppa.

'Robert, I've just taken a booking for two people, a Mr Priestley and his secretary. Do you think it could be the J. B.?'

Robert thought for a moment. 'I reckon it could be. Remember the visitors' book? This place might have special memories for him. Though, of course, it could be a coincidence.'

Sylvia moved into another gear. 'I'd better make sure everything is perfect in case it is him.'

Feeling rather guilty, she filled vases with blossom from a bush in the garden. Any flowers were a rarity in this limestone country with its shallow depth of soil, and they wouldn't live long when picked, but J. B. was worth that sacrifice.

Flowers in place, furniture polished to a high gloss with a sweet smelling sandalwood and beeswax, the table set, and lunch cooking: all was ready for the visitors.

Sylvia didn't see them arrive. It was Robert who welcomed them at the door and ushered them through to the dining room. She was busy at the Aga, but managed a brief glance as the pair passed through. He was grey-haired and grey-coated, and he walked slowly and slightly bent. His secretary followed. She too, seemed similarly colourless, but her face brightened as she caught Sylvia's eye.

'Robert, the food's ready to go through.' She proudly viewed the plates of baked ham, roast potatoes, whole onions with white sauce, carrot batons and, Sylvia's lifesaver, freeze-dried peas. 'Tell me if they look pleased with it.'

'Don't be daft, sis.' He picked up the tray of food and marched to the dining room.

'Well?'

Robert chuckled. 'They said they thought they were at the Ritz.'

'You bloody horror! You're lying!'

'Sorry sis, but you asked for it. Actually they just sat there.'

She felt disappointed. It wasn't easy getting a last minute booking, midweek, and with no fridge. Still, they'd be used to the best of everything and would expect no other.

She sent in the apple charlotte with lashings of thick cream, collected in a rush from Mark, and a great chunk of Wensleydale cheese. 'If they don't like that they can lump it!'

In spite of her bravado, she waited anxiously, desperate to know if she might have pleased the famous writer.

267

'They don't talk much. I don't think they've said more than two words over lunch.'

'Shush, Robert. They're coming out.'

Robert went forward to escort them to the front door. At the same time Sylvia grabbed Cassie's collar as she made a determined attempt to join the visitors. 'Oh, no you don't, madam.' Not everyone liked animals, even beautiful ones.

Robert returned smiling. 'They said thank you for the meal and that it was most enjoyable.'

She heaved a sigh of relief. 'Thank goodness! Where are they going now?' She dived to the kitchen window to see the pair cross onto the bridge. 'Robert. The secretary's stopped on the bridge. Now she's coming back to the car park. And he's carried on through the gate into the churchyard!'

'Move over. Let me have a look.' He squashed her against the sink. 'He's meandering round the graves. He's disappeared into the church.'

Sylvia stood absent-mindedly washing the pots whilst keeping the church door in her sights. Then she had an idea. 'Robert. The secretary must be waiting in the car for him. Why don't you go and ask her about the book he wrote when he stayed here?'

'Do you think that would be alright? I don't want to be rude.'

'Go on! She can only say she doesn't discuss his business.'

'Mm.' Robert walked out reluctantly. Sylvia turned to continue her watch on the church. At last the object of her curiosity emerged, and to her surprise he came out of the graveyard and slowly walked round to the path at the back of the church leading to the Quaker farm. He carefully climbed the steep and stony path for about 100 yards, then stopped and gazed, as though to imprint the view on his mind for eternity. His stance was as still as one of the huge chunks of limestone protruding from the scrubby pasture. He stayed there a while before dreamily making his way back down and across the bridge.

It only seemed seconds until Sylvia saw the roof of his car pass under the kitchen window. Somehow, she sensed a cloud of sadness surrounding the vehicle. Why should she have such a feeling? Robert changed her mood, coming in wearing a very superior expression.

'She's told you! Tell me what the book's called.'

'Well. It wasn't a book as such. It's a play called, 'I have been here before'. His secretary thought it had been published in 1936 or 7, but it was before her time.'

'That's great. I wonder what it was about?' She paused. 'Did you think he seemed sad?'

'Oh Lord, I don't know. He was quiet, but, he's a writer. What did you expect?'

They stood there in the kitchen, contemplating, until Robert sighed and shook the moment from him. 'Back to work, sis. Don't you think those sheep need checking?'

She'd all but forgotten the imminent births in the excitement. Quickly making sure Otti was comfortable and happy, she strode out on the trip round the eighteen acres taking particular interest in the view.

The job of sheep-minding had been allocated to her as she had more idea on birthing than the men. She fairly ran up the wall side of the pasture, bounding over rocks and harsh clumps of reeds. Nearly at the top she had to stop. She bent forward taking rapid lungfuls of air, desperate to quell her thumping heartbeats. At long last the noise in her chest and the fierce intake of breaths slowed. She straightened and gazed around the pasture. A whiter than white blob caught her eye. Oh my God. We've got a baby! All else disappeared. She approached the ewe and its lamb and to her delight found it was her favourite, Lucy. She sat proudly close to her newborn, but nosed at Sylvia's hand searching for a titbit. Delving deep into her pocket Sylvia found a couple of sheep nuts, escapees from the rough and tumble of feed-time. 'Lucy. You clever girl!' She offered the treat as she rubbed the bony head and carefully looked over mum and daughter. The lamb was clean and dry, so had been in the world for a couple of hours, and happily they both appeared to be fit and well. Excited, Sylvia continued her task. The rest of the flock were still in waiting, though one did look a little uneasy. She decided it would be best to repeat the trek in a couple of hours.

Robert was thrilled when she gave him the news and insisted he would take the next visit to see their first ever lamb.

Later, he donned his boots and jacket leaving Sylvia wondering if he would find the climb as arduous as she had. Though, to be fair, Robert hadn't her stupid bull-at-a-gate mentality, and he approached things at a sensible pace. It seemed only minutes before he returned, bursting into the kitchen looking agitated. 'Sis. I think you'd better come. One of them is in trouble.'

She pushed past him. 'Where is she?'

'Not far. About 100 yards away tucked under the roadside wall.'

Sure enough, the ewe was laid on her side panting weakly. To Sylvia's inexperienced eye, it looked as though the lamb was fast, or even dead. Her one thought was to get help. She ran. She was certain she ran the four minute mile back to Mark's farm. Fortunately, he was just about to drive off in his van when she breathlessly threw herself across the bonnet. 'Help, Mark! A sheep's going to die. She can't give birth.'

He smiled, shaking his head. 'J..jump in. A'l tek thee in t'van.'

Flinging herself beside him she disjointedly gave him the sheep's symptoms. He said nothing. As they reached the place where the sheep lay, he stopped the van and vaulted over the wall to the distressed animal. As quick as a flash, he laid his left hand on her heaving body and with his other hand felt for the unborn lamb.

'D'na worry,' he gave Sylvia a quick glance. 'It's breached.'

He deftly manipulated the tiny creature, and the ewe made one last desperate effort, giving an almighty push and brought into the world a fat, slime-covered, yellow-looking lamb. The ewe laid exhausted whilst Mark cleared her baby's mouth forcing it to breathe. There was a single bleat and it struggled to its feet, all floppety.

'Oh Mark…You angel. Thank you. Thank you.'

'Nay. A b..breached lamb be fairly c..c..common.'

'What's breached?'

'Backside fust.'

270

She grinned. They waited until the lamb began to suckle and the mum had recovered enough to start cleaning her offspring.

'There thou is. It'll be f..fine now.'

Sylvia was happy and their good fortune continued as the holiday weekend came upon them. Seven of the sixteen ewes had produced a single, healthy, lamb. She was relieved there had been no twins. One each was more than plenty under the circumstances.

The weekend brought with it beautiful sunshine and, its inevitable accompaniment, the hordes! They had never been so busy. Sylvia's day started at 5.30 a.m. with a dash round the 18 acres, then feeding the pigs and calves. The flock obliged by producing healthy lambs with no attendant problems saving her the worry she had experienced with the breached youngster. By the time she got back to start cleaning and preparing breakfasts, Robert had risen, but not John.

'Is John still in bed?'

'Where else?'

Robert's sarcasm wasn't lost on her. John liked his sleep and didn't care how he got it. He could fall into a sound slumber at the drop of a hat. She felt a bit peeved, but he did have his job so she must forgive him. Besides, he was good in the bar. The customers liked him even though he would keep them waiting as he chatted to some other interesting party. But that weekend took its toll. Sylvia knew she was running on empty. Her days became a blur. She was lucky if she managed more than three hours sleep. Breakfasts, coffees, lunches, afternoon teas, high teas, dinners, and in amongst, there was Otti demanding attention and the animals to feed. The days ran into one another; there were no boundaries.

The weather continued sunnily right through to Monday, when all residents departed and presumably all the trade. Sylvia felt dreadful, and looking at her jaded brother she knew he felt the same. 'Robert, I know you're exhausted, but guess how much meat, ham and fish we've got through this Easter?'

'God, I don't know. All I do know is that we've never bloody well stopped. How much then?'

271

'Over one hundredweight!'

'You're joking! No wonder we're knackered.'

John came in. 'Stop the racket you two. The vicar's coming.'

'Oh no. Not now, surely.'

The kitchen door opened slowly. There had been no knock. The rotund shape of Reverend Fullerton bowled in. He looked pleased with himself but raised a self-depreciating hand. 'Now people, I know you've been very busy, so I won't keep you a minute longer than I have to.'

They stood open-mouthed; what was coming?

'I think you will be happy with my news. Electricity will be with you at the end of this summer.'

Sylvia forgot all decorum and flew across the room to hug the clearly self-satisfied cleric.

'Why Sylvia! I knew you'd be delighted, but really…' He grinned from ear-to-ear.

CHAPTER 26

Sylvia couldn't come down to earth. Electricity was about to be installed! She was in her seventh Heaven. The thought of the ease it would bring to her could hardly be contemplated and planning and plotting was uppermost in her mind. 'Robert. We'll need to make room for a fridge and a washing machine.'

'Sis. For God's sake calm down. We'll only have to do a bit of a reshuffle. There's plenty of room if we plan. And... Sylv, I'm being deadly serious now. Please don't go off half-cocked and start buying stuff right away.'

'Of course not, but...'

'I know you. Give yourself time to think. The vicar says that Sam Holden, the electrician, won't be starting until October, so there's tons of time before any appliances could be used anyway.'

She looked crestfallen.

'Come on, sis. First things first. We've got to get the next lot of pigs to market.'

'Yes. And not in the car!'

'It's ok. John's organised Gerald for that run.'

'Did I hear my name mentioned?'

John walked in, seemingly full of the joys of spring, and Sylvia felt alarm bells ringing. 'Is something wrong John? You're back early. It's only three o'clock.'

'I've been busy organising a deal. It's worked out better than I expected.'

She waited for whatever bombshell he was about to drop. That kind of remark usually meant he'd been spending, or she would be landed with an extra workload.

'I think you'll like it, Sylv.'

Robert looked cautious. 'Not more stock?'

'No. I've found a top-class whippet dog to mate with Cassie.'

'You've what?!'

She couldn't believe her ears. How dare he? 'Oh no. Cass is not going to any dog.'

'But...' John glanced at Robert, trying to gain support, ... 'she's in season. I've nearly run over Mark's sheepdog twice this week keeping a vigil on the car park.'

That was true. Sylvia had kept having to shoo him back across the bridge, but that was hardly the point. 'I do not want puppies. Don't you think we've enough to do?'

Robert glared. 'You're not here struggling with folk, animals and young Otti. I hope you haven't fixed anything.'

Under his breath Sylvia heard him mutter. 'It's alright for some.'

John had the decency to look slightly guilty. 'Actually, she's booked in for tomorrow.' He went on with some haste. 'He's a wonderful dog. He's the son of a Cruft's winner. Just think, we could get about £10 per pup. And we do need the money.'

Without a word Sylvia took her jacket from the back of the door and walked out of the room with Cass at her heels. Outside, she clipped the lead to Cass, who had been showing signs of fancying a trip over the bridge to visit Mark's sheepdog. Sylvia hated to admit it, Cass had the makings of being a bit of a tart!

They walked up the road together and Sylvia contemplated John's underhand arrangement. Perhaps it might not be a bad thing after all. She had been told that it was good for a bitch to have at least one litter of pups, and a bit of extra cash was always welcome. Besides, it would be lovely to have puppies. Dreamily, she looked over the wall of the eighteen acres. The lambs had collected in a playful heap, running up a hillock and jumping high with all hooves in the air together, then dashing down the slope to a dead stop at the bottom. One decided it had had enough play and needed mum. It let out a pitiful bleat, which set off the rest to gallop away in search of their respective milk-bars. It never ceased to amaze Sylvia just how little time it could take for the right mum and babe to be reunited. She smiled at their antics, and at herself. She had done a complete turn-about. Ah well, lambs, piglets and now puppies; life was not boring.

On her way back she scrutinised the crop of would-be-hay in the meadow. It looked well as a breeze lifted the quite long grass sending it into a sea of gently rolling waves. The early rain followed by the long spell of sunny weather had produced a good yield. If the warmth continued hay-making and clipping would be close together. She'd better give both John and Robert a prod to get things moving before the weather broke. Determined to get action she walked briskly back and into the kitchen. The two men viewed her guardedly.

'I've been looking at the four-acres. The grass is growing well. You do realise we'll have to get somebody in to cut it for hay?'

John, obviously pleased he was not to be pilloried for his misdemeanour, grew an inch.

'That's ok, love. I've asked Gerald if he'll do the job when he cuts his front meadows. He was more than willing.'

The phone rang and John's expression of comfort changed. He made a dive to answer before anyone else could reach it. Speaking softly for a few minutes he placed his hand over the mouthpiece and turned to Sylvia. He hesitated. 'It's the lady with the whippet. She wants to know if tomorrow afternoon will be convenient for me to take Cass?'

Without even giving him the satisfaction of a glance, Sylvia said flatly, 'Ok.'

She kept up the wall of unfriendliness till well after opening time.

That evening a new face appeared in the bar. Sylvia heard him before she even set eyes on the man. The Geordie twang lilted down the passage making her curious. It was already ten o'clock, an odd time for a stranger to make an entrance. Robert came into the kitchen with a tray of glasses for her to wash. 'Who does that voice belong to?'

'Why aye lass,' he mimicked.

Sylvia slapped his hand. 'Stop it. Who is it?'

'Have you heard the locals talk about the twilight butcher?' She nodded. 'Well that's him. I think he's come to drum up some business. It might be an idea to give him a small order.'

'Why does he make his calls so late at night? Is that why he's called the twilight butcher?'

'I suppose so. I think he's a shop somewhere in the north-east and he comes down here after he's closed.'

'Gosh. He must work from early morning to late at night.'

'Much like us, sis. Much like us.'

Eager to view this paragon, she casually walked into the bar and sat alongside Carla and Albert.

'Would you care for a drink Sylvia?' Her artist friend was always polite.

'No thank you Albert, I'm awash with tea. In fact I'm just about floating.'

They laughed and Sylvia took the opportunity to cast a glance at the object of her curiosity. He was of average height with straight, nondescript coloured hair. It seemed to permanently flop over one eye which he annoyingly swept back with an elaborate gesture. His rather small, rat-like face was lit by piercing, pale blue eyes that missed nothing as they darted to all corners of the room. But Sylvia was mesmerised by his arms. Two powerful limbs extended from his rolled-up shirt sleeves. They surely belonged to a giant statue, white alabaster, mapped with a network of grey, protruding veins. They were fascinating yet repulsive. Sylvia felt uneasy about the man. He caught her scrutinising him and he held her gaze for a moment with an audacity she hadn't come across before. Standing, she made an excuse to Carla and Albert and made to leave the room. The butcher was sitting next to the passage door, she had to pass him. He lifted his head, looked straight at her and smiled, a self-satisfied smile that sent a shiver down her spine.

Robert followed her to the kitchen. 'What's up sis? You made a quick exit there, didn't you?'

'Just felt the need to get out. That's all.'

She didn't go into the bar again until all the customers had departed.

John called to her. 'Hey Sylv. Look what the twilight butcher has left you.' He passed her a parcel. 'Open it then!'

Even more uneasy, she turned back the wrapper to reveal three perfect pieces of fillet steak. John and Robert were impressed. 'By jingo. They're quality if ever I saw it. I'm glad I gave him a small order.'

'Robert. You didn't?'

She really did not want to encourage him. Her own butcher was fine. This man made her nerve endings jangle.

'Why ever not? A bit of competition's good for anyone. And I'm going to enjoy that tomorrow night.' He pointed at the meat laid on the table. 'It's not going to the residents. He said it was just for us.'

Sylvia decided to say no more. She picked up the package and marched it out to the dairy, holding it away from her as though it had been infected with the plague. Returning, she caught a movement at the corner of the barn, Mark's dog. 'Get off home. Go on, shoo.' She chased it over the bridge, waiting until he slunk through the farm gate. Perhaps it was as well that Cass was going to a proper dog, at least the puppies would be worth something. A sheepdog-cross litter would be worthless, and the way things were looking, that's what could happen if John hadn't intervened.

Her sleep that night was punctuated with vivid dreams of John losing Cassie in strange, man-whippet territory. She woke as though she had never been to sleep. Her mood was not helped when she came to say goodbye to her pet and had to entrust her into the hands of her husband, not always the best person in the world to rely on. He had the most awful habit of forgetting his responsibilities, and she feared things could so easily go awry.

When John returned that evening with a rather chastened Cassie, Sylvia was overjoyed and almost hugged the breath out of her soulmate.

'Was everything alright? Cass wasn't frightened was she?'

John started to laugh. 'No. No. But I've never seen anything like it. The job was done in the woman's kitchen…On a lino covered floor!!'

Robert seemed to understand the joke and a smile crossed his face.

'What?' questioned Sylvia, beginning to get impatient with them.

'It was so bloody funny. There was the dog…in all his glory… trying to catch Cassie, who gave him the run-around on the slippery floor. You've never seen such a scrabble. He couldn't get a foothold, his legs were all over the place. It was ages before he managed his job. The lino was covered in scratches.'

'Oh. My poor baby!'

John quickly replied, 'It's ok. Cass was fine. You might say, she led him one hell of a dance.'

Sylvia glared at him, he should have shrivelled with its intensity. She put Cass in her basket and gently stroked her head. 'Never mind Cassie. You'll love your babies.'

The next couple of weeks saw the departure of the second lot of piglets. This time transported in style in Gerald's trailer. Again, they showed a profit, though not as high as the first litter. The twilight butcher called religiously after ten o'clock every Friday, leaving them top quality meat. Generally, Sylvia kept out of the way when he was around, though she found she had no further uncomfortable incidents to confirm her original misgivings. In fact, he made one, mid-afternoon visit, just to show them how to get the best hay from their four-acres. Gerald had cut the meadow the day before and the weather was perfect, sunny with a slight breeze. The butcher, now recognised as Ken, taught her and Robert how to handle the wooden rakes and turn the rows of grass quickly and easily. He explained, laughing, how they would know when it became hay. 'Th'll hear it sing!'

'Sing?'

'Aye Robert. Tha'll know when it's ready. It'll sing t'thee.'

Sylvia and Robert barraged him with questions, but he would only laugh.

The ideal weather continued and Sylvia was able to let Otti roam with Cass in the shorn grass. He covered himself and the dog with handfuls of the loose hay until the pair of them closely resembled characters from the Wizard of Oz.

She and Robert became dab-hands at deftly flicking the rows over until the sun gave them the song of fresh hay. It was mid-afternoon, a breeze suddenly blew, lifting the drying grass into crisp swirls that danced in the warm air. Sylvia watched the blue-green strands intertwined with the soft colours of dried wild flower heads floating off her rake. She stopped to absorb the beauty of the little meadow by the river where a dipper bobbed on the stones at its edge and the leaves on the trees near the bridge whispered.

'Sis!'

She came out of her trance with a start. 'What is it?'

'Come here and listen.'

They stood together and Robert swished the row of hay. It whispered like the soft notes of a violin!

'There you go. That's the noise Ken said we would hear. The grass must be bone dry to make it rustle and sing. Now we know it's absolutely ready. We can start to get it into piles. Raking into hay-cocks was back-breaking, but by the weekend they had a meadow of tall green-blue hillocks standing proud. Sylvia's fingers were well blistered, but the joy of a wonderful crop of food for the winter eliminated any discomfort.

Fortunately the weather held over the weekend. They were too busy with trade to find time to get the hay from the field and into the barn, but Monday gave them the opportunity. Gerald brought his tractor and flat trailer for him and Robert to load up with the stacks. They were then brought to the barn where Sylvia stood in the loft ready to move the hay that Robert threw up. She worked most of the afternoon forking hay to almost fill every available space under the low roof. She was hot and tired, wisps of hay stuck to her damp arms and there was hardly enough floor room left for her to stand upright. It was a relief when Robert shouted. 'Sis. This is the last load. Have you room?'

'Yes! Thank the Lord. I ache all over.'

Robert sent up a sweet smelling shower that hit her amidships. Unbalanced, she fell backwards onto the softest bed in the world. The mattress of green tea whispered and sang, intoxicating her with the scent of nature's magic mix of herbs and flowers. She laid there, not wanting to move, but Robert's resolute attack to finish to the last fork-full forced her to arms.

'There you go. That's the lot.'

Yawning, she climbed down from the loft wondering what she could make for dinner when John's car drove up to the front door followed by another. Who had he brought? The last thing in the world she wanted was to cook for visitors. A young couple stepped out to join him and he led them towards her. 'Sylvia. Come and meet Dorothy and Nig. You remember them? They have that wonderful gift shop in Skipton.'

In spite of her tiredness, Sylvia took an immediate liking to the pair. She'd always admired their shop, it was full of tasteful and unusual items from all corners of the globe, though, she had only ever looked in the window on her rare visits to the market-town. John was the one who called in and had got to know them quite well. They wouldn't stay for a meal as they were intending to have an evening exploring. However, it was a full hour before they departed after coffee, scones, and bags of chatter. Sylvia was quite sorry to see the auburn-haired girl with the sweet disposition and her dark, live-wire husband depart. Female company was such a change, especially when they had got on so well. As they drove away Cheeky Charlie's old banger drew up. They were never going to get a proper meal.

He wound down the window. 'Just callin' t'tell thi', me an' Fred's cumin' t'morra t'clip thi' sheep.'

Meal forgotten, Sylvia was excited. 'Charlie. Will you teach me to clip? I want to do Lucy myself. Please!'

Charlie gave a huge grin. 'Aye. Missis. A'l teach thi'.' And off he went, chuckling to himself.

As promised, Charlie and Fred arrived late afternoon. The warm and muggy day had brought out the bane of Sylvia's life – *Midges!* They filled the croft in their thousands, hovering like swirls of smoke waiting for their next vampire attack on any innocent blood-filled being. Sylvia knew she was in for trouble. Insects of any kind found her a source of some kind of ambrosia. They would fight to inject their syringe and suck her dry, always leaving an angry red lump whose itch would drive her to distraction. But the hostile army had to be overcome if she was to clip Lucy.

Arms and legs well covered she climbed the steps up to the croft, the only suitable place to keep their little flock contained. The sheep were penned in a corner making a triangle of greyish wool overcoats waiting to be removed. They seemed to know they were to face the barber, they stood quiet and expectant with just the odd complaining bleat. Feeling a little nervous, Sylvia joined the flat-capped experts.

'Na' then missis. Cum' 'ere.' Charlie handed her a pair of sheep-shears. 'Git thi sen' used t'feel of 'em fust.'

She took hold of the tool of spring steel, reminiscent of handleless scissors. The two blades were held together with a piece of band. Glancing at Charlie he nodded, 'Tek of't string.'

The blades sprang open. They were quite difficult at first to bring together, but she kept opening and closing them until she became accustomed to the cutting movement. They weren't as heavy as she had anticipated, but she guessed her wrist would soon be aching from the action. Charlie watched her until he was satisfied that she would be able to cut the wool. 'A'l show thi' 'ow t'old thi' sheep. Thi' teks 'old o'its 'orn. Then thi' sits it on its arse wi' its back agenst thi knees.'

Sylvia watched anxiously whilst swotting the diving blood-suckers.

'Then thi' angs on t'wun o' t'orns so thi' can clip wi' t'uther 'and. See?'

He deftly started to clip the ewe with long sweeping cuts. In no time at all a shorn and very white ewe galloped off as though she had donned seven-league boots.

'Not a nick, eh?' Charlie proudly stood upright. 'It's thy tu'n na.'

She had managed to keep the midges at bay with her two hands free, but as she wrestled with Lucy she came under attack with no defence whatsoever. Determined to do the job she set her mind to ignore the pestilent swarm and concentrate on shearing her favourite sheep. At first she was hesitant. Then as her confidence grew, areas of Lucy's pink flesh sprouting short virgin-white wool increased, until she had the original shorn-lamb, sleepy, and quite settled, between her knees.

'Send 'er on then.' Came the command from her teacher.

281

Sylvia pushed her victim away and watched as Lucy ran, jumping with glee at the freedom from her winter overcoat.

'Tha' did well lass. Only a wee nick on 'er bum.'

She couldn't reply, the insect army had taken its toll. With her face in her hands she gave a half wave and flew indoors to the bathroom where she plunged her head in cold water. Her face, or rather a swollen red mass, was unbelievable in the mirror. A scarlet visage peered back at her through slits where once were eyes. She was in agony, even her ears were swollen. She heard John at the door.

'Are you ok, love? You did a good job out...' He stared at her. 'Oh God! What a mess. I'll telephone nurse Brown.'

He disappeared leaving her submerged.

'Syl, you've to put camomile on your face.'

A fat lot of good that would do, she thought, as she plunged underwater for the umpteenth time. Experience told her she'd just have to wait until the poison dissipated. In the meantime, how to keep hidden? Mentally she kicked herself. This was payment for her damned pride. She always had to show that she was able to match the men. Well...

One day, perhaps, she would learn!

CHAPTER 27

The effect on Sylvia's face by the attack of the particularly ferocious, Hubberholme, breed of midges gradually subsided, though she felt uncomfortable for a couple of weeks if anyone happened to give her a glance.

'I look as though I've had chicken pox,' she moaned to Robert.

'Sis, they're hardly noticeable. I don't know why you're so bothered. No one sees you in the kitchen.'

'Oh, hidden in the kitchen, eh?'

'C'mon, don't be so touchy. Why don't you take Cassie for a walk?'

'A good idea. I'll walk round the sheep. There's nobody to see me up there.'

She flounced out of the kitchen, but there was no Cassie at her heels. Anxious, she turned back through the door.

'Robert, is Cass alright?'

'She's sleeping in her basket. She did look up when you went out, then settled back down straight away.'

Sylvia rushed to her pet. 'Cass love, what's the matter?'

Robert leaned over. 'I think she's letting you know that now she's expecting she wants special treatment.'

'You might be right. Her nose is nice and cold, her appetite is fine.' Cass greedily ate a strip of crackling that Sylvia levered from the joint of pork cooked ready for the weekend sandwiches. But, the expectant mum refused, point blank, to get out of her bed and go for a walk.

Walking round the sheep without Cass seemed strange, Sylvia felt quite lost without her friend. She climbed slowly to the top, where to her consternation she spied a couple of gaps in the wall.

283

Hurrying to the first, she carefully replaced the few top-stones that had fallen. Lucy and her lamb came to view her handiwork.

'Now then, Lucy, that gap is now closed so you've no need to think about trailing off.'

She dug in her pocket to search for a treat. As she'd hoped a few stray sheep-nuts were hidden in the folds.

'There you are, flower. I'm off to mend the next gap. I hope it's not you doing the damage.' She gave the woolly head a rub then made her way to the next section requiring attention. Her heart sank. This was more than a couple of top-stones missing. There was a rough pile of stones of all sizes inside the pasture wall. That could only mean one thing, something had jumped in rather than any of their flock jumping out. Scanning the field, she could see no intruders, though the bottom was out of her sight. Better to close the gap first. Surely it shouldn't be too difficult? Studying the pile of stones for a moment she finally decided to stack the top stones and the 'throughs' to one side. She knew the 'throughs' were the longer stones used for linking the front and back of the wall. Never having tried her hand at walling, this was a first. Carefully building the stones at both sides and making sure they sat together neatly, she laid 'throughs' where she guessed were good points, then back-filled the middle with the small rubble. Gradually the wall took shape and at long last she reached full height and proudly set the top stones in place. Her back felt as if it was in half and her fingers were bleeding, but the wall was up and their flock secure. She stepped away to have a better view of the repair. It did look to have a bit of a bulge, though it seemed sound enough. She wrapped her hanky round the sorest fingers and began the descent.

To her surprise, halfway down she came face-to-face with a young red and white heifer.

'And who are you?'

The creature didn't wait to answer. She whizzed round and ran full pelt down the hill to the bottom gate. That's lucky thought Sylvia, it would be handy there for taking straight out onto the road to drive home, wherever that was.

She crossed mid-field back to the croft gate and through the garden, Robert met her at the door. 'Robert, we've a stranger in the 18 acres. A red and white heifer.'

He put down the crate of beer he was carrying, 'I know, sis. Gerald has just phoned. It's John Horner's from Buckden. He's on his way here right now,' he began walking towards the car park, 'though Mr Horner won't know where it is because Gerald last saw it above our land. I'd better try to catch him before he drives past the gate.'

Satisfied that the beast would soon be home Sylvia turned her attention to Cass, who viewed her mistress with a baleful eye.

'What am I going to do with you, young lady. Are you having me on?' She hoped Robert was right and that the mum-to-be wanted spoiling.

She didn't hear John's car stop at the front door.

'Look what I've got!'

His voice made her jump. 'Heck John, you gave me a start.'

'Sorry love.' He set down on the floor a bucket sized container. 'One of my customers had bought too much Snowcem for his needs. He's let me have this at half price. You said the place needed whitening.'

Robert walked in. 'Will you be doing it then, John?'

John adroitly ignored the taunt and rapidly went into great detail on the attributes of the product at his feet. And Sylvia, to avoid confrontation, ignored the pair of them.

It was a couple of weeks later before the opportunity and the weather gave Robert the chance to start the Snowcem operation. As soon as Sylvia had time she joined in. Filling a spare bucket, she began slapping the whitening on the end wall facing up the dale. She was halfway up the ladder when White Puss caught her eye waddling across the bridge towards her. Could she be? Clambering down to the cat she gently stroked her back, then feeling all round her fat belly, she knew she was!

'Robert, White Puss is going to have kittens.'

Robert, covered in blobs of Snowcem, came round the corner. 'You are joking!'

'No. Honestly. Have a look yourself.'

He glared at the cat as she rubbed against his leg, tail held high. 'You would, wouldn't you. Puppies, and now bloody kittens! I give up.'

Sylvia started to laugh.

'It's no laughing matter. We'll meet ourselves coming back, there's so much to do. And, I've run out of paint.'

'Oh no, I haven't enough to finish this wall either, and we've the chimney to do!'

At that moment a blue van appeared round the corner heralding, the twilight butcher. 'Sorry I'm early. Lord Markham needed meat f'sum' lunch party or t'other.'

The name still rankled. Sylvia's dislike of that landlord hadn't changed. She was quiet.

'Ye both look as though y've lost a p'und and f'und a tanner.'

'We've just run out of Snowcem for the last lap. It'll mean buying a full tin.'

'Well, I can remedy that.' He gazed at Sylvia with those disturbing pale eyes. 'Jump in t'van Sylvia. Old man Barker at Starbotton has a soft spot for thi'sen and he's doing the same job, Snowceming. He's got a stack of the stuff. I'm sure he'll let you have enough to finish off here.'

Sylvia hesitated but Robert jumped in. 'If you're sure, Ken. Off you go, sis. I'll keep an eye on Otti.'

She was torn. She didn't trust Ken, but it would be good to buy just enough to finish the job. 'You go Robert.'

The butcher butted in. 'Old Barker likes you Sylvia. He's partial to young ladies.'

'Well I won't do, then will I? Away with you,' Robert gave her a friendly slap. 'You won't be long.'

Sylvia climbed in the van. She was being silly. Nothing could go wrong between home and Starbotton. They chatted easily on the few miles to Mr Barker's farm and she began to relax. Driving into his yard she saw the elderly farmer in his khaki overalls busy lashing whitening onto the dairy wall. He turned as she climbed out of the van, and grinned like a Cheshire-cat, his old eyes twinkling. 'Why, it's Sylvia from t'pub. W'at can aye do f'thee?'

Her oldest customer held out his hand to greet her, and she held the thin gnarled claw whilst she explained her dilemma. He lost no time in filling a smaller can with enough Snowcem to finish the pub. He refused to take any payment but demanded a kiss, and a pint when he next called at the George. She obliged laughing. And she and the butcher departed.

When they reached Buckden, Ken took the top road at the other side of the river.

'Where are you going?'

'It's ok. I thought we'd take the scenic route down past Fairy Glen.'

He turned sharp left down the hill that led to Hubberholme and past the pretty glen where she had occasionally walked with Cass. Ominously, the van slowed to a halt in an open gateway. The road was little used, other than folk coming down the dale and going on to Cray. Nervously, she stuttered. 'Why have you stopped?'

He stared at her with those intense pale blue eyes. 'For a kiss of course! You gave one to old man Barker.'

Indignant, she made to open the door. 'That was a peck.'

Frantically her mind tried to deal logically with the predicament, but logic flew out of the window. She was pinned. He had seized her in a single lightning move. The back of her neck was held captive in an iron fist and her left arm in a vice. Her own right arm was trapped under his body, she couldn't move. Her head ducked to avoid contact with that rat mouth. Frightened witless, she desperately tried to free herself. The man seemed to have lost all self-control, his eyes had glazed and he was sweating. Thinking she would never get away, her luck turned. In an attempt to pull her nearer, he moved his hand from her elbow to her waist, momentarily freeing her arm. Acting on impulse, she tore her fingernails across his eye and down his cheek. Alarmed, she saw blood rolling down his face. Involuntary, he drew back, releasing his grip. In a fumbling panic, she managed to open the door and throw herself onto the grassy bank. Fear lent her wings. She was up in a flash, running for dear life. She vaguely heard the van motor start, but to her surprise it didn't seem to be following her. Slowing to a jog, she dared herself to look back. It would be best to see where he was going. The roof of his van was just visible over the wall top at the side of the road running up to Cray.

Relief flooded through her, leaving her as weak as ditch water. Standing in the middle of the road she stupidly panicked. What about the Snowcem? It was still in the van. Her gaze travelled down the hill to the gateway where they had stopped. She cringed. There was something in the road. She was too far away to be sure, but could it be the tin from Mr Barker? The butcher wouldn't want to keep it with him and he'd have to explain to John and Robert why he had it. Perhaps he would be hoping she would say nothing?

Slowly she walked a couple of hundred yards back. Surely it was a tin? Bravely she carried on, not wanting to return home without the tin, the reason for her whole horrible experience. Drawing nearer she was relieved. It was the Snowcem. She picked it up and trudged the mile back home. The tin got heavier and she felt drained. As she reached the front door it was dumped, unceremoniously, on the step.

'Robert, fancy a cuppa?'

'You look rough sis. Where's Ken?'

'Oh, he had to go.'

'Did you get the Snowcem?'

'Yes. I think there'll be enough to finish the job. But can we leave it till tomorrow? I don't feel like climbing on the roof to paint the chimney at the minute.'

'I'd go up but I'm just too heavy for the roof. We'll leave it then.'

Sylvia decided not to tell Robert or John about her ordeal. The last thing they needed was an altercation, and as sure as eggs were eggs the locals would get involved. Their custom was as tenuous as a thread in a spider's web, and couldn't be jeopardised. Men would back each other, she would be in the wrong. And the thought of her name besmirched up and down the dale was more than she could countenance.

It was a good few days later before they managed to finish the Snowceming. The weather cooled and the odd shower slowed down the operation. Sylvia conquered her fears and climbed onto the roof to paint the chimney. Surprisingly, she rather enjoyed the experience and the change in aspect of the views surrounding them. But she didn't enjoy the questioning from her men on the sudden absence of Ken on that Friday night.

'You were the last one to see him, sis. What was he like then? Did he give any indication that he wouldn't be coming?'

'No,' she whispered. The reason for his nonappearance returned vividly. She felt sick.

As she tried to gather her thoughts she absent-mindedly twiddled Cassie's ears, when it dawned on her that all was not well with the little dog. She had a diversion.

'Robert, I think Cass is starting to have her pups!'

It was 9 o'clock that night before the proud mum and seven puppies laid contentedly in a large wooden box at the far end of the kitchen. John and Robert went to bed after closing time but Sylvia refused to be moved and sat alongside Cass and her pups till well past midnight. White Puss joined her for a brief spell showing some interest in the new family, sniffing as she stalked round their nest with whiskers at full stretch. Finally Sylvia decided it was safe to leave the family. She stroked the cat and kissed the dog. It had been one hell of a day, what with the questioning on the butcher's nonappearance, and then the trauma of watching her beloved pet go through the agony and joy of delivering seven babies. Her feet dragged as she climbed the stairs. All she needed now was for Grace to pop up and that would be the end to end all endings. Fortunately, Grace spared her an appearance and Sylvia slept the sleep of the dead.

In the morning she couldn't wait to see Cass. She flew downstairs as soon as her eyes opened. 'Hello my clever girl.'

Kneeling beside the box she stroked Cassie's velvet head. Breakfast was in full swing, eager mouths searching for a place at the milk-bar. Sylvia smiled, watching them jostle, one, two, three…seven, eight… nine… ten!! She couldn't believe what she saw, there were ten bodies, not seven. Surely Cass hadn't produced another three after she'd left her?

Scrutinising the tiny creatures, she slowly realised the extra three were not the same as the rest. As she puzzled, White Puss came in through the cat-flap, a thinner, more streamlined version than the one from the night before. She minced past the box, gave it a cursory glance, then proceeded to eat the food in her dish she had left the night before.

'Puss? These are your babies. Aren't they? What on earth are you playing at?'

The door opened. 'You know what they say about folk who talk to themselves?'

'Oh Robert. Just look here! White Puss has had her kittens in with Cassie's pups. She's left them for her to look after. She's no intention of owning them.'

Robert knelt beside his sister. 'Oh dear. You're right, they are kittens. They're so much smaller than the rest.' He made a grab at mother cat as she walked by and unceremoniously popped her next to Cass. In a blur of white she flew out and away through the cat-flap.

'Well, that's that. They'll have to take their chance with the rest!'

'Poor things,' Sylvia murmured. She stroked Cassie's ears again and received a lick in return. 'Poor Cass.'

The days that followed developed into an emotional turmoil. Sylvia could hardly bear to watch the saga as it unfurled. Cass desperately tried to keep the kittens alive, encouraging them to feed along with the puppies, but the pups were stronger and pushed for survival themselves. The first kitten to die was reverently lifted out of the nest by Cass. She gently held it in her jaws, climbed the steps up to the garden and laid it on the grass. Quickly, her front paws dug a hole and to Sylvia's amazement, she dropped the tiny corpse into the earth and buried it. She would not leave until the grave was covered to her satisfaction.

The ritual was repeated with the other two kittens. At each little burial, Sylvia sobbed as though her heart would break.

CHAPTER 28

Cass was not amused when she and her seven pups were moved from the kitchen into the barn. The looks she gave Sylvia spoke volumes. It was obvious she considered her new accommodation third rate, even though the lovely straw bed suited her babies, who were beginning to play, and peer about with their bright blue eyes.

'Don't worry Cass. It won't be long before you're back next to the Aga.'

But Cass wasn't impressed. She turned her back on her mistress and buried herself in the straw. Sylvia missed having her pet near, but the puppies were growing and she knew the little family had to be rehoused outside. To add to the workload, John had come home one day with three new acquisitions in the shape of smallish, solid, black calves. Sylvia immediately christened the chunkiest, Buster, and the other two were allotted Henry and Ernie. She couldn't chastise John for the purchase, bull calves were dirt cheap, and these three had given them change out of £20!

The place seemed to be bursting with stock: sheep and lambs, pigs and piglets, Cass and puppies, Daisy and Buttercup, now young ladies, and the latest trio, all on top of a swelling summer trade. There was absolutely no spare time, though young Otti managed to stretch their elastic limits to breaking point.

It had been a particularly lovely week for the annual holiday of the six Halifax ladies. Most days they walked, covering miles of the beautiful countryside. They usually took packed lunches which gave Sylvia and Robert the luxury of a bit of a breather, but that morning they refused the picnic.

'We're going to walk over the top to Arncliffe and have a meal at the pub. It's a treat day,' Cynthia bubbled, the most garrulous of the six. Sylvia, laughing, waved them goodbye, thankful for the promise of a relatively free day. Perhaps she'd have time to take Otti to the other side of the river and let him play at its edge. He would enjoy the strip of sand left by the receding waters; rain had been sparse for quite a while. She busied herself with the usual morning tasks, taking her son with her while she made the beds and generally tidied upstairs. They had a little play of hide and seek, Otti squealing with delight as she hunted for him under the beds.

'That's enough now, young man. I've some baking to do. You'll have to play with Cass and her pups.'

The doggy family was contained in the corner of the barn next to Ariane's latest litter of weaned piglets, who were almost ready for market. Sylvia deposited her son in the doorway so that he could watch both the porkers and the puppies and fastened the temporary knee-high door.

'There you are Otti you can watch the piggies and Cassie. I won't be long.'

Happy that he was safe and she could hear him if he cried, she began baking scones and a meat pie for dinner that night. Absorbed in her task she didn't realise how the time had flown, and when Robert came in for morning coffee, guilt hit her with the kick of a mule.

'Heck, Robert. Otti!'

Running to the barn she could see no head visible over the small door, a makeshift barrier to let in maximum light and air. Perhaps he'd fallen asleep? But no, there was no sign of a small person. She fleetingly scanned the pigpen and the pups – nothing. Robert walked to the car park, peering in the coach house and the stable.

'He's not here, sis. I'll go over the bridge.'

Sylvia's heart missed a beat. Robert was going to look in the river! She stood stock-still. What if he'd been drowned?

Robert called to her from under the bridge. 'No sign of him down here.'

Relief swept through her. 'I'll have a look up the road. He might have gone under the pasture gate.'

'Right, sis. I'll have a reccy round the garden.'

She didn't reply, thinking the garden was far too obvious, every corner could be seen from the drive. Hurrying up to the pasture gate, her glance darted from right to left, over the wall into the meadow and back to where the sheep grazed. Perhaps he'd heard the lambs bleating and toddled up the road? Only Lucy and her lamb were at the bottom near the little copse. Sylvia became frantic not knowing where to search next. Then she heard a shout of triumph. 'Got him!'

Charging back to the car park, she was just in time to see Robert as he came down the steps from the garden, carrying at arm's length, a black, squirming child.

'There you are, sis. He's all yours!'

'Where on earth...?'

'I found him in the croft, in the middle of the muck-pile. Eating the stuff!!'

'Oh my God. He's plastered in it.'

Robert handed his slime-covered, wriggling nephew to his mother. Otti almost slipped from her grasp. 'How on earth can he stand the smell? It's fairly choking me, and to eat it! Gosh, I can hardly hold him.'

The muck-pile, an accumulation from both cattle and pigs, had been fermenting for months and was now a well-rotted stinking mass, which Otti had delighted in excavating. Sylvia began laughing hysterically. 'His mouth is full of the stuff.' She put her finger round his tongue, extracting what she could before he swallowed it. I'll strip him out here. We can't have that stench inside.'

Robert started taking off Otti's shoes. 'Steady, old girl. It's all ok now. A bit of muck won't hurt.'

The blathered infant had remained as quiet as a church mouse until the disrobing began, then it was all change. He bawled. His mouth, wide, and the whites of his eyes showing bright, contrasted ludicrously with the round, black-daubed face. Robert laughed. 'What a sight you are, Otti. I think we'll dip you in the trough.'

They had just about cleaned the worst from him when they were interrupted by Rev. Fullerton walking up the drive. He gaped at the strange trio before him as though they had come out of a zoo. Sylvia felt acutely aware of the sight they must look. Perhaps the vicar thought they'd been making mud-pies?

'What have we here? Have we had mischief at play?' He managed to smile benignly, 'I only came to tell you that Sam Holden, will be starting wiring the Inn on Monday.'

Monday! Sylvia didn't know whether to laugh or cry. She left it to her brother to deal with the pleasantries, her inside was in knots. They stood watching the cleric waddle back down the drive.

'We've no residents next week, but we've five booked for the weekend. The upheaval's going to happen earlier than arranged. It was supposed to be October not early September.'

'Don't knock it, sis. The job shouldn't take too long. We'll manage somehow.'

'I hope he doesn't make too much of a mess. I'll have to patch up until we can redecorate. What will John say?'

'Well, there's one thing certain. It won't effect him!'

'Robert, sometimes you can be so mean.'

She gathered her son under her arm and climbed the stairs to carry out the very necessary cleaning operation.

Monday arrived and Sam Holden was banging on the door at 7.30 a.m.. Sylvia was pleased. Hopefully it meant that he intended to get the job done quickly. She viewed the electrician critically, trying to assess his capabilities. He seemed normal enough, of average height and build. His complexion was sallow, his eyes had little life, and he had a habit of pushing his spectacles onto the bridge of his nose with a forefinger. She was surprised when he spoke. His accent was definitely not local, perhaps more Lancashire?

'I'll get started straight away. If that's alright? By the way, just to tell you that I have a slight problem with my wind.'

He marched past her and out to his van. Robert raised his eyebrows and Sylvia, feeling slightly embarrassed, giggled.

She thought no more about it until he started working in the kitchen and asked her if she could empty the cupboard under the sink. She rushed to clear it.

'Thanks, Mrs Bainbridge.'

She nodded, stretching her back, then turned to the Aga as Sam bent down. The most horrendous noise reverberated around the sink area. An extended *trumpet voluntary* rolled. He didn't lift his eyes, but just ignored the moment. Sylvia daren't look in his direction. Was this what he meant by a *slight problem?* Shocked at his blatant attitude, she opened the bar-passage door on the pretext of getting something from under the stairs. Before she had time to get through the performance was re-enacted, this time, even louder, and to her concern continued for an extended spell. The man neither blinked nor glanced in her direction, he merely carried on chipping on the wall at the back of the cupboard.

Bursting to tell Robert, she almost ran through the bar and out onto the drive. He was spreading clean straw in the pigpen. 'Robert, Robert. That man! You've never heard such a noise. He was unbelievable.'

Robert leaned on his fork. 'What noise?'

She ducked her head feeling a little uncomfortable. 'He farts! All the time! And not little ones. They don't seem to smell, well I haven't got a whiff yet.'

Robert started to laugh. 'Sis, you'll be the death of me.'

She thought he was going to choke with laughter. 'Is that all? I thought, at least, he'd knocked down a wall or something.'

'You can laugh, but it was so embarrassing. I didn't know where to look.'

He was serious for a moment. 'Obviously, he's got something very wrong with his innards. You'll just have to ignore it.'

'Easier said than done!'

The days that followed became something of a nightmare. Sam Holden's wind problem was at first a giggle, but as time went on it became an annoying nuisance. Sylvia found herself waiting for each subsequent gun salute, unable to concentrate on much else. To make matters worse, he was not the tidiest of individuals. She cursed his mess. Piles of plaster were left wherever he was working, which his feet seemed to find with unerring accuracy and spread throughout the place. The stair carpet suffered the most. Daily, Sylvia would find herself unable to breathe in the cloud of dusty plaster, created by her attempts to brush the stairs clean.

'God, I'll be glad when he's finished, though I've got to admit he is making a neat job and I've managed to touch up the bedrooms without too much bother. Thank goodness all the walls are white.'

The voice from under the stairs echoed. 'Well, he's almost finished. I reckon another couple of days and he'll be gone. I've finished cleaning the mess down here. He does do a good job. The fuse box is fitted beautifully in the corner.'

No sooner had the words left Robert's lips than the electrician appeared. 'I'm leaving early. Be back tomorrow.' And in a trice, he was gone.

'I wonder what brought that on?'

'Don't know. Don't care. When I've cleared this mess, I'll give Otti his tea early. Then...'

'Then...?'

'Well, it's ages since we had any fun. What about getting the old Remington down and having a bit of target practise? I used to enjoy going to the rifle club with John before we got married.'

'You little devil! What a good idea. I wouldn't mind having a pop myself.'

The outstanding jobs were cleared, then the pair of sharp-shooters checked all points of the compass to make sure there were no souls lurking in the undergrowth. Robert unchained the Remington .22 rifle from the gun-rack. It had not been touched since Peter Guy almost shot pregnant Jo. Reflecting on the near accident, Robert carefully inspected the gun. Satisfied all was well he gave himself a shake. 'All ok Syl. You go up to the croft and put these empty matchboxes on the wall top. We'll see who can hit one first.'

Sylvia lifted an eyebrow, then smiling, obliged. The heifers were in the 18 acres, nevertheless, she made sure no livestock had strayed into the croft. The fell rose steeply behind, so they had a good backcloth to fire into. She eagerly bounded back to the kitchen and opened the window wide. 'Bags I go first.'

Neither she nor Robert had any difficulty hitting the targets, but Sylvia soon got tired of running to replace the matchboxes on the wall.

'I'm bored with this, Robert. I'm going to see if I can hit the weathercock on top of the church and send it spinning.'

'Sylvia, *No!* You can't do that. It's sacrilege.'

Laughing, she taunted him. 'Since when did you become all religious. It's only a bit of metal. It's not Holy!'

With that she grabbed the rifle and opened the window over the sink, sliding it down to the right height so that the barrel would rest comfortably. She took careful aim and fired. The noise was deafening, more so than from the other window, but the weathercock remained stationary. It did not budge from due west.

'You've missed. No more now. What if the vicar hears you? What if he comes to church?'

'He'll be having his tea now. Anyway, he'll think it's somebody shooting rabbits. I'll just have another couple of shots.'

Robert sighed. 'Promise, only two more.'

'Ok.'

She blasted another three rounds, but the bird on top of the tower remained resolutely static.

'Gosh, I thought I would have been able to hit the damned thing.'

'C'mon. You promised. Give me the rifle. It's going back in the rack before you get yourself into some serious bother! Besides, that's John home. He'll be wanting his meal.'

They heard the car engine cut and John came in. 'What's to eat people? I'm starving. Hey! What's this? You've been shooting!'

Sylvia told him of her failure to hit the sacred target, which made him smile. 'Hang on a minute. I'll get the binoculars.' He lifted the lid of the wooden chest next to the bed-settee and delved in amongst Otti's toys to find the pair of ancient binoculars that had once belonged to his father.

'What are you going to look for?'

John walked past her and focussed them on the church tower. He started to laugh. 'Oh, oh, Syl. You haven't lost your touch after all!'

He handed her the binoculars. At first she could see nothing but a blur, then with a little refocusing the weathervane came clearly to her eyes. 'What am I supposed to see?'

'Look at it properly.'

'Oh, heck!' She put the binoculars down. 'I've peppered the damned thing!'

John was obviously amused. 'That's why it didn't swing. The bullets went straight through.'

Robert came over all serious. 'I told you, sis. Look well if the vicar sees it.'

'He'll never notice,' John said. 'He's hardly going to be checking the weathercock through binoculars, is he?'

Feeling contrite, Sylvia turned her attention to feeding the family.

Next morning when Mark brought the milk, Sylvia couldn't help but notice a change in his demeanour. He seemed hesitant. As he placed the can on the kitchen table, he faced her and nervously tugged at the lapel of his jacket.

'Is something wrong, Mark?'

He swallowed, 'Tha n..nearly killed mi' yesterd'y!'

'What! What on earth are you talking about? How?'

'W..well, a' wa' up at b..back o' church doin' a b..bit o' w..wallin'.'

A wave of nausea spread through her as realisation dawned. Had the bullets travelled so far after going through the cockerel? 'Oh, Mark.'

'It wa' like w..world war b..b..bloody three. A' 'ad t'jump o'er w..wall. B..bullets wa' flyin' all round. A' thought a'd 'ad it!'

Sylvia couldn't help it; knowing he was safe, she started to laugh. The mental picture of Mark hiding behind the wall and dodging her barrage of bullets was too funny for words.

'Mark, I'm so sorry. Thank God you're alright. I would have died if I'd hit you. Sorry. I can't say it enough, Mark, I'm sorry.'

Her sincerity seemed to change his mood and he began to chortle, ending in a full blown howl of laughter.

Robert, hearing the racket joined them, followed, surprisingly at that hour, by John.

'What's the joke then? Is it the farting electrician?'

'Oh, John. No it's not. I almost hit Mark when I was shooting. He was walling on the hill behind the church. And the bullets...'

Robert, triumphantly interrupted. 'There! I told you you'd be in trouble!'

'I know and I'm sorry. But Mark made it sound so funny. Like a comic film.'

John was patting Mark on the shoulder and the three of them were still chuckling, but Robert didn't join in.

'Aye,' he said. 'It might sound funny, but it could so easily have been a tragedy.'

Sylvia had a sudden twinge of conscience, Robert had seen accidents happen in the navy, including to him. She should have remembered.

CHAPTER 29

Sylvia sat on the edge of the bath, a pair of scissors resting in her hand. Her hair needed a chop. Robert had set the ball rolling when he announced that he would be taking a couple of bottles of beer up to High Greenfield, payment for the farm manager, the amateur barber, to give him a trim. She was glad he was going out, a change would be good. Since the shooting incident he hadn't been himself, and she wondered whether it had revived old naval memories, making him long for another way of life. They were imprisoned in the pub, there was no time at all to escape, it was just work and more work. A young man should be out and about, though Robert didn't seem to let that worry him.

Grabbing a handful of hair, she lopped off a couple of inches. It was a good job it had a natural curl to hide the hacking, for there was neither time or money for visits to the hairdresser. Not that it was an issue, she'd never been to a hairdresser in her life. Soon there was a pile of dark brown locks in the waste bin. Oh heck, she looked a bit like a shorn lamb. Still, it would grow!

Gazing sternly in the mirror she thought about Robert, Mark and the shooting. Her behaviour had been totally irresponsible. She firmly admonished her reflection – *No more shooting!*

Guilt had sat with her for much of the week, she could have maimed or even killed Mark. And to forget her son! That was unforgivable. But, soon her mind was on other things. Sam Holden would have the wiring finished any day, and she would have to steel herself, to accept that Cassie's pups would have to go.

Cassie had made it clear that she'd had enough of seven boisterous youngsters; she wanted her home comforts. Every morning when Sylvia went to the barn to feed the gang, Cass would sneak past her and tiptoe to the kitchen curling up in her basket next to the Aga. She'd stay there as long as she could, making sheep's eyes at her mistress for special treats, which were always supplied.

One morning, the dog family decided they would join mum. Seven spring-heeled pups jumped over the temporary, low door and charged past Sylvia and into the kitchen. Cursing and giggling at the same time, she followed the posse. She couldn't believe the scene that met her as she entered the room. It was incredible, and in a way alarming, twenty-eight legs seemed to have swelled to one hundred and twenty-eight. Bodies were airborne. They bounced on the table, the worktops, the bed-settee, grabbing cushions, loose rugs, Robert's slippers, in fact, anything that they could lift. Sylvia's impression was of a kitchen space full of flying missiles. Everywhere she looked there was a pup careering round at a frantic speed.

'Robert! Come and help me catch this lot!'

Robert dashed downstairs. 'Good God! he exclaimed as a jet-propelled body flew past him. 'They're mad! Why did you let 'em in?'

'I'd no damned choice. They barged past me. They followed mum.'

'We can't have this carry on, sis,' he panted as he won the battle, securing two pups under his arm. 'They'll have to be locked up, and I think Cass has had enough anyway, so she can stay inside.'

'Mm.' And that was the moment Sylvia decided the litter would have to go.

When John surfaced she asked him to put an advert in the local paper, puppies for sale.

'Leave it to me. I'll do it this morning. In fact, it might be a good idea to put one in a north-east paper. The miners up there like their whippets!'

As he drove off to work she waved him off with mixed emotions.

Cass appeared to settle now she was separated from her young family. Sylvia was surprised; she had expected her to fret. But Cass went back to her usual routine as though the past seven weeks had never happened. It was a relief; the job of sending the puppies out into the big world would be so much easier. Though that proved to be not as easy as Sylvia had expected. They had no enquiries! It seemed that whippet pups were not in fashion.

Sylvia began fretting. The advert had been in the paper for three nights and still no news. Then at about ten o'clock the telephone rang. John answered. There were long silences punctuated only by the odd yes or no. Finally he began writing on the note pad, then slowly replaced the receiver.

'That was a fellow from just outside Darlington. He wants to buy all the pups. But at his price.' He waited looking at Sylvia.

With an unexpected heaviness she whispered. 'How much?'

'£7 per pup.'

Robert chimed in. 'That's fine, surely?'

'That's what I thought. I said, Yes. He wants them delivered tomorrow evening.'

Sylvia sat down. 'Oh.' And a tear trickled.

John stroked her hair. 'C'mon Sylv, you can't keep them. You've always known that.'

'I know. But I'm coming with you. That's if it's ok with you, Robert?'

'Of course. I'll clear away after dinners and listen out for Otti.'

'Thanks love. It's a good job we've only four residents.'

John suddenly announced, 'I've had a thought. I'll see if Mark will lend us his van. It's so much bigger than the car.'

Van or no van, the journey to the outskirts of Darlington with seven puppies who wanted warmth and comfort from a mother figure, was one of nightmare proportions, almost as bad as taking their pigs to market. The pups refused to stay in the back of the van on their mattress of straw. Instead, they converged on Sylvia, vying for predominance of place, namely her lap. It was dark, and trying to hold the seven close on twisty roads proved to be a mammoth task. Her arms, neck, and back, lost all sensation that she could cope with, but the fear that she could be sending Cassie's babies to some horrible fate kept eating away in her mind.

Leyburn, then Richmond, came and went; she had just about seized solid. For some obscure reason, the picture came into her mind of the manservant who had held Charles the first or second, in an oak tree all night. God, he must have hurt. Here she was, only a couple of hours, not all night.

'This is the place, Sylv.'

She came to her senses, alert in a flash. In the headlights a skewed wooden gate led down a rough farm track to a dilapidated house. 'I don't like it, John. Let's go.'

'Don't be silly. The man sounded alright. In fact, quite kind.'

A little bow-legged man with a kerchief knotted at his neck stood in the doorway. At his side were two blue whippets. They looked superb and when he casually bent to stroke their heads, Sylvia began to relax. She kissed the sleepy bundle on her lap and gently extracted the two sleeping on her shoulders, passing them to John. 'I'm not getting out of the van, John. I don't want him to see me cry.'

'Ok, love. You stay put.'

He called out to the future owner of Cassie's pups, 'Can you give me a hand?'

Sylvia sat rigid, not daring to watch the removal of the little family. It seemed forever sitting in the dark waiting for John to come out of the house. Her thoughts tormented her. Why did this man want seven pups? He must surely be selling them on to make a quick buck. She felt ill. She had wanted to vet all potential owners, and now it was out of her hands.

The car door opened and John plonked in the driver's seat with a sigh.

'What's wrong? Are you thinking they're going to a bad home? Shall we get them back?'

'Steady on, Sylv. The man is alright. I'm not sure what he's going to do, but his dogs come first. So don't worry. They'll be fine.'

The journey back was made in absolute silence, neither uttered a word.

The days that followed seemed strange to Sylvia without the happy chaos of Cassie's family. Cass accepted the loss of the pups without a second thought, returning to the status of number one with eager enjoyment. Now she could have her little walks and cuddles in warmth and comfort.

Returning with her friend from a short amble, Sylvia was surprised to see the car belonging to Dorothy and Nig, sitting at the front door, then she remembered it was early closing day in Skipton.

'Hello there.'

Robert was sitting with the couple on the bed-settee and Sam Holden was working in the passage. It was obvious he'd been blasting forth, the grinning faces trying to hold a normal conversation gave the game away. Sylvia pulled up a chair to join the trio. The talk soon turned to the imminent switch on. Nig, an eager beaver, was particularly interested. 'What will you be doing in the bar? Wall lights?'

Before she had time to answer, he was on his feet and away to the bar, followed curiously by the rest.

'You want a proper bar in here, you know.'

Robert, a trifle indignant replied, 'We know. And we've discussed it, but it will cost an arm and a leg.'

'No. It needn't. This passage wall is not load-bearing, it's just laths, plaster and timber. We could have it down in a tick. And then...you could have a corner bar with pumps on the top.'

'Steady, steady,' Robert laughed.

'Seriously, Robert. Whilst you've got the upheaval with the wiring, now is the time to do it. I'll give you a hand if you like.'

Robert didn't seem to know what to say and Sylvia, full of enthusiasm, questioned Nig. 'I can see it wouldn't be too much of a problem taking the wall down, I've fancied doing it myself. But what would we make the bar from?'

Robert suddenly came to life. 'I know, we could build it like a stone wall. We've even got a pile of stones in the croft that would do.'

'Right. I've a few days free. I can start on Monday.' Nig was fairly jumping.

Sylvia was thrilled. John had told her that Nig had an excellent reputation as a joiner. The work he'd done in Dorothy's shop certainly bore that out.

'That's decided then? If you get one of your mates to do the wall, I'll make the bar-top with a flap so that you can get through to the cellar, and shelve out underneath it and on the wall at the back. We'll start Monday then?'

'Yes, please. I'll talk to John tonight. I know he'll agree.'

Monday came round faster than the blink of an eye. Sylvia could hardly contain herself. Dorothy and Nig would soon be with them, Gerald was already in the croft sorting out the stones he wanted for the bar, and John had taken a day off.

It wasn't long before the enthusiastic army were wielding hammers and crowbars, making a full blown attack on the passage wall. It gave up the fight with little opposition, other than filling the room and their lungs with clouds of dust. Dorothy and Sylvia got the job of filling the two barrows with rubble then wheeling their loads to a pile on the car park ready for Gerald to take away.

They slaved most of the day. John did his usual, escaping the drudgery by keeping them supplied with a constant flow of tea and sandwiches. At five o'clock all the rubbish was out, the room washed down, and the tables and chairs back in place ready for evening business.

'Gosh. The room looks enormous now, though it seems awfully bare.'

Nig, a terrier of a worker, was still full of beans. 'You wait a couple of days. You won't recognise the place.'

True to his word, by Wednesday night the room was transformed. Gerald had done a wonderful job of building a curved stone wall, encircling the door to the kitchen and the space under the stairs. Nig's woodwork enhanced the whole room. He had covered the bar top with a matt black Formica, matching the shelving behind. Now, the small window, overlooking the river, was exposed, bringing in masses of extra light. The whole place was opened up, giving a bright room, instead of the rather dingy aspect of before.

'What a transformation!' John exclaimed when he came in from work. 'All we need now is a stone fireplace to match the bar and it will be perfection.'

'Let's do it!' Nig bounded across the room to test the strength of the existing one.

Robert cautiously stemmed the flow. 'Don't you think we'd better ask the vicar? I know he was ok about the wall coming down but...'

Sylvia was indignant. 'Oh, c'mon. We're improving his property. Remember, we've asked him for nothing – or rather the church.'

John snorted. 'As if they'd stump up anything. If you're game, Nig, so are we.'

'Well. You're the landlord, John. It's your responsibility. Tomorrow then?'

And so the fireplace was built, a low slung affair with a hole to store logs. Sylvia was ecstatic. Now the room warranted new curtains and a lick of paint. John went another step further.

'I'm going to give Younger's brewery a call to see if they'll put in beer pumps for us. It would save the trips down to the cellar to fill the jug.'

'That's a good idea. Do you think they would?'

To everyone's delight, the brewery agreed, but with the proviso that only their beer could be sold. That was no problem. Younger's was all they sold anyhow.

A week later, the 'bar lounge' had been freshened with a coat of white paint, and bright curtains patterned with hunting and shooting scenes were hung at the windows. A new rush-mat lay in front of the rebuilt fireplace, red lampshades were resplendent on the wrought-iron wall lights, and the beer pumps sat proudly on the bar-top. Sam Holden and his wind had completed the wiring and he, together with everyone else, waited for switch-on, designated to happen as dusk fell.

Sylvia insisted that she would stand on the bridge to view the event. She walked across with Cass, not really knowing how she felt. The ease that electricity would bring went without saying, but at the same time there was a tinge of sadness. It was the start of change.

She breathed deep as she waited for the moment. In the dusk there were still movements from the odd bird and the buzz of an insect, and she could distinctly hear Lucy bleat. Without warning, all lights at the George were alive. A yellowish hue lit up the ancient building, shining from the windows like searching, questioning eyes.

Sylvia wanted to cry. 'Oh, Cass. I'm such a fool. I should be jumping over the moon!'

Cass leapt up as if trying to get a better view and Sylvia supported her out-stretched paws as the pair did a little jig on the bridge. When the whippet jumped down Sylvia realised that a figure was coming towards her out of the blurring glare. John was coming to find her and bring her back into the throng.

'Hey, sis, you can't admire your handiwork from out here.'

She swallowed her disappointment, and wiped her eyes as Robert came to wrap one of his long arms around her shoulders.

'It sure brings a lump to your throat, that's a fact.'

'Where's John?'

'Playing to the crowd. *His* bar, *his* electricity, *his* decorating...the usual.'

Sylvia smiled and slotted her own arm around his waist. 'John's John. The customers love him.'

'Oh, yes, he can tame the birds out of the trees, can John.'

Sylvia scraped her shoe across the loose gravel of the roadway, not wanting the conversation to follow this course. It didn't take much to bring back a stirring of jealousy over J- and there was probably nothing to be jealous about, nothing more than gossip and rumour.

'Do you think it will change Hubberholme, the electricity?'

'God, I hope so! No more filling oil lamps, no more fiddling with spluttering gas mantles...'

'I mean... well, people come to The George because of its olde worlde atmosphere. They like the adventure of the oil lamps and the spluttering gas mantles, beer being served from a jug.'

She felt his arm give her shoulders a squeeze. 'Visitors come to the George to enjoy the glorious setting, a comfortable place to stay, and...' he winked cheekily. 'Your cooking.'